Haeven

Book Two of the
Solarium-3 Trilogy

JOHN R. SPENCER

Overhead Diagram of the Solarium-3 Pods

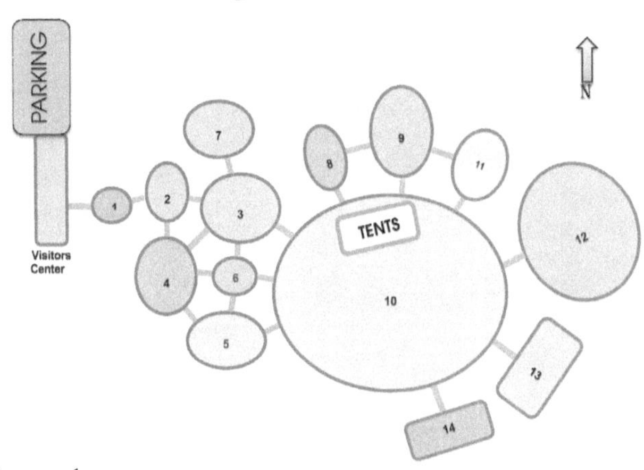

<u>Legend</u>

Pod 1   Entrance Pod
Pod 2   Communications Center (Comm.)
Pod 3   Research Center
Pod 4   Residence (House)
Pod 5   Recreation & Pool
Pod 6   Aviary
Pod 7   Infirmary
Pod 8   Maintenance Shed
Pod 9   Large Animals Housing & Research
Pod 10 Main Agriculture Area, Crop Fields
Pod 11 Small Animals Housing & Research
Pod 12 Ocean, Aquatic Plants & Marine Animals
             Research
Pod 13 Equipment Storage & Main Supply
Pod 14 Fuels & Fertilizers

1

"Hey, you awake?"

Mai Ker prodded softly at the back of Jimmy's neck with a dull finger whose nail had broken off in the field yesterday. Faint, early morning light was sneaking into the tents.

"Um?" came his almost inaudible response. He crinkled his eyelids tighter and unconsciously batted at whatever large bug was pestering his neck. In a half-dream state, he rolled his head around in the well-worn pillow, hoping he might disappear back into the happy oblivion of sleep.

"Jimmy?" she prodded again. This time, she shook a limp arm gently.

"Cut it out," he mumbled. "Knew I shoulda stayed in my own tent last night . . ."

"Would you take Sing and watch her for a while this morning?" Mai Ker asked with an irresistible plea. "I need some time off. Just take a long bath. Walk. Be by myself."

Jimmy rolled his head toward her lovely face, which was hovering just over his.

"You get more beautiful every morning."

"Ugly, you mean. You're asleep."

Jimmy chuckled gently. "No, ma'am. You took care of that."

Mai Ker smiled at him and kissed his cheek.

"You will? Huh?" she said, confirming what he wouldn't.

"Only because I love you. And you're so beautiful. And only if you make me breakfast first."

"You're a slug," she said, shoving him nearly off the bed.

She was on her feet, laughing playfully, pulling on a ragged-looking robe that was nearing its last days.

"Yeah. A hungry slug," Jimmy said, stretching arms and legs that reached beyond the edges of the small bed. "You need a bigger mattress."

"Oh, gosh. Remind me. I'll run to the store and get one tomorrow!" she sneered playfully.

"Yeah, let me see. Would that be the Mattress Market in the storage shed in Pod thirteen? Or the Little Spare Mattress Boutique behind the barn in number nine?" Jimmy teased. A quiet belch found its way up and out of his throat.

Mai Ker grabbed a brush and comb and headed for the lavatory tent, shaking her head.

"You figure it out, wise guy," she tossed over her shoulder.

"We could make one," he called after her, righting himself slowly on the side of the bed, trying to get his bearings on the new day and undo the cramp in his right leg. Mai Ker always snuggled so close to him through the night that he could never move, and one leg or the other nearly always managed to cramp up by morning. When he needed a good sleep, he slept alone or else with Pam, since she always slept at the far edge of her bed.

"I must be completely out of my mind," he said half aloud. The fuzz in his skull began to thin. "What in the world are we doing here?" he asked no one in particular. If anyone heard, they didn't reply.

The early October sun poured down on the tent roof through the Stellar plastic of Pod 10. Jimmy could feel that the temperature was going to top 90 degrees in the pods again today. Clouds OUTSIDE had been strangely thin or absent the past few weeks. Even through their sickened atmosphere, the sun was overheating the complex and the air conditioning units were running full tilt all day and half the night.

"Good morning, morning," he said, glancing in the mirror. He didn't care for what he saw. His deep brown skin seemed as dark as ever but somehow looked thinner. Older. Small cracks were appearing in the plaster of his personal facade. He wondered what old age was going to look like.

He turned from the mirror and went to see if Mai Ker was in the kitchen yet. His stomach gurgled.

THE PLANNING of the Solarium-3 project had been all encompassing and thorough. No details were ignored. Computer models had projected out thousands of possibilities, every likely circumstance. Nothing had been left to chance. So it had seemed, at least, to John Haskins and his team OUTSIDE.

They forgot one monumental detail. Not everything that is planned happens the way it was planned.

The universe, as usual, had spiraled on without mankind's help or guidance. For decades before the team was sealed INSIDE the Solarium, humans had been furiously busy trying—so they claimed—to save the planet. Rushing ever-faster trying to beat whatever clock might be ticking, most of them successfully avoided thinking about the central fact that, in the end, they couldn't even save themselves.

For the few souls INSIDE who escaped the great cataclysm, nothing had gone as planned, despite all the careful planning by some of the best scientific minds of the time. Four of the original seven Solarians survived. One of the three deaths was, ironically, completely disconnected from the terrors that confronted them INSIDE, and OUT. In the oddest place imaginable, the four survivors had escaped the devastation that had taken the human race—and all life on the planet. Solarium-3, the lone habitable place left on earth, now also held their two children, natives of the Stellar pods.

Why they were still here at all was a mystery to the Solarians. Perhaps, they felt, it was just one of those seeming accidents of history, one of those never-expected events that violently twist the rope of time, undo the knots, and throw the whole thing cascading over the cliff of unpredictability, where life—what was left of it—was carried downstream in a previously unknown river.

Bridget, Pam, Jimmy, Mai Ker, and the youngsters Herald and Sing looked out each morning at a dead world. And day by day they found nearly everything in their own little world to be just one more unmanageable challenge. Life went on, with no point.

They spent each day working hard, trying to keep the immense complex running and livable, and the air breathable. They had mastered the system, yet they knew only too well how easily—and quickly—everything could go wrong.

It was an overwhelming, numbing routine that filled their hours and minutes, months and days, with no sense of direction other than trying to stay alive. They took care of themselves and their Solarium. That was their life.

As big as the place was, the huge pods now felt much smaller. In some ways beautiful, the Solarium was nonetheless a cage. Knowing they were trapped here permanently, with no hope of change, time itself ran to a new rhythm, a tempo without any real beat or measure. The rules of life, the goals and expectations that had once driven them, were all suspended. Solarium-3 was, as far as they could tell, no more than a hardened-plastic coffin for the dying human race. They, its inhabitants, were in a sort of hibernation, a long wintery sleep isolated from the rest of history. To the adults who had known the world OUTSIDE, it felt like living in suspended animation, waiting, waiting—

for what, they couldn't see. Time no longer crept. It crawled as if through drying mud.

Still, though abandoned in their pods, there was a tiny glimmer of hope, a fragment of joy. They had become the source of new life, the infant beginnings of a new humanity. Their two delightful children were healthy and growing. "Why" was a question the adults avoided. To look back was out of the question. To look forward was the only choice.

BRIDGET HAD learned quickly, as moms do, that a 2-year-old toddler is one of the most dangerous creatures on earth.

"Herald, no! You can't play with that! You'll hurt yourself."

She grabbed the sharp knife from his hand just when he thought he had acquired the perfect sword. How a 2-year-old can even conceive the idea of a sword fight was a question that didn't occur to her.

"Here, honey, play with this," she said, handing him a large plastic ladle.

Herald was not nearly as impressed. But he wielded it mightily as if about to slay a dragon beneath the dining table in the kitchen tent. Everyone knows the fiercest dragons frequently hide under dining tables, and children's beds.

"Can I help?" Pam asked as she came into the kitchen. It was creeping on toward lunchtime and her stomach had been growling for half an hour. "Sandwiches?"

"Yeah, I just finished some fresh bread. Wanna cut it up for me?"

Pam did, because she could munch the scraps as she sliced the three warm loafs. The rich aroma filled the whole kitchen area.

"Jimmy and Mai Ker are finishing up in the supply shed. I bet they're hungry, too."

"Mai Ker made a great breakfast this morning," Bridget said.

She paused.

"Even eating gets boring. You know?" Bridget asked her.

"Everything is boring," Pam admitted. "If it wasn't for the kids, I don't know what we'd find to do with ourselves."

Bridget patted Pam's very pregnant tummy.

"Tell me that in a few days, mom-to-be," Bridget said, and she laughed.

PREGNANCIES AND babies had not been part of the plan. When the Solarium project was first conceived years before with the building of Solarium-1, the master plan was to create a fully self-contained environment where life could sustain itself with no outside support. Solarium-2 built on the successes of Solarium-1 but was designed with tighter controls and more restrictions on contact with the OUTSIDE. Both Solarium-1 and -2 were moderate successes for the Lifeline/New World Exploration Corporation, a for-profit group of entrepreneurs who envisioned the whole thing and raised the money needed to bankroll the hugely expensive projects.

But the first two ventures were too basic and relied on air exchange when needed with the OUTSIDE world. More extensive planning and more operational successes were needed before the Lifeline/New World partners could sell their master plan to the federal government or to any of the private space exploration firms that were beginning to pop up like August weeds. The new design would have to be not only perfect but tested, guaranteed to protect off-earth settlers from the hostilities of outer space and the unknowns of some alien planet.

So Solarium-3 had been built as the crown jewel of

the Solarium projects. Its design was far tighter and more controlled than the previous two projects, with improvements that grew out of mistakes made during those first two attempts. It had to be perfect. Everything in the complex would have to work over the long haul. To make the big sale, the corporate team would have to demonstrate that the complex would operate with no flaws, and no failures.

Under the oversight of project manager John Haskins, who had been onboard since Solarium-1 was only a few sketches on paper, the design and construction of the newest Solarium had gone perfectly, with one minor mishap. During the final press to speed up completion, a worker had been seriously injured. Such things were bound to happen, Haskins reminded himself. It didn't impugn the design or reliability of the Solarium itself. It was merely a result of the carelessness of a couple of workers. A little blood on the concrete of a podwalk. Nothing more.

Then, not quite a year after the Solarium-3 team was sealed INSIDE, John Haskins lay gasping for his final breaths. He was on his back on a skinny, rickety cot set up in a small basement conference room of the Lifeline/New World Exploration corporate tower in downtown Omaha. He gagged bits of mucus out of his windpipe and down his throat. The air around him was foul but still barely breathable, pumped in from sewer tunnels nearby. His final bed was near the emergency communications room they had set up in the basement to try to keep a link open with the Solarium-3 team as long as possible. Haskins had sent an email message to the team earlier that afternoon, though no one responded. He planned to send another later this evening. He planned, in fact, to send many more messages, to keep in touch. He wouldn't have that chance.

With lungs burning, pictures in slowly moving

frames ran through Haskins' mind as he tried to lay still, trying to overcome pains he had never felt before, whose source could not be found. He struggled to take in air that was so putrid it made him want to throw up with each breath.

He remembered those exciting months, a year earlier, as the opening of Solarium-3 approached. He knew he had a winner this time. He was confident that the years of research and development would pay off with a big win before congressional committees and with the directors of several private companies who had already shown their interest with very fat checks.

It would be the biggest sale of its kind. Haskins would personally get the project through its first few months, turn it over to his second-in-command, and take an early, lavish—and lucrative—retirement. A well-earned, and well-deserved, retirement.

That was his personal plan, and it, too, was perfect.

He choked in another breath and remembered the day when a 3-star general and a colonel from the U.S. Army walked into his office just two days before Haskins was to finalize his INSIDE team for Solarium-3. He assumed it was a social call. They had no doubt come to offer their congratulations on the launch of the new project.

He could not have been further off base had he been a base runner teasing a major league pitcher.

As he lay on his cot, and the single light above him seemed to weaken, he remembered the conversation that day months before, with a fear much deeper than he had felt even at the time.

"GOOD MORNING, John," General Francis Arnott had said as he made himself at home on a very comfortable leather sofa near the windows of Haskins' office. "Join us, will you?" Arnott sat back and loosened the tie of his dress uniform, which he loathed.

He smoothed his short, white, wavy hair back evenly along the crest of his head.

Haskins smelled a skunk. He was not used to people taking over his office like this, but the man had three stars on his collar and he was also the principle liaison between the U.S. government and the Solarium projects. No one, other than Haskins, knew the overall plan better.

Haskins got up from his desk, his damaged left knee making its usual complaint, and moved to a side chair near the sofa. Colonel Petar Roskovic sat in a chair opposite, sniffling from his early summer allergies. A messy but pure white handkerchief was only partially stuffed into his rear pocket.

"Glad to see you both," Haskins said with obvious uncertainty. It was a lie, of course. He wasn't glad at all because unannounced visits usually meant there was a problem. He hadn't even gotten a phone call. His antennae were up.

"Thanks for meeting on short notice, John," Arnott said. "You're limping. What happened?"

"Tennis. Guess I'm too old," Haskins said. *Short notice,* he thought. *How about no notice.* He repositioned his sore knee. *OK, John,* he told himself, *get over it.*

"Is there a problem, General?" he asked.

"With the Solarium?" Arnott asked. "Not that I know of."

Haskins breathed a little. "Well, good."

"But, yes. There is a problem." Arnott looked to Roskovic. "Colonel?"

Petar Roskovic was a man of few words. Normally. That he was about to break that rule, especially while fighting a miserably stuffed-up head, left Haskins with a deeper empty pit in his stomach.

"John, we don't have a problem. We have a major problem. Could be an insurmountable problem. We're still trying to confirm it. Really, we're still trying to understand it."

Haskins listened in silence, his forehead wrinkling down just slightly.

"And I can't explain it in the kind of detail I'm betting you'll want," Roskovic said. He looked over at Arnott as if for further permission. "But the long and short is, NOAA is certain that something catastrophic has occurred in the atmosphere."

"National Oceanic and Atmospheric Administration," Arnott explained rather pretentiously.

"I knew what he meant, thanks," Haskins said, trying to deflect any response from Arnott, a man who always had to demonstrate that his expert knowledge of everything was greater than that of anyone else in the room.

"Anyway," Roskovic was saying as if not interrupted, "this is big. It's ugly. And it's dangerous. In fact, if some of our guys are right, it's deadly. Don't know how else to put it."

Haskins had forgotten his stomach as a deepening frown settled across his face. At the word "deadly," he unconsciously rubbed a sore wrist that had also been injured, though less severely, in his most recent tennis escapade.

"What's happened?" Haskins asked.

"Well, it didn't just happen. It's *still* happening," Roskovic went on. "Our own researchers, and others around the globe, have detected something really bizarre. A little over a week ago. It was," he looked at his folder, "the 13th of May, to be exact. Seems we floated through some kind of matter, or anti-matter—or some such crap—that passed through our orbit. Whatever we hit—or hit us—triggered a depredation in the atmosphere. The *whole* atmosphere. We're not talking little pockets. We're talking the whole damn show. It's in a death spiral. And we have no idea how to stop it. Because we have no idea how it started." He stopped for a breath.

Arnott, who knew it all, was only half-listening. Haskins was stunned.

Then daylight began to dawn in Haskins' mind. The atmosphere was changing. But this was OUTSIDE. Now he knew why they were here.

"You think the Solarium is insulated from the problem. You think they'll be able to help."

"We do," Arnott said.

Haskins' mouth was going dry. He longed for a shot of something. Anything.

"We're thinking," Roskovic said, "since the atmosphere in the Solarium has been pretty much insulated—I mean, it was mostly closed in months ago—we can experiment in there. Once the team's INSIDE, we'll watch their air. See what happens. They'll be the test lab. At some point, once we know more—what's happening out here—we may be able to run tests INSIDE. See what kind of fixes might work. Or not."

"But we can't tell them any of this, John," Arnott emphasized. "This is strictly off-limits. From the team. From any media. We don't want panic."

Panic was already foaming inside Haskins.

"We use them as the lab, and depending on how testing goes," Roskovic said, "we may be able to develop some kind of protocol. A fix. For out here." He looked down. "Before it's too late."

"Wait," Haskins said. "Wait a second." He looked hard at Arnott. "You realize what you're saying? You're basically going to have them screw up their own air—on purpose—to re-create the problem we have out here? And they won't know it?"

"Essentially," Arnott said with no irony, or emotion, in his voice.

"It's making them guinea pigs," Haskins said,

emotion rising in his own voice. "I mean, they'll be locked in there. What if something goes wrong? They'd be sitting ducks. In a pressure cooker."

"John, we realize this is asking a lot," Arnott said. "But the fact is, we don't have many options. We don't know if they'll be able to work this problem through from INSIDE the Solarium or not. But they'll have a damn sight better chance than we do."

John Haskins sat thinking, all the while the names and pictures of the seven Solarians he was about to announce running across a screen in his mind.

"I don't think I can agree to this," he said firmly.

"We didn't come to ask," Arnott said, looking intently at Haskins.

"You mean, we're not talking options, we're talking orders. Right?" Haskins asked.

"Essentially," Haskins heard again.

"Look. This could destroy the integrity of the whole project. Any change in the designed routine, once we seal the complex—that could have really damaging effects."

"For God's sake, John, we're just looking for a little cooperation," Arnott said stridently. "I am your biggest supporter. You know that. Don't you?"

"But we're a private corporation, Francis. You can't just commandeer this project like it's your own." Haskins knew, in fact, they could do exactly that, if they wanted. But he had to at least make the effort of objecting. Had it not been for the bad knee, he would have strutted around the room in protest.

"Joint Chiefs think otherwise." Arnott paused. "And so does the Boss."

Haskin's mind changed gears. He was not a man to waste time, or breath, in a lost battle. He straightened his back a little. He pulled his thick glasses off and rubbed both eyes.

"What do you want?" he asked them, replacing the

glasses. Major problems were looming and his retirement party was receding.

"We need you to move up the start date. We need an earlier Seal-In," Arnott said. "Make it happen. Once they're in, and we see how it's going, a couple of my guys will work up some tests for INSIDE. We'll simulate whatever's happening out here. We'll have Colonel Jim Mahham onsite to look things over, before Seal-In. I want him to know the place close-up. All the operational details."

"You want him INSIDE?" Haskins asked, upset because he had already picked the perfect team.

"Nah," Arnott said. "He wouldn't do that if you paid him a million bucks. But he'll help coordinate things with you."

"What little we know so far," Roskovic said, "is that oxygen pressure in the atmosphere seems to be slipping. Nitrogen levels are pushing up. We'll need to set something like that in motion in the Solarium. Then—hopefully—we'll be able to find some fixes. That's why we've got to get them in there as soon as possible."

"And if it doesn't work?" Haskins asked them.

"We've lost nothing," Arnott said.

"Except maybe seven Solarians," Haskins pointed out.

"Chicken feed, John, in the big scheme of things. A loss—but trivial compared to what could happen to the rest of us." Arnott's face showed little emotion, but a subtle undercurrent of fear.

Haskins didn't like the chicken feed analogy but it certainly made the point. Seven, versus seven billion.

"I'll get the team in gear," he said. "Get them moving." He got up and limped back to his desk, and brought up the master project calendar on his screen. "I can maybe get them all there by June 12th. Soon enough?"

"And when for Seal-In?" Arnott asked.

"There's still lots of equipment and supplies to get in. Maybe we could shoot for the 25th."

Arnott nodded and punched a June 25th Seal-In date into his electronic calendar.

"It'll have to do," he said, "if it's the best you can do, John." He looked at Haskins, then stood and extended his hand.

Haskins shook it half-heartedly. It was the best he could do at that moment as he envisioned all his retirement plans flowing down a long, dark, endless tunnel.

A YEAR later as Haskins tried to lay still on his cot, pain burning not just through his lungs but his entire body as he struggled for his last few breaths, he desperately wanted to believe that what he had done in helping save the few Solarians might in some way be a very small part of some larger plan that was inescapably working itself out. What that plan was he could not see, but though blind to it, he felt somehow connected to it.

His own plans had gone up in flames but the Solarium and her inhabitants might survive. He came finally to his last moments—after days of confusion and increasing pain—and managed to hold his breath. He refused any more of the poison that had become their atmosphere. His lungs shuddered in a final, involuntary gasp and his heart, starved of oxygen, stopped. He died with the vague realization adrift in his mind that he had been a part of something that he didn't start and could not stop, nor had he in any way controlled it.

THE WORST fears of Arnott and everyone OUTSIDE had played out in ghastly detail. The reality turned out to be far worse than their fears. The planet was dead.

Humankind, apart from several souls INSIDE Solarium-3, was dead. Animal and plant life were equally dead. The earth was devoid of life, an empty steamer trunk floating through space, carrying only specks of debris from what had once filled it.

Solarium-3 had been designed as a perfect, self-contained environment where all kinds of living creatures could survive the hostile environment of another planet with no external supply of food, water or support of any kind. The planners had no way of knowing that earth itself would become the most hostile environment of all. Yet because the complex had been so designed—self-contained, and self-sustaining—it could now support not only humans but the other plant and animal life necessary for a healthy human life. All this it continued to do using only its own regenerating resources and what bit of the sun's energy that still reached it through the damaged atmosphere OUTSIDE.

When the special tests that Arnott had ordered Haskins to run INSIDE were over, their air was completely fouled. What Haskins and the others OUTSIDE should have realized, but failed to, was that the Solarium's air had already been contaminated during final construction, weeks before the Seal-In. So the special tests the Solarians ran for their bosses made their air unbearably worse.

Had it not been for the ingenuity of the team INSIDE, everything in this one remaining haven of life would long ago have died, too.

After weeks of panic, the Solarians managed to re-stabilize their air. Haskins realized that whatever the original plan had been, Solarium-3 would now have a totally different purpose. With the death toll rising OUTSIDE, the Solarium became the one hope for human survival.

THAT WAS four years ago. Against all probability, the Solarians—some of them, at least—had managed to stay alive. It was a hard-won survival that taxed their patience and stamina every day.

The heat in the Solarium throughout the afternoon climbed steadily. Mai Ker was walking with Pam toward the ocean in Pod 12 for a cool-down swim after several long afternoon hours in one of the garden plots in Pod 10.

Mai Ker's little vacation was short-lived.

"How are you doing?" she asked Pam.

"Can't stand being this fat."

"But it's not really you. It's the baby."

"Still fat."

"Not much longer, Pam. I know. Seems like it will never come to an end, huh?"

"It better. And soon," Pam groaned.

They knew she was carrying a baby girl from a sonogram done a month earlier. Pam was in her eighth month of pregnancy, a pregnancy the other Solarians had thought would never happen.

"The little gal is getting pretty rambunctious," Pam added, trying to make a joke of the pain. Her stomach felt like an inverted punching bag.

Almost as she said it, she stumbled slightly as her legs went weak under her. She folded to her knees and rolled sideways onto the ground alongside the stone path, protecting her stomach for all she was worth as she crumpled over.

"Ah-ahhh!" she gasped, unable to catch a breath. Her face wrenched into a doubled mask of pain and anxiety.

Mai Ker dove to her rescue.

"Pam, what is it? You OK?"

"Don't know. Kind of a shooting pain. Don't think it's labor. But I'm nauseated, too."

"Lay still!" Mai Ker tripped her intercom mic and

called for help. "Jimmy, Bridget, Pod 12—quick!"

Jimmy's hands were in grease and grime working on a tractor in the equipment shed in Pod 13. Bridget was in the tents and grabbed her radio.

"What's wrong?" she almost shouted, hearing the urgency in Mai Ker's voice.

"Pam collapsed. Don't know what happened. We were just walking over for a swim."

"Be right there," Bridget said.

"Me too!" Jimmy hollered over the intercom, greasing the mic key in the process.

They converged on the path that led down to the water in Pod 12. Bridget made it first, Jimmy not far behind her. Both were panting, as was Pam who was still on the ground, in deepening pain.

"Pam, tell me what's happening," Bridget said, dropping to her knees by the fallen woman.

"Pain. I just— All of a sudden, this stabbing pain. Sick too. May throw up."

"Jimmy, get a portable stretcher. We need to get her to the infirmary."

"No," Pam said. "Take me to my tent."

They all looked at each other, knowing each other's thoughts.

People die in that infirmary.

"You'll be all right, Pam," Jimmy reassured her. "Gonna be fine."

Bridget nodded.

"No need to worry, Pam. You're a nurse. Probably just something with the baby. Relax. That's the best thing."

"Easy to say when you're not the patient," Pam moaned. "Get me to the infirmary." The last word trailed off with another wave of nausea. Then she threw up.

"Crap," Jimmy muttered as he hurried off. He grabbed a portable stretcher they kept in a small shed in

#10 and ran back. Bridget and Mai Ker were both kneeling over Pam, supporting her shoulders. Bridget was wiping Pam's mouth with part of her own shirt.

They gently moved Pam onto the stretcher and Jimmy and Bridget carried her through Pods 10 and 3 to the infirmary in #7.

"Vitals," Pam was instructing Bridget, although Bridget knew what to check. "Jimmy, can you get some fresh water from the fridge? I need to settle my stomach."

"Sure." He was still trying to avoid the odor of vomit that lingered around Pam and Bridget. He didn't hold his nose because he didn't want them to see what a wimp he was when it was someone else throwing up.

Mai Ker hovered, trying to help Bridget. Pam spoke to them both.

"You're going to have to draw blood and I'll walk you through the tests. The computer will do most of it."

"Sure," Bridget said. She wasn't confident about her skills with a draw-needle but she knew she had no choice. Pam surely didn't want to draw her own blood.

Jimmy brought a cup of water from the small jug they kept in the lab refrigerator. Pam drank it and seemed calmer.

After some miscues with the needle, Bridget managed to get a large enough blood sample from Pam's arm. She started the lab work, following Pam's directions.

"I need something to eat," Pam finally said.

This was a good sign. Her appetite was not overwhelmed by the pain.

"I'll make something. Just tell me what," Jimmy said.

He was more interested right now in the kitchen than the lab and he knew it would smell better. Pam was the one who was pregnant and sick but Jimmy felt more squeamish than she did. Each time he thought about their baby, in fact, he got queasy with worry.

"Just something light," Pam told him. When Jimmy was out of the infirmary, she said quietly, "I can't lose this baby."

Mai Ker took her hand, and Bridget also came to her side.

"I know," Mai Ker said softly. "It will be OK. I hope." Only Mai Ker would have said it like this. But it was what all three women were feeling.

"What do we need to do, Pam?" Bridget asked.

"Give me the MedDxPad. On the desk there. I need to run symptoms and diagnoses, when the blood results are done."

Jimmy was back before long with a fresh sandwich and some milk. Pam got it down, but it was plain she was still hurting. They agreed she needed to rest. She and Mai Ker had worked hard throughout the afternoon. Maybe, Pam hoped, this was just fatigue. She worked on the sandwich and started running diagnostic quizzes into the MedDxPad. It would tell her what was going on.

Mai Ker stayed with her when Jimmy and Bridget left for the kitchen tent in Pod 10 to work on supper. They ate quickly, fed the kids, and made a sandwich for Mai Ker. Bridget stayed to tend the two children and Jimmy headed back to the infirmary.

Pam was pale and still not feeling good. She was half-dozing, as was Mai Ker in a chair beside the bed.

"How is she?" Jimmy asked softly, offering Mai Ker the sandwich.

Pam's eyes opened a little as if she was asking, *How dare you talk about me when I'm sleeping?*

"She's crummy," Pam said, humoring her husband. "And it's your fault, too." She smiled, but there came a sharp pain behind the grin.

"You'd better sleep in here tonight, Pam," Jimmy said. "I'll stay with you. Bridget and Mai Ker can look after the kids."

Pam nodded. She wanted this baby born. She wanted it now. She wanted it yesterday. She closed her eyes again and tried without much success to get some real sleep.

2

Friday, October 9th, 3 (NC)

Pam was still very ill this morning. Everyone was upset, most of all Jimmy, who felt helpless to do anything about anything. Bridget and Mai Ker at least were sitting with Pam, comforting her, reassuring her. Jimmy just walked in and out of the infirmary as if he was lost, or trying to think of some long-forgotten dream he had never had.

He had managed to sit by Pam's bed overnight, dozing much of the time, hoping that by morning his mere presence would make her feel better. When he awoke to her groaning and realized it hadn't worked, he went to the house tents to find Bridget and Mai Ker and said he needed a break.

As soon as Herald and Sing were fed and toddling around the pods, the two women went right to the infirmary. Jimmy stayed back, keeping an eye on the two kids. He walked and fretted. In the infirmary, Bridget and Mai Ker began to feel the same helplessness. Pam didn't seem to be getting any better, despite the medicine the MedDxPad had prescribed last night.

After two hours, Mai Ker was the one who needed a break. The worry on her face was like a stain. She knew Jimmy and Pam had tried a long time for her to get pregnant. If they lost this baby, the chances of Pam getting pregnant again were very close to zero.

Mai Ker quietly left the infirmary and found Jimmy. They stood staring out the north side of Pod 3 at the blank world around them, not really seeing anything beyond the plastic shell that held them. A gentle but steady rain had begun to fall OUTSIDE.

"Why is this always happening to us?" she asked Jimmy.

"What?" he asked.

"What do you mean, 'what'? Everything—always going wrong. Why can't anything ever go right?"

Jimmy knew what she was feeling. He had felt it often enough himself. But he had refused to give in to it in recent months. Herald and Sing were healthy and growing. The future, as always, was a blind. But Jimmy had begun to search for hope again, wanting to believe there was something more.

He looked at Mai Ker and took her in his arms.

"A lot does go right, Mai. I think we just don't notice when it does."

"You're just saying that. You think I'll feel better."

"What's wrong with that?" he asked.

"Are you really facing it, Jimmy? Look around." She gestured OUTSIDE toward the withered landscape and the darkened sky. She gave a sigh. "What could ever go right again?"

Jimmy didn't answer because he was distracted by a small, high yelp. Both of them turned and through the pod walls saw the source of the cry. Little Sing was standing, staring up toward the top of the Meeting Tent in Pod 10, upset and whining. Then they saw Herald, bouncing on the top of the large tent roof as if on a trampoline, 12 feet off the ground.

"Oh man—" Jimmy said, starting a fast jog for the podwalk that led to #10.

Mai Ker on his tail, they ran as fast as they could to the Meeting Tent.

"Herald," Jimmy was shouting as they came into #10. "Stop!"

If Herald heard, he ignored them. Only 2½ years

old, he was big for his age, inheriting his father's stature. How he got onto the tent roof they couldn't imagine.

"Herald, please stand still!" Mai Ker yelled as they lurched to a stop.

The shocked sense of warning in her voice finally got his attention. He bounced to a stop. Fortunately, the roof of this tent was heavy canvas and unlikely to rip through.

"Get him down," Mai Ker pleaded to Jimmy.

"Yeah, yeah!" he barked, trying to figure out the quickest way. "Wait here."

He ran into Pod 9, grabbed a tall stepladder from the side of the barn and ran back.

"OK, Herald, just stand still, OK?" he ordered.

Herald, finally realizing he was in trouble for some reason he couldn't understand, did just that. He became a miniature statue sagging about 1 foot down into the tent canvas as if sinking in quicksand. His smile was gone. He braced himself for whatever might happen next, as certain as a 2-year-old can be that it would not be fun.

Sing continued to fret but hadn't uttered another peep. Mai Ker grabbed her up and cuddled her, trying to calm her.

"Thank you, sweetheart! You're so smart to call Mommy and Daddy."

Sing had no idea what she meant. All she knew was she had been scared by Herald on top of the tent, thinking he might fly out through the pod roof into nowhere. Now her mom held her and she felt safe. Life is fairly simple for one that young.

Atop the ladder, Jimmy leaned as far as he could without careening into the tent roof himself. He coaxed Herald toward him. Herald moved stiff-legged like a wooden soldier and suddenly dropped himself into Jimmy's arms, which nearly sent them both flying off the ladder. Jimmy caught his balance and carried the wayward boy to the ground.

"How did you do that?" was the first question Jimmy hammered him with.

"What?" Herald asked in all innocence. It was one of the few words he knew, besides "Why?"

"How in the world did you get up there?"

"Rope." Herald said it as if any moron should have already known the answer.

"What ro—" Then Jimmy remembered. Two days ago, he had noticed that one of the brace ropes on the far side of the tent had come loose and was dangling toward the ground.

"No way could you reach that!" he told Herald. Jimmy hurried around to the far side of the tent. There, beneath the dangling rope, was a short bench from the Meeting Tent and on top of that was a plastic chair, its legs just touching the outer edges of the bench. The seat of the chair was about 3 feet below the dangling rope, enough for Herald to stretch up and grasp it.

"Unbelievable . . ." Jimmy muttered, taking the assemblage down.

Mai Ker had followed him. She shook her head.

"Well, at least he has a little scientist's mind," she laughed.

"Or an engineer's mind," Jimmy said, enjoying the humor now that the panic had worn off.

"And his father's courage," Mai Ker said, thinking of Clayton. "Sure miss that guy," she said sadly.

Jimmy nodded but said nothing. Clayton's death was still a very painful memory. He carried the bench and chair back inside the tent.

BRIDGET PROPPED Pam's head up a little more with a second pillow. Pam was still twisting slowly side to side trying to find a comfortable position, which she was finding impossible.

"Can you eat something, Pam? You must be starved."

Pam's head turn a little sideways as if Bridget had just asked her to swallow six slimy raw oysters.

"Can't. Probably puke again."

"Some soup, maybe? Try at least? You need something in you."

"OK. I'll try," Pam said with great uncertainty. Her belly ached inside and out. "No promise."

"I'll go warm something up," Bridget said.

She encountered Jimmy as he was coming back into Pod 7. He frowned as he explained what happened with her errant son.

"Didn't spank him," Jimmy said. "Prob'ly should have."

"I'll talk with him," she said. "Would you sit with Pam? I'm getting her some soup."

"She going to be OK?" Jimmy asked.

"I hope so." She saw it was the wrong answer. She tried, "I think so."

"We have to do something," Jimmy said. "We just can't lose this baby. Not this close."

"I know. But what can we do? The whole pregnancy's been hard. She's beat up."

"My fault," Jimmy muttered.

"No, it's not, Jimmy. We all wanted this. Just didn't realize how tough it was going to be. For Pam."

"If she makes it, we should give her a medal or something."

Now Bridget frowned.

"Jimmy, sometimes you talk like an idiot." She laughed. "What she needs most right now is a hug."

The idiot agreed and went into the infirmary and promptly delivered the prescription. It seemed to help. Pam forced a pained smile.

"Thanks, hubby," Pam said, and let out another little cry of pain. "Maybe you should pray to your God friend. I think I could use his help."

"Been prayin', believe me. All night." He let out a frustrated sigh. "Don't know what else to say."

Mai Ker had managed to tuck the two well-lectured kids into their beds for a nap and she followed Bridget back to the infirmary. Pam got down the soup and two crackers. Two crackers was her limit.

"Go on, Jimmy," Pam said, licking pasty cracker crumbs from her lips. "Say some prayers."

Bridget looked away. She wondered how Mai Ker would react. But when she looked back, Mai Ker was nodding slightly.

"Please, Jimmy," Pam said.

Jimmy had been leaning against a cabinet while Pam ate her bit of lunch. He walked over to the bed and took her hand.

"I'm not very good," he said.

"At a lot of things," Pam chuckled.

"OK." He paused, trying to think. "Lord God, you know I don't . . . I don't pray very good. But I ask you to be here and to help Pam, help her be well. And help our baby. Lord, we really want this baby. You know how bad we want it. I hope that's what you want, too. So, please help Pam. And please protect our baby." A pause. "Amen."

Bridget and Mai Ker both vaguely echoed the "Amen." Pam again nodded just a little.

"Thanks, Jimmy," Pam smiled.

There was no instant miracle, however. Pam continued to have severe stomach pain through the rest of the day and into the evening. She worried that all her twisting and turning was somehow hurting the baby, though she wasn't sure how. She tried to sleep a little more but it was impossible with the constant ache inside. She nibbled a couple more crackers late in the evening but besides two glasses of water it was all she could get down.

BRIDGET SAT with Pam through the rest of the afternoon while Jimmy and Mai Ker tried to find something to keep busy. When the children were up from their naps, they took them along as they cleaned around the horse corral in #9 and then did some cleanup in the equipment shed in #8. They continued to be amazed by how things in their little world could get so dirty, even in a completely closed ecosystem. Pod cleaning never stopped.

As the two worked, Sing and Herald stayed close and played aimlessly. Neither tried any new adventures. With the kids nearby, even with the little ones' very limited vocabulary and understanding, Jimmy and Mai Ker were careful not to talk about Pam or the baby. But she and the baby rarely left their minds, despite the busywork. Two years had passed since the terrible catastrophe OUTSIDE. And those two years had not even begun to numb the pain of losing Clayton, and Willy, and Sarajane. Another loss would be unbearable, though this fear never quite left their minds.

Today was October 9, 3 NC. "NC" was short for their New Calendar, the new period of history they were living in. With all the death and destruction they had witnessed—both at a distance, and close at hand—the surviving Solarians had decided to simply restart the calendar. What was done was done. History, as most of humanity had known it, was over. The old calendar died with all those who had been lost. So the year Herald and Sing were born became year "1." The next year became 2 NC. Thus they would measure whatever future they might have here INSIDE. Whatever was OUTSIDE was beyond thought or desire, and clothed in unthinkable fears. Everyone—everything—dead. The clear Stellar plastic of the pods had become at least mentally opaque to the Solarians. The only ones who ever really looked out with eyes to see were Herald and Sing. And their tiny minds could not plumb what they saw there.

What they incessantly saw out there was a still life of devastation. The high plains stretched out around them in depressing colors of browns and grays. The rubble of dead plants lay undisturbed, except when strong winds led a storm into the area. Most of the smaller trees had keeled over already. The larger ones were quickly rotting and would fall with time.

Some of the few appealing sights were the lush rainbows that sometimes followed a storm. The purplish sky seemed to intensify and alter the other colors of the bow. It was one of the few times they might look OUTSIDE with anxious hope, watching to see if a rainbow might arc itself across the sky. There was rain today. Their eyes would chance the depressing view as the price of perhaps seeing brief moments of rich color in the heavens.

BY LATE evening, Pam was still hurting but calmer. As 9:00 p.m. approached, Bridget was finding it hard to stay awake. She was hungry but didn't want to leave Pam's side. She tried to read, some of the time reading aloud to Pam, but the long day by the bedside had taken its toll. Bridget called on her intercom radio for Jimmy and Mai Ker.

"You guys take over, will you? I'll watch the kids tonight. I need some sleep." She looked at Pam. "No offense, Pam."

"It's OK. I understand. Believe me." She let out a yawn of exhaustion that, unfortunately, would not foreshadow sleep.

Jimmy and Mai Ker had just finished one of the regular inspection tours of all the pods, including those that were normally closed off, checking for any roof leaks. The drizzling rain had continued through the day and gave them a chance to watch for drips.

"Be there in a few," Mai Ker said over her radio as they pulled the podwalk door from #4 shut behind them.

Bridget was standing and stretching when they reached the infirmary. Jimmy gave her a hug and she left for the tents.

"Kids are in bed," Mai Ker told her.

"Small favors," Bridget said as she went.

Jimmy sat and took Pam's hand while Mai Ker busied herself with a thick medical book, looking at the pages that dealt with pregnancy.

"Remember when we got married?" Jimmy asked Pam.

"Yeah," Pam said vaguely.

"Me, too." He was looking intently at her. "You doing OK?"

"I am. Still hurting. But I'm better somehow."

"Really?"

"Can't explain it, exactly. But I know the baby's going to be OK."

Mai Ker looked worried more than ever. She closed the book and turned her face away from Jimmy and Pam. Was there a hint in Pam's voice that the baby would be OK—but she wouldn't? Jimmy sensed it, too.

"You're both gonna be fine," he told Pam. "Be fine."

"Yeah. I think it's all up to God, Jimmy. We did pray. Right?"

Jimmy smiled.

"Yes, we did."

The night moved on like a slug searching for food in the dark ground. Just before midnight Pam gave a yelp. This was a new kind of pain. It came suddenly and with full force.

"Aaa— Oohhh no! Can't—!" She choked. "Can't do this!"

"Get Bridget," Jimmy barked at Mai Ker, who had half-dozed off on the floor in a corner.

"What?" was her dazed answer. She stumbled to her

feet. She bolted for the door and podwalk. "Bridget!"

"Don't wake the kids, Mai!" Jimmy yelled after her.

"I think this is it," Pam was hollering. "I think our little girl is ready to show up!"

"It's too soon!" Jimmy babbled, starting to panic. The baby was not due for another month.

Mai Ker dashed for the house tent and found Bridget in bed, still sleeping, unawakened by her shouts. She roused her and hurried her back toward the infirmary.

Jimmy had ahold of Pam's right hand as if he might pull it off. Pam was writhing on the infirmary bed. Bridget broke in between them and got Pam into a better, semi-sitting position.

Piper Hansen-Algood almost didn't make it. Pam's labor started hard, eased off, then came on stronger again about 4:00 a.m. She was hyperventilating half that time. Bridget knew this wasn't good but she couldn't stop her. Pam pounded on the mattress as if she was trying to tenderize it, and poor Mai Ker, who knew childbirth all too well, grimaced along with Pam through the long hours.

About 3:30, little Sing came wandering through the infirmary door in her pajamas, half-asleep but wondering what all the noise and commotion was about.

"Mommy?" she whimpered.

She looked relieved to see her mother was not the source of the scary noises but the poor child was terrified at the state Auntie Pam was in.

Mai Ker hurriedly scooped her up and carried her back to bed. She managed to get Sing back to sleep, which was no easy task with a curiosity-peaked 2-year-old in the middle of the night.

3

Saturday, October 10th, 3 (NC)

Pam struggled through the last three agonizing hours of labor. Then, a little past 7:00 this morning, the baby's head crowned and the delivery went quickly.

Despite Pam being sick much of the pregnancy, and the baby being almost a full month premature, Piper seemed as healthy as could be. Just too small. The gripping pain Pam had gone through in the past few hours had not affected her baby. Piper, even with her eyes unopened, seemed radiant, a newborn glow that reflected the joy on Pam's face as she beamed down at her child.

Until she discovered she was pregnant with Piper, Pam had resigned herself to the fact that she would never bear a child. So there was a sense of the miraculous about Piper's conception once they finally knew it was certain. And even a few hours ago, Pam would have gladly sacrificed her own life to ensure Piper would be born healthy. Piper's life had depended entirely on Pam's. The Solarians were ecstatic they had both survived the ordeal.

Pam had chosen the name as soon as they discovered the baby was a girl, the name of a stage and film star Pam admired when she was young. Had she realized Piper Laurie's real name was Rosetta Jacobs, she would probably have thought twice. But Mai Ker immediately liked it, too, so the name stuck.

"We have a Herald. Why not a Piper? I love names that mean something. Most are so boring," Mai Ker told her.

"Like Pam?" Pam asked.

"What about Jimmy?" Jimmy interrogated her.

"Yes. Boring," Mai Ker said.

As he held little Piper in his arms moments after her birth, Jimmy beamed as brightly as Pam.

"Never thought I'd see this," Jimmy smiled as he cradled the newborn.

"You and me both, Papa," Pam chimed.

Bridget and Mai Ker stood by Jimmy, smiles bursting but hearts rending at the same time. Piper was a full month early. Her survival would be touch-and-go the next couple of months. They all knew that while each birth was in a sense miraculous, each also carried a sense of foreboding. What would these new little lives mean? What was *their* future likely to be? How long could the Solarium support them, not to mention the children these children might someday have?

These were the easier questions. Others were worse. What would happen once the older generation began to die off? How could anyone tell when that might be? Would they even live long enough to raise these children? The troubling questions kept piling up like wrecks in a junkyard.

At the moment, though, Pam felt only a sense of relief.

"Good Lord, I'm glad that's over," Pam whimpered. Her mouth was still dry, her voice raspy and straining. "How could something you want so bad hurt like that?"

"Like being cut in two with a machete?" Bridget laughed. "Tell me about it."

Mai Ker put on a pretended frown.

"You just make too much of it, Bridget. It is over very quickly." She was partly trying to convince herself, because she badly wanted another baby herself.

"Compared to nine months you mean?" Pam asked.

"That, too," Mai Ker laughed.

Jimmy just kept smiling, cuddling, hugging the poor

little creature almost to the point of suffocating her. It had been the same with Sing.

"Jimmy, don't kill her already," Mai Ker said, pulling the baby gently from him. "Let her breathe a little."

"Just lovin' her up," Jimmy said. "A most beautiful baby. Even if I am the dad. Can't understand it."

"Can I just hold her some more, too?" Pam asked weakly, drying her own hair and forehead with an edge of the bed sheet.

Mai Ker smiled and handed Piper to Pam. Little Piper was starving and would soon want to nurse but she and mom were both too exhausted right now to want anything but rest.

"I'll sit with them while they nap," Bridget said. "You two check the kids. Maybe get some breakfast together? It's been a really long night."

It had been. Jimmy's and Mai Ker's legs felt those long hours again as they trudged to the nursery to check on Sing and Herald.

BY NOON, after being cooped up in the infirmary so many hours, Bridget had to get out. She left Pam and the baby and went for a walk, wandering to Pod 12. She walked to her favorite spot by their artificial ocean, where she and Clayton used to sit and talk.

It wasn't the same anymore. Even though she could remember him vividly—and at times saw his face in her mind's eye—she could no longer sense his presence, even vaguely. He was just gone.

She stretched back onto the sand and looked toward the top of the pod. She tried to picture Clayton's face. He seemed always smiling, though in life he often wasn't. She also caught a glimpse in her mind's eye of little Caroline, his tiny nuthatch.

What ever became of her? Bridget wondered again.

None of the Solarians knew. They had just noticed one day she was gone. It bothered Bridget the most. She had actually gone and searched for the little creature. Caroline was not in the aviary, nor in #10 where she had often perched, watching the humans work. Nowhere to be found. She must have died.

"She was so cute," Bridget said to herself aloud. "And so sad. She used to perch on your bed, Clayton. After you were gone. Waiting for you to come home."

She forced her eyes tightly shut, pinching off the tears. Her half-smile faded completely. She missed Caroline so much because she had remained a living link to Clayton.

Bridget wished she could have found her. She would have buried the little creature in Clayton's plot, just above his coffin.

The memories were happy and tragic at the same time.

Guess it's always that way. That's death, she told herself.

She supposed death might be painful. But she knew it was those who were left who really suffered.

The thick smell of the sea air was refreshing. She could almost taste it. The scent always brought her a sense of relief, a reminder of happy times as a child. As she looked up, she imagined Caroline flying around near the pod roof. Clayton and his little nuthatch had been so connected. Vastly different species, yet kindred spirits.

"Wish you were back," she whispered to the Clayton who wasn't there. "You and your little friend." She let her mind drift for several moments. "I think it was your tenderness and love for that poor injured bird that first drew me to you, Clayton. A guy your size, with your brains, your muscle—being so caught up in loving something so helpless. Made me love you, I guess."

If Clayton Block had been there, he would have just nodded, and said nothing. So the conversation had a sense of reality.

"I wonder sometimes," she said aloud as if he could

hear, "if I'd have married you. If I'd known, I mean. That you'd be gone so quick."

It was one more unanswerable question, another wreck atop the junkyard. She floundered around for an answer. She found none.

She closed her eyes, wanting to see the invisible. She saw only a blank wall. What had become of him? Was he just gone, like Caroline? Did something of him survive? Bridget wasn't sure. She believed that something must survive when someone dies. She didn't know how. She usually didn't let her mind go to these places, where questions seemed always to have no real answers. It was too uncomfortable, wrestling with emotions that went this deep. Better to just let such things rest, she felt.

"Whistling past the graveyard," she could hear her grandmother saying. Grandma had said it more than once, especially as she aged.

"I still love you," she said quietly to the departed Clayton.

She remembered his touch, his kiss, his smell. In some way beyond her grasp, the connection they had was unbroken even by his death. She held onto that tether. She hated those long-ago days, the fears, the uncertainties, the gnawing not-knowing. Then Clayton's death shattered the one dream she had dared among all the nightmares of those months. Still, she clung to the memory of those terrible days to keep sane. For as bad as they were, they included Clayton, the father of her son.

She had given up trying to understand it all. She just wanted something—someone—to hold her.

Little Herald was her consolation. He could not hold her but she could cuddle him. She could share Clayton's love with his little boy. The boy he didn't get the chance to meet.

MAI KER and Jimmy were cleaning around the main house tent and the kitchen area. It had obviously been neglected the last couple of days. She had become more fanatical about things being clean. She felt better seeing things washed up and in place. It provided a sense of rightness, of stability, of calm amid the continuous storm that was their life INSIDE.

But today, for some reason, her mind had gone to worrying about the stability of the Solarium again. Maybe it was because they were living "outdoors" in the tents and had abandoned the house to help save energy. Maybe it was just general anxiety ramped up by the birth of the newest baby.

"How long do you think we can go?" she said vacantly to the air.

Jimmy stopped wiping a countertop, stared at her, and frowned, expressing with his eyebrows that he didn't have the vaguest clue what she was talking about. The first thought that popped into his mind was wildly astray.

"Go?"

"How long can we last in here?"

She had asked similar questions before and he hadn't liked it then, either. His normal solution, for himself, was to try to avoid all thought about anything long term and focus on the day at hand. Most days it worked.

"Why are you asking?"

"I don't know," Mai Ker said truthfully. Her eyes narrowed, as if she was peering off into some great distance. "I just wonder about it. Sometimes."

Jimmy took her hand and brought her over to sit by their transplanted kitchen table. He looked at her still-beautiful eyes.

"Wonder? Or worry?"

"Yes. I worry some," she said. "Family trait."

"Some? You worry a lot. Especially now. With Sing."

"Yes. But it is not just Sing. I want another baby. But then I think of it. And I'm afraid."

"Of what?"

"Is it smart? Jimmy," she said looking at him as if he

were a stranger, "I mean, how many of us are safe in here?" She looked around. "The Solarium was built to last. I know that. But they really only planned for four years. Now look. It's no good." She turned back to Jimmy. "It will never last."

Jimmy frowned deeply as he watched the tremors in her face. He made a little nod.

"Well, yeah, they planned out four years. But the place was designed to last a century or more—you know, as an outpost on another world."

"Still," she said, "it could be endless. Babies grow up. They'll have babies. Can it be endless like that? In here?"

"I don't know," Jimmy had to admit.

Mai Ker sighed quietly. She was thinking deeply about something else that she wasn't voicing.

"Is there anything we can do to improve the pods? Or increase our food production? Or animal production?"

He hated it when she pressed him like this with questions she knew he could not answer.

"Mai, we're doing the best we can. And we're already producing and freezing more than we'll ever eat. And we don't really need more animals sucking up our air. Right?"

"Yes, that's true." She peered off into the impenetrable darkness again. "But what if someday we end up with a couple of hundred people in here? It could happen. Right? Then what? We grow, then we falter?" She paused, shaking her head at the thought. "How are we going to support that many? If we raise more food and cattle—to have enough—will that ruin the air? Will everything go wrong again?"

"Right now we don't need more cattle. We need more kids."

"But is it safe? Is it wise? What if we do? What if we have more—and something does go wrong again? Then what? What have we done? To them," she winced a little, "after we're gone?"

Jimmy knew what she was feeling. He just didn't want to go down that trail at the moment. It was a happy day, with the arrival of Piper. He didn't want to spoil it with worry.

"Oh, I think a few more kids won't hurt," he reassured her. "We could sustain quite a few more mouths and sets of lungs. Honestly, I'm more worried about whether our babies can have babies. And how many. You know?"

"Yes. I think about it, too," she said. But then she got quiet and her face went somber. Mentally, she left the room.

"Yeah," Jimmy said aimlessly, acknowledging what he saw in her eyes. He gently rubbed her forearm. "We have to face it. That a day will come when we're not here anymore. It will just be the kids. And we have to plan for that. We've gotta train them how to take care of everything. The equipment. The crops. The animals. It's so much for us. How will just two or three be able to manage all that?"

"They can't," Mai Ker replied. Her mind was back in the room. "That's why I want another. We have to try to build things back up. So, yes. I worry. What if we overload everything? Especially, what if we end up breathing too much air, and it can't regenerate fast enough?"

"The balancing act we've been facing all along, sweetie. Nothing new. There's something else I've thought of, though. Don't know why we haven't done it already. You know, we never refilled all those air tanks and oxygen tanks we emptied out."

"No," she said. "I guess we didn't see any point. At first. Put bad air back in them, I mean."

"But the air's stable now. We could refill them. Everything we can find. Like before. Our emergency reserve."

"It worked once."

"Could work again." He paused. "And if we refilled

the scuba tanks, I could go diving again. Miss that."

Mai Ker looked dumbfounded.

"We just forgot with . . . everything else." She started to say "with their deaths," but caught herself.

But Jimmy knew what she was about to say.

"You're right. Why didn't we do it after that?" she asked.

"What do you call me all the time?"

"Dummy?"

"Yeah. Pretty stupid that we haven't refilled those tanks." He laughed and hugged her and planted a big kiss on her lips. His mind wandered to where it had started a few minutes ago. "No time like the present," he smiled, about to kiss her again.

But Mai Ker's mind had again gone elsewhere.

"Let's go check on Pam and the baby."

Bridget had moved Pam and Piper back to Pam's tent, where Jimmy had built a new crib for the little one. It was much like the wicker bassinet Herald and Sing had shared, but smaller. He made it new because he wanted Pam to feel it was special, for her and her child.

As they walked over to Pam's tent, Jimmy refocused his mind, picking up his conversation with Mai Ker.

"Our air is as good as it's ever gonna get. I've kept a close eye. Hasn't changed much the last year. We should definitely refill all those tanks. Some reserve is better than what we got now."

"None," Mai Ker said.

He thought a moment. "If we got creative, maybe we can figure how to rig some new kinds of tanks. Or air tents. Something."

"You know," Mai Ker said, pausing just outside Pam's tent and looking at it a little sideways, "there's dead space under the old house. That crawlspace where the pipes and electrical come in. Could we seal that good enough? To make it airtight?"

"Don't see why not. I think we'd have what we need.

Close some holes, some taping and caulking. It's pretty much closed in already." He looked at her. "That's a pretty smart idea, Mai."

"I am a pretty smart woman."

"Pretty, at least."

She smacked his arm.

"And smart," he added with a smile. He leaned forward and planted another long and loving kiss on her pretty smart lips. He wanted to head over to her tent.

"Let's see the baby," she said, putting him off.

Pam looked refreshed and rested, and was nursing Piper. Bridget had gone off somewhere, so Jimmy and Mai Ker planted themselves and talked with Pam. Pam's eyes were wide open for the first time in hours, and they were taking in the beauty of her little girl. She was nearly a bald little thing, and very small. They had no incubator, never having considered a preemie. So Pam's arms or their own would have to provide the nearly constant warmth her tiny body would need to adjust and thrive in the outer world. Pam had her well wrapped in two halves of a cotton blanket that had been cut down to baby-blanket size. Piper didn't understand nursing yet, but she was avidly trying to figure it out.

"She's perfect," Mai Ker said.

"We're very blessed, aren't we Jimmy?" Pam asked. "Didn't think this was ever going to happen. For me."

He was unconsciously squeezing Mai Ker's hand and self-consciously let go of it. This was one of his other wives. He kept forgetting. The addition of the child between them now brought a different sense of closeness to Pam, a sense that had been lacking. Still, Mai Ker would always be his first and his real love. His love for Pam and for Bridget was a duty and would always lack the depth of what he felt for Mai Ker.

"We are blessed," he finally said. "How, why, I don't know. Life is so fragile."

"But so very persistent," Mai Ker observed, the

scientist in her resurfacing.

"Very," Pam said, looking with delight at Piper.

4

Monday, February 8th, 4 (NC)

Not many months after Piper came along, Mai Ker discovered she was going to get her wish. She was pregnant again.

The test showed she became pregnant around mid-December, so the next arrival in the Solarium was expected in early September. She and Jimmy were elated again, as were Bridget and Pam when they first heard this news last night.

"Finally," Mai Ker said as she had given them the news, "maybe things are finally starting to go right."

All four felt excited. Maybe they could begin to dream again, to plan a future after all. The image of life INSIDE being renewed was faint and still distant, but it was there. Life persisted, even when all seemed completely dark and hopeless. It was a solid realization that had lurked in their hearts beneath the surface of reality. It was now beginning to resurface into consciousness as one of the few things they could really count on.

The Solarians gathered for breakfast this Monday morning at the large table in the middle of the kitchen tent. Sing and Herald were propped up with several books and a couple of cushions on wooden chairs, the children's makeshift highchairs.

None of the planners of Solarium-3 had expected a need for highchairs. In fact, the original planning team under Haskins had done everything they could to prevent such a need.

Jimmy and Bridget had rigged the chairs up to the

right heights so that the two kids were comfortable, if messy. Some of Herald's food was ground into his lap and Sing was spreading almost as much jam on her face as was on the toast.

Herald wouldn't need his highchair much longer if he kept eating and growing at this rate.

"Don't feed him so much," Pam joked. "He could eat a whole freezer-worth in a day if you let him."

"Growing boy," Bridget said happily. "Got his father's appetite."

At almost 3, Herald remained large for his age, as his father had once been, and he had begun to reflect his father's bold walk. He wasn't exactly hefty, nor was he small. His large childish frame was obviously the beginning of another oversized man. The only thing he seemed to have inherited from Bridget was her smile and the fact that, when he tried to think hard, his eyes narrowed into that sleepy look that was so characteristic of his mom. His wavy hair, which early on had been nearly blond, was darkening to a sandy brown.

Piper seemed happier than usual this morning. She always seemed happy, though she was only 4 months old. She was half-tucked into her wicker crib that Pam had carried in and parked by the breakfast table. The baby cooed quietly as Pam had breakfast. Pam was still nursing Piper but wasn't producing enough milk, so this morning she was about to break her in on some cow's milk, watered down a little. First mom had to eat. She was buttering a large chunk of fresh, warm bread.

"I've been thinking we should work on some new solar panels," Jimmy was saying.

"Why?" Bridget asked. "Something wrong with the others?"

"No, every one of 'em checks good. But it can't hurt to have a little more backup. We're adding kids. Little by little," he smiled at Mai Ker. "Over time, there's gonna be more." He said it with a confidence that outweighed his own hopes of producing many more children. He was ready to settle for being a grandfather. He looked at little Herald and Sing, and shook his head. That would be a very long way off—if ever. "Eventually we're gonna have to open back up some of the other pods."

"And it's your fault, too," Mai Ker laughed. It had become the women's standard jibe at him.

"Yeah, with lots of willing help," Jimmy replied, turning his head from woman to woman. He and Bridget had not yet succeeded in the child department, but not for lack of trying. "Anyway, I just think it would be a good idea. We boost our electrical production, it helps take some of the worry out of things. Who knows, maybe someday, we get comfortable enough, we turn some of the shut-down equipment back on, too. Heck. Never know what we might be able to do."

"Since we've got all the air tanks filled again, we should be thinking of other options, too," Mai Ker said.

"I thought closing in the crawlspace under the house was pretty creative," Pam said. "A giant air tank. I would've never thought of that!"

"Yes, but that's just one idea. Who says we can't come up with more? We've got a long time to think," Mai Ker said.

Bridget was already thinking quietly.

"You know," she said, "I was wondering, about underground. If there's some way we could tunnel down, maybe along one of the pod foundations. Maybe create some air spaces down there, too. We've got plenty of plastic sheets and tarps we could use to make it airtight."

"Soil leaks," Mai Ker pointed out. "Air would escape over time."

"But it would hold some. Right?" Bridget wondered.

"Prob'ly," Jimmy said. "Just got to be careful we don't go too deep. Remember, there's a catchment basin under the whole complex," Jimmy said. "That's part of what's keeping us safe from air leaking in from

OUTSIDE. Lined with lead, remember? We don't want to damage that lining."

"But we can stay inside of that, can't we?" Bridget asked.

"Sure."

"So there we go," Pam remarked. "You guys' brains run a mile-a-minute. I'd say you're way ahead of the population curve." She reached down and brushed Piper's thin, silky, light brown hair with her fingers.

"Well, that's exactly what we want to do," Mai Ker said. "We have to make sure we can support more life. Not just us. The plant life, and the animals. They're all important, too. We wouldn't last long without them."

"Well, I'm with Jimmy," Bridget said. "Let's get busy on some more solar panels. Hey, anything makes life easier—I'm in favor!"

THE WORK started that very afternoon. They assembled wood and metal edging for the framework and more 4-by-8 sheets of lightweight plastic from the supply shed in Pod 13. It was truly amazing how much stuff the planners had packed into this place. Just six months ago the Solarians had uncovered a couple of sealed, metal crates that contained special oxygen packs, small, portable oxygen bottles they never knew they had. These, they figured, were probably planted by the military guys who worked with Haskins at the last minute before the Seal-In to provide for longer-term survival, just in case what they feared might happen OUTSIDE did. As it had.

The planners hiding this extra gear so well was providential. Had the Solarians known about these oxygen packs before "the Grand Opening," they would have all been empty now. The team was pleasantly surprised when they stumbled across them. They now had a pure oxygen reserve for future medical emergencies. Planning often fails, but sometimes it pays off.

Over the next few weeks they built 16 new solar panels. This meant they could run all the basic equipment and fully charge the large storage batteries at the same time. On the scale of life's comforts, electricity still ranked pretty high. And it meant much less time on the exercise bikes they had connected to two small generators.

Jimmy and Bridget also spent time trying to design a foil-bladed windmill to generate more energy. The plan was to devise a tower with broad blades at the top covered in lightweight tin foil or plastic foil. The tower would sit in Pod 5 above the swimming pool and connect to a small generator on the ground. Jimmy thought that with the right materials the heat near the pod roof would make the blades spin. It was just an idea at this point. Scribbles and designs on paper. They hadn't actually tried to build it.

But the fact they were thinking like this again, beginning to dream a little, beginning to imagine a longer future, this alone was a sign of health among the team. Feeding little mouths helped, but learning how to once again rely on ingenuity was a step they all enjoyed taking.

OVER THE next several months they would also implement Bridget's other idea. Gradually, carefully, and with significant help from the small people among them, they began to tunnel down underneath several of the pods, where it was safest to do so. As they painstakingly enlarged these underground cavities, they lined the areas with plastic sheeting and tarps, gluing them together as best they could to make them reasonably airtight. As each cavity was completed, they sealed it off, except for a large plastic hose that would pump air into the cavern for storage. The air would get a bit stale over time, but they hoped it would remain stable. If their atmosphere INSIDE ever soured again, the caverns could be used to slowly, in a controlled way, bleed "fresh" air into the pods.

On the other hand, they desperately hoped they would never need to try it.

Time had crept by slowly through the recent months. The Solarians were gradually aging. This, as Jimmy and Mai Ker had begun to discover, presented new psychological problems. Pam applied herself to these new issues cheerfully, looking for ways to bring humor into the glum reality that none of them was getting younger. Humor helped, except when her own body ached early in the morning and didn't seem to work as well as it used to. And she was, she kept reminding herself, nowhere near middle age.

There would be no such thing as growing old gracefully in this place. They had to think things out. They had to get ready. If that was possible.

The good news was that every day they aged, so did the kids. That, they continually reminded themselves, was the one really joyful thing in the midst of all the turmoil, worry and uncertainty that had become day-to-day life in Solarium-3.

MAI KER was awakened somewhere after midnight by a strange sound. It was a voice, but a very small voice. And it was strained through an obviously deep anxiety.

"Jimmy, what is that?"

Jimmy moaned quietly.

"Mice . . ."

"No, it's one of the children. Come on."

She pulled him out of the bed and they stumbled toward the door of her tent. There, across Pod 10, almost invisible in the low light, was a tiny figure in makeshift pajamas. It was Herald. The noise was coming from him, a kind of cry-like, fretting sound that was not in his normal store of kid sounds.

"Herald," Jimmy called as they walked quickly

toward him.

The call woke Bridget, who sat upright in her bed, breathing hard for a reason she didn't yet understand. She sat for a few moments trying to decide if she was waking up or dreaming more deeply.

"Herald," Jimmy called a second time, but with no reaction from the boy.

As they got close to him, it looked like his little body was glued against the pod wall. His face and hands were pressed tightly against the plastic as if he might push his way out to explore this strange mystery OUTSIDE. His little mouth mumbling against the pod wall accounted for the strangeness of the sounds coming from him, childlike sounds of curiosity blended with fear and confusion.

As they got closer to him and the pod wall, Jimmy and Mai Ker began to see what he was reacting to. The light of several overhead pod lights now behind them, they could just make out through the plastic wall streaks of lights plummeting toward the ground OUTSIDE.

"It's a . . ." Mai Ker began.

"A meteor shower?" Jimmy wondered.

"Looks like."

Herald's face remained pressed against the pod wall. He heard Mai Ker and Jimmy coming up behind him but was not about to take his eyes off the spectacular and strange sight OUTSIDE. His curious, frightened moan continued.

Mai Ker reached him and picked him up.

"It's OK, honey. Just some falling stars."

"Falling?" Herald asked, looking straight into her eyes with a puzzled expression.

He had seen stars at night, dimly, through the pod roofs. He had never seen any of those little points of light tumbling toward earth.

"Did I do it?" Herald asked.

He was so used to causing problems and so expecting almost hourly reprimands from one of the parents that he was feeling sure he had done something bad before bedtime that caused this. He had gotten out of bed to go potty and several streaks of light high overhead caught his eye as he walked in small steps toward the latrine tent. As he looked harder, it appeared that whatever these strange lights were they were hitting the ground not far away, just the south of the Solarium.

He had wandered clear across the pod, watching. He had never seen anything like this before tonight. He was lost in wonder but was also frightened. It appeared the world OUTSIDE must suddenly be falling apart.

"You didn't do anything, kiddo," Jimmy assured him, laughing softly and coddling his head. He understood perfectly why Herald had leapt to such a conclusion. Jimmy remembered being a little troublemaker at that age, too. He laughed again. "It's just a meteor shower, little guy."

"The stars are taking their bath?" Herald asked, more confused than ever.

"No, honey," Mai Ker explained, "a shower from the sky. They're little rocks, from space, falling through the atmosphere."

"At-*what*?"

Mai Ker could see there was no explaining this simple phenomenon to a 3-year-old.

Bridget came up behind them, eyes half-open, fairly certain now that she was not dreaming.

"What's going on?"

"Herald spotted a meteor shower," Jimmy said.

"Don't worry, honey. It's OK. Part of nature," Mai Ker was assuring him. She looked out at the meteors continuing to burn up as they sped toward the soil of earth. "I don't remember seeing one for a long time, though."

She looked at Jimmy. He shrugged.

"Me either," Bridget said. "Pretty."

She took her son from Mai Ker and cuddled him, bouncing him a little, trying to relieve the anxiety in his young eyes.

"Don't worry, sweetheart. Everything's OK. You're safe."

"I can't remember a meteor shower since we've been in here," Jimmy said. "'Course, I haven't really been watching very hard. Out there."

"Yes," Mai Ker acknowledged. Preoccupation with the grind of life INSIDE consumed their attention most days, especially at night when they were all very tired.

"But that's odd . . ." Jimmy said, looking off to the right, toward the sky.

"What is?" Mai Ker asked.

"Well, look. See? There. Toward the west and southwest. Why is it so black?"

"Dummy, the sky is black at night. You awake?"

"No, I mean you can see stars all around—except over there." He pointed. "That whole area. Seems blank." He peered harder through the thick Stellar walls, certain they were impeding his vision. "Weird."

Bridget, with Herald wiggling in her arms still watching the meteor shower that he didn't understand, looked off toward the southwest, following Jimmy's finger.

"Yeah. I see it now. It's all black, over that way."

"No stars. Stars everywhere else," he said, motioning in a broad stroke with his arm. "But not there."

"But that cannot be," Mai Ker said, telling him what he knew perfectly well. "There's stars out there. We're just not seeing them."

"But why?" Jimmy asked curiously.

"You sound like Herald," Bridget laughed.

"Simple. Probably a bank of clouds over that way. They haven't reached here yet," Mai Ker said.

Jimmy looked again.

"Maybe. Looks spooky, though."

"I didn't know you were so easily spooked, Jimmy Algood," his first wife snickered. "Come on. I'm tired."

Jimmy took a last glimpse OUTSIDE as they turned back toward the tents.

"Like a curtain drawn across the sky, or something. A giant stage. And the curtain pulling closed."

"There is no curtain in the sky, Jimmy," Mai Ker said softly, shaking her head. "Maybe your imagination is more awake that you are."

Jimmy shrugged.

"Or," Bridget said as they walked, "maybe some chemical changes in the atmosphere. Different density of gases in that region? Blocking the star light?"

"Maybe," Mai Ker said, feeling very sleepy again. "Why is it such a big thing to you two?"

"I don't know." Jimmy pulled her close to him. "Something new. Different. Not much different, ever. These days."

A distant memory pulled at his mind. Something he half-remembered. Maybe something he had once read. What? It would not come to him. He shook his fuzzy brain. It didn't help.

"Maybe we can tell better in the morning," he said. "When the sun's up."

Mai Ker was even groggier and wanted nothing except to fall back into bed.

"It is morning," she said.

Jimmy looked down at his watch.

"Almost 3:30."

"Ugh," Bridget said and walked ahead, carrying Herald back to his tent.

Mai Ker rubbed her shoulder, sore from sleeping crooked on it.

"It's late," she said.

"Early," Jimmy corrected her.

"Well, I can't handle any more mysteries tonight."

"This morning," he said.

She punched his arm harder the usual.

Jimmy would be up with the sun, as tired as he was, too. But when he looked out, he would see that the sky looked just as it had yesterday. Whatever the meteor shower had brought, if anything, remained invisible.

5

"We've got to make more diapers," Mai Ker said to Pam. "I get tired of washing these things every five minutes."

Pam laughed.

"Yeah, I'm just glad Piper is beyond them. Why can't kids be born potty-trained, huh?"

Mai Ker threw the messy diaper from her youngest child into the receptacle that served as a diaper pail, an old metal bucket with a large pie tin for lid.

"I'd just as soon clean the horse corral," she said.

"Hey, your folks lived through it, right?" Pam laughed.

"Yes. Maybe this is my payback?" Mai Ker wondered, snugging the fresh cloth diaper onto her son Nathaniel.

Nathaniel Moua-Algood, the not-quite-2-year-old son of Mai Ker and Jimmy, was their second child. He was growing and healthy, but slow on the upswing of understanding the use of the facilities in their bathroom tent. Mai Ker, in most respects a very patient woman, found herself impatient with the little guy, wanting him to grow up a lot faster than he ever could.

"Why does everything take so long?" she commented to Pam pinning up the diaper with the handmade pins Jimmy had fabricated.

"Are we in a hurry to get somewhere?" Pam asked in reply. "I'm not sure what the point of hurrying with anything anymore is."

"Maybe," Mai Ker said. "I think I just want the future more than it wants us."

NEARLY SEVEN years had passed since the original Solarian team had been sealed INSIDE Solarium-3. Just over five years had crept by since they restarted their calendar on the first of January following their second year in the complex. Still, though they didn't realize it, the surviving Solarians and their children had made only the tiniest dent into what lay ahead, a minuscule scratch in the top of a mountainous future buried in uncertainty, the uncertainty they struggled to face each day.

As Mai Ker had sensed months ago, things had finally begun to go better for them. Life was still painfully difficult but improving in small ways. All the equipment in the pods was still functioning well, at least what they had up and running. The new solar panels had increased their electrical production to the point where they even restarted the old master computers in Comm. Center in Pod 2 and the Research Center in Pod 3. There was no one OUTSIDE to communicate with but restoring access to all the archived information and data in those systems, and the vast knowledge stored there, would be an indispensable aid in teaching the children as they grew. Trapped INSIDE, the kids would be doubly curious about what had gone on OUTSIDE, why they were trapped here, and what had become of the race they descended from.

The extra power generation helped the Solarians keep all their rechargeable equipment fully powered. Handheld radios, flashlights, portable computers and various testing gear was now always ready, in case something hardwired failed.

The biggest plus, at least psychologically, was their new air storage reserves under the house and in the underground caverns. All were holding the compressed air they had pumped in. This backup air supply gave huge comfort to the Solarians, the reassurance that if the air ever started to foul again they had a way to help bring it back into balance. To their surprise, the compression of air into the reserve caverns had almost no effect on the total air pressure throughout the pods. Most importantly, the oxygen and nitrogen pressures remained in normal balance.

Despite the natural complaints about too many diapers, their attempt at repopulating the Solarium was gradually showing success. On September 6th just over a year and a half ago, 04 under the New Calendar, Nathaniel had been born to Mai Ker and Jimmy. Mai Ker wanted a traditional Hmong name but Jimmy had already picked a name he had come across one evening in his Bible. Checking one of their many research archives, he discovered the name Nathaniel meant "Gift of God." In their present predicament, he thought that was a pretty apt name. When he told Mai Ker what it meant, she was easily convinced.

Nathaniel was not the only new addition. After many long months of trying, Bridget finally got pregnant again. She was near the end of her final month and just after 10:00 o'clock this morning the labor started. As with Herald, her labor went as smoothly and easily as any labor can. Braden Listner-Algood was delivered at midafternoon, and Papa Jimmy was beaming once again.

"Thank you Lord!" he said when the cord was cut and the little guy let out a half-hearted yelp. "Another baby, safe and sound!"

Bridget just smiled. She wasn't sure how much the Lord had to do with it, and felt sure she had done all the work. But she had also begun to appreciate Jimmy's bubbling—and apparently growing—faith in his God, even though she didn't see much merit in such things herself. As she took the baby from Pam and cuddled him close to her breast, she was relieved, still aching, but grateful that another child had made it into their sheltered world.

As awful as their existence was, trapped in the Solarium, they had come to accept that this was all they would ever have. They were alive. That is what mattered. They were having children. Like Mai Ker, Bridget hesitantly began to believe some kind of future might come along for them after all.

"Call it God if you want, Jimmy," Bridget said. "I just call it life." She let out a long sigh. "And love. Nothing more lovable that a noisy, messy baby, huh?" She hugged Braden close. "They're so little and helpless."

"Uh-huh. Kind of like us," Pam remarked.

"OK, you ladies continue to talk," Jimmy said, "this is going to get deep, I can see. And long. So I'll just find something useful to do in the fields."

"It's not like we talk a lot," Pam said.

"It's not like you *don't* talk a lot either," he said as he left the infirmary.

Jimmy already had another new crib ready. Braden would share the nursery tent with Nathaniel now, with moms taking shifts. Herald, Sing and Piper had graduated to a shared bedroom in the new "kids tent" the team had added to one side of the main house tent.

Parenting, not to mention managing the whole Solarium, was keeping them all more than busy. Some days they ran on exhaust fumes. Jimmy, in the opinion of the three women, got most of the fun and playtime with the kids, while they did most of the real work. But with three children his own—now four—and Herald essentially his son by adoption, the women figured Jimmy's role as super-dad was enough of a burden without giving him all the dirty work to boot.

"NOT EXACTLY what we hoped for, is it?" Pam

asked Bridget and Mai Ker as they ate snacks by Bridget and Braden's bed in the infirmary two hours later. She said it cautiously, not wanting to offend Bridget.

"How do you mean?" Mai Ker asked.

"We've been hoping for more girls. By this point. You know?"

"Easier to have more babies with more girls," Bridget admitted. "But I love my little boys," she added, cuddling newborn Braden and trying not to doze off.

"Sure. Of course," Pam said. "I didn't mean that at all. I love them, too. I just meant, it's going to be harder—a lot slower. For the kids to have their own children, I mean. With only two girls."

"Not to mention the boyfriend-girlfriend fights that are going to break out someday!" Mai Ker laughed. "Can you imagine?" She chuckled again.

"Yes, I'm afraid I can," Pam said.

"Nothing ever goes the way you think it will, does it?" Bridget said, wiping a little drip of gurgling saliva from Braden lips.

"We're not dead, you know," Mai Ker said. "Not yet. Still time."

"No," Pam said with a melancholy frown. "You're not. But I think I'm probably done. I know you've noticed."

"What?" Mai Ker asked innocently, as if she really didn't know.

"My menopausal symptoms." Pam grimaced. "Jimmy sure has. Poor guy. Has to listen to me raving like a lunatic sometimes. For no reason."

"Yes, but maybe—" Bridget began before Pam cut her off.

"No. My periods have all but ended. Yeah. I'm afraid I'm done."

Braden, who had been trying to nurse unsuccessfully, burped quietly. Bridget wiped a little more spit.

"Just means me and Mai Ker will have to work harder," Bridget said.

This thought was the last thing she wanted to entertain at the moment. Her whole belly, back, pelvis, and legs still ached with shadow pains that, like long-term motion sickness, would take hours to subside.

"We can have more babies," Mai Ker said. "And I know some things that are supposed to help get a girl instead of a boy. Maybe old granny fables. But there is no harm trying. Is there?"

"No," Pam said, wanting to feel encouraged.

The troubling questions continued to press in on them. Could they really expect to grow their conjoined family with just two girls and three boys? How long would they have to wait? They didn't want the kids having kids when they were still kids. None of the moms, not to mention Jimmy, could really imagine their children actually getting married or having children of their own. That would make them grandparents. That, in itself, was unsettling. Then there was the most troubling question of all. What if one—or both—of the girls could not conceive?

These were not new questions. These fears had plagued them for months, especially since an ultrasound showed Bridget's second child was going to be another boy.

"I've worked this all out," Pam said after a protracted silence.

Mai Ker and Bridget watched her carefully, waiting for her to continue. Braden was dozing, blissfully oblivious against Bridget's chest.

"Most of the children," Pam went on, "are in some way related by blood. Except Herald and Sing. They're the only two who don't share a parent. They're the only ones who could marry. Without directly mixing genes, I mean. So, I don't know where exactly that leaves us."

She frowned slightly.

Mai Ker, with a Ph.D. in genetics, corrected her.

"Actually, Herald and Piper don't share a parent either. So Piper could marry Herald, too."

Pam looked puzzled for a moment. She, for a selfish reason, hadn't even considered this.

"You mean, Herald would have two wives?" She looked offended.

"Not unlike us, Pam. Jimmy?" Mai Ker said, pointing out the obvious.

"Oh." Pam looked less blank. "Old-fashioned me. I just assumed all the kids should have only one husband or wife." Her eyes pleaded with them. "You know?"

Bridget now stated the obvious.

"You don't like the idea of Piper being a second wife. Behind Sing."

Pam's facial expression admitted this.

"No," she said awkwardly. Then her face came out of its shadow. "Of course, Piper could marry him first!" The tension in her neck and shoulders relaxed a bit. She smiled.

"No," Mai Ker said, "we can't afford to wait that long. Piper's too young. Two years younger than Sing."

"What are we talking about," Bridget blurted out. "They're all too young! They're just kids." She frowned as only a mother could.

"Won't be forever," Mai Ker said passively.

Pointing out the obvious was becoming both dull and irritating. They looked at each other. Minds spun, twisting uncomfortably between reality and common decency. It all felt too much. As they silently looked at each other's eyes, they realized they sounded like old hens clucking over the pickings.

Mai Ker finally spoke.

"When the time comes—and it's a long way off—Sing must marry Herald. First. We can't wait forever."

"What about Nathaniel?" Pam asked. "And

Braden?" she added even more awkwardly, nodding at the infant in Bridget's arms.

"No," Mai Ker said rather emphatically. "Everything else carries a risk. Besides Herald and Sing, and Herald and Piper, it's too risky. Not a certainty, but the genetic dangers mushroom quickly," she said, trying to chart out the unknown waters ahead of them, trying to imagine what she really *couldn't* imagine. "If Piper, say, married and had children with Nathaniel, her half-brother through Jimmy, we might luck out. It's safer than a full-blooded brother and sister having kids." She shook her head, almost immediately rejecting the idea. "But not risk-free."

"Only Sing and Nathaniel are full brother and sister," Pam said.

"Yes," Mai Ker said. "We could never allow that. That would be very bad. Genetically. Emotionally, too. There were very good reasons for all those laws against intermarriage between brothers and sisters. And cousins."

"Gene-wise, yes," Bridget nodded, her frustration showing. "But reality-wise, do we have that kind of luxury?"

"I know you're worried, Bridget. How can we ever rebuild? Right? But in the bigger-reality picture," Mai Ker told them, "we just cannot take those chances. If we let Piper or Sing marry one of their half-brothers, we could create a *huge* mess. If genetic problems erupt, everything would be infinitely worse." She shook her head firmly. "No. We cannot take the risk."

"Don't know how anything could get much worse than it is," Pam said sullenly, munching the remnants of a very old and stale soda cracker.

Mai Ker looked hard at Pam, then Bridget.

"Well, believe me, it could. But then it's the kids who suffer the consequences. Right? You want to do that to them?"

"I agree with Mai Ker," Bridget said. "We're in enough of a mess. Let's not take any chances. We just have to make do."

"Seems like 'make do' is all we do," Pam said like a pouting teenager.

But she expressed the heart of all three women. They were thoroughly tired of just having to make do.

"Yes. But there is new hope today, isn't there?" Mai Ker said, nodding toward Braden.

Despite it all, and the feeling of labor pains still echoing through her whole body, Bridget smiled.

Their conversation got even more complicated—and highly personal—after that, focusing on how Mai Ker and Bridget would try to have more children with Jimmy. And though it was many years down the road, they each began to think about how they would try to encourage appropriate relationships between the children, relationships that someday might produce a third generation INSIDE. The whole idea was embarrassing and very awkward, whatever jokes they told to try to diffuse it. The three women were glad Jimmy was far out of earshot.

JIMMY HAD finished cultivating one of the bean plots in #10 and had moved over to Pod 14 to do a fertilizer inventory. He had piled 20 empty 5-gallon plastic gas cans over against a wall, out of the way. They were keeping the empties with the plan to melt them down into more usable material. They hadn't yet found the time or interest to do it, let alone imagine exactly what they would use the plastic for once they had remade it. Jimmy planned to fabricate a metal pouring table where the liquefied plastic could be formed into sheets of various thicknesses. But he had too many other things on his mind. It seemed he had three "honey-do" lists most of the time instead of one and he was always looking for a break where he could play with the children.

Taking inventory of the fertilizers was discouraging. While they had enough for many years to come, he knew that at some point, however distant, they would run out. They needed to begin to seriously develop their own recyclable fertilizers from compost. He and Mai Ker had also begun to devise a plan to reclaim some of the chemical fertilizers from the soil in Pod 10. This wouldn't be easy, but they had discovered the procedures laid out in detail in the original Solarium-3 Operations Manual in the main computer. Someone had been planning ahead, for the long haul. Reclaiming fertilizers would be labor intensive and time-consuming but would be worth it, someday.

WHEN JIMMY got to spend time with the kids, it was mostly for fun. But he was also training up more workers. There were no child-labor laws in the Solarium complex. The kids were still very small but they were taught to help with every task they could manage. They started by helping wash dishes when they were 3 years old. They were diligent little workers, almost frighteningly so. They hadn't reached that point of laziness that older kids naturally slip into.

The older children's attempts at house "cleaning" always produced a certain amount of laughs for their parents. It was more "moving dirt from here to there" than actual cleaning. But they tried, and laughed along, and felt good about helping Mom and Dad and Auntie Whomever.

As the Solarians continued excavating the underground caverns for air storage, Sing and Herald proved invaluable help. The adults were surprised at how much early progress the two little ones made at the beginning of a new dig. Because they were so short—Sing especially so—they could work in the shallow opening of the tunnel until it got deep enough for one of the adults to take over the project. Jimmy was amazed at how much damage Herald and Sing could do with a small spade and shovel. The two could barely pick up the tools, but once they got ahold of the things they could cut through dirt and small rock with maniacal passion. The trick was to keep them from bashing each other's skulls in. Digging was sometimes the most fun part of the day for the kids. The parents got as much exercise laughing as the kids did digging.

THIS AFTERNOON was to be a different story. Sing had spent part of the morning languishing in bed while "Cousin" Herald was bounding around the pods playing hide-and-seek with himself. Sing was usually the first of the two to be up in the morning, but because the adults were preoccupied with the birth of baby Braden, they had paid scant attention to Herald and Sing.

When Mai Ker went in to the kitchen tent late in the afternoon she noticed the dishes were still not done from breakfast. Sing would normally have washed up, even without being asked.

Mai Ker went to look for her and found her back in bed, the smell of vomit nearby on a rug, and Sing looking sad and wan.

"Oh my goodness, sweetheart, what's wrong?"

"Sick, Mommy."

"Yes you are." Mai Ker felt her forehead, which was hot. "You should have called out for Mommy."

"Couldn't."

"Darling, I'll get you better. Can you eat?"

"No. I'm sick."

"Well, let me get you something light. Some juice? Or soup? OK?"

"OK," was followed by a quiet grimace of stomach pain. It was not a very convincing agreement.

Mai Ker could tell by looking that Sing's entire

demeanor was out of sorts. Her daughter had suffered through some usual kid illnesses but she had never looked this sick before. As Mai Ker tried to feed her some watery vegetable soup, Sing seemed to be wasting away before her eyes. Sing's whole personality had shifted from her usual bubbly and fun smiles to a withdrawn, frightened soul. Wherever Sing was, she seemed to be in hiding.

Mai Ker grabbed an intercom radio and tripped the voice-activated mic, calling Jimmy and Pam. Both came running. They heard the controlled panic in Mai Ker's voice. As they arrived, Sing had just thrown up again on the floor of the tent. Mai Ker asked them to stay with her while she got some cool water.

When Mai Ker got back, Pam was taking Sing's temperature and checking her pulse. Sing's breathing was too shallow, and her pulse was fluttery.

"Her fever is high."

"Try to sit up a little, darling," Mai Ker urged.

"It hurts," was all Sing could say, lying as still as she could with the pain in her gut.

"She's very hot," Pam said again. "One hundred and four. Try a little juice. Nothing else. Let's swab her down with some cool washcloths."

"I'll get 'em," Jimmy said.

"Should we take her to the infirmary?" Mai Ker asked, almost pleading.

"Can't. Can't be around the baby."

After an hour of cooling her off and coaxing her, Mai Ker finally helped Sing get a bit of plum juice down. Plum wasn't the best idea for a sick stomach, but Mai Ker knew she loved the taste and right now it seemed more important just to get something healthy into her.

The hours dragged slowly into the evening. Sing didn't improve. She seemed to worsen. She would hardly speak, even to Mai Ker. It was too painful to try to talk. Each little sound had a muted tone of suffering. Then without warning she would get stiff, her muscles contracting, reacting to the pain and the dehydration throughout her body.

Pam took some urine and blood specimens to the lab in Pod 3, hoping to figure out what was happening. Pam was in the dark. She guessed it might be some kind of bacterial infection but she wasn't sure. Remarkably, though not surprisingly, since the Solarians had been sealed into the complex they had suffered almost no viral infections. Either because they were now insulated from the OUTSIDE, or because of the dramatic atmospheric swings they went through early on, any really damaging viruses were apparently gone from their little world.

Pam was beginning to panic. Repressed thoughts of Clayton's final illness still haunted her. At this moment, the image of Clayton lying on the infirmary bed leapt at her like a hideous bogyman. The only thing that saved her from crying was the memory of Bridget now lying on the same bed cuddling her newborn. Ugliness had been replaced there by beauty and renewed wonder.

Still, whenever one of them got sick, the whole Solarium routine ground to a halt. The Solarians put aside all normal work to tend as best they could to the sick one. Any illness, INSIDE, was not just a temporary bump but a potential catastrophe. They had learned that bitter and tragic lesson with Willy, Sarajane and finally Clayton. Any illness, every illness, could lead to death. Every minor scrape needed to be treated and healed. As they struggled to repopulate their fragile race, they were not about to lose one more soul. Not if they could help it. An illness like what Sing now had—if it careened out of control—would destroy what little hope they held.

Even young Herald wanted to tend to Sing and

comfort her. Kept at a distance outside the tent he normally shared with her, he felt helpless throughout the evening and started crying. He was pretty sure, as a 5-year-old would be, that a hug could cure anything. But despite his tears, the parents would not let him close. The only thing worse than losing one would be the potential of losing two. They would not risk Herald catching whatever this was. And because of the very fact that they were all insulated from what used to be daily exposure to strange bacteria, the children's immune systems were not as resilient as they would have been otherwise. Even though the children were generally healthy, when they did get sick, they got much sicker than children in times past. This, too, was part of their new reality.

Pam's 3-year-old, Piper, eventually walked with Herald over to the swing set that Jimmy had built for the kids in Pod 5.

"I'll push you," she offered somberly to a very upset Herald.

"I'll push you. I'm a boy."

"Who was crying?" Piper pointed out.

Herald choked up again, and plopped into the swing.

JUST BEFORE 11:00 p.m., Sing's temperature spiked up to 106 degrees. She began to shake and had a mild seizure. Despite their efforts all evening, they had been unable to get enough liquid into her to stem the increasing dehydration. Finally, Pam grabbed her out of her bed to move her to the infirmary.

"Get Bridget and Braden over to her tent," she commanded Jimmy. "I need the infirmary!"

Jimmy did as he was told and rushed ahead to clear Bridget and the baby out of the infirmary. He found Bridget with one arm wrapped around Braden and Herald snuggled up in the other. Herald had been crying quietly on and off for hours. Sing was his favorite cousin.

"We've gotta move," Jimmy told Bridget. "Sorry. Sing's really sick. Gotta get her in here."

Still weak, Bridget managed to rouse Herald and Jimmy helped them all to Bridget's tent. They looked like an overly tired family wandering home late from a carnival.

In the infirmary, Pam started an IV in Sing's arm as Mai Ker watched in dismay. Pam opened the IV line, running a fast drip of saline solution into Sing, trying to get some fluid back into the little girl. She added some antibiotics into the IV line with a syringe.

Pam and Mai Ker were both frightened by how badly Sing had worsened in the past several hours. She was all but incoherent and, though still semi-alert, she was not responding at all when they spoke or tried to comfort her.

Jimmy returned. Pam, terrified, whispered to Mai Ker and Jimmy.

"The blood and urine didn't show anything definite. Must have an infection. But I don't know what."

Jimmy had been wracking his brain trying to think of what could have caused this.

"She and Herald were playing in the fertilizer shed. Day before yesterday. When I was cleaning up in there. But I was around most of the time. I didn't see them get into anything."

"And Herald's not sick," Mai Ker pointed out. "But I did notice she had a small cut on the back of her leg. Yesterday."

Pam lifted the sheet and looked. The small cut had reddened, and was starting to swell slightly.

"Could be that. Could be something we ate. I don't know," Pam said, expressing complete frustration. "Could've been something microscopic, something got into that cut. Or something she touched got in her mouth. You know kids. Trying to taste and smell the whole world."

"How do we help her?" Mai Ker pleaded. She felt she would overheat, too.

"We're doing it. We've got to get fluid back in her. I'll give her more antibiotic through the IV tonight."

"That's it?" Jimmy asked, certain they must do more.

"Jimmy, patience. This'll take time. She's very sick."

It was the last thing Pam wanted to say but there was no sugarcoating it. They were Sing's mom and dad. They were entitled to know the worst. Pam's eyes flooded as she choked out the words.

"We could lose her."

Jimmy leaned against the bed, then fell to his knees. He bawled.

"Oh, God. No. Not this . . ."

Mai Ker knelt beside him, and kissed his neck.

"Don't, Jimmy." She stuffed back her own fears. "We will hold on. We *will* get through this."

"Will we?" he asked blankly. He couldn't look at her. His eyes were burning holes in the tiled floor.

Making sure Sing was secure on the bed, Pam quietly knelt down by Jimmy and Mai Ker.

"Sorry, you guys. I just don't want to lie. We're flying blind again."

Mai Ker leaned her head against Pam's shoulder. The three looked like wreckage on a human freeway.

"We just need to watch her close all night," Pam said in hushed, still sobbing words. "The fever should break by morning. I'll give her as much antibiotic as I can. Right now she needs to keep resting. So do you." She voiced the most painful advice parents can hear. "She'll do better if you're not in here."

Jimmy and Mai Ker were upset but realized it was probably true. Their weeping and commotion would not help their little girl.

"This is weird," Jimmy said, getting to his feet and wiping his face mostly dry. "Just like when you got sick, Pam. Before Piper was born."

"Yes. But the symptoms are different. I don't know what I had. But I think this is something else. Her little system has just got to fight back."

"Call us if—" Mai Ker couldn't finish the thought. She turned away toward the door.

"I'll be right here with her," Pam said, giving Mai Ker a hug. "Just relax, and sleep. If that's possible."

Reluctantly, Jimmy and Mai Ker walked away.

"You rest, too, Pam. Don't need you getting sick," Jimmy said as they left.

Sing was lying still and very quiet now. The IV fluid was beginning to help. For good measure, Pam started a second IV in her other arm. Sing was so insensible at this point that she never felt the large needles. A small mercy for a very sick little child.

Pam watched Sing several more minutes, then went over to the lab table to re-examine the blood and urine results she had brought back from Pod 3 earlier. She started retracing the test steps. She pulled out the MedDxPad and started quizzing it.

Somewhere there's a clue, she thought. *If I can just find it.*

6

Sing had gotten worse between Wednesday and Thursday. Her fever wavered up and down by a couple of degrees and she was suffering deep pain in her abdomen. She lost weight for lack of eating and kept vomiting, though these were mostly dry heaves. None of the antibiotics or other medicines they tried seemed to help.

By Thursday afternoon, Mai Ker was at the end of her rope. She and Jimmy had fed Herald and Piper and had gone off to do chores. The tension had ramped up between them. Both felt helpless because of Sing.

"This can't be happening again! Why is this always happening?" Mai Ker wailed pathetically in a sour, angry voice.

Jimmy snapped.

"We're *not* gonna lose her!" he nearly shouted, his words harsh and angry. His voice echoed off the roof of Pod 11 above where they stood near a large turkey pen.

"Because you say?" Mai Ker responded, equaling his volume. "What makes you so smart?" she demanded angrily.

"Don't push me, Mai Ker! We're not gonna lose her. That's it! We're not!" He walked away several steps.

Mai Ker fell silent. She absently tossed some feed to the turkeys from a small pail. A small, jet-black, Bombay-mix cat hovering nearby jumped at the chance, poking its small head in through the fence, assuming it was entitled to some of the feed. A large tom almost took its nose off in the fight for one small pellet.

Mai Ker wanted to believe Jimmy, to trust what seemed to him certain knowledge. She was not as certain of her own understanding. She set the pail down and sat on a small stool, emotionally wrung out. She started crying, tears mixed with short gasps of air. Jimmy held his feelings in as best he could, which was not very well, and went to her. He knelt by her and held her loosely, letting her cry and trying not to himself.

In the infirmary, Pam was fighting Sing's illness as best she could and trying to comfort her little patient. The clue she had searched for all last night still eluded her. Even the MedDxPad held no answer. Sing had an infection, most likely some bacteria, but the blood tests were not conclusive enough to say which bacteria it was. So Pam's shotgun antibiotic approach was the best she could do. Whatever this stuff was, she hoped, the antibiotics should kill it. She just prayed the drug wouldn't kill off too many good bacteria in Sing's system, which would only make matters worse.

Sing was so hungry now that she tried on and off to eat a little dry cereal and drink a bit of water. Half the time she threw everything back up. She still was withdrawn. She wouldn't speak even when they held or hugged her. The child looked to be on the verge of wanting to give up.

For a 5-year-old who was this sick, it was impossible to understand what giving up meant. With no further comprehension, she simply wanted to go to sleep for a long, long time. She wanted everyone to quit bothering her, poking at her, and fussing over her. She wanted to be left alone. Her whole being was dropping into a well from which little hearts often can't return. Pam could see it happening and felt powerless to stop it. The hours in the infirmary felt darker as they dragged out.

Two things changed the desolate picture.

First, early Friday morning Mai Ker insisted that Jimmy pray to his God again, because it had worked before when Pam was so sick. This time Jimmy had less trouble forming his thoughts. He had been reading his Bible much of the night before—looking for what, he wasn't sure. It didn't really comfort him. If anything, it just raised more questions and made his anxiety worse. But it helped him now to find words of prayer.

He and Mai Ker and Pam gathered around Sing's bed in the infirmary. Mai Ker was bleary-eyed. She hadn't read all night but had lain alone in her bed, staring up at the tent ceiling for what seemed interminable hours, unable to sleep even a wink. Pam had spent all night in the infirmary again and was so tired her eyes would only half-focus. The entire inside of the infirmary had begun to look surreal, something a drunken artist might have cooked up while suffering the DTs.

Bridget would have joined them but she was still keeping herself and Braden at a safe distance, in case whatever Sing had was contagious. Herald and Piper were being kept away too, for the same reason.

Jimmy tried to collect his thoughts and overrule his emotions.

"Lord, Lord Jesus, I'm begging. I'm begging you, now. Save our little girl. Our beautiful little girl. She's our joy." His eyes were pooling tears, and the muscles in his face were at war. "She's our hope. Our future. I can't think about it. What it would be without her. Lord, I know you say everything is in your hand. Prove it to me now. Please. Save our little girl. I know you love her, too. Don't take her away. Let us keep her. Please, let us keep her." His mind began to wander and he didn't like where it was headed. He had said enough.

He stuffed back his tears. "Lord, please hear this prayer."

"Amen," Mai Ker muttered with the most hesitant hope.

Pam added, "Thank you, Lord."

The second thing was this. Late Saturday, just before sunset, as long, richly colored rays of light glanced through the pods sideways, Piper—fresh from a long nap and a short dream—crept quietly and unnoticed into the infirmary. Mai Ker was in a chair by a wall half-asleep, her head turned sideways in a very uncomfortable position. Pam sat with her back to the bed, fretting over the results of some new blood tests she had just run, still finding nothing certain about what was wrong with her little patient. She was seething with frustration, angrier than ever that she couldn't figure it out, but she couldn't let the others see this. It would only make them worry more.

Piper, barefoot and in the long, ragged shirt that served as her favorite nightie, stepped up quietly on the bottom frame of the infirmary bed and inched herself sideways along the caster rail until she was by Sing's head. She leaned up and forward—which was quite a stretch for a 3-year-old—and softly kissed Sing on the cheek.

"I love you, Sing."

Pam heard it and turned suddenly. Her reaction jolted Mai Ker from her nap. They both saw Piper—and panicked.

"My God, Piper!" Pam blurted out before she could stop herself.

Piper turned and froze with a petrified look, feeling she must have done something terribly wrong. Pam and Mai Ker lunged toward the bed together. Pam was on the same side as Piper and reached her first, about to snatch her away.

"Wait!" Mai Ker said in a hushed voice. "Wait."

Pam already had her hands around Piper's middle, but stood still. She looked inquisitively at Mai Ker, who was looking down at Sing.

Sing's eyes were stirring under their lids. Then, for a moment, she opened them not quite halfway.

"Thank you," she said to Piper in barely a whisper.

Piper said nothing, but beamed. Mai Ker came around the bed and picked Piper up.

"Piper, that was so nice." She gave her a gentle hug. "But, honey, you can't be in here," she added without anger. "Sing is very sick. We have to be very careful. You know what 'careful' means?"

Piper, who obviously didn't, remained paralyzed and mute in Mai Ker's arms. She drew her head back slightly and shook it with an innocent and helpless, *No*.

"We don't want you to get sick, too," Mai Ker said in that tone of voice that a 3-year-old is supposed to understand better.

"She'll be better now," Piper said. Her face unfroze and she smiled the most adorable grin at both Mai Ker and Pam, as if she had just made one of the greatest pronouncements in all history.

"Well, thank you, sweetie," Pam said, "but let's get back to whatever you were doing." She nudged Mai Ker. "Will you take my little girl back to the tents? Maybe she can watch while you make us all some supper."

AS MUCH as Bridget wanted to see Sing, she knew she couldn't risk any contamination that could be passed to Braden. The others were careful to wash their hands every time they left the infirmary, hoping to isolate whatever it was in that building. When Mai Ker got back to the tents with Piper, she not only washed her own hands, she gave Piper a bath—just to be safe.

Jimmy came back from the Research Center in Pod 3, closing the podwalk door as he left. He, too, had been scanning through medical files trying to figure this mystery disease out. He even went back through their own personnel and medical records to see if there was any clue in terms of some genetic or inherited problem that could have triggered Sing's illness. But he came back both tired and empty-handed.

"Why a bath this time of day?" he asked Mai Ker as she was drying Piper off.

"She snuck in to see Sing," she said in a measured, even tone that was supposed to be Jimmy's clue not to overreact.

"What!?" he exclaimed, overreacting.

"It's OK, Jimmy," she said, placating him. "She just wanted to see her. I'm sure everything is fine," she said, placating herself. "I just thought a bath wouldn't hurt. You know." She said the last two words with a certain inflection that was meant to tell Jimmy to tone it down and not upset poor Piper again.

"It's OK," Piper said, as if parroting her. "It is."

Bridget was in a different part of the tents in her own room, but the advantage—or sometimes disadvantage—of tents was that you could hear pretty much everything.

"What's Piper been up to now?" she called out.

"Hi, Auntie Bridget," Piper answered. "Is my new baby brother OK?"

"Of course, sweetie," Bridget called. She would have invited Piper to come and see the new baby again, but was not about to when she realized Piper had snuck into the infirmary.

Mai Ker suggested that Jimmy take Piper over to Pod 5 to the playground. Jimmy was happy to do it. He was going to watch her like a hawk the next several hours to make sure she didn't begin showing any of Sing's symptoms.

Mai Ker went into Bridget's room.

"So how's Sing doing?" Bridget asked.

"Still bad. I don't know. I'm really worrying this time, Bridget. I do not like it when she is sick. My nerves are fried. I keep crying."

"None of us like it. Is she responding at all?"

"No. That's what's odd. The medicine doesn't seem to be doing anything. Then, you know, Jimmy prayed for her yesterday. I made him. And I really thought that might help. But she doesn't seem any better today. Then Piper snuck in a little while ago. She gave Sing a kiss on the cheek."

"What?" Bridget was more alarmed. "Why'd you let her in there?"

"We didn't. I was napping, Pam was busy. She just snuck in."

"Dear God, I hope she doesn't get sick, too!"

"I gave her a bath. I'm sure she's fine. But you know Piper. Always spreading joy, got to be with everybody. Just trying to help, I guess. I'm sure she doesn't understand what's going on. She can't understand . . ." Mai Ker's voice faded and she swallowed an invisible lump in her throat. ". . . how desperate it is."

Bridget considered this for a moment as Mai Ker brushed several tears aside.

"I wouldn't be too sure," Bridget said, lost in some hard-to-reach thought.

IT WAS now Monday. As if emerging from a long nightmare, Sing had begun to show slight signs of improvement yesterday evening. By this morning she was awake and becoming more alert. Her fever had dropped dramatically to just under 101 degrees. Most importantly, she wanted to eat. Jimmy was giving her some milky, cooked cereal.

The first thing she asked her dad when he brought breakfast was, "Where's Piper?"

"I dunno," Jimmy said. "Wanna see her?"

"No."

Sing ate the cereal. She sipped some warm tea that Mai Ker had made, a special Hmong blend that was supposed to help her body heal. Sing looked away from Jimmy, out of the infirmary door.

"We were dreaming together," Sing said, as if this was the most natural statement in the world.

For a moment it didn't even register with Jimmy, who had lost a lot of sleep himself the last few days.

"You— What?" He looked at her through half-awake eyes. "Dreaming?"

"Uh-huh."

"I don't understand, sweetheart."

"You know. Like not asleep, but not awake? We went to the playground."

"Sweetheart, you've been here. In bed."

Unfazed, Sing ignored his matter-of-fact statement.

"Yesterday. No. Day before." Her little mind was trying to sift and sort through the lost hours and days.

Jimmy remained mum, watching her, trying to take this in. *Dreaming together?* The look on her face was as plain, innocent and sincere as any he had ever seen.

"Can I go home? I don't really like it in here." She faked a sad-face that was real.

Jimmy nodded. He left her with her tea for a few minutes and found Pam. Pam thought it would be OK to take her back to her own room, but insisted Herald and Piper should stay somewhere else for another couple of days.

"Maybe you and Herald could camp out by the ocean," she suggested. "Piper can go with you. Or she can bunk in with me."

Jimmy was ready for some fun. The thought of the sound of the ocean, which he hadn't bothered to enjoy for several weeks, sounded very inviting. He nearly fell asleep just imagining it.

He and Pam got Mai Ker and went in to talk it over

with Bridget. She needed to OK moving Sing back to the tents because of the proximity to baby Braden. As they talked, Jimmy shared what Sing had said to him about Piper a few minutes earlier.

"That is very strange," Mai Ker said. Her scientist's mind tried to digest the idea, without success.

"Piper and I were at the playground," Jimmy said. "On Saturday. But how could Sing have known that?"

"Um," Pam hummed, considering it. "Dreaming together. Doesn't make sense. But Piper did go see her. And Sing is getting better," she added, still vexed that she didn't know what had made Sing sick.

"Maybe your prayer worked, Jimmy," Mai Ker said, putting her arm around him.

"Maybe Piper's kiss worked," Pam suggested.

"Maybe they were the same thing," Bridget said.

7

Tuesday, September 21st, 15 (NC)

The years were passing, year following year, but they felt like eons. Time did not fly. It hovered, landed, and crept. To the Solarians it seemed nearly frozen, days stagnated between no beginning and no likely end.

General Francis Arnott had once commented to John Haskins that time was about to become a thing of the past. He had been an unwitting prophet. As the months and now years slogged along, time and history had become distorted, or were simply gone.

The full weight of the hours and days and weeks bore down on them like a boulder atop an egg. The few clocks they still ran moved like sickly snails. Their days, though busy, frequently deteriorated into boredom. They seemed to be going nowhere. There was nowhere to go.

Trapped in their small, carved-out bit of space INSIDE, they felt equally trapped in time. As days came and went, routines—almost ritualized— mercifully sustained them. Most days there was nothing particularly interesting to do other than those routines: keep the plant life healthy, feed and clean up after the animals, keep the machines running. The question they tried to avoid was, *Why?*

The Solarium had become a zoo where the keepers were also part of the exhibits, where the cages were constructed of thick Stellar plastic, and where they always felt someone was watching them, even though all those who used to gawk at them from the sidewalks

OUTSIDE were long gone. Like caged ferrets, the original Solarians knew where they were but had begun to lose the sense of who they were. They had no sense of what lay ahead.

Their days were hopelessly monotonous. Looking ahead from an early morning, a single day could produce a singular dread, like those dreams that run on and on and over and over, and seem like they should be about to end, but won't. Daily scenes repeated like nightmares—with slight variations, but always essentially the same—a nighttime phantasm that won't end even when daylight crests the horizon. Even the simplest tasks were, at times, infuriatingly tedious. Life felt pointless.

The sounds of the Solarium had become equally wearisome. The quiet purr of electrical equipment, once in a while a relay clicking in or out, the ventilation fans gently moving air through the pods and podwalks, or stopping to reverse and rev up in the opposite direction. The animal noises were also nearly constant, even the depths of night being disturbed by crickets and other thoughtless insects which didn't have enough common sense or decency to sleep when everyone else did. Jimmy, in particular, would awaken to these noises and then spend two or three hours fretting himself back to sleep.

One of the most pleasant sounds for Jimmy, his wives, and their children was still the washing of the waves along the beaches and rocks of their artificial ocean. Even in past years when electrical current had been at a premium, they could never bring themselves to shut down the huge wave machines that generated this beautiful sound. It was like milk and honey to starving souls. Just a few minutes, but especially a few hours, spent in Pod 12 made the world seem perfect and peaceful, if only they could avoid looking out on the lingering devastation that surrounded them

OUTSIDE.

But as the years passed, the finest sounds were those of young voices, their laughter, their hollering, their teasing, and even their tears. These were the most blissful sounds of life, sounds that generated deep contentment in the four first-generation Solarians. The sounds of their children rang like perfectly tuned chimes amidst the horrors of the dead world OUTSIDE. Those voices made getting up each morning possible. And, not surprisingly, these were the sounds that actually *did* awaken them most days.

OUTSIDE, just beyond the pod walls, the old horrors remained. Although everything out there seemed finished, the sun continued to rise and set. Storms came and went, seasons progressed and changed. The purplish air colored the moods of those INSIDE, although the air in the past several months seemed more of a peculiar shade than ever, as if someone had watered it down like cheap paint.

Still, life was still life. The Solarians were still breathing and the children, thankfully, were all alive and thriving.

MAI KER was working in a garden plot, cultivating soybeans along with her daughter, Sing. While Mai Ker herself had been a beautiful young woman, Sing was becoming a young lady of unusual beauty and strong character. She had turned 14 on August 8th, but she had a loveliness and maturity about her that seemed far beyond her years. Her long, dark-brown hair shared the texture of her mother's hair and flowed helplessly around the increasingly grownup beauty of her face and ever-smiling eyes. Getting some of her dad's height, she had passed Mai Ker by several inches over the last year, and her growing height added strength to the loveliness of her emerging figure.

Sing was at the moment, in keeping with her name,

singing some notes she had made up, mixed with others that took the form of an airy whistle. Since a very young age, she had shown a gift of music in her soul that, with no instruments other than her mind and voice, provided musical joy for the rest of the Solarian family. Rarely were there words, but invariably she was singing or humming. Her melodies were simple, expressing what life was like for her in the Solarium.

Mai Ker looked over and smiled.

"What tune is that? I don't know it."

"I don't either, Mommy," Sing said. "Just something I made up."

Mai Ker paused. She listened. She looked around nostalgically.

"You know what I miss?"

"What?"

"The birds. I miss them so much. Not that I don't miss Clayton, and Will, and Sarajane. But I miss the beautiful birds. And their songs. So beautiful. So simple." Her chest felt hollow and drained. "And then they were all gone."

Despite the fact that a few hearty birds survived the near-fatal air problems early on in the project, all had died out over the years. Mai Ker attributed it to damaged reproductive systems, loss of a mate, or maybe just being cooped up so long INSIDE.

"I've seen pictures of some," Sing said.

"You know, you can make the computer play their sounds. There's recordings of their different voices."

"I never tried that." There was a hint in her voice of asking, *What would be the point?*

"I bet you would play the sounds if you had ever heard the birds for real," her mom smiled. "I especially miss little Caroline."

"Who?"

"No, you wouldn't know about her, I guess," Mai Ker said. She sat down on a large bucket and wiped sweat off her face. She brushed bits of weed and dirt off the cultivating fork. "Caroline was Clayton's pet. A little nuthatch. He brought her in here when we first came. She must have died before you were born," she said. "I'm not sure what happened to her."

Sing nodded and said nothing. She began to hum softly, a different melody.

"I don't really know what happened to her." Mai Ker looked sad, but then joy came back to her face. "The birds meant so much to me growing up. When I was your age. I could sit and listen for hours. That's why I loved to camp out."

"Like in the tents?"

"No. I mean, really camp out. Outdoors."

"OUTSIDE?"

"Yes. I'd sit in the woods, or by a lake. There were always birds. Like the invisible background of a beautiful painting. Depth, and meaning. Something I couldn't see any other way."

"Sounds pretty."

"Yes. Even when I didn't really hear them, out in the forest, I heard them in my heart." She listened. "I still hear them." She looked at Sing. "I think you were given to us to replace them. Maybe that's what made me think of your name."

SING'S ALMOST unnatural beauty and appeal was not lost on young Herald Listner-Block. In fact, while Sing worked with her mother in Pod 10, Herald was in the Research Center, skimming through the computer archives, supposedly studying history but mostly daydreaming about Sing.

Since infancy, they had been physically and emotionally close, like brother and sister, though they actually weren't. But in the past few months, Herald began to recognize changes that were taking place, subtly, slowly. Sing had always been winsome and attractive, but her little-girl cuteness was changing, morphing radically into something very different, into a new kind of beauty that made Herald light-headed if he stared at her too long. And the changes were not just the physical ones. Their relationship was changing. She was becoming more interesting, as a person. It bothered him that she seemed so much older than him, although he was actually several months her senior. But he felt their relationship was definitely changing. He didn't understand why. In fact, he didn't want it to change. Then, of course, she was so astonishingly pretty now. How could their life together stay the same, he wondered? He felt drawn to her now in ways that had no real reason—that he knew of—but the attraction was real, and getting stronger.

While daydreaming about Sing, Herald had abandoned his study of Greek city-states and was browsing through old music files in the computers. Her name, he thought, must have suggested it. He himself could barely croak out any truly musical sounds, but listening was fun.

He had stumbled into what sounded like ancient religious music and had played through several songs. He switched on his voice-activated intercom mic and his voice blared out over the speakers throughout the pods.

"Mom, you there?"

"Yes, son," Bridget said, answering into her own mic. "Turn the volume down. You're blasting us again."

"Me or the music?"

"Both."

"Hey, I found this song in the archives. Something to do with something called 'Christmas'? You won't believe it. Me and Sing are both in the first line!"

Bridget laughed.

"Yeah. I know the one you mean."

"What's Christmas?"

"Hum." She felt stumped. Slowly she spoke into the mic. "Guess I haven't ever explained that, have I?"

Silence, as Herald waited for more.

"I'll explain after supper," she said.

Jimmy chimed in on his radio from the maintenance pod.

"If you'd just sit and read with me some evening, you'd get the idea. It's all in the big book."

"You talking to me or Mom?" Herald called.

"Both."

"That big book you read at night?" Herald asked.

Mai Ker and Sing were starting to cover their ears, because the background music still blared over the speakers every time Herald spoke.

"That one. All there," Jimmy replied.

"Not tonight," Herald said, "Sing and me are going to play volleyball. Or, maybe it was dodge ball. Don't remember." Sounds of bronze bells and some trumpets crackled over the speakers.

"Actually," Sing told her mom, "I wanted to go swimming."

JIMMY WAS patient. *What else can you be in this place?* he thought as he chewed a last piece of potato. His patience went unrewarded. Bridget managed to avoid the subject of Christmas all through supper, and Herald didn't ask.

Jimmy followed Sing and Herald over to Pod 5 after dishes were done. He sat on the pool deck and tried to referee the two-person volleyball game, which was next to impossible since only the two players' opinions seemed to count.

His eyes wandered OUTSIDE toward the west. A more radiant blue than he had seen for a long time was trying to squeeze in between the red and purplish rays of the sunset. A hint of a strong thunderstorm brewing far to the southwest also caught his eye. Several weak, distant flashes of lightning punctuated the clouds.

The kids, huffing and sweating, finally flopped onto a couple of deck chairs by Jimmy when they finished what they considered a full game. No one knew the score by that point. They swigged down large, recycled bottles of water in large gulps.

"So, you still want to know about Christmas?" Jimmy asked Herald.

"I guess." His tone said, *Not really*. He had already lost interest, as any typical 14-year-old might.

"I do," Sing said.

"Must have been big," Herald commented. "There is *tons* of music about it."

"Big would be one way to put it," Jimmy said. "It was a celebration, of a birthday."

"Whose?" Sing asked.

"Jesus, the messiah."

"The what?"

"It's a word the Jewish people in ancient times used for the great king they hoped would come someday and save them."

"Save them?" Herald asked. "From what?"

"From all the mess of the world," Jimmy explained.

Both kids nodded but said nothing. They waited, watching Jimmy.

"It's all in my Bible. I don't just read it, you know. I pray, too."

Neither of the children had any concept of prayer. They guessed it was something from a past age, when there was still a world OUTSIDE. They had only very rarely heard the word mentioned by their parents.

Jimmy wanted to go on but felt stumped. He wasn't sure how he made the leap from Christmas to prayer, or where his mind was trying to go. This was worse than trying to talk to Herald and Sing about the birds and the bees, another subject he had so far successfully avoided. He plunged on, awkwardly.

"See, when I pray, I'm really praying to Jesus. Because he's God."

"Wait," Sing frowned. "I don't get that. You just said he was born. So he was a man?"

"Yes."

"So he's not God."

"It's complicated," Jimmy said.

He had now not only fumbled, he had completely lost the ball. He didn't know how to answer this. He wasn't sure, in fact, that he knew the answer. Time to punt.

"I'll explain some other time."

He let it drop. He was out of his depth. The kids were cooled down and both had that specially rehearsed teenager look that said they were really anxious to be somewhere else.

"Want to go swim now?" Sing asked Herald.

"Yeah," Herald said, standing. "Let's go change."

Jimmy just nodded incoherently as they walked away. He looked out to the west, his mind stuck, as he watched the sun finally disappear.

HERALD FOUND Sing fascinating to look at, even clad in ragged, cut-off jeans shorts that had once been her mom's and a tied-up shirt that belonged to her dad.

Sing and he had stopped at the tents to change, then walked to Pod 12 to the far side of the ocean near the south edge of the pod. Within the Solarium, it was as far as they could get from everyone else and gave them a moderate feeling of solitude. They both loved an early evening swim. With the lights of the pod turned down, a dreamy sense of happy unreality filled the place. It was quiet here. The younger kids were somewhere else with the parents. The two of them could just hang out and have fun together. It's what they had done as long as they could remember.

They swam for half-an-hour and were now resting on the small beach on this side of the pod. The soft overhead lights in the pod were soothing. While a bleak, darkly clouded sky scowled at them from OUTSIDE, peppered by lightning and the first drops of a rainstorm, it was a perfect evening INSIDE.

Sing was lying on her stomach, her arms curled under her face. She was humming something. Herald lay on his back looking up through the pod roof. Occasionally he would turn his head toward Sing, listening to the soft tune she was humming. Her face was toward him and each time he looked her way, she smiled.

Herald felt a sudden urge to show off for her. He didn't feel this urge much, but it had become more common in the past several months. He usually ignored it. They knew each other just about as well as any two young people could. He didn't need to impress her, or prove himself. But this evening he acted on the strange impulse.

"Wanna swim across?" he asked her.

"Across where?"

"The ocean."

"You nuts? No. It's too far."

Herald jumped to his feet, stretched, then immediately plopped down again into the sand right next to her. He pushed her arm gently.

"Come on. Don't be chicken."

"Not chicken." She craned her head and looked out across the full width of the ocean, several hundred yards across. "Not stupid, either."

Herald stood again, stretched himself to full height, looked, and nodded.

"Yep. Not that far. We can do it."

"No." She rolled on her side, and frowned at how ridiculous he looked at the moment.

"You don't think I can do it," he chided her.

"Didn't say so. Just don't want you to. Dummy. It's too far."

She studied Herald. Like his father, he was over 6 feet and was already pushing a stocky but muscular 180 pounds. He shared Clayton's handsome looks and Bridget's smile. His waving brown hair was a little too long for her liking but it showed off his blue eyes. Always active, perhaps a little hyperactive, he was a very hard worker and could help the adults with almost any chore or bit of work.

She liked the fact that he was so good looking. But now he was acting stupidly. He was flexing his arm and leg muscles, getting ready, apparently, for the long swim. She had never known his father, but wondered if maybe Clayton's genes or brain cells were now at work in his son.

"Come on," Herald said one last time, not to be defeated.

"No. Don't you, either."

"Cluck, cluck, cluck . . ." he laughed at her. "Do I just hear a chicken 'Singing'?"

He laughed, thinking his pathetic joke was actually funny. There was definitely a strong trace of Clayton Block in him.

Sing shook her head and said nothing. She sat up, but stayed planted.

"Herald, come on. You can't make it across. Not all that way."

"I can."

"You ever try before?"

"Not yet."

"You're an idiot."

That straw broke the camel's back. Herald's need to prove himself took over. He shook his head in denial and plunged into the water. He was a strong swimmer and was soon 70 yards out. But their ocean was big. He wasn't yet a quarter of the way across. He swam hard, not pacing himself, but making it a sprint. He tired quickly. Both arms began to strain.

Sing stood and started to gather her things and Herald's towel to walk back. She watched him a bit longer. He had slowed down but was pushing forward in a strong crawl. But as she started to walk in the direction of the podwalk, his head dipped and jogged like a bobber on a fishing line. Then for a moment, it wasn't there. She stopped, staring hard, searching. She guessed he was just behind a small wave. As she watched, his head bobbed up again, then an arm lifted, but not swimming. It was an arm struggling.

"Oh, crap!" Sing cried out. She yelled as loudly as she could. "You OK?"

There was no answer. His head was gone from sight again, then the arm came up again. Only one.

"Oh, crap!" she yelled again, louder this time. She panicked. She dropped everything and started into the water. But she could see he was too far out. She loved to swim but was not that strong. She couldn't reach him and she knew it. Her heart was in her throat and she wanted to cry but didn't have time. Breathing hard, trying to watch Herald and figure out what to do, she searched around. About 50 yards to her left, one of the aluminum boats they used for fishing and marine maintenance was tied to a post on the shore. Trying to keep an eye toward Herald, she ran hell bent for the boat. She almost fell into the boat when she reached it—and saw there were no oars. Now she began to cry. She untied it, shoved it out and jumped in, and clattered to the bow.

She looked again and couldn't see anything but gentle waves in the direction she thought Herald had last been. She was disoriented from the run, was out of breath and wasn't certain now which way to head. She didn't care. She leaned as far over the bow as she could and started paddling with both arms. A sharp spur on the metal edging around the bow cut into the underside of her right arm. She barely felt it. She pushed on. She began shouting his name. Finally, she spotted his head off to her right, just above water, and one arm working back and forth, trying to keep himself afloat.

She finally realized she should call for help. Then she realized the intercom radio they brought along was in the pile of gear she just dropped on shore.

"Daddy! Mommy! You guys!" she began screaming as loud as she could. "Help! Help me!"

She continued paddling and screaming. The bow of the boat dipped up and down with each stroke but she made slow progress. She didn't take her eyes off Herald's position. She paddled harder. She had no idea if help would come.

As it happened, though, she and Herald had left the inner door of the podwalk open when they had come into #12. Usually, they were careful to close it. Orders from Jimmy. Tonight they had been careless. Blessedly careless. Bridget was in her tent brushing her hair and was the first to hear Sing's screams. She bolted from her dressing table and began hollering, too. In a few long seconds Jimmy, Mai Ker and Pam were running with her toward the sound of the cries.

As Sing got closer she could hear Herald's pained cries between her screams.

"I'm here!" she called. "I'm getting to you." It crossed her mind how well she knew Herald. A mean thought struck her. "You better not be faking!" she yelled.

The sound of his next cry assured her he wasn't. It sounded as if a large fish had just bitten off his foot. One arm continued to work and flail, the other arm unseen.

A slow trickle of blood ran from Sing's arm into the water as she plowed toward him. Thankfully, the Solarium planners had decided against keeping any sharks or predatory marine life, so the blood would not attract more trouble. They had enough at the moment. She was almost to him.

"Sing," he cried, "hurry!" He spit water from his mouth.

She worked her arms harder, trying to reach deeper, her chest raking against the bow.

Bridget, Jimmy, Mai Ker, Pam and Piper all came barreling through the podwalk at once, saw the boat, and ran to a position as close as they could get to it on shore. Without even thinking, Jimmy ripped off his shirt, kicked off his shoes and was in the water. Bridget called to Sing.

"What's wrong?"

She didn't answer. No time. And she was too out of breath.

"Jimmy!" Mai Ker called after him.

"Get the other boat!" Pam shouted, pointing to where it was tied to the dock at the far side of the ocean.

Piper and Mai Ker ran for it. Their short legs moved faster than anyone would have believed possible before this moment.

Bridget and Pam paced, stepped into the water, stepped out. They couldn't see any way to help. Pam said a prayer. Bridget stomped and cussed under her breath.

"Where is he?" she pleaded. "Where is he?"

Sing reached him. She dove over the edge but had the presence of mind to grab the front anchor rope around her arm before she dove in. It tethered her to the boat. She grabbed at Herald's one flailing arm and caught it on a backswing.

"Cramp!" he was crying in severe pain. "Won't let go!"

Sing pulled him close. She couldn't tell how much of the wetness on his face was salt water and how much was tears.

"Hold around my neck," she ordered him.

She had no life-saving training. None of the kids did. Yet. She moved from pure instinct.

Herald clung to her with what strength he had left in his arm. The other hand held his cramped-up leg, trying futilely to relax the cramp and straighten the leg. It would not budge and shot pain every time he tried to straighten it.

Jimmy—panting and mouth half full of water—was pulling close to them. He called out.

"Can you make it?" Sing called back, now worried about him, too.

"Think so!"

"Can you get up into the boat?" she asked Herald.

"Dunno."

"Try?"

"Yeah."

He grimaced in pain as the cramp constricted again.

"Feels like a knife in my leg!"

"Come on, try!" she pleaded.

His arm almost choked her as he tried to pull himself over her and toward the boat.

"Wait," she said, pain creasing her neck. "Won't work. Wait." She untwisted the anchor line from her arm and shoved it toward him. "Hold on. I'll get in first."

Herald took the rope and wound it around his free forearm. Pain shot up his calf muscle again and through his thigh, searing clear into his hip. He wanted to shout out a curse, but wouldn't with Sing so close.

Sing pulled herself up and into the boat. Her own muscles felt like steel at the moment, bands of indestructible stuff that could surmount any obstacle. Where this sudden strength came from she had no idea. She reached down along the rope, pulled it, and took hold under Herald's arm. Blood dripped from her own.

She finally noticed it and frowned, but didn't stop to consider it. Her one object was to get her beloved friend up into the boat.

"Almost there," Jimmy called with serious fatigue in his voice, completely winded.

"Crap, have to save him before long," Sing said under her breath. She pulled Herald's arm harder, without success. "Take a big breath," she ordered him.

He did, and the extra buoyancy this produced in him was just enough to help Sing to drag him up and over the edge of the boat. He rolled into it on his back, almost kicking Sing in the face with his cramped-up leg.

"Ahh!" he screamed.

"Baby," Sing said, falling back against the bow and clamping a hand over the small but bloody cut under her arm. She heaved breaths in and out. Adrenaline kept rushing through her whole body, bouncing into her brain like a rush of angry bees. She stopped breathing for just a moment, trying to collect herself.

As she lay gazing upward, a tiny point of light caught her eye. The sky OUTSIDE was dark and still raining. For a moment, she was sure it was a meteor falling swiftly to earth. But it was no meteor. It slowed, then stood still. Then—frightening more breath out of her—it seemed to come toward them. Finally, it appeared not to be OUTSIDE at all, but high up INSIDE the pod roof.

Her eyes widened as she stared. Herald was still groaning loudly. The pinpoint of light momentarily broadened into a small orb, and was gone.

She kept staring, confused, at where it had been but suddenly remembered her dad was still in the water. As fast as she could turn that way to look, a hand came up on the edge of the boat, and Jimmy's face appeared, sweating profusely under all the seawater.

"What in the world are you two doing?" he whined.

"World" was not the word he wanted but he wouldn't let himself swear at them. He huffed in several breaths and spit the saltwater from his mouth.

Herald was now working the leg with both hands, rolling on his back like an upset sea turtle, still grimacing every two or three seconds.

"You want up?" Sing asked her dad.

"Not unless you can pull me."

"Not right now," she said, still breathing heavily. "Give me a minute."

"I'm fine, sweetheart. Just glad you guys are."

"I'm not a guy."

"Sorry, sweetie. You know what I meant."

They both laughed. Herald was on the verge of tears.

"Can't make it stop!" he complained to Sing.

She shook her head at him.

"Serves your so-stupid-self right," she said, stumbling over her own tongue.

She crawled over to him, took hold of his foreleg, and began to gently rub the rock-hard calf muscle that was still in a tight spasm.

"Just try to let it relax, Herald," she coached. "Let me rub it."

He finally let go of the offending leg as Sing massaged it. He closed his eyes and took several deep breaths, coughing out more water as he did. In half a minute his leg began to relax.

"Panic," Jimmy said to him over the edge of the boat. "You panic, just makes it worse."

"Can't tell him anything, Dad," Sing said.

"What were you doing clear out here?" he asked Herald.

Herald was not about to answer. Sing was happy to.

"Thought he could swim the whole thing."

Jimmy eyes widened. He wiped dripping mucus from his nose.

"Clear across? You nuts?"

"Where have I heard that before?" Sing asked, chastising Herald with a fond look.

"Yeah. Well, thought I could make it," Herald said. "Guess it's farther than it looks."

"Tell me about it," Jimmy said, still trying to catch his breath.

He pulled himself up and into the boat.

Bridget yelled from the shore.

"Everything OK?"

Jimmy waved, too winded to yell that far.

Sing let go of Herald's leg and he was finally able to straighten it most of the way.

"Let's go in," Jimmy said. He looked and realized there were no oars. "How'd you—" Then he finally noticed the blood on Sing's arm. "Sweetheart—"

He saw blood on the bow. He moved over to her and held her. He pulled off one of his drenched socks and used it as a makeshift bandage around her upper arm.

"Sorry, Sing," Herald said as he watched this. "Didn't want you to get hurt."

"Didn't care if you drowned yourself, though, did you, stupid!" she spit out, anger finally catching up with her heart rate.

"Well, we're OK," Jimmy said. "Let's get ashore." He looked at the ailing Herald. "Can you paddle on that side?"

Herald was not about to refuse, even though his leg still burned in pain. At least the cramp had gone.

"'Course," he said, trying without much success to sound tough.

With Jimmy on the opposite side and Sing leaning back against the bow, they made their way toward where Bridget and Pam stood. Piper and Mai Ker were heading toward them in the other boat and soon caught up. They had oars.

"Do I want to ask?" Bridget said with a glare as she helped her son out of the boat.

"I don't think so," Herald said, looking away.

"I'll be happy to tell all about it," Sing smiled. "Soon as I get in some dry clothes. And fix this," she said, proudly holding up her blood-streaked arm.

She gave Herald a little shove from behind and pushed past him, walking with a ladylike swagger toward the podwalk. Piper jumped out of the other boat and caught her, peppering her with quiet questions, awed by the fact that Sing was bleeding but seemed unfazed.

Herald could feel her smug smile, even though her face was away from him. He took hold of Jimmy's arm and limped toward the podwalk on the sore leg, promising himself he would never try to impress the girl again.

8

Wednesday, September 22nd, 15 (NC)

Herald hid most of last evening in the tent he now shared with Jimmy, while Sing gathered with the others in the Meeting Tent and described in elaborate detail her daring rescue of Herald. Piper, Nathaniel and Braden listened with fascination to every word. They especially liked the part where Sing's arm—as she told it—bled profusely into the water and how she very nearly passed out from the excruciating pain. It was the best entertainment they had had in a long time.

This morning the breakfast conversation was subdued. The children chattered quietly between bites but all four adults were ruminating—all about the same thing—though no one voiced the real concern.

They were deeply troubled because they all knew they had almost lost Herald yesterday. Losing him wouldn't have just devastated them emotionally, it would have devastated their plans to rebuild the remnant of humanity surviving here in the Solarium. He was the only child whose father was not Jimmy Algood. Without Herald's genetic line, it seemed impossible to imagine how a viable race, however small, could be re-created.

Bridget finally broke through the adult wall of silence, looking at Herald with genuine love but also with great sternness.

"No more he-man exploits, Herald. OK?"

He looked at her, nodded guiltily, and took a renewed interest in the bottom of his near-empty cereal bowl.

"So. What did Sing tell you?" he asked the others, without looking up.

"Only that you were being very silly," her mom said, greatly curtailing the long, embellished story Sing had spun last evening.

Jimmy looked at Mai Ker, and grinned.

"I think the word 'stupid' came in somewhere. Didn't it?" He gave Herald a friendly, stepfatherly look.

"I'm just happy they're both OK," Piper said. "I guess water is dangerous, huh?"

"Yes it is," Pam said, nodding at her daughter. "You children need to remember that. The world's a dangerous place." She looked around. "Even this little part."

Her comment quieted even the chatter among the younger kids. They all finished breakfast in silence like monks. Herald felt badly that he had precipitated such a morose mood among everyone. He promised himself to stop and think a little before he attempted any more escapades like the one yesterday.

"DO YOU think I'm terrible?" Herald asked Jimmy.

It was midmorning and they were in Pod 14, checking the shrinking store of gasoline in four large underground tanks.

Jimmy looked at him as if he didn't understand the question.

"How do you mean?"

"Because I was so stupid yesterday. Could have drowned out there."

"Terrible? No. A little reckless, maybe."

"Didn't mean any harm. Just not thinking clearly, I guess."

"So why'd you do it?" Jimmy asked, pulling the long wooden measuring rod up out of the third tank.

Herald really didn't want to answer, though he knew the reason plainly enough.

"I guess—" He gave in, thinking, *Why not tell the truth?* "Trying to impress Sing," he said as if this was something to be ashamed of—especially since he was talking about Jimmy's daughter.

Jimmy shrugged.

"I can see that," he said matter-of-factly. "You like her, don't you?"

Herald choked a bit, and nodded.

"She's a pretty girl," Jimmy said.

"No. She's beautiful," Herald said.

"Yeah. She is. No reason you wouldn't want to impress her. I mean, try to get her to like you." Jimmy checked the fourth tank. "But, you know, I'm pretty sure she already does." He smiled, his back to Herald.

"What did she say?" Herald asked hopefully.

"Oh, nothing. All you gotta do is look at her. I can see it."

"But it's kinda . . . I dunno. Weird. She's—like—my sister."

"Yeah. But she's not. Not even actually a cousin. Just an old roommate."

"Yeah, and I'm sure glad you let me move to your tent last year. It was getting—" He reached for a word. "—impossible."

Jimmy laughed.

"Living with a woman is like that. Sometimes."

Herald laughed.

"Man, you oughta know."

"Yeah," Jimmy said, reading the measuring rod again, "I sure oughta."

Herald's respect for Jimmy suddenly grew about three light-years. Beginning to feel as he did about Sing, he couldn't imagine how Jimmy managed the complicated relationships with his mom, Mai Ker, and Pam.

"Gettin' low," Jimmy said.

"Why you feeling low?"

"No, Herald. The tank. Number four is getting low. We're down to about forty thousand gallons of gas. Between the four. Someday we're gonna run out."

"Oh." He changed the subject back. "So how do you do it, Jimmy?"

"Measure the tanks?" Jimmy said jokingly.

"Come on, don't change the subject all the time. How do you manage to get along with three wives?"

"I think it's that they manage to get along with me."

Herald considered this.

"Kind of a two-way street, isn't it?"

"Kinda like a six-lane highway. With no exits," Jimmy groaned.

Herald sat on a crate near the door. In case Jimmy tried to escape.

"Explain."

Jimmy wasn't in the mood. But he knew why Herald was asking, and knew he wouldn't stop asking.

"Well, don't take offense. I mean, I love your Mom. I really do. But, see, Mai Ker is really my wife. My real wife. Your Mom and Pam, they're like—well, surrogates isn't the right word. I mean, we're married and all. We tried to do this right. But I just don't have the same kind of feelings for them. Like I do for Mai Ker. Understand?" He was watching Herald's eyes, which were studying a spot on the far wall.

"Yeah. I think so." But then Herald frowned. The question that had been tiptoeing up behind them for several minutes surfaced. "Am I going to have to get married?"

Jimmy laughed loudly.

"You make it sound like an execution," he said, still chuckling.

"No. I mean, am I going to have to get married— more than once?"

This immobilized Jimmy's brain in mid-thought. He had, until this moment, fairly successfully avoided thinking about this, though he knew the women had talked at length. He had, for a long time, envisioned Herald marrying his wonderful daughter, Sing. Now, a sense of jealous protection for her suddenly leapt into his consciousness.

"Well, I . . ." He stuttered slightly. "I, ah, I haven't really thought that far ahead, Herald. Surprised you have."

"You kidding? I don't want to think about it at all. I don't even want to marry Sing!"

This caused a sharp recoil in Jimmy's heart.

"And why not?" he asked, sounding just a little indignant.

"No, I mean— Not like that! I mean, she's so sweet. And special. And, and she's the most beautiful thing I can imagine. But I—I don't know. I can't explain it." He was waving his hands in the air in front of him as if trying to paint a picture he couldn't see. All he could see was Sing's face, and the look of panic that was there yesterday as she pulled him from the water. It hurt him that he had frightened her so badly.

Jimmy sat on an empty fertilizer barrel opposite Herald. His allergies were acting up, and he tried sniffing hard to clear his nose.

"Let's just go slow here, OK? First, you're only 14. And Sing, too. So, it's not like we're going to rush into something. OK? Relax. Second, I don't know the answer to your other question. Too many unknowns. Yeah, I suppose someday maybe you and Piper might want to marry, too. It's just—" Jimmy broke off. He wasn't sure where to go with this, or how far.

"Just what?"

"Well, I'm not crazy about this thing."

"Thing?"

"This whole multiple wives thing."

"Jimmy, you've got three!"

"Yeah, I know. My point. I just told you, I still only think of Mai Ker as really my wife. I guess that's wrong, somehow. It's all wrong, somehow. But we were forced into it. Sometimes . . ." He was being careful. ". . . sometimes, realities limit your choices."

"OK. What about this reality? What happens someday?" Herald asked.

"Someday?"

Now Herald was trying to be careful.

"Yeah. Someday. Like someday when you, and Mom, and Mai Ker, and Aunt Pam—when you're all gone?"

Jimmy wanted to leave but Herald would only stand up and block him. Herald pressed on, exploring what little he could see of his future.

"And that leaves, what? Me, Sing. Maybe a baby. Or several. And Piper, and Nate, and Braden." He shook his head. "Piper, Nate, and Braden. You're their dad. All three. How could they ever marry?"

"Well, they won't. Mai Ker explained that to me a long time ago."

"So, no more kids. Except who me and Sing might have. Unless, I marry Piper, too."

Jimmy was starting to feel Herald's anxiety.

"Feel like a lonesome bull in the meadow. Don't you?" he asked Herald.

"You should talk."

They were both quiet. Jimmy scratched at an itch on his forearm. Neither had the answers. Neither wanted to continue the conversation.

"Can we take this up some other time?" Jimmy asked with an apologetic tone.

Herald now shrugged.

"I guess. But just you and me. Not Mom. Not Sing."

"Just you and me."

Jimmy stood and put an arm on Herald's shoulder,

which was already 3 inches higher than his own was. They shut off the lights in the fuel shed and walked back through the podwalk into #10, to face the mob.

AFTERNOON SCHOOL time was held in the Meeting Tent. The grownups tried, not always successfully, to devote at least two hours a day to schooling the children.

Mondays and Wednesdays were history days and Bridget was the instructor today. Pam was also there and Jimmy sat near the back of the tent reading *Wuthering Heights* on an electronic reader.

In the middle of a discussion about the Renaissance, Braden, the youngest student at 9, raised his hand.

"Did they build any more of those big church places?" he asked with excitement in his eyes. He wanted to see more of the pictures.

Bridget didn't find any connection to what she had been saying.

"Son, maybe just listen better. We were talking about how modern printing was invented, and how books flourished."

"Didn't they have computers?" Piper asked.

"No," Braden interrupted, ignoring Piper, "remember? On Monday you talked about how in the 'Middle Ages'—I think that's right—people built those huge, big building things? A kind of church?"

"Cathedrals," Herald helped him.

"Yeah. Well, why?" was what Braden really wanted to know.

"That's where people gathered. Kind of like we do, here. In the Meeting Tent," Bridget said, reaching a bit.

"Why?"

"Well, mostly they went there to pray, I think."

Braden looked at Nathaniel, who looked blank, too. He looked back at Bridget.

"Do we pray?" Braden asked, apparently not really

knowing the answer.

She had to be truthful.

"Yes, well, not much. Mostly by ourselves."

"Oh." This seemed to satisfy Braden. "OK."

Bridget was anxious to go on when Sing interrupted. Apparently the Renaissance was not a hot topic today.

"Can you explain to us about praying?" Sing asked.

"Maybe your Mom could do that," Bridget suggested, mentally dodging sideways.

"Doubt that," Jimmy said from the back without looking up from his novel.

"You started yesterday," Herald said, turning to Jimmy. "Wanna finish?"

"Finish what?"

"You told Sing and me about this Jesus you pray to. Christmas. It was really confusing. That stuff about how he was man, but God, too? Wanna start there?"

Jimmy really didn't. The agreement the original team had made when they first arrived at the Solarium was to keep their religious views private and to keep religious celebrations out of the picture. With the exception of the weddings, and the funerals, they had pretty well stuck to that plan.

The plan was starting to unravel. They were now confronted with five children who had almost no religious instruction yet seemed to be curious about God. Sing, in particular, had always been curious about why her dad spent so much time reading his Bible.

Jimmy held his hands toward Bridget and Pam in a gesture of helplessness.

"Ladies?"

"It's all right, Jimmy," Bridget nodded. "We are studying history, right? I guess this is part of it."

Jimmy put his e-reader aside and came to the front of the tent. He sat on a short stool, close to the kids.

"OK. Sing and Herald and I were chatting yesterday."

"About Christmas," Herald explained again.

"Yeah. So Herald asked what Christmas was and I was trying to explain." He paused and watched the children's eyes. Their eyes didn't leave his face but no one said anything.

"Jimmy. Don't make this hard," Pam said.

"OK. Christmas was a time each year when we celebrated Jesus being born. We'd give gifts. That sort of thing. And go to church and pray."

"Well, some people did," Bridget added.

"So," Sing said, "this Jesus, he was a baby?"

"Yes," Jimmy said with just a shade of sarcasm, "men tend to start out as babies."

Sing frowned.

"But yesterday you said you pray to him because he's God."

"It's kind of hard to understand. He's both. That's what his followers believed," Jimmy added.

"Who's God?" little Braden wanted to know.

Wow, Jimmy thought. *The original question.*

"He's the person who made the world."

"Who made him?"

"Nobody. God always has just always been there."

Braden had that look that said he was not about to be fooled.

"How can there be a person, before there's a world?" This was a perfectly obvious question to Braden.

Nathaniel nodded agreement. Jimmy looked from Bridget to Pam but neither offered to help. Pam was smiling but it was a smile that said, "Too bad for you."

"Uh, because he's not a person like us. He's God. He doesn't have a body like us."

Jimmy gestured toward his chest and hips, as if this would help. It didn't. It just confused the kids more.

"Look, God made us. Well, first he made the world," Jimmy said, struggling, "then he made us. And since he made us, he loves us. But people wouldn't live the way God wanted. Everything went bad. So finally God sent Jesus, his son, to be a human. Like us. So Jesus could make things right." He watched their eyes. "See?"

"So, it didn't work, then," Braden observed.

"What do you mean?"

"Well, OUTSIDE, Daddy. If Jesus came to fix things up, looks like it didn't work."

This took the last puff of wind out of Jimmy's sail.

"Maybe we need to get back to history," he said lamely.

"Wait. I have a different question," Sing said.

Jimmy let out a sigh of relief.

"Sure."

"If this God made the world, why did he make it so messed up in the first place?"

Jimmy wanted his sigh back. He was thinking of his answer when Pam finally jumped in.

"I don't think he messed it up, honey," Pam said. "I think we did that."

"So, we made the air go bad?" Sing pressed.

"That's a tough one, honey," Pam admitted. "I don't know. I don't think people caused that. But I'm not sure God caused it, either. I just don't know." It was the only honest thing she could say.

"If God's so big and powerful, why didn't he stop what happened?" Herald asked, taking sides with Sing.

"Good question." *So good it hurts,* Pam thought.

She looked at Jimmy. His eyes said he did not want this ball back.

"Maybe he's just mean," Sing said.

"No. He's not mean," Jimmy said. He wasn't sure why he felt he had to defend God. "He must have some plan. But maybe since we're right in the middle of it, we're too close to see it all."

"We're sort of—flying blind, you mean," Herald

said.

"Flying *what?*" Braden asked, his eyebrows bent down.

"Never mind," Herald told him.

"Yes, Herald. I guess we're flying blind a lot," Jimmy said. "And maybe that's not all bad."

"You want to live in the dark?" Bridget asked, siding with the kids.

"No. I mean, maybe it's better that we don't know some things. Before they happen," Jimmy said.

Bridget looked at him, then at Herald. She remembered how quickly Clayton had taken sick, and how quickly he was gone. Leaving her pregnant. She had to admit to herself that Jimmy might be right.

The questions had gotten far too deep and were bound to get worse if they went on. Besides, Jimmy didn't want to admit in front of the kids that he had struggled with these same questions, after the catastrophe descended on them.

"Let's let Bridget finish her lesson," he said. It seemed like a safe way out.

Braden wasn't ready to bow out, though.

"Daddy, didn't the people who built this place have a plan?"

"Yes, they did. But things happened."

"Everything got wrecked," Nathaniel said.

"Yes. But then you guys—" Jimmy caught himself. "—then you gals and guys came along. By surprise. You know, you can plan, but then something else happens instead. Gotta take things as they come." He looked at the children. "But I wouldn't trade any of you for the world."

"Are we done?" Braden asked, starting to jump up.

"Can I ask something else?" Herald asked, taking hold of his brother's arm and pulling him back into his chair.

Why not, thought Jimmy. *We're in the deep end*

now. "Sure," he said.

"You pray, right?"

"Yes," Jimmy said cautiously.

"Why don't you ever pray with us?" Herald asked, genuinely curious.

Praying was one thing. Praying with his children, or wives, that was another.

"You and I, we're gonna talk later, right?"

Herald remembered their conversation this morning. "Oh. Yeah."

"Let's talk about it then," Jimmy said.

Pam had walked to the back of the tent. She gave Bridget a head bob, gesturing toward the door. Bridget understood. They needed an escape plan.

"Recess, kids," she said.

Jimmy felt the weight lift off him.

"Let's go play," he smiled.

THIS EVENING Jimmy was staying with Mai Ker. As she was getting ready for bed about 11:00, she sat down beside him on the loveseat they had brought to the tent from their old house. He was still trying to finish *Wuthering Heights.*

"So, Herald said you and he had quite a deep conversation this morning."

"He did?"

"Yes. I saw he was moody earlier this evening. When they were getting ready to go run. I sort of pried it out of him."

"Um," was all Jimmy said.

Mai Ker reached over and switched off his e-reader.

"Why'd you do that?" he said in an annoyed voice.

She didn't respond, just went on with her own train of thought.

"I think it is good. They are starting to have a lot of questions. And truthfully, I don't want to answer them."

"Well, neither do I," Jimmy confessed.

"But you try."

"Have to try. It really started yesterday, with him and Sing both. Questions about Christmas, and God, you know. But some of the questions, I'm still struggling with. I think about this stuff, but I just get frustrated."

He looked at her. The look of her face told him he wasn't making much sense. He stroked her neck, then cuddled her head against his shoulder.

"It's not just questions about him and Sing. It's about, you know, why we're even still here." He kissed her gently on the cheek. A pang of emotion hit him. "What's gonna happen to us, Mai? And them?"

"I know," she said, the same worry in her voice.

"I really don't *know* why we're still here."

"We're alive. What else matters?" she wondered.

"Yeah, well you should have been at school today."

"I hear that got pretty deep, too."

"Oh, man. My head hurt! You know me, Mai. I've always been a believer. Not a very good one maybe. But I never doubted there's really a God. Or that he's really in charge. And that he cares. But how am I supposed to know some grand, master plan?"

He leaned back into the cushion and straightened his legs, tired and feeling drained from his head to his toenails. The muscles in his back and shoulders were sore from the sudden, panicked swim yesterday evening. He mumbled on.

"I don't even know why I get out of bed some days. I wanna believe. But at times, I feel lost."

"You're rambling, Jimmy Algood."

"Sorry. I mean, I start doubting God. That's why it was so hard today, with the kids. I always thought there was a plan. But, like Herald said, if he's so powerful—if he's really in charge—why didn't he stop what happened?"

"You are asking me?"

"Yeah. Yeah, I am." He leaned away, watching her, waiting for an answer.

"Well. Suppose . . ." Mai Ker was stumped, casting around for an idea. ". . . suppose there is this great God person you say. Suppose he has his plan. And the whole, big disaster was part of the plan."

It sounded completely foolish even to her.

"Mai, that's crazy! Why would he just—kill . . ." He searched for another word. ". . . just . . . take all those people?" Jimmy got up, agitated, and walked away several steps. Then he turned back with large question marks crumpling his eyes.

"You are the one who asked," she said. She looked at the floor. "OK, it sounds crazy." She pondered this outrageous possibility. "Maybe to us, he seems crazy."

"Now you're insulting God!"

"No. I don't mean anything about him. I mean, about us. Maybe he seems crazy to us—because we don't understand."

It hit Jimmy that this was almost exactly what he had told the children this afternoon.

"Oh."

He sat on the edge of the love seat.

"You say his ways are deep. What if the soil in our minds is too shallow?" she asked.

"Still. That's so hard to believe. That he would just—"

"Well. You did ask me."

Jimmy stood again and wandered the room aimlessly for several moments, reflecting on all the troubling questions of the day. He stared out the tent door toward the darkness OUTSIDE. His mind began to empty like a storm drain after the downpour has passed. The apparent futility of everything bore down on him.

Finally, he came back and sat by Mai Ker and put

his arm around her again.

"Sorry. Been a long day. Very frustrating." He wiped his nose with a small rag that doubled as a handkerchief, his allergies still bothering him. "Why can't I work it out? Why can't *we* work it out? We're all supposed to be so smart."

He looked at her beautiful eyes, which, despite the tone of their conversation, were smiling at him.

"Smart doesn't always matter much," she said.

"Well, it makes me mad I can't get it."

"So, you're mad, and your God is crazy. 'This is certainly another fine mess you've gotten us into,'" she said, trying to sound like one of her favorite comedians. She meant it half-seriously.

Jimmy laughed and hugged her tightly.

"Like you say. We're alive. That's what matters," he said.

"And the children."

"Yes. They matter most."

Mai Ker got up and finished changing into her bedclothes. She got into bed and lay back against her pillows. She patted the mattress, inviting Jimmy to stop trying to think so much and come to bed.

But while he finished changing, her own curiosity got the better of the moment.

"There's one thing though," she said.

"What?" Jimmy said as he lay down carefully by her, turning toward her on his side.

"You told me once this Jesus person—this one you claim is your crazy God, by the way—you said he was supposed to come back. In your big book, his friends keep saying, 'He's coming back.'"

"Yeah?"

"Well, dummy?"

Jimmy looked at her, bewildered.

"Well what?"

"Well, why didn't he?"

Jimmy frowned. He looked across at the tent wall. He reached over the top of Mai Ker and turned off the bed lamp on the side table. He laid back.

It was not a new question. He had asked it of himself a hundred times. He had no answer.

"Why didn't he come back?" she prodded him. "Before it was too late?"

Jimmy's feelings moved from confused, to completely stumped, to irritated.

"I don't know," he said sharply in the darkness.

"So, if you thought he'd come back and rescue us—before all this mess—I can see why you'd be upset." She rolled against his chest. "If I believed that, I'd be upset, too."

He leaned across her again and flipped the light back on.

"You're worse than the kids. You know that?"

"What?" she asked, now the irritated one.

He stopped himself before he wandered into real trouble and said what he was thinking. He was here with his first and most beloved wife. He just wanted some quiet, loving time with her. He found he needed that more and more these days. He didn't want to mess it up.

"What?" she repeated curtly.

"Nah. Let it go."

"Maybe you take this stuff too seriously, Jimmy," Mai Ker said. "Maybe, after all, it's not really real. Maybe the stuff in that book of yours—maybe it is just made up."

"No. I don't believe that."

"Why?"

"It's— It's hard to explain. I just know. I admit, I look around—at what happened—it doesn't make much sense anymore. But I still *know* the things I know. You see?" He was looking straight ahead, nodding his head as if answering his own questions.

"It's a sense I have. Maybe it's from God. But it's real." His eyes narrowed.

"You're rambling *again*."

"Yeah, well, it's what I'm good at."

Mai Ker looked at him with a peculiar amazement. She gently stroked his cheek, trying to calm him but also to connect with this man who seemed so distant and lost at the moment.

"With all that's happened? You still say that."

"Yes. Even when hell breaks loose, some things don't change." He looked into her eyes. "Like the way I love you."

9

Wednesday, August 14th, 18 (NC)

Three years had dragged by. The children kept growing. They had each become unique and special to the parents who shared the job of caring for them all. They were, as Jimmy had said more than once, the most valuable resource in Solarium-3. More important than the plant life, or the livestock, or the solar panels, were their babies who were no longer babies.

Not quite 15, Piper was becoming a lovely girl. Certainly not as striking as Sing in appearance, Piper possessed a rather ethereal beauty that was attractive simply because it was so plain. Hers was a beauty mild and fresh like a flower that has not yet quite fully flourished. She was moderately framed with long arms that were somehow light, more nearly like wings. Through some genetic fluke, she had been given very light, sandy hair that curled in every direction with no pattern or reason. She had Pam's blue eyes, though Piper's were a more intense blue, a hue that belonged more to the sky—before it had turned purplish—than to eyes. The richness of their color made them penetrating when she looked at anyone, as if to create a connection of personalities, as if she could see inside.

She was definitely Pam and Jimmy's daughter, but in some way belonged to all of them, even the other children. Perhaps it was just the way Piper carried herself, but her whole personality was radiant. As Pam had noticed for years, it was not Piper's looks so much as what was hidden behind them that made her a joy to be around.

Nathaniel, on the other hand, Sing's "little" brother who was taller than her, was the rambunctious one. He was about to turn a snotty 14. Being a teenager wasn't what it used to be. INSIDE, everyone had to become a little adult pretty early on and pull their weight with all the work. Still, Nate managed to act out his adolescence in typical ways, mostly in trying to sound a little rude when he didn't really know what that was. And if any of the kids was likely to be out of sorts, it was likeliest to be Nate. He had a temper that was sharper than anyone else in the Solarium. Some of this trait no doubt came from Jimmy, who could get hot at times, but Nate seemed to get mad for almost no reason. Added to this, he had neither Jimmy's good looks nor Mai Ker's beauty. He was, in fact, a bit odd looking. Caught between Mai Ker's short frame and Jimmy's height, Nathaniel was much shorter than Herald and much lankier, but just as tough. His eyes were just a little too big for his face, which was fairly round, and his frizzy, dark brown hair just sat on his head and did nothing.

"YOU'RE IT!" Jimmy squealed as he tagged Braden and ran toward the other side of the pool.

He and Braden had been supposedly cleaning the pool but had lost interest and got caught up in a game of tag.

"No fair! You snuck up," Braden laughed, and took off after his dad.

His legs were not yet long enough to make a serious pursuit, so Jimmy purposely ran a little slower.

Either because he was the youngest, or because he was just cute, Braden was Jimmy's current favorite, his youngest son with Bridget. He had turned 12 in May. Jimmy loved to spend time with him. They would play hide-n-seek, tag, or whatever they could make up on the spot. When Braden laughed, the grin accentuated his long, narrow face, which was topped with a mat of straight brown hair that seemed, in the right light, to have a kind of orange tinge to it.

"It's gotta be your side," Jimmy once told Bridget when she noticed it. "Sure as heck didn't come from me."

Braden shared his sister Sing's even, pleasant personality. Although they were only half-siblings, they were much alike with a friendly, natural affinity for others and were not very self-conscious. They would help with anything and rarely turned out a sour word to anyone.

Braden caught up to Jimmy and tagged him at the beltline. Jimmy turned and reared like a giant grizzly about to leap on its prey, than let out a bellowing laugh and rubbed his hand through Braden's crop of hair.

"Let's go see if we can sneak an early snack," he said to his son. "I don't think the ladies will be back to the kitchen this early."

Braden grinned, needing little encouragement.

ON MARCH 3rd this year, Herald had turned 17. A week ago, on the eighth, Sing reached the same landmark. At 17 she was prettier than ever and continued—unconsciously—to turn Herald's head and hold his attention whenever she was around him.

Trapped in the haze and ambiguity of their humdrum lives INSIDE, but driven by the need to survive and continue growing their family, the Solarians finally arrived at the first pinnacle in scaling the treacherous rock face of their uncertain future.

With Sing and Herald both turning 17, Bridget, Mai Ker and Pam had been conspiring for months. They were careful and delicate about it but their intentions were clear enough. Jimmy managed to avoid most their little quiet conversations, knowing pretty well what the topic of discussion was. Sing was still his baby girl. He didn't really want to think about these things.

About 10 days ago, though, just a few days before Sing's birthday, Mai Ker roped Jimmy into the conversation. The kids were all off doing things somewhere else around the pods. Piper was with Sing looking for flashlight batteries in Pod 13. Nathaniel and Braden were in the back of Pod 9 behind the stable trying to build some kind of new contraption that had no design, and no earthly purpose. Herald had already finished his chores and, as he often did, was listening to old music at the Research Center console.

Just after lunch, Mai Ker asked Jimmy if he would sit down with her and the other two women. Jimmy got a look on his face like he was about to be tortured.

"Sure," he said, though he didn't mean it. He rubbed his head between taut fingers as they walked to the Meeting Tent. "Got a caffeine headache."

"Too much?" Mai Ker asked.

"Not enough."

"Yes. Start getting used to it. Coffee is going to run out one of these days."

"Yeah," he said, shaking his head, "With all their great planning, how come nobody thought about coffee beans? Huh? Coffee beans? All this ground up, canned stuff. Not a single bean that we could plant. Dumb."

"Well, there's a lot of things that are going to run out. Eventually."

"Yeah. The big question is, when will we?"

They found Bridget and Pam in the Meeting Tent and gathered on a couple of sofas. Jimmy sat, but said nothing. The three women smiled at him but it was more a conniving smirk than a smile. They knew something he didn't. But then, they always did.

"We've been talking," Bridget began.

"I'm shocked," Jimmy said placidly.

"We think Sing and Herald should get married," Pam

said.

"Sooner. Not later," Bridget added hastily.

"We thought you'd probably agree," Mai Ker said.

It was like listening to a set of bells chiming out a well-planned piece that was meant to entertain him, and hopefully put him in a cheerful mood.

"Yeah. I figured that was it," he said, eyeing his first wife.

"And?" Mai Ker asked.

"Well. OK. Yeah. I mean," he shrugged and exhaled a little more forcefully than normal, "it seems a little soon to me, that's all."

"Twenty years from now will still seem too soon for you, Jimmy," Bridget said, her chin down as if she was addressing one of her children.

Jimmy had to laugh at himself, because she was right.

"Yeah." He nodded. "And when were you ladies planning to discuss this with the kids?" He could feel an odd little tingling in the back of his neck.

"Right after her birthday," Mai Ker said. "We think that would be good. It will be another milestone. She's so proud that she's about to be so old."

"Not so old," Jimmy said with a typical fatherly melancholy.

Pam blew a little puff of breath out into the middle of nowhere and spoke.

"Look, Jimmy, we understand this. How you feel. It's natural. But she's not just your little girl, you know. She's the same to all of us. Our darling little Sing."

"My God, who'd've ever thought we'd be talking about stuff like this?" Bridget blurted out with flawless irony. She looked at each of them. "None of us thought we'd ever make it this far ourselves. Let alone the kids."

"Yeah. I remember," Jimmy said. "We almost didn't."

"So we should be happy," Mai Ker said, pushing him with a playful jab. "*You* are an old man, Father Jimmy.

Look what you've done."

"It's all your fault," Bridget added playfully.

"All right!" he snapped. "All right. I get it. I'm an adult. We can handle this." He looked at them. "We can *all* handle this. Right?"

"Of course," Pam said, and smiled.

They were munching some of her fresh cookies, which made most everything more pleasant, if not any easier. She offered one to Jimmy. He ignored it.

"The point is, can the kids handle it?" Jimmy asked.

"Well, yes. That's the issue," Bridget said. "And we've been talking about that. And we think—"

"You mean, *you* all think," Jimmy pointed out.

"Yes. *We* all think that we should talk to Sing first, and kind of break the ice with her. I mean, this could be a bit of a shock. She's so sweet-hearted. I don't know how she feels about Herald. I mean, not like this."

"I know she loves him," Mai Ker added. "I just don't know how she loves him. Do you see what I mean?"

"Yes. I know," Jimmy said with the same discomfort in his voice.

"So? Is that OK with you?" Bridget asked.

Mai Ker stared at him. Pam studied the subtle movements in his face. This was not going to be easy.

"I guess. If you think," he said. "Then I'll talk with Herald."

"Well," Bridget said, "actually, we thought we should all four talk to Herald. Together."

"And why, can I ask?" Jimmy said, his eyes on Bridget. "Or do I dare ask?"

"Jimmy, you're a great father . . ." she began.

"But Herald is a pretty soft-hearted kid, too," Mai Ker said. "I have no idea where that came from," she added, smiling, as they all thought of Clayton. "Anyway, we thought it would be easier for all of us to talk with him together. You do the talking. The three of us just sit in."

"We thought he'd feel—more comforted," Pam

added. "In case . . ." She hesitated slightly. ". . . it doesn't go well. Having his 'Moms' there, you know. It will reassure him."

Jimmy thought about this for several moments. He tried to imagine the scene, himself being Herald. Here he would be, being sat down by his stepdad Jimmy, his mom, and his two aunties, and trying to take it all in. Overwhelming.

"Look," he said. "I'm sure you've thought about this a lot. Bet you've talked about it endlessly. But I think you're wrong on this one."

"Why?" Bridget asked. "He *is* my son."

"Oh, yeah. And he's also a teenage boy who has grown up in the most bizarre, abnormal world that could exist." Jimmy started getting a little heated. "Trapped in big plastic bubbles? With three more-or-less moms, and then these other kids running around in his hair all the time. And frankly—unless *you* all have talked about sex with him—I mean I haven't—not in any detail. I mean, he's probably clueless." Jimmy was upset now, trying to think how to protect Herald's feelings. "So, I just think it's safer—and easier—for me to talk with him. Alone."

"Easier for who?" Pam asked.

"For him!"

"OK, Jimmy. Don't blow a gasket," Bridget said in a calming voice, her palm raised.

The three women were taken aback by Jimmy's intensity. They had worked all this out in their heads. They were certain Jimmy would be fine and fall in line with how they had mentally arranged it all. They didn't expect him to want to tackle any part of this alone. He was, after all, a truly shy person even with his own wives, and they couldn't quite picture him discussing anything about marriage or sex with Herald without backup.

Mai Ker shrugged, trying to agree.

"If you think that is best, let's do that. OK?" she asked, looking at the other two women.

Pam nodded her OK. Bridget still had to think for a moment. This was her son.

"I suppose," she finally said. "You are a man. I guess this is 'man talk.' But you'll tell me if there's any problem, Jimmy," she insisted.

"Well, sure," he said, "In half-a-heart-beat."

ON THE 10th, just two days after Sing's birthday party, the three women sat down with her early, just after breakfast. They were in the Meeting Tent again.

"You all look so intense," Sing said to them, wondering if she was in some kind of trouble.

They did look intense and all felt a sense of urgency but awkwardness. None was in a hurry to start. In their private discussions they had pictured this being a lot easier than, in fact, it was.

"Sing. Sweetie," her mother began, "we want to talk about something. It's very personal. So if it's awkward talking with all of us, tell me."

"Sure looks awkward for you," Sing said, more worried now. She made a kind of nonchalant face that said she could talk with them about anything. "You're my Mom. And you're my family."

Silence. Sing was really getting nervous, the women more hesitant. Sing's lips began to tremble a little.

"What's wrong?"

"Nothing's wrong, darling," Bridget said. "We want to talk about you—and Herald."

"What did we do? Are we in trouble?" She began to hold her breath, her lips quivering now like she would start to cry any second.

"No, dear, nothing. You haven't done anything," Mai Ker said, thinking to herself, *I hope not*. Then her eyes widened just a bit. "You're not, are you?"

"Not what?"

"Well, in some kind of 'trouble'?"

Sing had not the faintest inkling what her mom was

talking about.

"No, I—I don't think so."

"Oh. Good. Then, no, there's no trouble."

"It's—" Bridget started in again but fumbled for words. Pam rescued her.

"We're wondering how you feel about Herald," Pam said matter-of-factly, tired of dillydallying. "You know. Do you like him?" She thought bluntness was best now.

"Like him?"

"As a boy."

"Oh . . ." Sing suddenly looked incredibly relieved. The quivering broke out into a broad smile. "Oh, you mean, do I *like* him. Yeah. A lot. He's great!"

"Have you thought about what your future might be," her mom asked. "You and him?"

Sing considered this. She shook her head *no.* Then she reconsidered.

"What do you mean, 'future'?"

Mai Ker saw no profit in dragging this out.

"Well, we wonder, I mean if you think you really do like him, we wonder if you and he would—" She spun invisible yarn in the air in front of her. "—if you would want to get married."

It took several seconds for this to fully sink in.

"Oh, my gosh," Sing said with a little playful ring in her voice. "You mean . . . ?"

"Yes. You'd be husband and wife," Mai Ker said.

"So, you mean . . . ?" Now Sing spun the yarn.

"Yes, Sing," Bridget said. "That, too."

Sing was laughing before she or they realized it.

"Oh, that would be so funny!"

Mai Ker just stared at her.

"What do you mean?" her mom asked, confused.

"Oh, funny. You know. Like it would be very *strange,* but very fun."

All three women began to grin, though they all suppressed it. They were trying to keep this serious. But with Sing, life was never that heavy—just light, joyful, good, and fun. She had never known firsthand what it was like, before. She had never had any personal tragedy touch her. She had known nothing but the Solarium and her little family. Life was just what it is. And now, this idea of she and Herald being man and wife, though it sounded peculiar, almost bizarre, would simply be, as she put it, fun.

"It's all right with me," Sing finally said. "It would be perfect." She smiled broadly. "Perfectly all right."

The warm pod immediately felt warmer. The scents of everything growing around her in #10 just beyond the tent walls suddenly smelled closer, richer, more alive. She looked at her mom and aunties quizzically.

"Is that what *you* want?" Sing asked, wondering.

"As a matter of fact," Bridget said, "it is what we want. We've talked about it, and we talked with Jimmy. We think it's time. And it's OK."

"So what did Herald say?"

They should have known this question would come but they had not prepared for it. Mai Ker tried to make it sound like they had.

"Sweetie, um, we haven't talked with Herald. Not yet."

"Wow, you mean I get to choose? I get to decide? For both of us?"

"No, honey. He gets to decide, too. We just thought," she looked at Pam and Bridget, "well, we thought it would be good to discuss this with you first."

"Why?" Sing looked puzzled.

"Well, in case you didn't like the idea. And said no."

"We don't want his feelings to be hurt," Pam added.

Sing laughed again as if this was the funniest thing yet.

"Why in the world would I say no?" Her whole face sparkled. "I can't wait!"

Mai Ker gulped slightly.

"You sure she's Jimmy's, Mai Ker?" Pam laughed.

"What do you mean?" Sing asked, suddenly serious.

Mai Ker backhanded Pam's arm, not lightly.

"Auntie Pam is just trying to be funny, dear. And you know she's not very good at that." She raised her eyebrows toward Pam.

"Well," Pam said, toning it down, "that's good, then." She took in a full breath and exhaled slowly, relieved. "That's settled."

"Well," Bridget reminded them, "not really. We have to talk with Herald."

"Of course we do," Pam agreed. "I just mean, it's settled with Sing. Sing, you're such a dear girl." She went over and gave her an excessive hug.

"But I have a question," Sing suddenly asked, surfacing from the hug.

"Sure, honey," her mom said.

"What about Piper?"

"What do you mean?"

But quiet panic rippled through Mai Ker and the two aunties. They instantly knew what she meant. And they hadn't thought this one out either. They were silent.

"I mean, you all married Dad. To have children. Right? So, will Piper marry Herald, too?" Sing pondered, looking puzzled again. "Or would she marry Nathaniel?" She shook her head, wondering.

The women were stuck. They should have seen this coming.

"Well, honey, Piper's not even 15 yet," Pam said. "So, it's not really time. To worry about that. And, well—"

"We've talked things over," Bridget cut in, gathering her courage, "we're not really sure. It's complicated. See, Piper and Nathaniel are actually brother and sister. Well, half. They're both Jimmy's."

"But Herald and I are brother and sister, too. Aren't we?" Sing asked, her world suddenly shifting.

"No. Not in the same way," Bridget said, trying to weed her way through this. "You know, we all basically act like you are. Brother and sister. But you're not. Jimmy isn't Herald's real Dad. He's a stepfather. Clayton was his father."

Sing nodded that she understood. "I get it."

"So," Bridget said, "you and Herald aren't brother and sister by blood. You're only kind of related. Since I'm married to Jimmy."

"Yeah. I forgot." Sing thought. "So what about Piper, then?"

"Well, I guess she could maybe marry Herald later."

"We haven't really gone that far," Mai Ker said. "But she could never marry Nathaniel—or Braden either. It's not good for a half-brother and half-sister to marry."

"It can cause problems," Pam added.

"You mean fights?" Sing asked.

"No, sweetie," her mom said. "Worse. Problems for the babies."

"Oh," Sing said. Her eyes narrowed and she bit lightly on one corner of her mouth. "Oh."

"Are you worried, honey?"

"Just, more—wondering. You know. If I would have to share Herald with a second wife. I love Piper. I do. But . . . I don't know if I'd like that."

Mai Ker looked keenly at Sing. Bridget and Pam looked sideways at each other.

"Well," Pam said. "Now that's interesting."

"Why?" Sing asked innocently.

"Just interesting. That's all."

Bridget intervened.

"We'll talk with Herald, Sing," she said warmly. "Then we'll figure it all out."

"Talk with him today?"

Bridget smiled.

"I don't think we'll have any problem finding him."

SUFFICE TO say, young Herald Listner-Block needed no encouragement whatsoever to collude with his parents' wishes. He was deeply in love with Sing, though he had never told her that, or anyone else. He had no idea how to express this strange feeling for her. He could not describe, even to himself, the unique bond that had developed between them over the last year and a half and his growing attraction to her. To Herald it felt like a disease. If he had to go work in a different pod for several hours he felt mildly alarmed, like he might not be able to find her when he came back. Whether he was working, playing music at the computer console, or just walking, he could not keep her face out of his mind.

So it went much easier for Jimmy than it had for the ladies.

"You're serious?" Herald asked, his eyes getting bigger, not to mention very excited.

"Sure," Jimmy answered. "Very serious. We think it would be great if you and Sing marry."

"How long do we have to wait?"

This seemed to be the common theme between the two youngsters.

"I don't know." Jimmy thought about it. He and the wives had not discussed the exact timing. "Not long, I guess."

"Great. Tomorrow?"

Jimmy laughed.

"Maybe not."

Herald was beaming. He began to imagine all kinds of things that he had tried really hard not to imagine before. Jimmy almost lost his attention completely.

"Herald?"

"Huh?"

"Soon, I guess. But it's not set. The women have talked with her. But, I mean, you have to ask her."

"Oh." Herald looked shaken. *"Me?"*

"Herald, if she's going to be your wife, you have to

ask her. Not us."

"But you just said they already asked her."

"I know. I mean—" It was so awkward, talking like this about his own daughter. "You're supposed to ask Sing. Yourself. That's how this works."

Herald smiled at a devious little thought.

"Why can't she ask me? If she knew first?"

"You are being way too much like a teenager, Herald." Discomfort crawled up and down Jimmy like a giant centipede. "Just take my word for it. You have to ask her. And you've both got to agree. You need to look each other in the eyes, and agree."

"And then we're married?"

"No. Then you're what's called engaged."

"In what?"

"You know, I can't tell if you're trying to be funny, or if you actually meant that."

"Huh?"

Jimmy could see that Herald's mind was drifting somewhere else again. He was pretty sure where. Herald's face was moving through several conflicting expressions, an explorer lost in the wilderness and wondering why there was no map.

"Let's just go find the ladies. And I think the other kids should be there, too."

"Be where?" Herald asked, with a rough landing.

"When you ask her."

"Sure. Can we do it now?"

"Wait." Jimmy's throat got a little tight. "There's something else, Herald."

"Yeah?"

"Well. You understand, we're kind of rushing this. You know? You're both pretty young still. But it's . . ." Jimmy hated awkward moments. "Look. You're grown up enough. You should be able to have children. And, honestly, that's really why this even came up."

Herald got quiet, and very still. Wondering and

fantastic daydreaming was one thing. Stopping in his tracks and thinking about the actual reality was something very different. Living with Sing. Sleeping with Sing—in the same bed. This suddenly felt very, very strange. Just as suddenly, he felt very uncertain of himself. What if she didn't really like him, the way she seemed? He couldn't begin to conceive of anyone calling him "husband." Least of all, Sing.

He looked like a dull knife was slowly pushing into his right side.

"So . . . you want us to have a baby." He felt something like a toothache in his stomach.

"Yes." Jimmy didn't dare say more.

"OK." Herald was trying to breathe normally, but it showed that he was not having much success. He shook his head quickly. He simply couldn't let himself think about it anymore. "Can we go talk to her now?"

"No time like the present."

"What's that mean?"

"Forget it."

BRIDGET AND Pam quickly straightened some things around in the main living room area then went about tracking down the other three kids for the big announcement.

After a short search, Pam found Piper and Nate swimming in the ocean in Pod 12. Piper was up high on one of the large rocks, about to dive in. Pam held her breath at the same instant Piper did, as Piper plunged down—head first—into a spot where the water that was only about 6 feet deep. She belly-flopped.

"Piper!" her mom shouted from the doorway of the podwalk. But Piper was under by then and didn't hear the panic in her mom's voice. She surfaced quickly with a big smile.

"Way to go, klutzy!" Nate hollered. Although he liked Piper, he was not about to show it.

Pam hurried quickly to them and chastised Piper.

"Darling, you know you shouldn't dive from that high where the water is shallow. You could get hurt!"

"I'm OK. It's fun!"

"Fun or not, it's dangerous."

"What is?" Nate asked, barging unwanted into the conversation.

"Forget it for now," Pam said, frustrated. "Just bring your towels and come dry off. We're having a family meeting."

"Again?" Nate whined in annoyance. "Seems like every day we have to have a stupid family meeting."

"First, Nathaniel, it's not every day. You're exaggerating. As usual. And second, this is really important."

"Hardly wait," the boy said.

"Come on, pokey," Piper said as she pushed past him, shoving him on purpose as she went by.

"OK, now you're gonna get it!" he yipped and began the chase.

"Kids!" Pam yelled, to no avail. "Kids," she said reflectively as she watched them chase each other into the podwalk to #10.

Piper ran gracefully, if not very fast. Even running and soaking wet, she had a waiflike look. She turned laughing toward Nathaniel. Her personality, at one moment bubbling and the next sedate, was unique. The older Solarians never knew quite what to make of it. They all had to work at being pleasant. For Piper, this came effortlessly.

"Gonna catch you!" Nathaniel hollered.

As he passed Piper and bumped her aside, he gave a laugh and a little snide smirk back at her. He ran clumsily, but was still faster.

Bridget had looked for Braden without success. She was back in the living room area of the main tent trying to make it look nice. It had to be just right for a grand announcement. She paged Jimmy on the intercom and asked him to find their son.

Jimmy started where Bridget had not looked but where Jimmy thought was likeliest. He found Braden in the Comm. Center at one of the computer consoles playing an old world-conquering video game called "Bankrupt!" It would have been a complete dinosaur by now if the world of video games had not, along with everything else, come to a screeching halt.

Even though Pod 2 was kept closed off, Braden didn't hesitate to sneak in when he was sure nobody was watching. He once tried to get his dad to play "Bankrupt!" with him but Jimmy declined. Built around a concept of large corporations purposely gobbling up smaller, younger, undercapitalized companies by driving them into financial ruin, the game reminded Jimmy too much of the "real" world that he remembered only too well.

Jimmy came up behind Braden and rattled the back of his chair.

"Hey, buddy, need you to come home. We've got stuff to talk about."

"Whaddid I do now?"

"Nothing, kiddo. Somebody else this time."

Braden frowned at his game being interrupted when he was just about to win a huge pile of make-believe cash and bury two of his imaginary opponents forever inside an unused bank vault. He looked up at his dad, then set down the game controller and got up.

"I guess," he said. "Could'a waited five minutes, though."

Jimmy scrambled Braden's hair again.

"Well, this is more important stuff. You'll be surprised."

Only now did he consider how surprising it really might be to the other kids.

Piper and Nate, not happy about their fun time being

interrupted either, were wrapped in large beach towels and sitting on the floor in the living room. Jimmy and Braden came in and everyone else sat down. Everything was set.

Jimmy asked Herald to stand up in front, and have Sing stand by him, which they did.

"So, ask her," Jimmy said.

"Already did."

The parents gawked at him and at the huge grin that spread across Sing's face.

"Whad'a'ya mean?" Jimmy asked.

"You guys were all in a flurry, running around. Setting the stage kind of thing. You know, like we sometimes play-act on Saturday afternoons? But I didn't think this was play-acting. So I snuck Sing over behind the old house. And I did what you said."

"He asked me," Sing said. Three simple words, perfectly musical without notes.

"Am I supposed to kiss her or something? Like you guys?" Herald was hoping for a yes.

Jimmy was still trying to recover his dad-like dignity.

"You can kiss her," Mai Ker laughed. "Just once."

And he did. It was a bashful kind of kiss—but a lot longer than the parents had expected. Mai Ker winced.

Braden's nose turned up like he smelled something bad. Nathaniel was preoccupied, still brushing sand off one toe that had a nail partly torn off.

Piper got up from the floor and went over and hugged Sing and Herald.

"I am so happy. This makes me so happy. You two are my best friends."

"Your only friends," Nathaniel said.

Even in Solarium-3, kids were very much kids.

IT WAS a very short engagement. Anything else, under the circumstances, would not have been wise and would have driven poor Herald crazy.

The wedding was set for today, the 14th, at 2:00 in the afternoon. Mai Ker and Pam hastily sewed up a wedding dress for Sing out of the best material they could find, which was some old bed sheets stored in the upstairs of the house in Pod 4, and a waist-circlet of lace taken from a blouse that had been Sarajane's.

They planned a simple party for after the ceremony, swimming, dancing, and whatever special treats they could throw together. It was not like there could be a honeymoon. Life was the honeymoon.

Piper was dressed up as Maid of Honor in a patchwork piece of various fabrics Pam had stored up from bits of old clothing. The bodice was made from pieces of old shirts that had belonged to Clayton and Willy along with frilly lace from one of Pam's old nightgowns. The skirt was dark pink material that had been an old work blouse of Bridget's. Piper seemed pleased with the very creative design, odd as it was.

Nathaniel, much to his displeasure, was tapped to be Best Man. He mulishly agreed to a clean pair of jeans, but nothing fancy. Putting on slightly large, leather shoes that belonged to his dad seemed completely abnormal but he finally gave in.

Once everyone was gathered around a small table just outside the main tent, they adjusted their positions a little to give some idea of formality. Braden, the odd man out, stood with his mom and Auntie Pam as witnesses.

Jimmy, with Mai Ker at his side, opened his Bible to the only thing he really could find easily that he knew was about getting married. He stopped at, "That is why a man shall leave his father and mother and be joined to his wife, and they shall become one flesh."

He asked Herald to take Sing's hand.

"Her right hand," Jimmy corrected.

"She's left-handed," he said.

"Her right hand, in your right hand." He whispered to Herald, "Don't argue."

Herald looked very solemn and said his vow.

"I take you, Sing, as my lawful wife, to have and hold forever, better or worse, rich and poor, sick or healthy. Till we are parted by death."

Mai Ker took the next part.

"Sing?" she asked.

"I take you, Herald, as my lawful husband, to have and hold forever, better or worse, rich and poor, whether sick or healthy. Till we are parted by death." She looked at Herald. "And you really love me?"

He smiled.

"I *really* love you, Sing."

It couldn't have been better in a storybook.

"Can I sing something?" she asked. "I made it up for today."

What she sang was perfect. Whatever she sang would have been. It had the sound of a mother bird reassuring her brood in the dark of a storm. Sing knew her own mother would like it. The song of a living bird with a human voice.

A shiver ran through Mai Ker. It was so real. Her ears touched the sound. Then she remembered, just briefly, a moment when she was a little child, out in the woods listening to the birds, imagining how one day she would marry a wonderful, handsome man and live in a big, beautiful mansion. She looked at Sing. She listened to her daughter's beautiful music. And she was stunned at how her wish had come true. Come true in a way she could never have conceived, in an artificial world she could never have imagined as a child. Mai Ker wept happy tears.

Jimmy took her close and held her. In the middle of all the tragedy, for those few moments there was renewed hope, a sense of expectation. And there was joy. And there was a real future rushing toward them.

The party lasted late into the evening, a shadow of days and evenings past. Even Nathaniel and Braden finally broke into the fun and were dancing with Piper and with Sing, and with everyone all together. For a while the children felt like adults, and the adults were again like children. Slowly the night wore down, and their energy slipped away until finally they noticed that Herald and Sing were nowhere to be seen.

Mai Ker swigged down the last of her fruit drink and walked over to Jimmy, taking him around the waist in her arms.

"Sure miss your old rocket fuel."

"Too many kids," he said.

"I love you, Jimmy Allll-Goody-goooood."

"I love you, Miss Mouuu-aaaaaah," he laughed.

Years of fear and trials cascaded together and compressed down into a moment of perfect joy. Jimmy and Mai Ker stood close, looking intimately at each other, soaking it in.

Pam and Bridget had given up. They were reclined on the floor with the younger children, and were not thinking very hard about getting back up.

"Maybe just sleep here on the floor tonight," Pam said half-drowsily.

But eventually they got up and got the younger children to bed. Then they and Mai Ker and Jimmy all went off to their own separate tents and slept in their own separate beds, in respect of the occasion and to honor the newlyweds.

Four different kinds of prayers went up toward the pod roofs that night from each of their tents, looking for answers, hoping for the best, and caught up in the sheer impossible wonder of this day that had just passed.

10

Saturday, November 23rd, 18 (NC)

The weight of days INSIDE Solarium-3 remained heavy and humdrum. Most days were dreary and alike. But not all.

On the 24th of August, just a week and a half after the joyous wedding, the routines had been overthrown, at least for a few terrifying minutes.

Nathaniel and Braden were riding bikes through the pods. Jimmy had the podwalks open into pods 3, 4 and 6 for cleaning and some routine maintenance work. When they should have been helping their dad with the work, the two boys decided instead this was a great opportunity to test their bicycling skills and have a race.

They nearly ran over Piper and Sing as the girls weeded a pumpkin patch near the west side of #10. The girls threw several choice taunts and some dirt clods after them but neither boy, laughing louder than usual, heard the girls, which was good since they weren't terribly ladylike words.

Braden bounced his front wheel hard up over the edge of the sidewalk in front of the old house in Pod 4 and left a skid mark in the turf near the side porch as he slid sideways trying to sneak around Nate. It didn't work. Braden flipped sideways and smacked against the lattice work that closed in the area between the grass and the porch floor. He wasn't hurt much. Nate sped on, thrilled that he now had a lead that would be impossible for Braden to make up. He would be the hands-down winner.

As Braden was getting to his feet, he thought he was

seasick. He knew seasickness from spending long days in the boats with Jimmy and Mai Ker testing the salt water and checking marine life. But here he was standing on solid ground. He thought.

He stood as still as he could but the ground wouldn't let him. He let out a yelp, and stumbled.

"Daddy?!"

Jimmy, nearby in pod 6 pointlessly putting fresh paint on the bars of the empty aviary cage, heard Braden but didn't reply. He stood frozen, frightened himself. He grabbed onto the bars of the cage. The tall cage was shaking, slightly at first, then violently.

"Oh God!" was all he could think of.

He didn't want to look up, but he did. The beams and plastic roof sections of the Solarium seemed to be heaving gently one way, then another, as if he was looking at them through a shallow pool of water. He felt sick.

"Daddy?!" came Braden's cry again, now a poorly controlled scream.

Jimmy let go of the cage and turned and ran toward Braden's voice in #4. He emerged through the podwalk near the front of the house and saw Braden to one side, standing like a little tree ripped from the Petrified Forest. His legs were bowed and his arms were out to the side as if he was walking a tightrope.

The earth shook violently under the Solarium and for miles around. Jimmy was shaking, too, realizing they were in danger of a final catastrophe. If the Solarium gave in, it was the end.

He ran and knelt by Braden and held him and tried to calm his son's panicky tears.

"What is it?" Braden demanded.

"Gotta be an earthquake—or something," Jimmy said as carefully as he could, not wanting to frighten the child more.

Bridget's out-of-control voice crackled loudly over

the intercom system.

"What the hell is it?!"

Her voice was tight, peppered with fear. It was not what Jimmy wanted the kids hearing at this moment.

"Be OK!" Jimmy called back over the intercom radio. "Everybody stay calm. Be OK." He almost added, "Stay in the open," until he realized there was no such place. Huge structures hung over their heads. Anything could fall any moment.

The movement of the ground under the Solarium was subsiding. The quake lasted a mere 40 or 50 seconds that seemed like an hour. There would be several more, smaller jolts. But the worst had passed.

"Everybody to the tents," he heard Mai Ker shout over the intercom.

Braden was still shaken but willing to go pretty much anywhere else this second, if only his dad would stay by his side. They hurried quickly through the podwalk to #10 where Nathaniel had dumped his bike and was kneeling, trying to steady himself. Jimmy collected him and they met up with everyone else at the main tent.

"What was that?" Pam was saying to anyone and everyone.

"Obviously a quake," Bridget said tersely.

"Can't be! Not around here," Mai Ker said with the authority of research behind her. "That was one reason for putting the place here, so isolated. There were never any earthquakes around here. Supposedly."

Bridget let out a laugh.

"Supposedly-a-lot-of-things."

"Will it do it again?" a shaken Sing asked her dad.

"How the heck am I supposed to know?" Jimmy said. "Like your Mom said, this isn't supposed to go on. Around here."

They all fell into silence for several moments. Nathaniel and Braden had both plopped onto the tent floor, afraid of another shaking. Piper was holding Pam's arm with a face that said she never wanted to feel that again.

"If there was this one, there could be more," Bridget finally said. She looked around the tent. "It hurt anything?"

"Who cares about the tents? I wanna know about the pods!" Jimmy said. "We need to walk," he said, taking Mai Ker with him. "Let's do some checking," he said to her quietly, still trying not to frighten the kids.

"Can I go?" Herald asked.

"Guess so," Jimmy said, nodding.

They left the tent.

"You think we're OK in here?" Pam asked Bridget.

"In the tent?"

"In number ten," she said as she loosened Piper's fingers from around her forearm, "It's the biggest. If something came down—I mean, there's a lot more to come down. In here."

Bridget reacted immediately. Fear was back in her voice.

"Pam, if *anything* comes down—if any of the pods go—it won't matter." She said it as quietly as she could with a *Don't you get it?* look in her eyes.

Pam was sorry she asked. She was not going to say any more with Piper and the other children there. She looked around. A lot of things that had been on shelves and tables a few minutes ago were now on the tent floor.

"Would you all help me straighten up?" she asked the children.

It seemed like the only thing to do.

THERE HAD been three small aftershocks that same afternoon. Then calm returned. Jimmy felt they were beyond any trouble. He, Mai Ker and Herald spent over four hours that day walking every pod, looking for any damage. Apparently the Stellar plastic was more than up to its name. It had strained and moved gently with the swaying of the main beams. They could not, even with binoculars, see any damage. Their shelter was safe.

Jimmy and Mai Ker also spent two days after the quake going back through early site research files for the complex. Surely something had been missed by the engineers, some soil fluke, some rock fault that was maybe noticed but ignored.

They found not the slightest hint or record of any site problems. Nor did they find any record in the historical files of an earthquake ever hitting anywhere near where Solarium-3 was situated. The planners had done their homework.

"There were some minor jolts up around Denver," Mai Ker said, reading from one archive file. "Late 1960s. The government was pumping stuff—some kind of waste—into underground caverns at an old arsenal north of the old airport. When they realized this was destabilizing the substrata, the pumping stopped. So did the quakes."

Jimmy listened as she read. Interesting, but far too long ago to have a relationship to what happened on the 24th. Everything had settled down. There was no damage. His air monitors showed no fluctuations or pressure changes. He was sure they were safe.

"Just one more stupid darn thing for the record book," he finally told the rest of his large family. "Planet's dead. But she still can't settle down, I guess." It was an attempt at humor. It didn't elicit even a single smile.

Life returned to day-to-day normal. As normal, that is, as it ever got INSIDE. The tedium and monotony returned. Until November 2nd.

THIS TIME it came just before sunup. Everyone was still asleep. Jimmy was sleeping in his own tent. Herald, snoring quietly, was curled up by Sing in their "Honeymoon Tent," the one Sing used to share with Piper.

Everything shook this time. They rocked, even in their beds. Braden, who had been lying on his side near the edge of his bed, fell off and landed hard on the floor, coming up with bloodied nose. Nathaniel, trying to wake up, thought it was a nightmare and felt paralyzed. In their tent, Pam and Piper both yelped, too terrified to really scream.

The Solarium shuddered, moving more violently than the last time. The beams strained, groaning with a sound that would have frightened the most evil spirit. The horrid sound terrified Jimmy even in his still-half-conscious state as he imagined the whole Solarium collapsing in.

Bridget and Mai Ker in their own tents grasped their beds and watched their tent roofs move side-to-side like overwrought hula dancers. Mai Ker got sick to her stomach with fear. As she lunged for the safety of the floor, she threw up.

This quake lasted much longer than the first. Almost four minutes. It was long enough to deepen the fright in the children and for the anxiety to bubble over in the adults. As it dragged on, the kids got more scared. They looked for something safe to cling to but there was nothing that didn't seem to move.

In the corral, two of the horses were bucking and kicking at the rails, wanting to be somewhere else, safe, and running. Trapped, kept, they rebelled against what felt like the end of the world to them, sudden destruction about to come crashing down. The groaning of the pods awakened in them a deep horror, some equine fear of imminent destruction, triggering a cry for freedom or pity, or both.

All the smaller animals were reacting, too, each in a unique way. Two yellowish cats, descended from earlier domesticated pets but now essentially wild, clawed at a tree as if to tear it down before it fell on its own. Hissing gave way to several short fits of spitting at the air, at whatever invisible thing was trying to kill them.

Jimmy rallied everyone into the Meeting Tent. It was at one side of the tent complex and he thought it was least likely to cave in from the movement of adjacent tents, all of which tied together at several points.

Just as they gathered into a large human knot, the shaking began to subside. He and the women were trying to calm the children while trying to calm themselves.

"Why is it happening again?" Mai Ker demanded plaintively.

Exasperated, Jimmy snapped at her.

"You always ask me stupid questions you know I can't answer!"

"Sorry."

"You know as much as I do!" he said, overlapping her apology.

"It wasn't a real question," she explained. "Thinking out loud."

"Yeah? Well stop it," he said intensely, nodding toward the kids.

Every nerve in every Solarian was frazzled. They felt absolutely powerless. Illnesses, air problems and such they could try to figure out, look for solutions, maybe fix. An earthquake was so far beyond their control that their abject helplessness was oppressive. They had one choice. Stand fast and pray the whole complex didn't come crashing down around them.

They sat together on the floor. They sat in silence for at least ten minutes. No one could think of anything to say. Nathaniel and Braden were valiantly trying to stifle tears. Herald was sitting between Sing and Piper, holding both of them close as if he could somehow protect them.

When it was certain the thing had finally stopped, Jimmy got up and walked to the tent door. He was afraid to look, sure he would see beams broken loose or sheets of Stellar plastic dangling from the pod roof. It had been that violent.

To his amazement, the mammoth dome appeared to be intact. Running into the Meeting Tent minutes before, he had seen the beams wrestling, fighting each other for supremacy. Now looking up, he couldn't believe nothing had broken loose or come down.

"Unbelievable . . ."

Bridget and Mai Ker were behind him now.

"Well?" Bridget asked.

"What?"

"Any damage?"

"Can't tell. Can't see any. But, man—after that—it'd be a miracle if something didn't break."

A lot of things that didn't belong there were now lying on the floor or the ground, wherever they had fallen. The Solarians let them lay. In teams of two, they spread out over the complex and began, on empty stomachs, to search for any sign of structural damage. After a full two hours of walking, looking, straining, and stomachs harassing them for food, they reassembled in the kitchen tent.

"Well?" Bridget asked once more.

"Anyone find anything?" Jimmy asked the whole group.

Heads shook, *no*.

"Us either," he said of his and Mai Ker's efforts.

"Can we eat?" Nathaniel asked.

"I don't know. Can you?" Mai Ker asked back.

"You kidding?" he said. "I could eat a horse."

"Luckily, nothing broke loose and crashed onto the corral," Jimmy said, "so you won't have to."

Mild laughter broke the tension that had held them in its grip for the last two hours. They scrambled to make breakfast.

Through the rest of that day, November 2nd, and for several days after, the whole family kept watching, searching for any damage they might have missed. Miraculously, so it seemed, their little haven in the deadened world was intact. Amid what was a vast graveyard OUTSIDE, their life could go on.

No one slept very well that night. But each night that followed, they relaxed a little more and begin to fall asleep with less and less anxiety of being awakened like that again.

TODAY WAS the 23rd of November. The newlyweds, still acting conspicuously like newlyweds, were working in the Rec. Pod, straightening up around the playground Jimmy had made when they were little. Though it wasn't getting used much these days, Herald and Sing hoped a day would come soon when it would get used a lot, by their own children. Keeping it nice now was a down payment toward that day. When they finished the playground, they picked up the mess around the pool left from a swim party last evening.

Except for the terrors of the two quakes and several aftershocks, life was happy for the young couple. They had discovered a deeper love for each other, deeper than they ever felt in the months before their marriage. Attraction had grown into true desire, and a solid bond.

They were, as Jimmy's Bible had put it, becoming one. They understood their charge. Their parents expected babies, lots of them. But then, committing to this duty was not exactly work for Sing and Herald. Day by day, they grew more deeply in love.

At meals, the other children would watch them as if examining creatures from another planet. Their parents looked at them in a new light, too, beginning to finally feel a sense of possible permanence in their Solarium world.

Sing and Herald enjoyed each other's company so much that they found themselves spending less and less time with their folks and more time alone, enjoying the joys of each other. They had also identified several new spots around the complex that were secluded and unlikely to be visited by parents or siblings in the early evenings. They sometimes snuck off to one of these favorite spots to practice what they called their "baby-making aerobics."

They finished cleaning up around the pool and started the walk back to the tent village at the far north side of Pod 10. They strolled between various crop plots like their parents, always keeping an eye on the health of what was growing in each plot. Herald bent down over some rhubarb plants. Sing was humming a new tune quietly as it leaked out of her mind.

A cloud shadow passed over her and she looked up through the pod roof to see a huge thunderhead OUTSIDE, billowing several thousand feet high, moving quickly southeast. A storm system was approaching from the northwest. Sing followed the movement of the cloud as she sang. Then, because just the right angle of purply, yellowish sunlight popped out from behind the cloud, her eye caught something that seemed odd, something she had never seen before and hoped she wasn't seeing now. There appeared, for a moment or two, a razor-sharp line in the plastic pod roof, about 20 feet from one of the support beams.

She stopped singing abruptly. She frowned. Without looking down, so as not to lose the exact location, she reached down, found Herald, and pulled him up by the back of his shirt.

"Quick. Look." She pointed up.

"That's a really big cloud."

"No. Closer. See?"

"See what?"

"See? That line thing."

Herald stared, but saw nothing out of the ordinary. He didn't know it, but his uncorrected eyesight was not as sharp as Sing's. The Solarium planners had thought of most everything, but not eyeglasses. Several of the team came in with soft contacts, but these had long ago worn out. Sarajane had brought reading glasses, but these had been lost track of years ago.

"Wait," Sing said. A trailing, smaller cloud had partially cloaked the sun's brilliance. She took hold of Herald's chin and directed his gaze toward the faint line just before this cloud passed on.

"There!" she said, pointing again.

"Yeah." Now he saw it. "What is it?"

"A scratch?"

"Don't know."

"Did something hit the OUTSIDE of the roof? Maybe?" Sing wondered hopefully.

"Can't tell. Stay here. Let me get Jimmy. And some field glasses."

He found Jimmy stretched out on his bed trying to nap. Herald insisted that he had to see something. Jimmy, half-dozing, was sure he had seen everything there was to see in the Solarium but he played along because Herald was so emphatic.

Herald ran and grabbed a pair of binoculars from his room that he used to study the night sky. He liked to try to locate stars, if the night was reasonably clear OUTSIDE and, of course, watch for meteors.

He grabbed Jimmy, who was still trying to wake up just outside his tent, and hurried him toward Sing.

"It's still there?" Herald asked as they arrived.

"Yes," Sing said. "Can only see it at times. When the sun's just right." She squinted. "Wait a second."

As soon as Jimmy saw her staring toward the pod roof he got a sour feeling in his stomach. He had continued to watch the pod roofs almost continually since the quakes, looking for any sign of damage. As he looked up now at the huge dome over their heads, the highest in the Solarium, he saw nothing.

"Look," Sing said, "there."

Herald pointed, too. Jimmy looked, squinting hard. As the sunlight surged a little, he saw the unmistakable line.

"Is it a scratch?" Herald asked, hoping.

Jimmy didn't answer. But it was not a scratch, he was sure. It was a crack in the plastic. He had seen this before. The roof was damaged. The only question was whether it went clear through the Stellar sheet, or not.

He called the women over the intercom. In a few minutes they were all standing, looking up. Piper and Nate joined them.

"What is it, Daddy?" Nate asked, without his usual sarcasm but a genuine sound of apprehension.

"Not sure yet, son," Jimmy said. "It's gotta be a crack. But from this far, it's hard to tell how bad it is."

"What do we do now?" Mai Ker asked. "I am not climbing a pod again." She looked at the tremendous height of #10's roof. "Especially not this one."

Jimmy took the binoculars from Herald. He looked, adjusted the eyepieces, looked again. He strained his eyes, which didn't help.

"Herald, get the telescope. In the back room in the Research Center. The big one."

Herald hurried off, Sing running alongside him.

"Why's everyone so upset?" she asked him.

"You don't see?" Herald asked her as they hurried into Pod 3. "This could be really bad. If the plastic's cracked—clear through—air could get in."

"OUTSIDE air?" Sing asked with sudden alarm.

"Yeah."

They rushed back with the telescope, Herald carrying the scope and Sing awkwardly carrying the tripod. Jimmy quickly set it up. Braden had heard the intercom chatter and he, too, was standing alongside his mom, his arm around her waist. It wasn't certain who was holding whom.

Jimmy cranked two adjusting knobs until the large lens brought the spot on the pod roof into perfect focus. He didn't look very long.

"Crap!"

"Jimmy," Mai Ker complained, nodding toward the kids.

"Shoulda said a whole lot worse," he said looking at her, and pulling at a taut muscle in his neck. "Look."

Mai Ker did.

"Bad?" Bridget asked.

"Take a look," he said.

Bridget looked. Pam was about to take her turn, but stopped and stepped back.

"No thanks."

Each face dropped as it pulled away from the eyepiece. They all knew what this meant. Herald and Sing understood, too.

"Now what?" Pam asked.

"Sing, why don't you and Herald take the kids over to the corral," Mai Ker said. "I think the horses haven't been fed enough today."

They took the hint and the other kids and left.

"We've gotta try to fix it," Bridget said.

"Yes. But how?" Mai Ker asked. She had already given her opinion about climbing again. Their previous climb in Pod 9 had nearly ended in disaster.

"Same way we did last time," Jimmy insisted, ignoring the protest on her face.

"But if Mai Ker won't go, well— Who?" Bridget asked.

"Don't know. Maybe I'll go up by myself," he said.

"That's stupid, Jimmy," Pam said. "You can't handle all the gear and all that stuff by yourself!" She shook her head. "I'd try—but you know I'd never make it."

Bridget was shaking her head.

"You know how I am about heights, Jimmy."

Jimmy stood looking at them.

"Might put a rope on all three of you and haul you all up there."

He waited. Mai Ker studied a spot on the ground.

"If I have to, I have to," she said.

Jimmy was thinking. He looked back through the telescope. His mind was working, but painfully. Mai Ker had kids now. It was different than before. And he had kids. Everything was more complicated. It was not just fears, or feelings. Now it was practicalities, and far-reaching implications. Things that were too confusing for him to contemplate right now.

"Maybe we need to think this one through," he said.

As the leader, he knew they would respect his decision. But no one was in a hurry to hear it. They knew, though, that they could not just ignore the threat. There was real danger, to them, to the kids. OUTSIDE air could be fatal. Even a small leak could send their atmosphere INSIDE into another tailspin. And once in that spin, there was no guarantee of pulling up.

"OK," Jimmy finally said. "Let me do some close monitoring for the next 24. I mean, the thing's probably been there a while. Since the quakes. And we just missed it. Let's see if there's any air changes. Before we go crawling up there."

"Good idea," Pam said, relieved. She remembered the last time, too. She and Bridget had nearly been sliced and diced by a sheet of Stellar.

Bridget looked through the telescope again.

"I thought the damn stuff was s'posed to be indestructible," she said bitterly.

"Anything made by man will eventually break," Jimmy said.

"You think air is getting in?" Mai Ker asked.

"No way to know yet. I mean, depending on what's happening with the air pressure OUTSIDE, our air could be leaking out."

The others had not considered this.

"But that's not good either," he added. "It would reduce the ambient pressures in here. We don't want that either."

"Even if air is leaking out, though," Bridget said, "a

pressure change out there, it could reverse and push in. Right?"

Jimmy nodded, looking up.

"Maybe till we know, maybe we should wear masks for a couple of days," Pam said. "We have those little air bottles in storage. And there's extra oxygen masks in the infirmary."

"Not a bad idea," Bridget said.

"They're not airtight," Pam hedged.

"No," Jimmy said. "But the air in the bottles is going to be cleaner than anything from out there. If there is a leak."

Mai Ker's mind went to the kids.

"Yes. We should do it. Just in case."

She stared up at the crack again, then back at Jimmy.

"You won't make me go up there, will you?"

He looked at her more closely and seriously than he had since Herald and Sing's wedding day. Then he put his arm around her and pulled her tightly to him.

"Not if I can help it."

"Good."

PAM BROKE out enough of the small medical masks to fit up each of the Solarians. They used small oxygen tanks that had been refilled with regular air, keeping the ones found in storage on hand in case they needed purer oxygen. The air tanks would protect them to some degree if any bad air were creeping in.

It was a little surreal, especially for the kids, trying to work and walk and talk with the masks on. But Braden thought it was fun. He imagined they were walking in space.

"I want to be a spaceman, Daddy," he told Jimmy through the air mask as he sat with his dad in the Research Center that afternoon. Jimmy at a computer was running through various monitoring programs, checking their air quality. He was afraid to rely just on the sensor alerts. He didn't really catch Braden's comment through the mask.

"What's that?"

"What's what?" Braden asked, perplexed, then looking at the computer screen.

"What did you say? 'Spacemen'?"

"I wanna be a spaceman."

Jimmy stared at him. *Where'd he get this idea*, Jimmy wondered. They had never talked about it. But he knew there were a lot of historical records about space exploration in the computer archives. That was part of what had driven the creation of the Solarium projects in the first place. He thought for a second. He didn't want to discourage any dreams.

"Well, buddy, I don't think that's a problem." He put his arm around Braden's shoulder and pointed at the ceiling of the research building.

"The ceiling?"

"No. Out there. OUTSIDE. See, you *are* a spaceman. You're kinda flying through space right now."

Braden's expression let his dad know he was sure he was being lied to.

Jimmy chuckled.

"Look, earth is really just a big space ship. Right? It's flying through space at thousands of miles an hour. Pretend the Solarium is our ship. And you're in it. See?"

Braden really didn't, but he didn't want to question his father—who he was sure knew absolutely everything. So he nodded with just a little uncertainty.

Jimmy's attention went back to the air-testing programs. After several minutes he spun Braden's chair toward him.

"I've gotta go talk to the Moms. You hold down the fort, huh? And don't mess with this program that's running. Here." He pointed. "OK, spaceman?"

"OK," Braden said, pleased with this great trust.

Jimmy called to the women over the intercom to meet

him on the porch of the old house. The kids rarely hung out there since the pod was still normally closed off. The kids thought the house was ancient looking, and creepy. Tents, they were convinced, were much better and more normal.

Jimmy got to Pod 4. He looked around to make sure Herald and Sing weren't holding some private rendez-vous. The pod was empty.

The women joined him on the porch chairs. Pam sat in the swing.

"So?" Bridget asked.

"I can't find any major change. But the oxygen pressure *is* down. Just a smidgeon. Could be just heat fluctuations, that sort of thing."

"Or, maybe not?" Bridget prodded.

"Yeah. Could be we've got a leak. If air is leaking out, the oxygen or nitrogen pressures might just notch up or down a little. But I don't see anything major."

"But nothing leaking in?" Mai Ker asked.

"Honestly? I can't tell. 'Cause we don't know enough about what happened. OUTSIDE, I mean. We didn't ever get any really good numbers on how things were out there at—" He hesitated. "At the end." He shook his head in frustration. "And we got no way to know what the air pressure is out there now."

"So, air *could* be leaking in, and we just can't tell," Pam said.

"Yeah. Maybe." Jimmy was all uncertainty at this point. Hoping for the best, he was worrying about the worst. "I think we just watch it another day or two. And see."

"I hate these masks," Bridget said. "And Nate keeps pulling his completely off. I'm worried about him."

"Nate will be the first to get cranky if he doesn't feel good," Mai Ker said. "If he needs it, he'll keep it on."

"Well, we have to just force him," Jimmy said. "No chances here but one."

Mai Ker reconsidered.
"OK."

11

The rest of the weekend Jimmy had closely monitored the air throughout the pods. Braden, his sidekick, missed little.

"You look worried, Daddy," he said.

"Um."

"We going to be OK?"

As much as Jimmy wanted to say *Yes,* he wouldn't lie to his favorite child.

"I hope so," was his compromise.

The air balance had not changed since Saturday. The oxygen pressure remained a bit low, but was constant. He wasn't sure of the cause but he couldn't dismiss it.

"Tell me about the other time," Braden said.

Jimmy really didn't want to revisit it, but Braden's staring eyes broke his resolve.

"Well, it was raining real hard one night. OUTSIDE. And we found a drip."

"Mommy said you almost killed her."

Jimmy could clearly imagine the look on Bridget's face when she had said this to their son.

"No. I didn't. A piece of Stellar almost did, though."

"The stuff in the roof?"

"The stuff we live in, son. The pods are just big upside down plastic tea cups. Now we've got another crack."

"Why?"

"Had to be those quakes. Probably on the 2nd. Last time it was the nuclear blasts that cracked the roof.

Remember? I told you about it in history class."

Braden nodded that he did remember.

Jimmy remembered several of their history lessons with the kids. Many involved painful memories for the teachers. One back in early October came to his mind.

HE HAD been trying to teach them about the 20th century and why all the wars happened.

"I don't understand history," Sing interrupted. "It makes no sense."

"Sure it does," Jimmy said.

"No, it doesn't. It all ended up so pointless."

"Wait—" Jimmy tried to say.

"It makes no sense," Sing insisted again. "All that making stuff, and building stuff. And the fighting. All those wars. What was the point?"

Jimmy hesitated because the question was so big and his answer could end up so long.

"That's a really good question, Sing. I've asked that a lot, myself. What *is* the point?"

Jimmy knew his only real answer was in the realm of his faith, which the kids would not understand, since it was so little talked about. He pressed on anyway. He could not just ignore the question that was now in every child's eyes.

"I guess, my real answer, Sing? Because I still believe in God. Somehow, to him, it must all make sense." He watched their eyes closely. He hesitated, not out of doubt but to challenge their young minds. "I know you guys wonder about that. But if God's not real, if he's not finally in charge—or he really doesn't have a plan—well then, you're right, Sing. There is no point."

"Like I said," Sing said, not in meanness but drilling her point with simple earnestness.

"Look, kids," Jimmy said, getting gut-honest with them, "I've struggled with this, too. Especially when everything went wrong. Out there," he said after a poignant hesitation. "But I still believe in God—I still trust him. Maybe I can't explain it very well. But that's why I pray. 'Cause it works."

There were a few moments of quiet reflection. Sing and Herald both knew the story of the time when Sing had been so sick they all thought she would die. They knew one key point of the story—related to them, remarkably, by Bridget—was that Jimmy prayed very hard for Sing and not long after that she got well. Sing loved the story, although she remembered almost nothing of the actual events. Herald was still skeptical. But then he was awfully glad that Sing was still around.

He found himself looking at her, taken by how pretty she had become and how lucky he was to have her as his new wife. At that moment, on that day in October, he felt himself on the verge of saying "thank you" to someone. To whomever it was who made her get well. But he knew nothing of prayer and had no idea who he might pray to.

He turned his head and looked up at Jimmy.

"Dad, tell me again. Why do you pray?"

"I pray, because . . ." It was a very good question, one Jimmy had never considered in great depth. But he knew where to start. "Like I said. It works. And I learned to pray when I was very young."

"So, it's for kids?" Nathaniel asked.

"No, I didn't mean that. I mean, it became part of me, when I was young. My family prayed together. And we always went to church and prayed with other people."

"Why?" Herald asked.

"Like I said. I believe in God. And I think he wants us to talk with him. Praying is how you do that."

"How do you know who you're praying to?" Sing wanted to know. "How do you know there's even anyone listening?"

"You been talking to your Mom?" her dad asked her.

"No."

Jimmy considered how to answer this.

"That's why I read my Bible. It tells about God. What he's said to people about himself, what he's shown us. Over many centuries."

"Back when there was still history going on?" Nathaniel asked sincerely.

Jimmy smiled.

"Yeah. Back when there was history."

"Ooh, you mean, like the night when all the bombs went off?" Braden asked. "Remember? You said everything boomed and rattled?"

"Yes," Jimmy said. "What are you asking?"

"Maybe God was knocking and you forgot to answer."

Jimmy wanted to laugh except he wasn't sure this was actually funny. Or that Braden meant it as a joke. The boy certainly looked serious.

"You've been reading my Bible, haven't you?"

Braden smiled.

"It's a weird book, Dad."

"Not weird."

"Yeah, weird. All those strange people. With funny names."

"Like 'Nathaniel'?" Jimmy asked.

Braden laughed.

"Yeah, like him!" he laughed, pointing at his frowning brother. "That was good, Dad!"

BRADEN'S VOICE brought Jimmy back to the present.

"So, you think it was the second quake. The big one? That cracked the pod?" Braden asked.

"Yeah. Probably. Anyway," Jimmy said, "whatever caused it, we've got a crack in number ten. And we're gonna have to fix it."

"You need a big ladder."

"Something," Jimmy said.

He remembered that night years before when he and Mai Ker had climbed to the top of Pod 9 to patch the first leak. A tingle ran up his spine. He didn't want to make a climb like that again. And compared to Pod 9, Pod 10— 130 feet high at its pinnacle—was a monster.

Jimmy gathered the women together late that morning, again on the porch of the old house.

"I can't see much change in the air numbers since Friday. Oxygen pressure is still a little low. Not convinced what that means. Could get worse. Might get better."

"Well, I think we need to ditch the air masks," Bridget said wearily. "It's next to impossible to get the kids to keep them on tight. They're a nuisance."

"The kids?" Jimmy asked.

"The masks."

"We're probably OK without them," Pam agreed.

Bridget looked at the others cautiously.

"I been thinking the last couple of days. There's obviously a crack. And our air hasn't really fouled much. So, I'm wondering. Do you think maybe that's a good sign?"

"About what?" Mai Ker asked.

"Well, maybe the air OUTSIDE isn't as bad. As it was. Maybe it's changed. Gotten better."

"There's no way we can know that," Pam said. "Is there?"

"No," Bridget said. "Not without going OUTSIDE."

"What?" Jimmy said. He lurched forward a little on his chair, staring at Bridget. "You nuts? You really want to venture out there?"

"Just thinking," Bridget told them. "I mean, it's been a really long time. Maybe it's tamed down, or cleared up, or something."

"Well, we're not about to find out," Jimmy said

emphatically. "It's too dangerous."

"I was just thinking," Bridget said, not giving up, "it might be easier to climb the OUTSIDE of the pod than the INSIDE."

"But we can't *go* OUTSIDE," Jimmy repeated.

"But, if we could—with good rubber shoes, and some ropes over the top—I mean you could pretty much climb the pod slope without too much trouble. Couldn't you?"

It was a very tempting idea, but Jimmy was not swayed.

"Out of the question." He looked straight into Bridget's eyes for a third time. "No."

Bridget was undaunted.

"Look, Jimmy, I know you're not crazy about climbing up there again. That high. I just thought, if you could work a rope up over the top of the pod OUTSIDE, a safety rope, you could use it to help climb up. It would take a lot of rope—"

"Bridget, for the last time! Nobody's going OUTSIDE!"

"I would much rather have to climb the beams in here," Mai Ker said without hesitating, "than be out *there*."

"We have plenty of air tanks. If we can use them in here, why can't we use them out there?" Bridget insisted.

"Look," Jimmy said, passing his boiling point, "we've been through this all before. If we open the entry pod, there's no going back. We break that seal, we don't know what that'll trigger. No way to know. 'Cause we never had any good idea what the air was really like out there."

"I agree with Jimmy," Mai Ker said, "We can't foresee the consequences. And we've got little lives to think about!"

Bridget listened and remained composed.

"Just a thought," she said apologetically. "Just trying to weigh out our options."

"Well, that's not one of them," Jimmy said hoarsely,

anger foaming around inside him. His mouth was dry.

Pam tried to rescue Bridget.

"The air seems a little less purplish out there the last few weeks. Have any of you noticed? It's gotten more peachy color, seems to me," Pam said. "I wonder. You think Bridget might have something?"

"Don't you start, too," Jimmy said. "Man! Why in the world anybody would want three wives is beyond me!"

He got off his chair and stomped down the porch stairs and headed toward the podwalk to #2. He went toward the Comm. Center, not sure where he was going, or why.

Maybe Braden will be there playing "Bankrupt!" or something, he thought. Maybe he could recover some male sanity.

MAI KER went looking for Jimmy early in the afternoon after he skipped lunch. He was in Pod 13. Not surprisingly, he had several ropes piled up on a crate, along with a single rappelling harness.

"Why did you not eat?"

"Needed time to think."

"And what do you think?"

"Can't decide. I know we gotta patch the crack. It's just too risky to ignore it. Just not crazy about making you climb up there."

"Yes. I am not crazy, either," she said.

"So. I'm gonna do it. First thing in the morning," he said, turning away.

She stared at him, took his arm and turned him back.

"No, you are not, Jimmy. You cannot do it alone. It was almost impossible last time with both of us."

"Yeah. Oh well."

"So I have to help."

"Said you wouldn't. And I don't want you to."

"I know I said it. Who else is there? Who else would do it?" she asked.

"Don't know. I don't think Bridget could make the climb. Pam for sure could not."

"So it's me."

Jimmy sat on a crate, his mood hushed. It seemed for a moment he might cry.

"Why does it have to be like this?"

"It is always like this," she said.

"But everything was going so great. The kids are healthy. Life was getting almost normal. If that's possible."

"I know it."

"Now this."

"We have to do this, Jimmy. You and me."

He looked off across the shed.

"Herald could do it," he said, thinking aloud.

Mai Ker almost choked.

"No!"

"Why not, Mai? He's strong. He's a good climber. He practices all the time. Why not let him use it?"

"Jimmy, I do not want to go up there. But I will not let him go up."

"You're not being reasonable."

"Has nothing to do with reason," she almost barked. "He is married now. He needs to have children. Don't you understand?"

"Why can't he still have children?" Jimmy was no longer thinking clearly.

"Dummy! What if something happened?"

"Mai, that's why we've got the ropes. Nothing will happen."

"No!" she barked again. "Don't even dare say it to him. I'll— I won't talk to you ever again if you do!"

Jimmy realized how serious she was but couldn't stop the laugh.

"Wow, you're still a tiger, aren't you!"

"You say one word to Herald, you will find out!"

She felt like storming out of the equipment shed but

stood her ground instead. Until she had an answer.

Jimmy looked into her eyes, which were burning and moist.

"OK, sweetie. Miss Tiger-lady. Your way." He laughed lightly again but tried to swallow it. "Hope you're in shape."

"You would know if anyone would, huh?" she joked.

"Yeah. You're in shape."

He nodded approval. He took a deep breath and let it out like it was too much to hold. Then he went back to a deep shelf and pulled more climbing gear together, along with a second harness.

"Would you carry some of that stuff over by the podwalk between number ten and number five? That's where I'll start from in the morning."

"You'll start?"

"Yeah. You're gonna have to start opposite. At the other side."

"What do you mean?"

"Because, where the crack is, it's not close enough to any beam. We can't reach it. We'll have to attack it from two sides."

"And you, you crazy person—you thought you could do this by yourself?" she laughed.

He didn't.

"We'll go up opposite sides and rig out a sling between us. We'll stretch it tight and work from that."

Mai Ker was feeling queasy already. She imagined looking down to the pod floor from 130 feet up.

"We need to get plenty of sleep tonight," she told him.

"Yeah. I'll be in my own tent." He came over to her and hugged her. He looked down into her eyes. "I was hoping all day you'd change your mind. And offer to help. Just didn't want to ask." He made an innocent shrug. "Knew darn well I couldn't do it by myself."

"That's why we love each other," she said.

"We do, don't we."

"Yes."

Mai Ker began carrying some of the gear across Pod 10 toward the side near the podwalk into #5. Herald saw her from the front of the main tent where he was watering grass and came over to her.

"Whatcha doing, Mai Ker?"

She looked away.

"Helping Jimmy."

"He going up there?" Herald said, gesturing at the roof.

"Yes. In the morning."

"Great. Where is he? I wanna tell him I'll help him."

Mai Ker stared at the ground and kept stacking rope. She had hoped Herald would not offer to help. *How to put this gracefully*, she was asking herself.

"No need," she said, without looking up.

"Whad'a'ya mean? He can't go up there by himself," Herald pointed out.

"Yes. You're right. But I'm helping." She continued coiling a long rope on the ground.

"Oh, I don't think you should, Mai."

"Why?" she said sternly, standing and finally facing him. She straightened her back up, trying to match his height, a lost cause. "You think I'm too old, don't you!"

It was a gentle scolding but she hoped it would work.

Jimmy was coming toward them from Pod 13. Herald looked at him for a second, then back at Mai Ker. He didn't know what to say that would not insult her.

She had set it up well.

"Well . . ." He was stuck. Now he looked at the ground. "Nah, you're not too old." He looked for a way through this. "But obviously, you think I'm too young."

"You are too young."

"For what?"

It was a loaded and poignant question, considering he had just married her daughter. Still, Mai Ker was not about to give him the real answer.

"I just don't think it is a good idea."

"You mean, you don't think I can."

"No. I did not mean that. I mean, I don't think it would be smart."

Her thoughts were wandering but she didn't want to admit what she was thinking about.

"Just wanted to help. You know I love to climb," Herald said, pressing the matter.

"I know you do, sweetheart. And I also know your wife would probably wring her mother's neck if I let you climb this pod," she said, pointing to the towering pod roof.

"Why would Sing care?" Herald asked rather stupidly.

It was the wrong thing to say.

"Herald, when you have been married more than a couple of months, you will discover your wife has a whole lot of opinions about a whole lot of things. You just don't know it yet." She laughed. "Anyway, it's been decided. It's Jimmy and me."

"Jimmy decided?" Herald asked, just as Jimmy reached them.

"We decided," Mai Ker said. "Didn't we, Mr. Algood?"

Jimmy was profoundly stuck. He had just received his wife's stern warning not to say a single word about the climb to Herald, and here she was, stacking the gear and talking about it with—Herald. He took the easy way.

"Whatever it was you said." He smiled at Herald. "Whatever *she* said," he added, looking at her.

"Man, nobody trusts me even a little," Herald whined.

Sing came out of the podwalk from #11, where she had just finished feeding the bunnies and cleaning their hutches. She saw Herald, Jimmy and her mom and wondered what the pile of gear was at their feet. She nearly ran to them.

"What are you doing, Mommy?" A jumbled fear

showed in her eyes.

"Your Dad and I are going up there to work on this problem. Tomorrow." Without looking up, she pointed up.

"I wanted to help," Herald groused.

A second wave of panic struggled across Sing's face.

"You're going up there, too?" she demanded of Herald.

"No, he's not," Mai Ker said flatly. "Your Dad and I."

Herald started to stomp away toward the tents.

"Man, you'd think I was still a baby."

"Nah," Jimmy said quietly when he was gone. "But still pretty much a kid."

"Exactly my point, Mr. Algood," Mai Ker said.

Sing hadn't moved.

"Why?"

"Why can't he go?" Jimmy asked.

"No. Why do you guys have to?" she pleaded.

"Um." Jimmy looked toward the top of the pod. He gave a little nod. "Gotta be done," he said in a very unenthusiastic voice.

Sing turned without another word and followed Herald, her insides churning.

HERALD CONTINUED to mope all evening.

"Come on," he said to Sing not long before bedtime. "Let's go walk."

"Where you two going?" Mai Ker asked as they left the living room.

"Out."

Herald didn't turn, just took Sing's hand. They went for a long, private walk. Herald thought he had grown up. He thought the adults respected him as one of themselves. He realized that would be a while coming, now.

"What's wrong?" Sing asked him.

"It was easier being a kid," he said quietly as they walked hand in hand.

12

Herald didn't sleep much. He was still fretting. Tossing during the night, he had thoughts about talking to Jimmy privately this morning to see if he could climb instead of Mai Ker. Sheer size and strength, he thought, should count for something. He couldn't understand why Jimmy didn't stick up for him yesterday.

Herald turned his head. Sing was not in bed. She also had a restless night and had gotten up early to go help make breakfast. Herald dressed and found Sing in the kitchen helping her mom and Pam with the food.

He looked around. Jimmy wasn't there.

"Jimmy around?" he asked Sing quietly.

"Why should I care?" she said. She was upset with her dad, too, for a different reason.

Herald grabbed a piece of toast and went looking for Jimmy. He was in Pod 13 getting several more hundred-foot coils of rope.

"Jimmy?"

"Hey, Herald."

Jimmy had loaded the armful of gear onto a small cart. There was a 30-inch square sheet of half-inch Stellar on the cart along with some tubes of glue. Jimmy went to a cabinet and got out several small propane torches.

"Lot of gear," Herald commented.

"Yeah."

"Sure I can't help?"

Despite Mai Ker's injunction, Jimmy knew he had to answer.

"No. We'll do OK."

"How come you'll let Mai Ker help and not me? She's a woman."

"That's rich," Jimmy said. He set down the gear in his hands and looked at Herald. "Look, if it wasn't for what she did the last time we had this problem . . . well, you would probably not be standing here right now." He continued loading gear. "She can handle herself."

Herald saw no way forward without insulting Jimmy's most beloved wife. They all knew, even the children, how he felt about Mai Ker.

"Whatever," Herald said. "Can I at least help you move the gear?"

"Sure. This pile goes to Mai Ker's side. About halfway between the Pod 11 and Pod 12 walks. OK?"

"Yeah."

Herald took the cart and started toward the spot.

Jimmy followed but went to the kitchen for the breakfast he had skipped.

Sing saw Herald moving the cart into the east side of #10. She confronted Jimmy at the door of the kitchen tent.

"I thought you promised—" She grabbed his arm and pulled him outside the tent, out of everyone's hearing.

Mai Ker watched with curiosity. She, too, saw Herald moving gear and thought Jimmy had changed the plan.

"Jimmy!" she called to him.

Jimmy ignored her. His head was bent down toward Sing's near the door of the Meeting Tent. He held a hand out to Mai Ker to tell her to be patient. He shook his head *no*, and Sing looked relieved and ran toward Herald.

Mai Ker expected an explosion when she reached her husband. But oddly, as Sing said something to Herald, Herald looked for a moment like he was just hit in the back of the head with a board. Then he grabbed Sing into a hug, and wouldn't let her go.

"Now what?" Mai Ker asked Jimmy.

"Ask Sing," he said.

Herald and Sing were walking toward the kitchen. Mai Ker waited for them in the doorway. Jimmy stood a couple of feet behind her.

"Now what?" she asked the children.

"You tell them," Herald said with a very peculiar look on his face.

Sing half-smiled and half-cried.

"I think . . . I have a baby." Now she did cry.

"Oh my gosh," Mai Ker blurted out as she hugged her. "Sweetheart. When did you know?"

"Well, a couple of weeks. But I wanted not to say anything yet. I wanted to be really sure. Now I'm pretty sure. I think I started in late September."

Herald couldn't find any words but was beaming with amazement that he was actually a part of this.

"But when I thought Herald was going up there," she pointed toward the cathedral-like roof of Pod 10, "I had to tell." She looked squarely at him. "You're not. Are you?"

"'Course not."

"I need you. I don't want you taking any chances."

"Don't worry, Sing," Jimmy said. "He's staying right down here by you."

"Not much consolation," Sing said. "You're my Mom and Dad. Not much difference."

"Well, let us be that, then. You're still my baby girl!" Jimmy said, giving her and her baby a warm, long hug.

Mai Ker gently stroked Sing's hair.

"We'll be careful, honey," she promised.

Herald was still beside himself. He put his hand gently on Sing's stomach as if it might electrocute him.

"Really?" he asked.

"Yes. Pretty sure."

"I love you." He said, hugging her.

The two of them hurried to tell Pam and Bridget Sing's exciting news.

ALL THE gear was in place and ready by 9:30. Jimmy helped tighten Mai Ker into her harness and then went to his spot and got into his. He felt pressed to get on with this. The crack may have been there for several weeks, but once discovered it seemed like a giant ogre hovering over them, waiting to pounce.

Mai Ker started up the far side of the pod just to the east of their tent village near the podwalk into #11. Bridget and Herald were her ground crew. Jimmy started a minute later from across the pod near the podwalk into #5. Pam and Sing were his crew. At both sides, the ground crews would manage a safety line for each climber. These lines, threaded through safety loops along the beams as they climbed would act as tethers as they inched their way up the beams. More importantly, they would become rappel lines to lower Jimmy and Mai Ker back to the ground when the work was completed so they would not have to make the tiring, painful hand descent down the beams.

Herald held Mai Ker's line and let out slack as she climbed and Bridget backed him up as the final anchor. On Jimmy's side, Pam held the line and Sing was the anchor.

Piper had been given the assignment of chief babysitter for Nathaniel and Braden to keep them out from under foot, but this was like herding cats, especially with something so exciting going on. The kids had watched Jimmy, Mai Ker and Herald do short practice climbs before but no one had ever attempted the 130-foot-high roof of Pod 10. It was the Mount Everest of the Solarium complex. The interlaced steel beams worked their way from ground to roof in an elaborate web that managed to support the massive weight of the plastic panels that formed the exterior of the pod. The Stellar panels were a full inch thick. The sheet Jimmy had cut the patch from was half-inch Stellar, backup stock that had been laid in by the planners for, as the Solarium manual put it, "minor repairs."

The plan, as before, was to scale the pod, pull the repair sheet up with ropes, use the special glue to tack it into place over the crack, then heat the patch with the gas torches to super-dry the glue. With one mishap, this had worked perfectly when they patched the roof of Pod 9. The difference was that #9's summit was only 65 feet above the ground. Pod 10 was twice that. Twice the climbing, twice the effort, twice the time.

The other difference was that Jimmy and Mai Ker had been able to climb Pod 9 together, leapfrogging their way up the beams until they reached the damaged spot. It had been within easy reach of one of the support beams. This new crack was nearly 20 feet from the nearest beam. As Jimmy had explained to Mai Ker, they would approach from opposite sides and by carefully tossing ropes back and forth would weave a netlike sling between the two nearest beams. They could then climb out onto the sling to do the repair.

The two beams they would anchor the sling to were roughly 25 feet apart so it would take a lot of time to weave enough ropes back and forth to make a safe work-sling. Difficult, Jimmy had told everyone, but it could be done. When they got to the middle of the sling, they would drop ropes to the ground teams to ferry up the plastic patch and other gear in large buckets.

The biggest difference, though, was that Jimmy and Mai Ker were both 17 years older. Jimmy had done quite a bit of practice climbing with Herald to keep in shape. Mai Ker hadn't done as much.

The whole team faced the prospect of a very long and tiring day. They hoped to complete the work before suppertime. But, as Jimmy said again quietly to himself as he started up the beam, "Gotta be done."

"How you doin'?" he called across the pod to Mai Ker from about 20 feet up.

"OK. But I have to go slow. Don't want to tire too early."

"Go as slow as you want," he hollered back. "Just be careful."

The support beams had 1-inch holes every foot or so to facilitate climbing since the planners knew such climbs might be needed to repair fans, lights, or other equipment suspended from the pod roofs. As Jimmy and Mai Ker progressed, they attached short rope loops to these holes with carabiners every couple of feet, at about an arm's reach. They used the loops to pull themselves up, or to stand in like a stirrup. Most importantly, they threaded their safety lines through these loops every 20 feet or so as they went. To do this, they had to briefly unhook their safety line from their harness, quickly thread the line through one of the loops on the beam, then snap the safety back onto their harness. That was the tricky part.

Jimmy had rehearsed this with Mai Ker on the ground.

"Just be darn sure you have a really solid grip on the beam before you move your safety line. And don't move till it's secured again. OK? Not an inch."

"Worrywart," she said. "I know the routine."

By continuously threading these safety lines through loops on the beams, the ground crews could catch them if they slipped. It was the safest way they knew to make this kind of climb.

After about 15 minutes, Jimmy was already winded and his legs were beginning to feel wobbly. His fear of heights didn't help, but he tried not to look down. He kept his sight trained most of the time on Mai Ker inching up from the other side. She was making good progress and was actually a little ahead of him.

"You OK?" Bridget called up to Mai Ker.

Mai Ker caught a long breath, which was getting more difficult as she climbed.

"Tired. But OK."

Mai Ker knew from previous climbs that she wasn't afraid of heights. It actually thrilled her. Looking down didn't bother her. She smiled down toward Bridget then looked across to Jimmy.

"Jimmy?"

"Yeah?"

"How are we doing?"

"Pretty winded. But we're doing fine. Just keep going."

Mai Ker did. She, too, was tiring rapidly and wondering how she was going to handle weaving the sling ropes back and forth once they reached the top. They guessed that part would consume at least an hour, probably more. She dropped a small rope down to Bridget and Herald and called for them to send up another 20 rope loops.

Having to stop every 15 or 20 feet to rethread her safety line through these loops, though necessary, was adding a lot of time to the climb. She thought about cheating this a little and just threading it every 30 or 40 feet. But Jimmy saw what she was doing and yelled, "Safety! Closer together!"

She nodded, took a deep breath and a tight hold, and unhooked the line from her harness. She reached up as far as she could and threaded the safety line, then reattached it to her harness and moved on.

"Pain in the neck," she said under her breath, though no one was remotely close enough to hear.

They were about 80 feet above the ground where the beams began to angle quickly toward the peak of the dome. They were getting close to where the crack was, which they guessed was at about 115 feet. They could begin to see the end of the climb. Then would come the really tricky work of creating the work-sling.

Jimmy relaxed a little. He hooked another loop with a carabiner to the beam he was on. Carefully, hanging tightly with one arm wrapped up around the beam, he unsnapped his safety line and threaded it through the loop. The line was too short to reach back to his harness.

"Feed me some more slack," he called down to Pam and Sing. Sing loosened the anchoring end around her waist and Pam fed up another 20 feet of slack. Jimmy pulled up the extra line and fumbled around with it, re-snapping the safety line back to his harness. His arms were as rubbery as his legs now and beginning to tremble. The climb was much harder than he expected.

With straining arms, Jimmy pulled himself several more feet up the beam. Because of fatigue, he didn't realize that the large carabiner securing the safety line to his harness hadn't snapped shut completely. The rope was caught in the interlocking teeth of the carabiner. Holding tightly to the beam, he pulled one leg up toward the next stirrup but his sweaty hands lost their grip. His full weight jerked against the safety line and he hung suspended for half-a-second. The rope tore violently against the half-closed carabiner—and ripped loose.

Apart from his short, gasping curse as he plummeted from the beam, there was not a sound until the sickening noise of his unconscious body hitting the dirt at the edge of one of the fields. Everyone stood paralyzed, helpless, watching. They gasped in unison, too stunned to speak, except for Braden who cried out a wretched, horrified, "Daddy—!"

Mai Ker didn't see him fall. Her head was turned, working with her own ropes. She heard the anguished cry from Braden. The fall was so fast that Jimmy was on the ground before she could turn her head. As she did, she froze. She became sick. Her eyes were blinded by fear, anger and swelling tears.

"God, no!" Pam cried as she let go of the limp safety line and ran toward Jimmy.

Sing stood, frozen in place, still holding the safety rope as it cascaded back down through the loops like a hideous snake seeking its hole in the ground.

Bridget and Herald were stuck. They couldn't move because Mai Ker had passed out and was now dangling by the safety line they held in their hands.

"Sing!" Pam called, still running. "Get the children out of here!"

"Pam . . ." Sing sobbed in protest.

Pam stopped and turned angrily toward Sing.

"Don't argue!"

The crushed, helpless look in Pam's eyes said it all. Sing tried to swallow her tears and couldn't. She felt a wound inside she had never felt before. Feeling not only devastated but unwanted, Sing forced herself to do it. She ran blindly to the far side of the pod, bypassing Jimmy by only a few feet. She corralled Piper, Nathaniel and Braden and hustled them off into Pod 9. She took them around behind the barn and started hugging them and trying to quiet them, which was unbearable and, at this point, completely impossible.

Pam had knelt, hovering over Jimmy, checking for a breath, hoping for a pulse, anything. But she was certain from the angle of his head that his neck was broken. There was no sign of life.

The only consolation she could garner in that moment was that he had likely blacked out before he hit. But it was little comfort.

She forced herself to her feet, crying loudly. She looked toward Bridget and Herald, then up the rope where she saw Mai Ker dangling. She rushed toward them. Her first thought was to tell them Jimmy was dead. But as she realized what they were dealing with, she couldn't. In any case, the words would not come. And surely they knew.

Bridget and Herald were working Mai Ker's rope, trying to lower her, but a buckle of her harness had snagged in the rope loop that held her safety line to the beam.

"Herald, how do we get her down?" Bridget was

crying out in a hoarse voice as Pam reached them.

"I'm going up," he said.

"No!" his mother said. The muscles throughout her body trembled now with a new fear.

"Shut up! I'm going!" he almost shouted.

Bridget bit on her quivering lip and said nothing more. Pam realized what Herald was doing. She grabbed his anchoring end of the safety rope that held Mai Ker suspended.

Herald sprinted to the equipment shed and grabbed another harness and another hundred-foot length of rope. He raced back. As quickly as his feet stopped, he was belting the harness on. He tied one end of the rope to a large fence post nearby. He grabbed a shorter piece of rope, slung it around his shoulders and started up the beam toward Mai Ker. Bridget and Pam were beginning to strain holding Mai Ker's safety line.

Had it not been for his incredible strength and presence of mind, Herald could not have made the ascent as fast as he did. He pulled himself repeatedly past several of the safety loops that were holding Mai Ker's line without bothering to thread his own safety line through them. About 40 feet up he finally stopped and threaded his safety through a loop. He knew this was foolish. If he fell, one or two loops might not hold him. But he was out of breath, his mind was blurred, and he had no time. He clamored up the beam as if some giant hand were pulling him.

He stopped only twice more to thread his safety. In just over 12 minutes, he reached Mai Ker. With the second, short piece of rope, he quickly tied her off to the beam.

Since he had left the ground, two conflicting sets of emotions had been at war inside him. He wanted to be alongside Sing, comforting her over Jimmy. But he wanted to save Mai Ker. His heart was wrenching backward and forward in his chest, pounding like it might explode. He tried his best to keep from looking down across the pod to where Jimmy's body lay. He found this impossible. But each time he looked, he dug deeper for courage and strength to get Mai Ker down because he knew that's what Jimmy would want most.

With Mai Ker secured to the beam, he tried to wake her. It was much hotter near the top of this huge pod and that didn't help. Herald was sweating like he had never sweat before. He reached into the small pack on Mai Ker's back and pulled out her water bottle. After swigging down several gulps himself, he sprinkled some on her face. Slowly, she came around.

"What are . . ." she mumbled.

"Don't, Mai Ker. I'm gonna get you down. We're gonna tie together and rappel down."

"No, not— You can't," she tried to say, slurring her words. She was all but incoherent. Her physical daze was aggravated by the emotional daze of seeing Jimmy on the ground. "We won't make it." She began to almost shriek between the tears. "We won't make it!"

"We will. Hold on. We'll make it."

Herald said it with conviction for her sake, but fear lurked in his mind as he glanced down. It was a long way. Whether the small safety loops attached to the beams would support them both he couldn't be sure. But there was no other choice.

He also realized, too late, how foolish it was that he didn't thread his own safety rope through every loop coming up. His line would be held by only three loops. It would put incredible strain on them. Her line might hold. His might not. His mind became a jumble. He forced himself to stop thinking about it.

He shouted down to Pam and Bridget.

"Tie off her line to the fence! By mine!"

Then an idea struck him. He lowered a lighter-weight cord that he carried up on his harness.

"Tie another hundred-foot line on, so I can pull it up!"

he shouted to the ground.

When he had pulled the new rope up, he double-tied it securely around a crossing beam about 2 feet behind them to be a separate rappel line. He gave Mai Ker a hug.

"We're starting down," he told her. "I'm going to untie you from the beam."

Mai Ker nodded weakly. She was in no shape to lower herself down. Her eyes and nose were dripping from near hysteria. The adrenaline that had rushed through her system just before she passed out had now subsided, and she was shaking and nauseated. Herald would have to manage them both. It would require juggling rope and fear in mid-air.

"Here's where it gets iffy," he said to Mai Ker but mostly to himself. He untied the short rope that had held her to the beam. "I'm gonna use this rope to make a slide-knot around this big rope," he said, pointing to the rappel rope that now ran from the beam to the ground. "Then we're going down. I'll hold pressure with this knot to control our descent speed." He was tying the special knot Jimmy had taught him.

Mai Ker stared at him with watery red eyes and amazement. He had grown up ten years in the last ten minutes.

"Should I hold the rope?" she asked.

"If you can. Keep pressure on it as we slide down. This slide-knot will do most of it. Don't hold too tight. You'll burn up your hands."

"OK," she said, though at this point she didn't remotely care.

"We'll go slow," he assured her. "Untie the safety lines," he shouted to Pam and Bridget. "Keep hold of them till they're too high!"

Pam and Bridget didn't understand what he was doing but weren't about to argue. He seemed to know.

Pam gripped Mai Ker's safety line. As they started down, the end of the rope, still fixed to Mai Ker's harness, rose up. Bridget held onto Herald's.

Herald said a little prayer to himself. Where it came from, he wasn't sure. They began the descent. He kept tight pressure on the slide-knot. His father's strength and physique helped. They slid down about 5 feet per second. It was nerve-wracking.

Herald suddenly realized he was exhausted from his frantic climb. He was getting light-headed. His stomach turned. He hid this from Mai Ker as best he could. He didn't want to frighten her more.

His strength was nearly played out when their feet touched the ground.

"Let me go," Mai Ker said.

Herald didn't want to because he knew she would run to Jimmy's body. But it was pointless to try to prevent her. He let go of her and freed her harness from the rope.

As they all expected, Mai Ker made a weak and wobbling run toward Jimmy. Pam and Bridget hurried after her. Herald plopped onto the ground, trying to regain composure, just now recognizing the danger he had been in. *Thank you God,* ran through his mind. He was grateful that Sing was still out of sight in Pod 11, so she couldn't have seen what he just did. Then he realized she probably did, through the clear roof of #11.

Oh well, he thought. He was breathing heavily. Sweat soaked his shirt and shorts and had trickled down into his socks. He wanted a bath, but more than anything, he just wanted to lie down.

Mai Ker knelt down by Jimmy's body.

"Jimmy," she whispered, hoping he might hear. "Jimmy." Her voice was quiet but drenched with emotion. She broke down completely. The love of her life was suddenly gone. As strong as she was, he had been part of her strength in facing all the crises that had become normality in Solarium-3. She wept bitterly, wanting to somehow bring him back. She was ready to curse the God he had worshipped.

She couldn't understand this. This, of all things. What kind of God would take him like this? Now? In an instant all their life together as husband and wife was over, and suddenly seemed futile.

AFTER ABOUT 15 minutes of alternately sitting and lying on the ground, Herald got up and went to the infirmary for a stretcher. He brought it to where the three woman knelt by Jimmy's body. Bridget and Herald, straining, managed to carry it back to the infirmary.

They cleaned the body up as best they could, considering their own emotional state. Pam gently straightened his neck. Mai Ker brought dry, clean clothes to put on the body. Pam helped dress him.

They were all a wreck. They couldn't face a long, drawn-out goodbye. Once his body was as presentable as they could make it, they carried it to #10 and placed it on a cot just outside the main tent.

Sing had brought the other children back to their own tents. She, Braden and Nathaniel came out and stood around. They looked like castaways in a wilderness on some far distant planet devoid of humanity. Their young eyes were flooded. They barely looked at each other, or the moms.

Even Nathaniel was sobbing. After standing hesitantly at a distance for almost 20 minutes, he finally went up and hugged the lifeless remains of his father.

"Love you, Daddy," he said.

Sing and Braden watched, but didn't come close. They were confused, their minds trying to quell unknown emotions. Death was something new, and fearful. They had never imagined losing their father ever, let alone like this. They held arms around each other in quiet grief, then sat down in the grass about 25 feet from where their dad's body lay.

Piper appeared last. She had only one dress, the one Pam had made her for Sing and Herald's wedding. She had put it on. She had brushed out her hair, then came out and sat behind Sing and Braden. She was praying silently. Jimmy had taught her the Lord's Prayer and some other simple things he remembered from church in his childhood. She prayed. But she also asked God an angry question.

Why?

OF EVERYONE in the Solarium this evening, Piper was the one most at peace, yet the bitter, nagging question pressed in on her, a question for which she had no answer. He was her dad. She already missed him terribly. It felt almost as if he had never lived. Nothing, she thought, could fill the gaping cavern in her heart. She felt hollow.

She had cried for three hours. Still, her spirit was in tune with something far beyond the tragedy, far beyond the Solarium. Beyond the bleakness INSIDE and OUT, something was reaching toward her. She tried reaching back, but touched nothing.

Lunch had been missed and supper was a bust. Pam heated some leftover soup and put together some sandwiches. Everyone just picked. Mai Ker tried to get down some soup but ran from the tent and threw it up.

Piper sensed that she should try to console her family, Mai Ker especially. She found her sitting on a chair again by Jimmy's body. She walked over and took Mai Ker's hand and stood by her. She leaned her head down on Mai Ker's head.

"He loved us all so much. But he loved you most."

Mai Ker tried to smile. It was forced, yet genuine. Piper had touched a nerve.

"I don't know why people have to die at all," Piper said. "It doesn't make any sense. But I know what Daddy believed. And I think he's OK."

"He's gone, sweetheart," Mai Ker protested gently. "You have to face it."

"Yes. I know. But he's OK. He's with God."

"I don't even know what that means," Mai Ker said, deep distress in her voice.

"He's gone. I know. But not forever. Someday we'll get to see him again. At least, that's what he always told me about people who died."

Mai Ker finally turned and looked up at her. Piper's eyes looked deeply into hers.

"I wish I could believe that," Mai Ker muttered. "I want to believe it. More than anything."

"That's the thing, I guess" Piper said. "Believing. But it's so hard. At least, it's hard for me right now."

"If Jimmy's God is so great, I wish he would make things plainer."

"Me, too," Piper said, squeezing her hand. "It's funny, though. As far back as I can remember, I can't think of anything I really know that's very plain." She screwed up her mouth a bit. "I wish I could make us feel better. I don't know how."

Mai Ker shook her head, *No,* agreeing.

"But I'm like Daddy," Piper added. "I think there are some things that are real, but we can't see."

She bent and gave Mai Ker a tight hug, and held on. Mai Ker raised an arm around Piper's and held on just as tightly, as to an anchor. Pam and Bridget had come over and hovered by them. They had heard the conversation. They felt just as lost as everyone else.

Piper looked for a long time in silence at the body that had been her daddy just hours before. The words drained from her like they didn't belong.

"What a horrid thing it is."

Mai Ker looked at her.

"Death," Piper said. "Why is the world so awful?"

13

Thursday, November 28th, 18 (NC)

Wednesday had been brutal. They had put Jimmy's body into a walk-in cooler in the equipment shed in Pod 13 overnight. They held a short, simple burial early this morning.

It had been so many years since they last buried anyone that the women weren't sure how to proceed. If anyone would have remembered, it would have been Jimmy.

Herald read some verses out of Jimmy's Bible, from several Psalms that sounded fitting, one about strength and one about comfort. Piper led a short prayer. Then they buried Jimmy's remains. No cross this time. That tradition had been lost.

The remainder of the family went back into the main tent and fixed a late breakfast. No one felt like eating beforehand. Pam said maybe they should fast, anyway, right before the burial. An act of respect, she called it. But hunger had set in. Because of the unthinkable tragedy yesterday, they felt a renewed need to stay strong, even if only by physical nourishment.

The grieving was multiplied this time because, except for Herald, every remaining Solarian was either married to Jimmy or one of his children. Instead of one widow there were three. Bridget, now twice-widowed, bore the grief with a much deeper sense of resignation. But Mai Ker was in the worst state. She would hardly talk. She did eat, but little. Weeping came at unexpected moments.

The children weren't much better. Herald tried

valiantly to step into the void of fatherhood that Jimmy had so abruptly vacated. But he wasn't having much success. His own heart was still young and tender. Although Jimmy wasn't his father, they had been very close. And Herald was still trying to adjust to the idea that he would soon be a father himself. He wanted to just go hide somewhere and let the others work through their grief privately. Yet, as he looked into the sad eyes and depressed emotions around him, he knew he had to stand fast and support them. The three moms would never again have a husband, but he could try to be the best son he could be.

They had spent last evening trying to adjust to the radical change. When Clayton had died and Jimmy was chosen as the new leader, it brought a sense of relief, a feeling of comfort that somehow things would be OK, that life would go on. Now the emotional and spiritual abyss seemed deeper, a dark place one could fall into and never climb out.

They all felt it. Life again looked suddenly bleak. The joys of recent months, even Sing's ecstatic surprise about the new baby, vaporized overnight.

After breakfast, Pam asked for a family meeting later in the morning. She wanted to talk about their grief and try to begin to deal with it. She, best of all, knew it would be a lot harder this time. Of the first generation Solarians, only she, Mai Ker and Bridget remained. And they shared, now more than ever, a sense of impending doom, trying to crush down the unutterable fear of another untimely death, and another, and another.

Worse, this time young hearts were involved. The children, still not fully prepared for a long-term future trapped INSIDE, might become desperate. Who could tell how they would react, and what destructive thoughts might creep into their fragile minds?

When they finished the thin breakfast of toast and dry cereal, they all went about daily chores. The animals had been ignored all day Wednesday and were starving and thirsty. There were messes to clean up. There was also the mess in the infirmary from yesterday afternoon to clean up. Pam took this one upon herself.

An hour after breakfast, they all sat down in the main living room. Pam started things. She tried playing the role of spiritual counselor, but she needed so much guidance herself that she was only fumbling through it.

Braden sat aside by himself. He was weeping softly. Every time he heard Jimmy's name, the soft crying got a little louder. Surprisingly, Nathaniel went over and sat by him, put an arm around him, and did his best to comfort his younger brother.

"You'll be OK," he told Braden.

He scrubbed his palm through Braden's hair, just as Jimmy always did. It seemed to help. Braden leaned against Nathaniel's shoulder.

Sing and Piper sat together, with Herald just behind. They were quiet, thinking. Herald and Piper, though the others didn't know it, were both praying, asking God to help them all get through this, to give them understanding—but mostly courage. Their young lives had been altered irreversibly, like arms and legs jerked from their sockets. Some injuries go so deep they are never fully repaired.

"I don't know, really, how we go on from here," Pam was saying. "But we have to. Somehow. And we have to help each other."

"Why?" Mai Ker asked. Her depression had settled deeper over the past 12 hours. Waves of nausea kept washing through her. She felt like she wanted to end her own life, if that could somehow bring her closer to her Jimmy again. But she didn't let anyone know this.

Pam thought. Despite her *We must go on* platitude, she hadn't yet asked the "why" question herself. In fact, she had studiously managed to avoid it.

"Well, thanks for being so honest, Mai. You know, I

don't have an answer. Not one you want, anyway. I guess we go on today for the same reason we carried on yesterday, and the day before. We're here. We have a purpose. And we have beautiful children. In fact, we're going to have more." She smiled at Sing. "Whatever else runs out, we can't run out of love for each other."

"Pam, that's pretty profound," Bridget said. "It's what I was thinking. Last night. I couldn't sleep. I got to thinking about Clayton, and how I felt when I lost him. I thought, 'I'll have no one to love.'" She looked around and choked up. "Boy, was I wrong. If there was only one other person in the whole world, there's someone we can show love to."

"Even if I was all alone," Piper said quietly, "I could still love God."

Mai Ker jerked her head toward the girl.

"I don't need any more of this God talk! Every time we hurt, we think he's going to fix it. Why can't we just hurt for a while?"

She shook with an intensity that took Piper and everyone else back. But there was no real anger in Mai Ker's voice, just frustration, confusion and loss. It was a very real question that demanded an answer. From someone.

"We all hurt, Mai," Herald said softly. "We all do."

"I got over losing Clayton," Bridget said. "I don't know how. I still love him." She pondered. "Maybe more. But it just kind of happened. The weeks passed, and then the months without him. His love was gone but the memory of it grew. Our love seemed more intense after that." Her lips were quivering. "I realized how much more I loved him than I showed him." She got quiet. Her eyes narrowed as if she was looking through the tent wall toward their old house. She couldn't find any more words.

"Children," Pam said, "I know this hit you very hard. We've told you about how the others died. But now it's real. It kind of changes everything. From an idea—to a very sad fact. It's always a bitter loss."

Braden whined louder, Nathaniel held him a little tighter.

"Why is Daddy gone?" Braden asked. He was begging for an answer that no one had. He was turned inward. He wasn't really listening to anything being said.

"Honey, he's just gone. We all die," Pam tried to explain, "someday. It's just who we are. We don't last forever. And Daddy died too soon. But it was going to happen. As it will to me. And someday—" She started to say "you, too" but caught herself. "—to all of us."

"Where is he?" Braden wanted to know.

"He's just gone, honey."

"But where?"

Pam knew only the answer taught her as a child.

"He's in heaven."

"Can he come back?"

"No, honey. You don't come back from heaven."

It wasn't a good answer, but it was what she thought.

"I don't want to die," Nathaniel said with a tone of absolute rejection in his voice. "Why can't we just figure a way to stay alive forever?"

It was one of those typical 14-year-old questions: stupid, yet unreasonably profound.

"Nate, that would be great," Bridget said. "But we take life as it comes. We have to go on, like Pam said. As long as we're able."

Piper was quiet through all this. In her heart, she knew there was something missing, something in the background that either no one knew, or no one spoke about. In her moments of sadness over the past few hours, she had also felt an inexplicable sense of joy. Not happiness, but real joy.

She had listened many long evenings to her dad reading from his New Testament. She didn't begin to understand it all. But it was all about new life. Some kind of life that was exactly what Nathaniel was demanding, and what she, in her own spirit, knew was right. She sensed it was real, one of those invisible things that is also real, like her love for her father. But at the moment, for some reason, no one saw it. A ghost would have been more substantial.

Piper had no desire to see her daddy as a ghost. That was not who her daddy was.

Pam was still talking, still trying.

"I think it would help us if we choose someone to succeed Jimmy," she said. It was awkward, but she felt strongly.

"Succeed?" Sing asked.

"As leader," Pam explained.

"We can't wait?" Mai Ker asked. She was deeply offended.

"Why?"

"Pam, Daddy's barely in the ground!" Sing answered, also hurt.

"I know," Pam said as gently as she could. "But waiting won't make it easier. Maybe harder."

Mai Ker was ruminating, rolling all this through her own heart and spirit. Though it bothered her, she actually found something relieving about Pam's suggestion. A sense of release. Yes. It would be right. Because it would be what Jimmy would do. Keep things running. Stay on a schedule. Make things work. Most of all, try to stay optimistic.

She could see Jimmy running the show wherever he was now. Push the grief away. Send it packing. Let it go find its own misery somewhere else.

"I agree," she said abruptly.

"Which part?" Bridget asked.

"Choose a new leader." Mai Ker looked around. "I think Herald."

This caught most of them by surprise—most of all Herald.

"Oh, I don't—" Then he muttered a simple, "No."

"Why not?" Mai Ker asked him. "You're Clayton's son. Our original team leader. You're smart. You're obviously pretty brave." She pointed upward, to where she had dangled near death only yesterday. "Why not?"

As awesome as the responsibility sounded, and as much as he liked to be challenged, Herald felt a hole inside him that kept saying *No*. Someday maybe. Not now. He didn't need to rationalize it. He knew.

"No. Thank you, Mai Ker. I can't." He kept shaking his head. "I'm not ready."

He really had grown up.

They looked around.

"Bridget was our choice once," Pam said. "She refused, too. Maybe we shouldn't let her refuse twice."

"That is true," Mai Ker said.

If there was ever a swift and uncontested election, this was it. Bridget sat still thinking for several moments. Her eyes almost closed, then opened more brightly. She didn't want this before. She found she wanted it now.

Herald and Braden smiled. Their mom. How great it would be, they thought, if she were the leader of the whole family, responsible for the life of the whole Solarium.

"OK," Bridget finally smiled. "But you, young man," she said to Herald, "had better be watching close—and taking notes. You won't escape this forever." She became very solemn. "Like Pam said. Death's gonna knock on my door, too. One of these days. You better be ready." She looked around at the children. "All of you."

That was school for the day, a lesson more powerful than any they would ever learn.

The quick decision brought relief to them all. The grief didn't go away, and would not fully wane for weeks. But making this decision whispered that there still was a future in their future. And they could face it.

NATHANIEL AND Braden were walking around the far end of the ocean in Pod 12. Bridget had sent them supposedly to collect water samples so they could check the salinity. What she really wanted was for them to have some brother time together, to talk through what was happening.

Braden, being just two years younger than Nathaniel, found him more kindred than their older half-brother Herald who, now married, seemed distant and like a real adult.

"Why do people have to die, Nate?" Braden asked him as he bent over the water with several test tubes.

They were both dressed in ragged shorts that had once belonged to Jimmy. Being far too big in the waist, the shorts were held up by belts of heavy twine.

"You already know I don't know. I don't like it either."

"But isn't there a reason for everything? I remember Daddy saying that. 'There's always a reason for everything.' So he was wrong?"

"Braden, I don't know. Here, give me those tubes and fill these three."

They exchanged the full ones for empties. Nathaniel put two filled tubes into a little pouch. The third one he held up to the light and shook, looking closely at the sediment floating around in the captured water.

"It must have something to do with why we're born," he said to Braden. "You know. We just suddenly are here. No explanation. Then suddenly we're gone. No explanation."

"Why can't the grownups explain?"

"'Cause they're in it, too. They're in the stream. Like, if you walk out into the water here, and keep walking and walking, you're gonna drown. Right?"

"Yeah?"

"So, like that. You arrive out of nowhere—"

"Out of Mommy stomach's, though."

"Well, yeah. But still, you know, sort of out of nowhere before that. And you're here. And it's like you're wading through this water all the time." He was pointing out into the ocean. "And you keep wading and walking and after a while you're in deeper. But you keep going. So pretty soon you're in really deep. Too deep. And you drown. And you're gone. Dead. Get it?"

Braden had stood up and handed him the last three test tubes.

"No."

His expression was confused skepticism that said, *Someone must have a better idea than this.*

"That's all I know," Nathaniel said. "I can't tell it any better. You just have to take it. Like when we wrestle, and I punch you too hard, and your nose bleeds. Tough. You just have to take it. Mom makes me say I'm sorry. But you still bleed."

They headed toward the Research Center where Bridget would do the water tests. Braden's mind continued to wander into the confusing woods of death. He found his way out only by trying to decide what particular computer game he could play later. Nathaniel kept thinking about it, too, but said no more.

PIPER AND Sing were having their own conversation on a couple of stools in Pod 11 by the raccoon cage. Their talk was quite different from their brothers'.

"You really believe all that stuff?" Sing was asking. "About living somewhere. After we're dead?"

"Yes."

"To me, sounds like nonsense."

"Nonsense that Daddy believed, though."

"Yeah. But so?"

"Daddy had a deep heart, Sing. You know that. Why would he tell us, and teach us, if he thought it was wrong? Or not true?"

"He wouldn't."

"Sure. He wouldn't. So I listened. I remember—I must have been about 6. I started to pray on my own. And it kind of sinks in. The more I pray, the more I listen for God around here. And the more I listen, the more of a sense I get that he *is* here. He hasn't left us."

"Daddy?"

"God."

Sing struggled to make sense of this, just like her mother. Saying things, for her, didn't make them so. She wanted this God to show himself, if he was so real. And she *had* looked. It wasn't like she never tried. She had listened to her dad. But she never saw any sign that any of it was real. Like her mom, she teetered on a fence between skepticism and belief, dangling precariously between knowledge and feelings, wanting proof for whatever she thought might be true.

"Well, then he needs to show up."

"But don't you see. He has."

"No, he hasn't!"

"He showed up when you were born."

"How would you know?"

"Because I look at you—and there you are. Why else would you even be here?"

"You're nuts, Piper."

One of the raccoons was reaching his claws out through the wire cage begging for food. Piper reached into the pail and tossed him several small chunks of food that he caught gracefully in midair.

She turned back to Sing.

"Look, Daddy said God makes each one of us. We are his first, then our parents'. So if you're here, God's here."

"Piper, you talk in circles. You make no sense."

"Sing, you're so beautiful. Next time you look in the mirror, look deeper. Maybe your beauty gets in the way. Maybe you see your beauty and not yourself. Next time, look. See your soul. You're in there."

This made Sing think. It was true. She was so

beautiful she was taken with her own looks. She felt this was probably bad, yet couldn't help it. But Piper was right. She wanted something more, deeper, solid. She wanted to *be* something more than just pretty. She wanted to feel real. It had begun to haunt her. When she looked at her mother, she could see that her mom's beauty had started to fade. Slightly, but still passing away as a day winds down slowly into evening, and day becomes night. Like a sunset transforming from brilliant orange and red into purple, blue and then grayish nothing. Flat, irrelevant, gone.

Sing realized her own beauty would pass like that, too. Not for many years. But it would. There would be a day she would look at her mom and realize she was old, and no longer beautiful in the way Sing remembered her when she was a child. That scared her. If it was true of mother, it must become true of daughter. Sing shivered. Her eyes were open but she wasn't seeing beyond them. She reached unconsciously into a second pail and tossed some more food to the raccoons. Two fought frantically for the last piece.

Piper was watching her. She could sense the troubled thoughts racing through Sing's mind. Sing stared vacantly at the cage, not really seeing the animals there. Piper left her quietly, and unnoticed.

PAM AND Bridget were back in the kitchen planning a late lunch. The long talks today had thrown everything behind schedule. Chores were not likely to get finished.

"The crack is still there, Bridget."

"Yeah. Trying not to think about it."

"We have to."

"What do you think?" she asked Pam, seeing the worry in her face.

"It has to be fixed. And I think we need to rethink your idea. About fixing it from OUTSIDE."

"You mean, climb the pod from out there."

"Yes."

It was Bridget's idea but even she wasn't very keen on it. She cut some thin slabs of roast beef for sandwiches.

"Jimmy didn't like it much," she said.

Pam looked straight at Bridget with a strained expression. It was not accusatory, but essentially said, *And look where that got us.*

"Right," Bridget said, reading her perfectly. She nodded. "Risky. But not as bad as another attempt in here." She was spreading homemade mustard on about 20 pieces of bread.

"I agree," Pam said.

"Wonder how Mai Ker will feel?"

"I'm pretty sure Mai Ker's the last one who will want to go crawling back up those beams."

"Yeah." Bridget finished out several sandwiches. "What you said. You really think the air looks different?"

"OUTSIDE?"

"Yeah."

"Uh-huh, I do. It still has that purplish tinge. But doesn't it look thinner, or lighter or something?" Pam said.

"Truthfully, I haven't been looking. I don't look out there much. Too painful."

"And I've noticed," Pam added, "that especially after a good rain the air looks less dense. More regular."

"Regular?"

"I mean, like we remember it. Before."

Bridget rinsed the knife in the sink. She walked to the tent door and looked OUTSIDE, up through the pod roof. She looked with sharp eyes for the first time in months. Pam stood by her. Bridget shook her head.

"Trouble is, been so long since I really looked, I can't remember how it was. Like two or three years ago."

"I think it's definitely lighter," Pam said. "Still that purplish tint. But brighter. Like more sun is getting through."

Bridget squinted to try to see better.

"Might be, Pam."

Pam started setting plates and potato wedges out on the kitchen table. It would be a quick buffet lunch.

"So, maybe we should try what you said," she told Bridget. "Go out. With air masks, of course. Try to fix the roof. Maybe run some tests."

"Jimmy was pretty adamant. About breaking the airlock seal in number one, I mean."

"I know. And I've been working on that in my head. Maybe we can find a way to double seal it or something," Pam said. "I think it's worth a try."

"If it means we don't have to send somebody up in number ten again, I'm in favor."

"Or," Pam was still thinking, "we could just all start wearing air masks again. All the time. If bad air is leaking, they'd help protect us."

"But we'd run out of tanks, eventually."

"We could just refill them." She stopped. "Oh, no. Of course. I'm stupid. We'd be putting tainted air back in them." She grinned. "Guess that's why you're the leader and not me."

"We've got to deal with this problem. Get it over with. Sooner, not later. Or we'll worry ourselves to death."

"What if we screw up?" Pam asked.

"Guess I'd rather face that sooner rather than later, too."

Pam sat by the table. Her head drooped a little.

"Sometimes I just get so tired of it all. You know?"

"Um. Me, too," Bridget admitted. "Welcome, everyone, to the fabulous marvel, Solarium-3," she crooned like a carnival barker.

AS SOON as lunch was done, the three moms and Herald met in the Comm. Center in Pod 2. Braden was there playing computer games, albeit in a very depressed mood. Going through the motions. Wanting normality. Wishing his dad was here. It wasn't helping. He had a heartache he couldn't understand and didn't want. He half-smiled when the others came in, but it wasn't a happy smile.

They shooed Braden off to do some chores and the four sat down to talk. After an hour of hotly debating the hazards of breaking the air seals between Pod 1 and OUTSIDE, they decided on a plan. Herald suggested it. Mai Ker opposed it, mostly because Jimmy had opposed it so vehemently. But eventually, she came around. Trying to fix the crack from OUTSIDE had been Bridget's idea in the first place and she ultimately would settle the issue if they didn't agree. So there was no point in Mai Ker being stubborn. She would just be overruled in the end.

They would send out a small work party. Who, was not yet decided.

The party would gather into Pod 1 carrying extra seal material. Both the inner and outer doors of Pod 1 were designed with their own high-tech seals. Pod 1 was designed as an airlock. That had always been its primary function. But they didn't want to rely just on those door seals, especially because of their age.

The members of the work party would wear tightly sealed air masks. The INSIDE air would be slowly flushed out of the pod. Then OUTSIDE air would flow in to replace it. What it would feel like, this air, no one yet knew. It was the same air, as far as they knew, that had killed 7 billion humans, along with everything else. They had no idea if it would burn, if it would smell, if it was still inflamed with radiation, or if it would get past their air masks.

It was all a huge risk. They knew this. But they also knew no one wanted to climb the INSIDE of #10 again to fix the crack.

The plan was to make extra seals for both sides of the inner door of Pod 1, and a third set for the outer door. They would make these removable seals out of soft rubber cores, about 3 inches square, wrapped in soft, pliable tape. These could then be fitted and taped into the corners of the doorjambs. Two would cover both sides of the inner door jamb of #1. Then, once the work party was out, they would place the third set OUTSIDE the main door that led into the hallway to the Visitors Center. Someone INSIDE would unlock and relock the doors as the workers passed through each.

This process, they hoped, would increase the seal capacity to ensure that no OUTSIDE air got past Pod 1. If the seals between the inner door of Pod 1 and the rest of the complex held tight, they would be safe.

"When do we do this?" Mai Ker asked, worried, but finally giving in.

"Tomorrow morning," Bridget said. "Early."

"What?" Mai Ker cried.

"Why wait? We don't know how long the crack's been there. We don't know yet if we can even fix it. We don't know what's coming in, or what's getting out. We need to get it done."

"She's right," Pam said.

"Mai Ker and I can get to work on the seals this afternoon," Herald said, trying to put a pleasant face on. He was as nervous as the rest. "I know we have the stuff in supply. Finding it, that's another thing."

"I have a pretty good idea," Mai Ker said. "Done lots of inventories with Jimmy." His name rang like a cracked bell and resulted in a moment of hushed waiting, as if he might answer.

"Let's get to it," Bridget said. "Pam, you talk with the rest of the kids and let them know what we're doing. If any of them volunteer, tell them no. I'll decide who goes out." She looked at them. "I'll take the blame if anything happens."

As they watched her eyes trying to hide stifled tears, they realized the danger facing them with this little exploration. But they all knew they were going to do it.

BRIDGET REMAINED alone in the Comm. Center. She made the list. It was very short.

Not a lot of choices.

At least three had to go out. Two had to be good climbers. If one fell, the remaining one would need an ally to make sure they got back INSIDE before the air tanks ran out.

She would go. No one would be sent out unless she herself was willing to take the risk. It was, after all, her stupid idea in the first place.

Herald would go. First, she knew there would be no dissuading him. Second, he was an experienced climber. He had proven his courage rescuing Mai Ker. Lastly, he was her own child. She simply couldn't ask the other moms to send a child OUTSIDE. And at least one mom had to stay INSIDE.

Lastly, Pam would go. She had only one child. She was older. She was steady. She could help carry gear and, once they were ready to try the real climb up #10, she would be the ground crew for Bridget and Herald.

Bridget tried to press the thought back out of her mind, but there it was.

She has the least to lose.

Bridget kicked herself for even thinking it. But the reality of what they faced was brutal.

The work party was set. Tomorrow they would go out and try a short test climb. She would tell everyone this afternoon. As she doodled on the slip of paper, the muscles of her neck hurt. Her head ached. She was tight all over. She felt a deep anxiety throughout her body.

Why did I agree to be leader?

This was not fun. Every step, every choice, every turn seemed to lead to hardship and new fears.

If nothing else, getting OUTSIDE for a few minutes might bring some kind of relief—even if that meant death.

So be it, she found herself saying as a prayer.

Despite all the tragedy, she had become convinced there really was a God. Jimmy's love and patience had been a large part of changing her. But who this God was, and why he acted the way he did, she was far from understanding, let alone accepting. Still, she felt compelled to pray. Her hands were far too small to manage even their tiny piece of the world's wreckage.

It was late November in what used to be southeastern Colorado. It might be mild OUTSIDE or it could be chilly. The weather had been erratic ever since the great destruction. They would wear warm jackets until they could tell. And rain gear. It could rain at the drop of a hat out there. This time of year, depending on temperature, there could even be unexpected snow. Jackets and rain gear. And good boots, with soft rubber soles for climbing.

She added items to her list. She felt like a kid going to her first summer camp.

14

Bridget, Pam and Herald didn't sleep well. This would be a day they would not soon forget. Their minds could not stop racing all night.

Pam and Bridget had not been OUTSIDE since before the original Seal-In. Herald had never known a world beyond the Stellar domes of Solarium-3. It was at once terrifying and exhilarating.

None of the others had slept much, either. Mai Ker was fretting, working in the kitchen. The younger kids hovered in the background, partly to keep out from underfoot but mostly because after Wednesday's disaster they didn't really want to know too much. They knew who was going OUTSIDE but they weren't sure they wanted to watch.

Sing was agonizing, too, because her husband, father of her not-yet-born baby, was about to do the stupidest thing of his short life.

"You'd better be OK," she said intensely but under her breath as he shoveled down eggs and toast. "You'd better be OK," she repeated.

"Sing, we're being careful. As careful as we can. You know that."

"I know," she said grudgingly. "Doesn't help."

"Sing," he said taking her chin, "look at me. Nobody—except you—wants to see our baby more than I do." He kissed her. "I'll be here."

She was not reassured but resigned herself to it. She forced a little smile but her bottom lip was trembling and she couldn't hide her feelings. She knew a lot of thought had gone into the decision. But two days ago she had lost her father. She was terrified her husband might be next. Then what?

"The plan," Bridget said, going over it again at the table, "is, as soon as we get OUTSIDE, we take some air samples. Then Herald will try free climbing a little way up one of the pods. To see how the surface feels. If our climbing boots will adhere. Really no way to know how the surface has reacted to everything that's gone on out there. If the test climb goes OK, we'll go down to the river and get some water samples. If there's time, and everybody's feeling OK."

"I've got two of those clamp-on suction cups for climbing," Herald said. "For my hands."

"Good thinking, son."

"With the rains lately, there should be current in the river," Pam said.

"That's what I hope," Bridget said. "I really want to find out the radioactivity levels in the air and water. That's as important as the general state of the air gases."

"I could carry enough rope to try getting one over one of the shorter pods," Herald said.

"No need, Herald. Today's just a test. We're mainly exploring. You can free climb as far as you—" She noticed Sing's worried eyes. "—as far as you can make it safely. With no risks."

"No risks," Sing parroted quietly. "That supposed to be funny?"

Mai Ker took her arm.

"Sing, honey. They know what to do. They're being careful."

"So my husband says," Sing answered sharply. "Hope you're right, Mom."

"Any questions?" Bridget asked.

"No," Piper said, coming up to the table. "But can I say a prayer for you guys?"

Bridget was surprised, but then not really.

"Certainly can't hurt today," she said.

Piper tried to cuddle the three members of the work party into her arms. They didn't quite fit.

"Dear God, please go out there with them. We need them back safe. We trust them to your care today." She paused. "And please keep taking care of Daddy." She paused again, as if listening. "And please help us understand what's going on. Amen." Her words sounded like one of Sing's tunes without music.

Pam smiled. Sing was still frowning. Nathaniel and Braden nodded, whatever that meant.

WHEN THE air and water sampling gear was assembled along with Herald's climbing gear and the new seals by Pod 1, the party assembled and got their tanks and air masks on. They were hospital-type oxygen masks from the infirmary. Once on, they taped them tightly to each other's faces. They couldn't tape over the small expiration holes in the nose of the masks or they wouldn't be able to exhale. Bridget hoped the constant air pressure inside the masks would keep any OUTSIDE air from seeping in.

They each had a voice-activated radio mic clipped to their jackets that could pick up their voices through the masks.

Nathaniel and Piper were standing by to put the inner seals in place once the party was in Pod 1. Nathaniel was fairly tall for his age, a gift from his father, but Piper wasn't. They had a step bench handy just in case she couldn't reach what she needed to.

Mai Ker was stationed at the pod control panels in the Comm. Center. Braden hovered over her shoulders, having received strict instructions not to touch anything, which, for him, would be an enormous challenge.

Sing stayed back at the tents. She didn't want to

watch and refused to be anywhere near that OUTSIDE door when they broke the seals. As awkward as she found it, she too was praying for them.

"If anyone is listening, I pray they'll be safe," she said in a hushed voice as if she didn't want to offend or disturb the listener. She repeated it several times. Over the next hour, she uttered similar short prayers, hoping against hope there was a God who cared enough to listen.

Mai Ker typed several commands and unlocked the inner door of Pod 1. The three explorers went in with two sets of the extra seals. The door was closed and relocked and Nathaniel and Piper hurriedly taped their seals into place, sealing every crack as best they could. Inside #1, Pam and Herald put one set of seals into place around the inner door. Bridget monitored the air with a handheld sensor. Nothing changed. This meant the outer seals were intact. A first bit of good news.

"Ready?" Mai Ker asked over the radios.

"Yes," Bridget said very formally, but with an edgy voice. She sounded as if she were about to begin a college entrance exam.

"Here goes," Mai Ker said. She keyed in the air exchange sequence and hit "Enter."

"I feel the air moving around us," Herald said with a kind of sick thrill.

"Keep going," Bridget said.

"Done," Mai Ker said. "Here goes." She keyed the next sequence to draw OUTSIDE air into the pod. The Comm. Center air pressure sensors showed the pressure quickly rising to normal. But they weren't able to read the air quality.

"OK?" she hurriedly asked them.

"So far," Bridget answered.

"I feel a funny tingle. Up my back," Pam said. "Probably just me." She looked like she shook a giant bug off her back. "Just ignore me."

Herald rubbed his hand up and down her back.

"You'll be OK," he tried to assure her.

She smiled under her gawky-looking mask and took a deep breath.

Bridget was getting antsy. These last moments of waiting were unbearable.

"Open her up, Mai Ker," she ordered.

Mai Ker keyed the unlock sequence. A "clacking" noise announced that the OUTSIDE door was unlocked.

"Can I go first?" Herald asked.

Bridget stood almost frozen. The many years INSIDE now came flooding by as fleeting images through her memory. All that had happened. All they had been through. The deaths. The births. She had planned to go out first. But she was stuck.

"Be my guest," she gestured to her son.

He had not gone a step when she jerked him back by the shoulder.

"No antics today!"

His eyes gleamed.

"Sure, Mom. Come on."

He took her hand from his shoulder and pulled her along as he pushed the door open and strode through. Pam, more afraid of being left back than of going out, followed carrying the third set of seals and the tape. They quickly closed the outer door behind them and taped the seals in place.

Mai Ker had relocked the outer door. She stepped away from the console long enough to peer out a window and watch their progress. She watched them tape the seals in place, then saw them move down the hallway toward the Visitors Center.

"Everybody OK?" she called over the radio.

"So far," Bridget answered.

She already felt a million miles from Mai Ker and the safety of the Solarium even though they were barely 20 feet down the glassed-in hallway.

"I'm right here," Mai Ker assured them. "Standing by." She moved nervously. "Keep talking to me, you guys."

"We're OK, Mai," Herald said.

"How does it feel?"

"Weird," he said.

"I mean the air. Does it burn or anything?"

"Not yet," Bridget said.

Pam wasn't talking. She was breathing hard, a nervous panic trying to take hold of her. She resisted it with every fiber of her being. She was not about to become "the problem" out here.

"A little slower?" she pleaded. "So I can keep up?" It felt like her boots had lead weights in the bottom. She thought her leg muscles were ready to cramp. Both were anxious illusions.

They were almost to the door connecting the hall into the Visitors Center.

"Sorry," Bridget said. "Didn't realize how fast we're moving." She pulled on Herald's hand to slow them down. Then she jerked him to a stop.

"Honey," she told him, "you know there might be—" She hesitated. "—people in here."

"Bodies, you mean? Yeah. I know."

"Let's go slow."

Herald stood aside and offered his mother the door handle. She took a deep breath from her tank and went through.

Enough daylight poured through the high windows of the Center to show them that the place was deserted. No bodies. No animals had gotten in either. It was remarkably clean considering the years it had sat unattended.

"Must have good door seals out here, too," Bridget mused.

"Look," Pam said.

The vending machines at the far end of the building

had all been broken open and ransacked.

"Probably our final visitors," she said.

The memory of the refugees who tried to break into the Solarium that day long ago flooded her mind. The pathos of that day, the horror of having to refuse them entrance, still felt like a fresh wound. Did they do the right thing? Pam still wondered.

"At least they got a little food," she said.

"Who?" Herald asked.

"It's all right, honey," Bridget said. "We've never talked about it with you kids. Maybe some other time."

Herald frowned. But he knew better than to press his mom when she spoke with that particular tone of voice. "Some other time" usually meant "never."

"Let's start getting some air readings outside. It's got to be all stuffy in here," she said, leading them to the main entryway. "It feels stale."

Herald, who had been warned about antics, swept ahead of her to the main entrance doors at the north end of the Center, made a swift, deep gentlemanly bow like he had seen in old time movies, and pulled the door open as if for a queen. She frowned at him, then laughed. He made a second equally deep bow for Pam and held the door for her, too.

"Thank you, Sir Herald," Pam said.

They hovered near the double doors, just outside the Center. Bridget checked the air sensor. Pam opened two large airtight canisters that had been purged and vacuum-sealed in the lab that morning. She swooshed them through the air to get "fresh" OUTSIDE air into them, then capped them shut. As she finished, Herald was checking her pulse and his mom's pulse.

"Mine's a little fast," Pam said. "Just nerves."

Herald had basic first aid training. All the kids did. Jimmy had insisted on it. Herald could still hear him saying, "Never know when an emergency might happen." Herald checked his own pulse. Despite the excitement, because he was in great physical shape, his pulse was almost unchanged. Like Pam, he attributed the slight increase to nerves. He would check them all again once back INSIDE to compare.

Bridget tapped the air sensor lightly a couple of times and looked puzzled.

"All right, we've got sufficient air samples," Bridget said. "You both feeling OK?"

"Yeah," said Herald, "Good," said Pam.

"Let's try your boots on one of the pods," Bridget said.

They walked across the parking lot past where their own cars and two guard trucks were still sitting, covered in filth and dirt. They walked toward Pod 2. Mai Ker watched them from the door of the Comm. Center.

"Everything OK?" her radio crackled.

"Fine so far," Bridget answered.

"Gonna try a little climbing," Herald said. He gave Mai Ker and the kids a little wave.

He took the two large suction cups from his backpack. They were designed to clamp onto the stellar plastic INSIDE to hang temporary gear from. He slapped one against the pod wall as high as he could reach, and twisted the locking arm down. It suctioned itself tightly onto the pod.

With Bridget and Pam giving him a boost behind, he pulled himself up the pod a few feet, reached up with his free hand, and slapped the other suction cup to the pod. He clamped it in place.

"You're on your own from here," Bridget told him.

"Not going far," he said. The irritation of the tape holding the air mask to his face was getting annoying. As he climbed and breathed harder, the tape wanted to pull loose from his face. The sweat didn't help. With both hands engaged, he couldn't do much about this, except to pray the tape would keep the mask tight enough.

He made another 10 feet. Because Pod 2 was

relatively small, the incline angle of wall and roof was not as steep as #10 would be. After another 15 feet, he was convinced they could do it.

Pam and Bridget were standing below him like two doctors competing to deliver a baby. Mai Ker had walked over and stood beneath him on the INSIDE as if this would somehow help. It was like watching a spider crawl across her ceiling. It was more eerie because Herald was not a spider, and Herald did not belong OUTSIDE in the first place. She could tell he was struggling a little but knew firsthand how strong he was. She saw him fidget a hand toward his mask once or twice.

"Your mask OK, Herald?" she called on the radio, a sound of not-very-well-hidden panic in her voice.

"Yeah," he said. He gave a little half-nod, though he was not so sure himself. He was over almost 30 feet off the ground now.

"He looks OK," Bridget answered Mai Ker.

"Coming down," he hollered through the mask. It boomed over the radios.

"Careful," his mom urged.

His experience climbing INSIDE with Jimmy and Mai Ker was paying off. Between the suction cups and his rubber-soled boots, he had just as much adhesion coming down as going up. Bridget and Pam waited to cradle him down but he jumped over them at the last moment and stumbled to the ground on one knee.

"Not too bad," he said as he got up and brushed himself off.

"You're winded a little," Bridget said.

"Yeah. Well, it's new, you know? And my stupid mask feels like it's gonna peel loose."

Pam quickly inspected it. She pressed at the pieces of adhesive tape.

"Looks OK."

Just to be sure, she pulled a role of the tape from her jacket pocket and taped over the original pieces. The second layer was more irritating to Herald than the first.

As he finished brushing his pants off, Bridget frowned at him.

"You weren't supposed to get unnecessary dirt on you, remember? Radioactivity?"

"Oop," he grimaced. "Forgot."

"You'll have to strip down to your undies before we go back into number one. Those pants stay OUTSIDE."

"But they're my favorite pair!"

"Should've thought of that, I guess."

"Moms," he said under his breath.

"OK. You both OK?" Bridget asked them.

Both nodded.

"All right. It's a short walk down to the river. We've got time. Let's get some water samples."

"And you're worried about radiation in my pants?" Herald joked.

"We'll isolate the samples in the test cabinets in the Research Center before we open them," Bridget told him. "So we don't contaminate things."

"Can we go?" Pam asked. "I'm getting a little nervous being out here."

"Sure you're all right?" Bridget prodded again.

"Yes. Just want to get back in," she said a little breathlessly.

Bridget checked the air gauges on their tanks. Pam's was lowest but they all had more than enough air.

"You know, we meant to bring a backup tank out," she said, remembering.

"Forgot," Herald said. "We'll be OK."

"Let's get to the river."

The sky was partly overcast but the sun peeked through from time to time. It was the same sun they had seen every day, but seeing it without the Stellar barrier seemed to make it more rich and inviting. It certainly felt warmer and more natural.

They circled back around the west side of the Visitors

Center and made the short trek down to the bank of the Arkansas. As they crossed the parking lot, Herald peeked into the cab on one of the guard trucks. It was unlocked, but no keys.

"Mom, you gonna teach me how to drive someday?" he said as a joke.

"Maybe," she answered, then realized what she had said. "No."

The river was low, which was normal this time of year. But it was flowing, not stagnated. Bridget scooped up two 1-quart containers of water, capped them, and handed them up to Pam. Without thinking, she had knelt to collect the water. As she stood up, Herald was grinning.

"Looks like you're goin' back INSIDE in your undies too, Mom."

She laughed with him. His humor always reminded her of Clayton.

They made a hasty retreat, retracing their path through the Visitors Center. Being at least back in the building brought a moderate sense of security. As they walked back toward the hall that led to the Solarium, Pam stopped. She put her hand over the voice-activated mic on her radio.

"Bridget?"

"What?"

"Those trucks."

Bridget covered her mic, too.

"What about 'em?"

"Well. Two trucks. Two guards."

It was the last thing on Bridget's mind right now but she saw the earnestness in Pam's eyes.

"Should we go see?" Pam asked like a little child begging for a last snack after being told three times to go to bed.

"Why?"

"I don't know. It's like we owe them. You know?

They stayed to the end. To take care of us."

Bridget remembered.

"Should we?" she asked Pam.

Herald had picked up their meaning. His face puckered up like he smelled something really foul.

"It's not like I love seeing dead bodies," Pam said. "I just feel, you know, it would be kind of disrespectful to walk right through here—over their heads—and not at least check."

Bridget was torn. But Pam looked very grave.

"I guess," Bridget said after a long hesitation. "Herald, stay here."

"No way, Mom."

"Cover your mic. Yes, you're staying. It won't be nice."

"No kidding," he said deadpan. "I'm not a kid."

"Yes. You're my kid." She looked at him and shook her head with parental frustration. "All right. Come on."

She led them toward the south end of the Center where a door led into the basement stairwell.

"What's happening? Where the heck are you guys going?" Mai Ker boomed over the radios. They had been out of sight too long.

"We're OK. Just going to check something." Bridget didn't say what.

They reached the door. She tried the handle. Locked.

"Should've figured," she said.

"Wait," Pam said. She uncovered her mic and spoke to Mai Ker. "Mai Ker, when they shifted all the lock controls over to us INSIDE, did they shift *all* the locks?"

"Why?" she responded suspiciously.

"Can you unlock the door in here that leads from the main floor down to the basement?"

"Why?" she repeated, more suspiciously.

"Can you?"

Mai Ker frowned.

"Let me check."

Their air supplies were still fine but all three were now breathing harder. Pam looked at Herald's face. Sweat was still working away at the tape seal around his mask. She took out the roll of adhesive tape and put a third layer in place around the top of the mask. He resisted, but she kept at it.

"There. That should be OK till we're back in." She laughed. "You look like Halloween."

Bridget laughed, too.

"What?" Herald asked, in the dark.

"Never mind," Bridget said. "Mai Ker?" she asked impatiently.

"Checking. You didn't warn me about this. Have to look it up." She paused. "I know what you guys are doing. Do *you*?"

"Sorry to say, but, yes, we do."

"OK, I found it." She keyed the lock code for the basement door. "It work?"

"Nothing," Bridget said.

"Wait," Herald said. "Dad told me that when you guys moved to the tents, you powered down all the unneeded systems."

A light came on in Bridget's eyes.

"You're absolutely right."

"Must get that from you," he smiled.

"Or your father," she said absently. "Mai Ker, you've got to power up the electric line to the Center. We shut it all down. Remember?"

"I do now."

Mai Ker scrambled through more computer screens and found the switch links for the OUTSIDE power cables that linked to the Center. She keyed in several more codes.

A red exit light blinked to life in the Center by a side door. One vending machine across the room behind them tried to come back to life, the lights momentarily flickering. But a torn wire caused by the rampage of the refugees quickly shorted out and fried the circuitry, shooting off a stream of sparks in the process. The machine stood like a dead sentry again.

"Unplug it, Herald."

He went over and pulled the plug. He looked.

"Mom, what's 'orange soda'?"

"Not now. Mai Ker, try the lock again."

This time it buzzed like an angry bumblebee. Bridget, her hand on the handle, flinched, then opened it.

"We're going downstairs, Mai Ker."

"You people have lost your minds."

"Probably," Pam responded.

A bright, bare fluorescent light in the stairwell had blinked to life. They walked carefully down. The stairway, too, was clean. Almost pristine.

"Built this place pretty well, too," Bridget commented. "Not airtight. But pretty close."

They came to another locked door at the bottom that led into the OUTSIDE Control center.

"Mai Ker—"

"Yes. Got it." She was ahead of them. "Just waiting to hear you're still alive down there."

The lock buzzed.

"Thanks," Bridget said. "We won't be long."

"That's what people always say when they don't mean it," Mai Ker said. "You guys are making me really nervous!" She turned around. Nathaniel and Piper had joined her and Braden in the Comm. Center. "You kids go find some snacks, would you?"

"Mom! Now?" Nathaniel protested.

"Just go, young man!"

The three left with unhappy scowls, but the idea of snacks quickly relieved their disappointment. They ran toward the kitchen.

Bridget made Herald stand outside the Control Room door as she went in to take a look. Pam followed and stood just inside the door. Herald did his best to peer over her shoulder. It wasn't pretty, but it wasn't too horrid, either. Two guards had stayed to the end. Either their families had already died, Bridget guessed, or they had none.

One was lying peacefully on a night cot near the door. A light blanket was over most of him. His face had a slightly pained expression frozen into it, but he had apparently been sleeping when the last breath left. What Bridget hadn't expected was that he was almost perfectly mummified.

"Ugh," was all Pam could squeak out of her dry throat. It sounded worse through the mask. "Didn't expect that," she said.

"Me, either," Bridget said. She walked to the door where Herald was still holding but still peeking.

"It's kinda grim, son. But I think you can handle it. The dry, stale air has mummified him."

"You mean, he didn't rot," he said, not as a question but an observation.

"Yes. He didn't rot. Well, that is, he rotted in a kind of freeze-dried way. Without the freezer."

"So?" he asked.

Bridget realized she was still blocking his way.

"I guess."

She stood aside.

Herald walked toward the cot. His guts wrenched inside. He looked down with childlike sympathy in his eyes.

"They stayed to protect you guys. Didn't they?"

"Yeah. And to stay in touch. Give us someone to talk to out here."

"That took guts," Herald said.

He looked down the room where a second body sat slumped half-sideways in a chair by one of the consoles. He walked to it. It was dressed in an official royal blue SOLARIUM-3 guard jacket, squared pockets with an expensive-looking "S-3" logo stitched over the right breast. The stretch-dried skin had contorted the jaw and face into a pathetic expression of agonized pain that had witnessed some forbidding but indescribable horror.

What was almost indiscernible, except for the styling of the rusty-red hair, was that this had been a woman, the last guard sent out to replace one who had died.

Herald turned to his mom.

"Can I touch it?"

"I rather you didn't," she said. "We still don't know what we're dealing with. We're probably completely contaminated already. Let's not take another chance, son."

"OK." The closer he looked, the more he was sure that he didn't want to touch the mummified corpse after all. "I saw some pictures of these in the archeology files. They look a lot different in real life."

"If that's what you'd call it," Pam said quietly. She went and put an arm around Herald's waist. "You OK? Sorry I dragged you down here."

"I didn't witness any dragging," Herald said.

She smiled through her mask and gave his arm a gentle squeeze.

Bridget had walked further down the room, noticing a rock-hard, half-eaten candy bar still partly in its wrapper lying on the console by a computer station. Scrawled on the bottom of the computer monitor frame with some kind of permanent marker was "P. B. was here—for what good it did."

"Look," she said to Pam, at first confused. "Oh. Of course," she said, as it finally dawned on her.

"Of course what?" Pam asked.

"Paul Bishop. We sent him down here—to chat with us in the Comm. Center."

"Who's Paul Bishop, Mom?" Herald wondered.

"Same story, son. Tell you later."

"They took whatever was left in the refrigerator," Pam said. "Did you notice the mini-fridge over there?

Door was left hanging open."

"They the ones who rifled the vending machines upstairs?" Herald asked.

"Probably," his mom said.

"Maybe we should go now," Pam said. "I'm starting to feel creepy all over. Like a tomb."

Bridget nodded.

"Come on, son," she said, nudging Herald back toward the door.

"Should we do something for them, Mom?" He looked at her.

"Don't know what to do. Right now. We'll see. Maybe later." Her heart said drag them up and bury them, INSIDE or OUT. But she wasn't prepared to deal with it. "Let's wait. Let's just get back in ourselves." She gestured toward the door. "Come on, I've had enough."

After his mom and Pam turned toward the door, Herald quietly and carefully adjusted the body in the chair into what looked like a more comfortable position. *We owe her that at least,* he told himself.

They made their way up the stairs. No one spoke. It felt like they were leaving friends, yet had never met them. As they reached the upper door out of the stairway, Bridget checked their tank gauges. Over an hour left each.

An idea struck her.

"Wait here," she said. Then she called on the radio. "Mai Ker, unlock the Control Room door again."

"Bridget!" Mai Ker called back.

"Please!"

"Oh, my God," Mai Ker mumbled.

Bridget went back down to the Control Room. She didn't want to disturb the body under the blanket. She walked to the other one. She stopped, and frowned.

"You moved," she said curiously. Then it hit her. "That boy of mine . . ."

She reached carefully into the side jacket pockets.

Nothing. Carefully, so as not to disturb the fragile remains, she worked her hand into the right pants pocket. She felt a small ring of keys and pulled them out. Two different keys had a manufacturer insignia that matched the two guard trucks.

"Just in case," she said aloud to herself. She looked at the body. She straightened it a little, too. She wanted to straighten up the head but was sure it wouldn't move.

She rejoined Pam and Herald upstairs. They looked at her. She smiled her way past them and led them back through the Center hallway that led back to the Pod 1.

"We're ready," Bridget called to Mai Ker.

"About time!" Mai Ker said impatiently. She called over the intercom for the kids, who had gone off playing. "Need you guys, now."

Homemade jelly and a glob of peanut butter were on Braden's cheek when the three arrived back at the Comm. Center.

"Go get ready to pull the seals," she told them. "Braden, you stay with me. And wipe your face."

The OUTSIDE party pulled the outer seals from the doorjamb and set them aside in the hall. Then, remembering at the last moment, Bridget and Herald shed their pants and threw them in a heap by the wall.

Mai Ker unlocked the outer door. They moved into the pod and pulled the door tight behind them.

"Everybody in?" Mai Ker asked.

"Good!" Bridget responded.

Quickly, Mai Ker relocked the door and keyed the purge sequence. The OUTSIDE air was pumped out. Circulation vents from the inner side of the pod started to hiss quietly.

"Fresh air coming," she radioed them. She readied the command that would unlock the inner door once the air exchange was complete.

"Keep your masks on until we're INSIDE and we're sure," Bridget ordered them.

All three quickly took their boots off and sealed them into plastic bags. Slowly the warmth and the moisture of the Solarium air began to flow around them. It felt like a warm, welcome bath.

"That feels so good," Pam said breezily.

"A lot better coming in than going out," Herald said with relief.

"Is the outer lock secure?" Bridget radioed to Mai Ker.

"Yes. Secure."

"Pull the seals," she said over the radio.

Pam and Herald pulled the seals off from their side while Nathaniel and Piper pulled the seals from the podwalk side.

Braden's head was almost attached to Mai Ker's, watching the computer action. A green square on the screen showed INSIDE air had refilled the pod.

"Here," she said, pointing Braden's hand toward the keyboard. "Hit ENTER."

He did. He was ecstatic he got to help. The simplest things are the truest pleasures to kids.

"We're good," Bridget called to Mai Ker.

"Opening," Mai Ker answered.

The locks clacked in the inner door. Herald pulled it open quickly, they hustled through, and just as quickly he shut it behind them.

They were home, and alive.

MAI KER and Bridget spent the afternoon testing the air and water samples in the lab in the Research Center. Herald watched and learned. It was very much like the weekly tests they performed on the INSIDE air.

The test results on the air samples astonished them. The nitrogen pressure was still higher than normal, about 81 percent of the total pressure, but this was much lower than they had expected based on what they had heard from OUTSIDE, just before the end. More importantly, the oxygen pressure had returned to almost 19 percent, very near normal. And the ozone level was only slightly elevated above its old norm.

Bridget stared at the printouts. She read them over twice. She remembered from the last reports they had gotten years ago from OUTSIDE Control that most of the oxygen molecules in the lower atmosphere had broken down, and the ozone levels had skyrocketed.

"This can't be right," Bridget said with an expression that suggested someone had just smacked her head with a board.

Mai Ker took the printouts and scanned them. She frowned.

"You got a bad sample," Mai Ker said. "You must have."

"No, Mai Ker. We were very careful," Bridget told her.

"The sampling containers must have been contaminated with INSIDE air."

"I don't think so," Bridget insisted. "Pam and I suctioned and vacuum sealed them. Just this morning. There's no INSIDE air in those samples."

"You're certain?" Mai Ker pressed her.

Bridget was still perplexed but getting irritated.

"Yes, I'm certain! What we're looking at is air from OUTSIDE."

"But how?" Herald asked.

"What in the world is going on?" Mai Ker wondered, not even hearing Herald's question. She began to feel confused. Her face expressed her disbelief.

"I have no idea," Bridget admitted. "It's impossible. I mean, almost miraculous."

"But we know there is no such thing as miracles," Mai Ker responded, the scientist inside her protesting the evidence in her hand. "Right?"

Bridget was silent for several moments. Herald

watched her, then Mai Ker. It looked to him like there was a battle of some kind going on in their heads, but he wasn't sure who the adversaries were.

"This just can't be," Mai Ker said, handing the printouts back to Bridget.

"Uncanny," Bridget added. She began to waiver. "Maybe we did do something wrong."

"Everything is dead out there," Mai Ker said. "No photosynthesis going on. So how could there be this much oxygen built back up?"

"Don't know," Bridget said.

"It's not possible."

Herald kept watching the mental ping-pong.

"Well," Bridget said, exasperated, "so we have what's not possible, versus what we're holding in our hands."

"I mean— Well, I wonder," Mai Ker said, and fumbled to a stop. She didn't know what she meant, or what she wondered. Her scientific scruples were trying to overrule her own eyes and the unmistakable results of the computerized tests.

Herald finally managed to wedge in.

"This is kinda weird, Mom," he said. "What's it mean?"

"It means we need to recheck it again tomorrow. If this is right, if it holds, we may be OK. The crack in number ten won't be a problem. Because this air is almost normal. Still thin on oxygen, but breathable."

Bridget's legs felt like lead. She had been on them most of the day. She plopped into a chair.

"No. I still think we must fix the crack," Mai Ker said.

"Why?"

"The air went bad before. We're not sure of its current state. We cannot tell if it might go bad, again. We have to fix the roof."

"OK. But I don't feel so urgent, now. At least I'll sleep a little tonight. We don't need to rush."

"I'm gonna find Pam. She'll want to know," Herald

said.

Mai Ker tested the water samples next. Then she scraped bits of dirt from the bottoms of the boots they had worn OUTSIDE to check soil radiation. When the tests were complete, she and Bridget rejoined the family in the tent for supper.

Pam had made a wonderful, hot supper of lamb, potatoes, and a large veggie salad. Piper and Nathaniel helped. Nathaniel in the kitchen was always a bit of a challenge but he liked to help and it meant he wasn't off stirring up trouble somewhere else.

"This is fantastic," Pam said of the air readings as they ate. "I don't understand how it happened, though. I mean, nothing looks changed out there. Except the lighter color in the air."

"Yes, I know," Mai Ker said. "But we rechecked the samples three times. Same result. Unless the equipment is malfunctioning, the results are good."

"Amazing," Pam kept saying. "You mean we could breathe out there? Without the masks?"

"Well, I'm not confident of that, yet," Bridget said. "But if we get more samples, and the same results, it means things have changed for the better.

"That would be wonderful," Piper said.

"Lot less worrisome," Sing added. She looked across at Herald and was finally able to smile.

"Incredible," Pam said. "But I can't understand how."

"Me, either," Bridget said. "But there it is."

"You always told us the air was so bad out there," Nathaniel said. "How come?"

"It was bad, Nate. It was horrible," Pam assured him.

"Why did it just get better?"

"I have no answer." She looked at Mai Ker and Bridget. "You know, we never knew what went wrong in the first place, did we?"

"Haskins said it was something in space, some strange, unknown stuff. Corrupted the atmosphere," Mai

Ker said.

"I remember."

"They knew pretty certain when it happened. You're right. They did not know exactly *what* happened."

"Does that help, Nate?" Pam asked.

"I guess," he said, meaning "Not really."

"I wonder," Bridget said. "Whatever happened before—maybe happened again. But in reverse?"

"You mean, it reversed the damage?" Herald asked.

"I don't know, son. Just guessing. What matters is that the air seems to be getting back near normal."

"But when something's gone wrong like that, how can it just—fix itself?" Pam asked. "I mean, short of a miracle or something."

"Depends on what you mean by a miracle," Bridget said.

"Maybe we can't explain everything," Piper chimed in. She had been anxious to ask. "Mom, can I go out tomorrow, too?"

Pam looked at her and frowned.

"Oh. I'm not sure, honey. Maybe we need to be more sure first."

"I'd like to go with you. Can I? Please?"

"We'll talk about it later."

This was Pam's usual way of saying no. Piper looked very disappointed. Now that the possibility of roaming around in a whole huge world was floating around, she found it hard to resist the idea. She wanted badly to go along.

"I'm happy to stay in the Solarium," Sing said with conviction.

"Well, we're happy with that idea, too," Bridget said. "No taking chances. With your baby."

"What about the water?" Pam asked.

"We forgot to tell you," Mai Ker said. "Not such good news. It's very oxygen starved. And it still carries high radiation levels. From the blasts. Though I think the radiation is much lower than it probably was at first."

"We found radiation in the soil samples, too," Bridget added. "They were surface samples. The deeper soil may not be as contaminated."

"Could it ever be cultivated again?" Herald asked.

"Who knows? Maybe someday there will be a life OUTSIDE," Bridget said. "Too soon to tell."

Life OUTSIDE. It was a completely strange, alien concept to the children.

"So, right now, we can breathe the air, just can't drink the water?" Nathaniel asked.

Pam laughed.

"Kind of what my travel agent used to say when I went to Central America!" she joked.

The older women laughed jovially. The children all looked blank.

"I don't get it," Braden said.

"It's an OUTSIDE joke," Bridget laughed.

AFTER SUPPER, the three women and Herald went to the Meeting Tent to plan tomorrow's exploration.

Bridget told them she had found the pickup truck keys. She thought maybe they should drive to one of the nearby towns, do a little looking around, get a better picture of what was left out there.

Even though the air seemed fairly safe, Mai Ker insisted they take no chances. She made Bridget promise they would wear the air masks, and that they would remember to take along extra tanks.

Piper was in a corner of the room reading. She listened quietly. She couldn't keep her mind on her book. When the little group was breaking up, she caught her mom.

"Could I please go along, Mom? Please?"

"Why are you so insistent, Piper?"

"I don't know. I just want to go. I feel like—" She was hesitating to say it. "I need to be looking for something."

"What?"

"I don't know. Just a sense I have. You know, like I get sometimes?"

Pam did know. She knew Piper had not only a sixth sense but a seventh and eighth. She had made insignificant predictions in the past. They almost always happened as Piper expected.

"It's a big risk, honey," Pam said. "Bridget will take some convincing. She's trying to minimize risks."

"Can I talk to her?"

"Of course, sweetheart."

Piper caught up to Bridget changing in her tent. Not only Piper's insistent mood but something about the piercing look in her eyes persuaded Bridget. Bridget, too, knew Piper was different from the other children. She didn't demand things for herself. She seemed to Bridget the most altruistic soul she had ever known. So her asking to go along OUTSIDE was not, Bridget felt, out of any selfish motive or to impress the other kids. Piper was insistent, even though, as with Pam, she couldn't quite express why she felt she must go.

"So, can I?"

"I guess. If you really want to. Your Mom say OK?"

"If it's OK with you."

"OK."

"Thank you, Bridget."

"But you've got to promise. Have to be really careful. It's not like running around in here."

"I know."

"We don't know what we'll run into. What hazards are still out there. Some things might be . . ." She hunted for a word. ". . . unpleasant."

"I understand."

"And if I give you an order, no talking back. Understood?"

"Yes," Piper said with a polite smile. "I love you,

Auntie Bridget." She hugged her.

Bridget actually, and oddly, felt reassured that Piper would be going along. She couldn't explain to herself why.

IT HAD been a long, tiring day for those who had gone OUTSIDE. But it had been equally tiring for Mai Ker and those who stayed back because of the worry the whole time they were out there.

Braden and Nathaniel had disappeared to their tent an hour ago. They were talking quietly. Mai Ker looked in on them on the way to her tent.

"You looked tired, Mommy," Nathaniel said.

"Yes. You?"

"Kinda."

"Maybe put the light out. Get some sleep."

"Mommy?"

"Yes, Nate?"

"Is Daddy OK?"

The wounds were still very open and very raw in all of them.

"Sure he is, honey. I guess. Why are you asking?"

"All that stuff they were saying. About where he is. That stuff. I don't understand."

"He's gone," she said as gently as she could. "That's what we have to get used to." She sat on the edge of his bed. She rubbed his cheek.

On his own bed, Braden had rolled on his side and was listening intently.

"He's in heaven?" Braden asked.

Mai Ker wasn't sure and didn't know how to explain.

"He's gone," she said again.

"Piper said he's with God."

"Yes. Well, that's how she understands it."

"Does God take care of people who die?" Braden wanted to know.

"Daddy said so. Didn't he?"

"Yes," Braden said.

"Then I trust what your Daddy said. I don't know any more than that."

"My stomach hurts when I think about him," Nathaniel said.

"God?"

"No. Daddy."

"Yeah. Me, too," Mai Ker said. "But it's my heart."

"I wish Daddy would come home," Braden said. He rolled on his back and stared at the blank canvas ceiling.

"I wish he could," Mai Ker agreed. "But that's not how things go."

She leaned down and kissed Nate's head. She went over and kissed Braden, too.

"Try to sleep," she said.

Easy words.

15

Saturday, November 30th, 18 (NC)

Through the night, Mai Ker tossed around, trying to unwind, trying to find a comfortable position on her bed that she never found. Sleep eluded her. Her mind twisted and wound back on itself, fretting about her talk with the boys.

Why do I feel so lost? she wondered somewhere after 2:00 a.m. She was and always had been a strong, independent person. Yet the loss of Jimmy was crushing her spirit. She was determined to stay positive around the kids but she had failed to bring any light or hope last evening with the boys. They obviously felt abandoned, too, and she was no help to them.

Sing had also not slept much. Despite the news about the air, her worries over Herald being OUTSIDE intensified her sense of helplessness triggered by her father's death. Like the other children, she had no experience with death. It felt as if a foreigner with a different language had moved in among them, an unwelcome guest who was consuming their emotions like a thick, delicious dessert.

Death had arrived uninvited and had to somehow be confronted and answered. Neither Mai Ker nor the children had the words.

Unintentionally, Jimmy's death was quickly becoming an out-of-bounds topic for everyone. Emotions were raw. Answers were few. Anxieties about who might be next were intolerable.

IT DAWNED today a cloudy, almost sunless morning. A gray radiance barely showing through the light purple air OUTSIDE flooded over and into the Solarium.

Bridget had measured the temperature in the upper 50s yesterday and expected about the same today. The four explorers, now including Piper, dressed in jackets, long pants and heavy work boots. There would be no climbing today, so Herald wore his regular boots, a well-worn pair inherited a couple of years ago from Jimmy.

They gathered their breathing gear and extra air tanks by Pod 1. Several handheld air sensors, more air and water sampling canisters, and a small package lunch for each were set there as well.

The team gathered outside the Comm. Center. At the last minute, Bridget felt around in her pockets.

"Hang on. Almost forgot."

She ran back through Pod 3 and across Pod 10 to their tent village. She had left the truck keys sitting on top of her bureau.

"Ready?" she asked everyone as she returned.

"Got your driver's license?" Pam joked.

Bridget laughed.

"Don't know if I'll remember how."

"I'll drive," Herald said excitedly.

Bridget didn't answer but shook her head.

Braden was with Nathaniel this time to place the seals around the inner door of Pod 1. Mai Ker had persuaded Sing to join her in the Comm. Center, in case an extra hand was needed. Sing followed her in and carefully closed the door behind, hoping this might somehow insulate them from the OUTSIDE air that would soon flood Pod 1.

The four explorers entered Pod 1, the seals were placed on both sides of the inner door, and Mai Ker transitioned the air. Soon they were in the OUTSIDE hallway, sealing up the cracks of the outer door and picking up all the gear. They all had their air masks on before going into #1. The masks were again taped in place, for what good that would do.

They walked through the Visitor Center, almost to the door.

"Mom," Herald said through his mask. "I had an idea last night."

"Yes?"

"Well, there were radio transmitters down in the Control Room. Saw 'em yesterday. I've seen these in the technology archives. Would it be worth a try?"

Bridget hadn't thought of this at all. His suggestion of trying the transmitters had only one purpose. To see if someone might be alive somewhere, and might answer.

"Anything's worth a try, I guess. But don't get your hopes up," she said. "Mai Ker, let us back down to the Control Room."

"Now what?" came the predictable moan from the Pod 2.

"Piper and I will stay up here," Pam said judiciously.

"Good idea," Bridget said.

She and Herald went down to the Control Room. Near the console where the mummified lady was perched, Bridget saw two radio systems. Each had a mic on a stand, so they were indeed transmitters.

"Never knew these were here. Good eyes, Herald."

She carefully rolled the lady's chair away several feet and pulled up a different chair. She studied the console, found a power switch and flipped it on. A short static buzz in one of the radios was replaced by a quiet hum.

"Might be shortwave," she said.

"Tunable?" Herald asked.

"Yeah." She looked at him. "How do you know all this stuff?"

"History, remember? Jimmy spent a lot of time with me at the research computers."

She examined the controls.

"It's got a scan button."

She pushed it. The low hum continued, broken periodically by a kind of electronic hiccup. Twice there was a funny swooping, piercing sound as if an electric eagle was diving after its prey then twisting into a sudden climb. Both times this lasted only two or three seconds.

"Try saying something," Herald urged her.

"Don't know what to say."

"In the old movies, they'd always said something about May 1st."

"May Day— Yeah." She pressed the mic key. "May day, May day."

She tried a couple more times. Each time she keyed the mic, a digital readout locked temporarily on whatever frequency it had hit. They waited. There was no response.

"S.O.S.," she said. "S.O.S."

Herald didn't know this one. She saw his look.

"Save Our Souls," she explained. "Used to send it out from sinking ships."

"Sounds like we're the only ship still afloat," he frowned.

"It does. No big news there, huh?"

"There's another one. They used it with Morse Code. C.Q., C.Q."

"What's that mean?"

"Seek you, seek you."

"Sure," she said, "go ahead."

Herald leaned down and keyed the mic slowly as if it might bite him.

"C.Q., C.Q., C.Q." He waited. "C.Q., C.Q."

Still silence.

"Try that other one," he said, pointing.

The other radio had a small plaque on it that said OMAHA. She rolled her chair to it, powered it up, and tried the mic. As she let go, there was a brief static sound like two drunks belching over each other.

For an instant, she was sure she made out a word or two. But it was only what she wanted to hear. It was static gibberish, not words.

She tried several more times. Pleadings, acronyms. No response. She sat for several moments, wondering.

"Everything OK?" Mai Ker's voice called.

She was tracking everything through their voice-activated radios and got nervous if there was a long silence. Pam and Piper hadn't said a word since Bridget and Herald went downstairs.

"Yeah. We're fine," Bridget answered. "It's no good," she told Herald.

"Just a hope. You never know."

"Hate to say it. I kinda did."

They went back upstairs and joined Pam and Piper.

"No luck, huh?" Pam said. "We were listening, too."

"Nope. Let's get on with it. Air samples. Then water samples. Then deep soil samples. At least 18 inches down, Herald."

He waived the small folding hand-shovel he had brought.

They carried the extra air tanks they had brought out and set them by one of the two pickup trucks, then began collecting samples. Herald went off toward an area of dead grass beyond the parking lot and started digging. He brought kneepads this time to keep the soil off his pants.

They had all the samples they needed in 15 minutes.

"Anybody for a ride?" Bridget said.

Herald and Piper both shot their hands up. The tape on their masks was already starting to irritate their skin but they could put up with a little itching if it meant exploring.

Pam watched, still dubious, but she could see that the kids' enthusiasm for going was starting to grow.

"Sure," Pam finally said.

"You guys put all the samples inside on that big counter marked 'Information.' I'll check the truck," Bridget said.

Pam and the kids carried the samples into the building

and rejoined Bridget. As they walked toward the guard trucks, Bridget was stretching her arms in the air as if she had just woken up. Then, with no warning, she pulled her air mask several inches away from her face. She took a deep breath.

"Bridget!" Pam screamed, running toward her.

Bridget inhaled and exhaled again, deeply.

"Have to find out eventually," Bridget said. "There's only one sure way."

"Not like this!" Pam said heatedly.

Bridget pushed her mask back against her face, patting the tape back in place.

"The readings on my sensors are just as good as yesterday. Haven't picked up anything odd. Just thought I'd try a little."

"You're crazy! Please don't do that again. Give me a heart attack!"

Pam turned to the kids. She didn't care if Bridget *was* the leader, she was being foolish.

"You kids don't dare touch your masks!" Pam barked.

From the looks in their eyes, they were not about to.

"Look," Bridget was saying, handing her an air sensor. "Doesn't look dangerous. Even smells normal."

"I don't care, dammit! You're the one who said no risks!" Pam challenged her.

"You're right. Kids, listen to Pam. Here, wanna tape me up better?"

A very annoyed Pam pressed more adhesive tape on extra hard just to express her irritation. She was furious that Bridget was giving ideas to the kids.

"OK. We'll be fine," Bridget said. "Everybody breathe normal. So we don't use more air than we need to." She gave Pam a sideways hug, smiling through her mask. "We're good, Pam."

Pam was still frowning.

The four squeezed into the seat of the one guard truck. Bridget turned the key. The engine was silent. It wouldn't start.

"Let me check," Herald said. "Jimmy and me worked on the tractor batteries a lot. Cables might be loose. Or dirty."

He got out, opened the hood and propped it up. No battery.

"Shoot."

"What's wrong?" his mom asked.

"Battery's gone."

Bridget frowned. Then she remembered.

"You know, on the farm, when grandpa wasn't gonna use a vehicle for a while, he always took the battery out and stored it in the truck somewhere. So it wouldn't drain down."

Like a search party, the four Solarians looked every place in and on the truck where a battery might be hidden. They didn't find it.

"I don't get it," Herald said, puzzled.

"Maybe they knew they wouldn't be leaving," Piper said somberly.

"Maybe," her mom said. She looked around. "What about that little storage shed over there, by the corner of the building?"

"I'll look," Herald said.

With a little effort he pushed the rusty shed doors open. There on the plywood floor sat the two truck batteries.

"You're brilliant, Pam," he smiled as he carried one back.

While searching for the battery, they had found a small wooden toolbox with several rusty but usable tools behind the seat in the cab. Herald took the toolkit and set it on top of the fan housing. There were no socket wrenches. There was, however, a large set of pliers. He set the battery down on its platform and clamped the two cables back in place.

"Try it, Mom."

Bridget got back behind the wheel. This time, two faint lights tried to come on in the dash. She turned the key further and the sound of a very tired bear in a midwinter snore greeted them.

"This isn't gonna work," Bridget said with frustration.

Piper and Pam stood alongside the truck watching all this, both thinking it was time to go back INSIDE.

"Wait a second, Mom," Herald said.

He looked at the two battery terminals more closely. Both had a light beard of greenish corrosion. He dug deeper in the toolbox and found an old, ratty wire brush. He took the cables off the battery again and brushed the terminals and cable heads thoroughly. As he finished, he bumped his pliers with his wrist. The tool grounded out against both battery terminals and sparks flew.

"Herald!" his mom shouted, jumping out of the truck.

"OK, Mom! Calm down. Just a little spark." He smiled to himself. "Got some juice, at least."

"Maybe we should give this up," Pam said.

"Almost there," Herald assured them.

He brushed both cable heads one last time for good measure and reconnected them to the battery.

"Try again."

"But no sparks?" his mom asked.

He frowned at her.

She nodded, got back in and tried the key. This time the bear snored loudly for a moment, then rolled over and went back to sleep.

"Guess we're not going for a ride after all," a disappointed Piper said.

"Hang on," Herald said. "Jimmy taught me more tricks than that."

Jimmy's name carried over the voice-activated radios back to Sing and Mai Ker in the Comm. Center. They looked at each other. Sing took her mom's hand. They were stuck at the computer console, not going anywhere, either.

At least we're safe, Mai Ker worried.

Herald crawled under the right front wheel-well of the guard truck with the large pliers and banged several times on the starter motor. Powdery bits of rust dropped off the shaft and out of the motor housing. He whacked it three more times.

"Try it now!" he hollered to his mom.

Bridget turned the key. The bear snorted, then woke, and growled loudly. The engine started. Invisible horses pulled at their reins, ready to go.

"You did it!" Piper said clapping Herald on the back as he got to his feet. "Smart guy!"

"Thanks to your dad," he smiled.

In the Comm. Center, Sing winced.

"Why can't they stop talking about Dad?" she asked her mom, who had no helpful way to answer.

Back OUTSIDE, Piper hugged Herald and tried to kiss him on the cheek through their masks. Bridget shook her head and smiled.

Herald dropped the toolbox into the bed of the pickup and they piled back in, Piper next to Bridget, Pam next, Herald by the passenger door.

Bridget was in the saddle and raring to go.

"OK, Superman. Where to?"

"Daddy said people used to drive to go get ice cream," Piper said.

"Nice wishful thinking, honey," her mom said. "I think the ice cream man is out of town."

"The road goes east or west," Bridget said.

"East," Herald said. "Toward the sun."

"East it is."

It still felt extraordinarily strange for Bridget and Pam to be OUTSIDE again. They felt it even more than yesterday. Out here the purplish air, seen for years through their Stellar pods, was now less purple and seemed almost natural. The difference took on a new reality. Everything around them was more bold. Looking out on a dead world was one thing. Being out and in it was at once exhilarating and frightening.

They drove the quarter mile north toward the highway, passing the abandoned guard booth that stood near where their road met the main road. Bridget turned east along old Highway 194 toward what used to be Las Animas. It was here that Clayton had spent his last night of freedom before reporting for work at Solarium-3. The highway wound through several curves, then straightened out. Bridget's driving was as rusty as the starter. And the truck was not in the best shape. All four tires were low. They should have pumped them up but that would have meant going through the whole ingress-egress operation again just for a tire pump. She took it slow. It was still early in the day. They had plenty of time and extra air tanks.

Bridget had noticed there was just under a quarter tank of gas. Driving slow would help conserve it. But the biggest reason for going slow was that the road was in very bad shape. It had never been much in the best of its days and the years of weather, freezing, cracking, and no resurfacing had broken whole chunks loose along both edges of the road and down the center where the two strips of asphalt met. The recent earthquakes had not helped. In places, deep slices tore through the pavement and soil, as if a giant had been pruning its toenails with a huge knife and slipped.

"We're gonna be out of radio range," Bridget called to Mai Ker.

A garbled response came.

"We'll be OK," she added.

No response.

The highway ran along the north side of the Arkansas River and came into the north end of Las Animas. They turned south on what would have been Bent Avenue, if the signs had survived.

They crept slowly into town. They had passed only a

few abandoned farmhouses along the highway. Now, coming into a community, it got scarier. Piper had a grip on her mother's knee that could have held her to the bottom of an airliner in flight.

Herald had been fiddling with the radio tuner on the dash, still hoping to find a signal from somewhere. It seemed his compulsion today. The only sounds were atmospheric static.

As they pulled into the main part of town, Herald began to pay closer attention to things around him. Here was a world he and Piper had seen only in pictures. Piper was equally awed. Both were fascinated by the number of houses and stores, although many had been vacant long before the final catastrophe had come. Especially intriguing to the children were the signs. Painted signs, old electric signs, signs carved deep into planks of wood with stained-in letters, signs of all kinds. Even some of the old cars and trucks had signs painted on them.

"Why did they write on everything?" Piper asked.

"Used to call it advertising," Pam said. "Some even used their license plates."

"What's a license plate?" Piper wanted to know.

"Keep an eye out for somewhere we can find gas," Bridget said. "We could use some."

"We've got fuel back at the pods," Herald said.

"We don't want to use that out here. If anything, we should see if we can find some to take back, to replenish our supply."

"That looks like an old station," Pam said, pointing to a ramshackle building with two weathered, rusted gas pumps out front.

"Let's try."

Bridget pulled in and stopped near the pumps. They all got out. In just seconds, they realized this would be futile. The pumps had been run by electric motors. There was no electricity.

"Could we hotwire a pump to the truck battery?"

Herald wondered.

"Wrong voltage," Bridget said. "The pumps would have been 110. Maybe 220."

She walked around behind the building and came back smiling.

"There's an old beater truck back there. Got a siphon pump in the back. Like they used on farms. If we can push it to one of the underground tanks, the hose might reach deep enough to draw some gas."

In the meantime, and without Pam realizing it, Piper had gone exploring, against her better judgment but in service of her growing curiosity. She went around the opposite side of the building where she saw two large metal caps embedded in the battered concrete. She just barely heard Bridget say something about tanks.

"Are these them?" Piper asked. No one heard her. She started back around the building. She happened to glance, again against her better judgment, through the front window of the station. Her eyes went straight to a hand sticking out of a shirtsleeve on the floor. But the hand was only dried bones. The rest of the arm, and whatever it was attached to, was hidden behind a beat-up, dark-brown counter. Piper ran to the truck, pulled herself in and slammed the door shut. She gulped air. She was sitting, pale and frightened, when the others came back around the other side of the building.

Pam looked at her face and tried the door. Locked. She tapped the window. Piper rolled it down nervously.

"I think I found the tanks," Piper said.

"Why are you so frightened, honey?" Pam asked.

Piper swallowed a bunch of saliva that had pooled in her mouth.

"Think I maybe saw a man."

"Someone's alive?" Bridget said, astounded, turning wide-eyed.

"No. Used to be," Piper said.

Pam gave her a little hug through the truck window.

"Honey, you need to stay in the truck," she said.

Their words sounded strange, muffled through the air masks. At times it sounded like they were choking when they weren't. But at the moment, Piper was still gagging a little.

"Over there," she pointed. "Through that window."

"You sit here. I'll help with the fuel," her mom told her.

Piper was perfectly thrilled to stay in the truck. She rolled the window back up.

None of the others were anxious to investigate inside the station. They went back behind the building and with a straining effort managed to push the old service truck over to the underground tanks. Herald ran the 20-foot hose down into one of the tank necks. Bridget began cranking the siphon pump. In seconds, it was pulling gas out of the ground and feeding it into the 100-gallon storage tank in the back of the old truck.

When they had about 40 gallons, Bridget drove their truck alongside. She put the outlet hose from the storage tank into their truck tank and let gravity fill it up.

"Pretty slick Bridget," Pam said. "You're so inventive."

"Spent time on my grandparents' farm one summer. Up in Canada, when I was a kid. Things just come back to you."

The gas tank full, they decided to drive around town a little more. Piper was looking at the floor now more than the scenery. Once in a while, she would look up.

This excursion turned very gloomy. So far, except for the hand in the gas station, they hadn't seen any bodies. Everyone apparently had found a quiet, private place for their last moments. Most. But as they turned down one street along a row of 80-year-old homes, they saw several bodies outside on the porches.

Two were precariously balanced in a porch swing and looked like they may have been holding hands. They could have been young, or old. It was impossible to tell.

In front of another house, they saw the remains of a man who had stretched himself out on his lawn, maybe for his last night. A figure in an old-looking cotton dress was in a rocker on a porch across the street from this one. What looked like a knitting bag was by her chair. Whatever her knitting project had been, it had been shredded by some animal that survived longer than she had.

It was unnerving and grim, and quickly becoming sickening. Bridget decided to turn back.

"Let's go home," she said almost inaudibly.

They went back north on Bent Avenue. At the junction where 194 turned west and old Highway 50 went east, Herald read another sign.

"John Martin Reservoir, 17 Miles." The arrow pointed east along Highway 50. "What'd'ya think, Mom?"

"Think we better get back. We're out of radio range. Mai Ker's probably worried sick."

"But a reservoir. Bet it's bigger than our ocean."

"Wouldn't be hard," Piper said.

"Can we?" Herald pressed her. "We could get more water samples. You know, a lake instead of a river."

"Yeah," Bridget acknowledged. "Might show us something different."

She slowed the truck to a stop and pondered. Curiosity is a powerful thing.

"OK. But let's not spend a lot of time. We've gotta get back."

She headed east, past an old hotel that was in ruins, the whole west end burnt to the ground.

"So eerie," Pam said. She was having trouble keeping tears back.

"Yeah," was Bridget's only response.

"Used to be so much life. Wish you kids could have seen it," Pam said. "The world was so alive. Millions of different kinds of plants and creatures. Big and small."

"Most too small to see," Bridget commented.

"Every place out here was teeming with life. And everything worked together. Like a huge puzzle." The wonderment in her voice masked the pain of seeing it all gone.

"Must have been something," Piper said, looking south across the dead landscape. There were no bodies visible out here, just endless terrain.

"It was. Yes, it was something. People working, creating, building." She looked at the two children. "Having kids." Her eyes scanned the landscape around them. "The world was alive."

This region had never been as plush as other parts of the world that Pam remembered. Now it was even more barren. Before, sparse, high desert plant life struggled to thrive here. Nothing survived. Only dry, dead prairie grass and the withered stems of long-dead brush and cactus were visible now, beaten down onto the decrepit soil by the poisoned air, the lifeless rains and the icy, blowing snows of winter.

"Now it's silent," Pam said, her unplanned soliloquy ended.

Herald stared out the truck windows, too. The sound of the air pushing through the open windows melted in with the purr of the old engine. Herald secretly wished he could take off his air mask for a while. After Pam's earlier reaction, he knew he would get smacked.

In just a few minutes, a large body of water came into view down a meandering embankment to the right. Bridget watched for a turn but there didn't appear to be any good access road. She kept going.

Finally they came to an intersection where a little group of houses and a rickety, abandoned store sat hovering near one corner. The sign over the door of the store, as best they could make out, read HASTY STOP AND SHOP.

"S'pose that's the original convenience store?" Pam

joked.

Piper saw a village sign as they turned right onto the side road. HASTY.

"I think it was the name of the town, Mom," she said.

Bridget pulled into the gravel parking lot.

"We better change air tanks. It's been way over an hour."

With Herald's help, she exchanged all four of their tanks for full ones. They had four more, just in case.

They loaded back into the truck and drove south along the broken asphalt road toward the water. Past the last house, the road sloped down radically. The pavement ended. They went down through a sharp dip. Without warning, Bridget slammed the brakes and stopped.

A few hundred feet away from them, spread over a large gravel area near what was once the water's edge, were a group of cars and trucks. Several old pickups had camper units in the back. In the middle were two military-style trucks. To one side of the parking area was an old delivery van with the words JUST DESSERTS SNACKS & BAKERY fading from its side.

"Oh, God," Pam said, swallowing the hushed words.

Piper looked at her.

"What's wrong, Mommy?"

"Of all the bad luck," Bridget was saying over Piper's question.

"Mom?" Herald asked her.

The kids might as well have not been there.

"Is it?" Pam asked Bridget without looking at her.

"Can't be. Must be." She surveyed the cluster of vehicles closer. "It is." The words fell like bricks.

She let her foot off the brake almost unconsciously and the truck jerked forward down the short hill into what had once been a water's-edge camping area. She felt something draw her against her will. It wasn't curiosity.

"It is," Pam confirmed. "I remember that truck. The name."

"Yeah," Bridget echoed.

"Seemed so ironic at the time."

Pam and Bridget both felt the need to explore the camp. They had to know, to be sure. The bodies in Las Animas were just bodies. This was different. This was more personal.

Pam's mind ran back to that day. The guns. The screaming. The pleading. The confusion. The emotional chaos INSIDE the Solarium and inside themselves.

Bridget brought the truck slowly to a stop 20 feet from the nearest car. She took a deep breath in her mask, mustering courage. She got out. Like Pam, she was caught up into the immediacy of the past. She actually forgot for a moment that Herald and Piper were there. Her eye caught them as she shut the pickup door.

"You two stay here," she ordered them.

"Mom—" Herald began.

"Both of you!"

Both frowned, deeper than usual, wanting an explanation.

Pam and Bridget walked toward the vehicles without another word, as if in a daze. They walked carefully past several cars, peering in, walking as if land mines were about to blow them to another world. The cars were empty, except one, where a ragged blanket on the back seat likely covered a small body. Nothing human showed.

"Maybe just a pet?" Pam asked, trying to avoid the reality.

Neither was keen to find out.

They came to a beat-up camper in the bed of a pickup. They looked at each other. Bridget tried the door handle on the camper. Locked from the inside.

"Let's look over there," said Pam, pointing to a camper trailer sitting helpless, unhitched from whatever had pulled it there.

This time Bridget found the door unlocked. Shoving

down a whole pile of emotions, with great unease, she stepped up into what had been someone's last home. Pam reluctantly followed.

The scene was much worse than the Control Room under the Visitors Center. Here were skeletal remains of at least two families. Three adults, six kids. The women couldn't smell much through their air masks, but a stale, rancid odor seemed to permeate their skin. The trailer had been shut up for years, sometimes under an intense sun, and was far from airtight. Heat and chemistry had taken over.

The bodies had not mummified. They had simply decayed. What was left was mostly bones and teeth. They had been spared the usual kind of destruction inflicted by various rodents since all those little creatures had been destroyed by the poisonous air, too.

"This was a bad idea," Bridget said with flat expression.

Yet they found it hard to leave. They had been unable to help them before. They could not help them now. The pain in their hearts cut twice as deep.

Odds and ends of these folks' lives lay piled or scattered around the trailer. There was still food in the cupboards. Pam and Bridget debated if they should take anything that looked usable.

"Better not," Pam advised. "Don't know when the stuff was canned. Could've been contaminated by the air. When it was being processed."

"You're right," Bridget said. "Probably couldn't eat it anyway," she said, looking at the pathetic scene. Then she forced herself to reconsider. "Would it maybe help, though? Longevity-wise? For the kids?"

"Not worth the risk," Pam replied. "Anyway. It'd be like robbing a grave. We can grow what we need."

Bridget nodded.

Just as she was about to say, "Come on," they heard footsteps behind them on the step of the trailer and jumped with fright.

"My God! Herald! You scared me to death!" his mother squealed.

"Sorry," said Piper from over his shoulder.

"I told you to stay in the truck!"

"We were worried," was Herald's weak excuse.

"No, you were curious!"

"That, too."

"It's all right," Pam said to Bridget. "They might as well see. Or they'll just keep asking." She wiped dusty sweat from her forehead.

"Do *not* touch anything!" Bridget commanded.

The two children stepped in but stayed just inside the door. They looked around cautiously. Both were nervous but curiosity had, indeed, gotten to them. Herald's eyes filled with inquisitiveness, Piper's with a deep sorrow. It was like walking into a neglected mausoleum, though neither had any experience of what that would be like. Here there were no fancy coffins or expensively embalmed bodies, no memorials recited at their deaths, no lovely flowers on brass stands. Just sadness and stark, barren death.

Piper looked at two of the adult remains. It occurred to her that her daddy might look like this before long. It shook her badly. It was not right. As much as she loved God, this felt wrong.

Why, God? They should have lived, she thought. She said an unusual prayer, silently, because she thought it might be blasphemous. *God, you better make this right. Help me understand. I don't understand why you would do this.*

Herald meanwhile was looking, being careful not to touch. There was an old radio but he didn't bother it. There was a small boxy thing that looked like an old-style computer monitor but was actually a television. There were two books, badly worn. And there were some large, flimsy paper things with lots of print on them and some grainy-looking pictures.

"What are those?" he asked.

"Newspapers," his mom said.

"What?"

"They used to print them every day. For news," Pam explained.

"Why?"

"People read them."

Herald was sure Pam was making this up. With computers and rich colored graphics, who would look at grungy, ink-smudged paper?

"Didn't they have that—what did you call it—the internet or something? To get their news?"

"They did," Pam said.

"So, why would they read these things?" he wondered, pointing at the papers.

"Old habits," his mom grimaced. "Hate to tell you, son, I was one of those old-timers."

Suddenly, the weight of age crept over her like a shadowy animal crawling up her back. She felt anxious. The sense of the smells in the place which she really couldn't smell was getting oppressive.

"We could take some of these back," Pam suggested, looking through several newspapers. "They kept us so much in the dark. Till the end. We might learn something."

Bridget quickly scanned one. The papers from various cities bore dates spread over the two months after the Solarians got the heart-rending news from John Haskins. They might fill in some gaps, or at least give some hint of where these people had come from and what drove them to seek refuge in Solarium-3.

"Enough," Bridget said somberly, indicating Herald and Piper with her eyes. "Let's get out of here."

She went out, the others following. The air outside felt better, even if they couldn't really taste or smell it. It was cooler.

"I still wish we could have helped them," Pam said absently as they walked to their truck.

Herald and Piper didn't understand what she meant.

"Shouldn't we bury them?" Herald asked.

"My gosh," Bridget said, "it would take forever. You realize how many bodies are probably here?"

"No."

"Well. I'd rather not tell you."

"We buried Daddy," Piper said.

"I know, honey. But this is different. We don't have the time, for one thing. And there's only four of us. We're tired. Our air would run out." Any excuse would do.

"Maybe we don't need the tanks," Herald said, hinting, and looking at Piper.

"Look, that was stupid of me earlier," Bridget said, "when I pulled my mask off. We haven't fully tested the samples from this morning. Let's just get back. Mai Ker and the other kids will be in full panic mode soon."

"If they're not already," Pam added.

"I guess," Herald said.

"Can we at least say a prayer for them?" Piper asked, lagging back.

"Kind of too late for that," Bridget said as sensitively as she could.

"Maybe," Piper said. "I'd still like to."

Bridget looked at her. They stopped and faced back toward the camp. The early afternoon sun had broken through the clouds. Sunrays bore down on the iron and tin and wooden graveyard. The day was heating up.

Three of the four expected Piper would start a prayer. But she was silent. After what seemed like two minutes, Pam finally spoke.

"Father in heaven, I pray for all these people who died. And all those we don't even know about. We ask you to keep them in your arms, and be merciful. Keep them in your care until . . ." She was stumped. *Until what?* She didn't know. "Keep them in your care always, amen."

It seemed a good enough prayer. Considering the mix of emotions raging through Pam and Bridget, it was wonderfully simple.

They walked back to the truck in silence and loaded in. Bridget turned the key, but the bear had gone back to sleep. There was one short, quiet snort. The engine wouldn't turn over.

"Oh no," Bridget said with muffled fear. "We don't need this." She looked across the campground. "Not here."

"Try again, Mom," Herald said.

She did. This time there was a brief *click-click-click*, then nothing.

"Now what?" she appealed to Herald.

"Alternator must not be working right," he said. "Didn't charge the battery up enough while we drove."

"Great. How do we get home?"

Herald considered this, a problem he had never before confronted. He shook his head.

"Dunno. Unless we can find a better battery." He looked at the floorboard, then out across the campground. "Let me get the tools."

They all got out again. Herald took the toolbox from the truck bed, looked around, and started for the two big military trucks parked in the camp area. Bridget went, too, checking the gauge on his air tank as they walked.

"We only have half-an-hour on these tanks. Those next ones are the last, Herald."

He nodded and kept walking, trying to breathe normally. They reached the first truck. He got the hood latch to unlock but fumbled trying to get the hood up. It crashed back, almost eating his right hand. Bridget made him step back. She felt around through the rusted steel grill, found the latch and raised the hood. With Herald's help, she propped it up.

The battery was gone.

They went to the other military truck. Same thing. No battery.

"What's with everybody hiding the dang batteries?" Herald said, smacking his lips with irritation.

"Well, like the guards did, that was smart," Bridget said. "If they're disconnected and stored, they're more likely to last."

"Gotta be here somewhere," Herald said beginning another search.

They scavenged around for several minutes and finally discovered the battery shoved in a side compartment near the rear of the truck.

"Can you carry it?" Bridget asked.

"Sure. Let's see if the other one has one."

"You're a smart young man," she said.

"Wonder where I get that from?" he grinned.

Two batteries would be like insurance. They went to other military truck. Not bothering under the hood, they found the battery in the same compartment at the rear of that truck.

"These guys were definitely military," Bridget said. "Everything like clockwork."

"Like what?" Herald asked, in the dark, as they started back with the two batteries.

"Just a figure of speech, son. When we had mechanical clocks."

They got back to their truck. Bridget set the extra battery in the bed. Herald brushed off the terminals of his and switched it out with the old battery, which they also threw in the bed. Bridget got in and tried the key. The truck fired up almost instantly.

"Hard to believe that battery was made by the lowest bidder," she said nebulously.

"What?" Herald asked, again confused.

"It's just—"

"I know," he said, stopping her with a hand. "A figure

of speech."

Pam kept looking back over her shoulder as they drove up out of the shallow river valley that held the remains of the reservoir and the refugees.

Wonder if we could have saved them? she kept asking herself. It troubled her for miles, until they reached Las Animas. Then she realized there were probably more lost here, even in this tiny community, than had come to the Solarium that dreadful day. It hit her hard that just a few miles from here, they themselves had survived.

The truck bumbled along the broken road. Because she couldn't help herself, her mind began to wander further, to the larger towns and cities in the region. Her brain, resisting, began to do the math. The final magnitude of the whole catastrophe came into focus for Pam in a way it never had before, while she was cooped up INSIDE. Thousands. Millions. Billions. She felt awe, but mostly anger, much as her little girl had felt earlier. Pam remembered. She had prayed to God during those dark days that he would do something. Just a few minutes ago, they had prayed again to the same God, the one who let it all happen. Or, worse, made it all happen. She was confused like never before, and almost in despair. Then she thought of Jimmy.

"I just don't understand," she muttered.

The other three looked at her. Piper put a hand on her arm.

"What Mommy?"

She looked at the children. She thought about what they had just seen. She couldn't deal with it here.

"Never mind," she said. "Just thinking out loud."

Bridget guided them slowly west again along the river road. The sun played hide and seek behind dark, mountainous thunderheads, then disappeared completely. Lightning began to strike a few miles west of them. As they eased along on four low tires, one bolt struck violently not far beyond the Solarium, whose domes they could see again.

At almost the same moment, a violent wind struck the front of the truck. By the time they reached the sharp left bend in the road that would lead toward the complex, a new horror jumped up to meet them. Bright orange and yellow flames cloaked in dense brown, roiling smoke was being fanned toward the Solarium by the violent winds. A wildfire had been unleashed.

"Must have been lightning," Bridget said, anxious and trying to drive faster. "We've gotta hustle."

Piper let out a tearful cry. She had seen a few similar fires from INSIDE, off in the distance. She had never been this close—and exposed.

Bridget gunned the engine and hoped the tires would stay with the rims.

"Kids, you gotta help us get those air tanks in the back into the building as quick as we can! Can't let the fire get them. Could explode."

"OK," was their simultaneous response.

"What about the other battery we found?" Herald asked.

"Have to leave it. Won't be time." She pictured the next couple of hours. "Truck may explode, anyway."

The gas tank was still nearly full. The wildfire flames, like a stampede of yellow, angry, bucking stallions, were bearing down on Solarium-3.

"We've never had a fire come this close before!" Pam nearly shouted as the growling roar of the fire approached.

They were all thinking the same things. *Can we get INSIDE in time? Will the smoke get us? Will the pods stand the heat?*

Herald pictured the burned-out hotel they had seen. What would happen to the Solarium if struck by raging fire? He tried not to imagine it.

They made it to the complex moments ahead of the flames but the wind-driven smell was far ahead of the fire. The rancid odor pushed into their masks. Bridget keyed her radio as they were rolling to a stop.

"Mai Ker, quick, open up!"

There was no answer.

"Mai Ker," Bridget called again. "Where are you?"

Several moments of silence ensued. Finally, Mai Ker's voice came, rushed and breathy.

"Sorry, you guys. I was with the kids. They're afraid of the fire. It's never been this close!"

"Not as close as it is out here!" Bridget yelled. "Get the kids to number one and pull those seals. We've gotta beat the smoke!"

The truck slid to a stop almost slamming into the doors of the Visitors Center. Each grabbed two air tanks from the back of the truck and bolted through the doors. Piper dragged hers.

At the last second, Herald set his tanks down, ran to the pickup bed and grabbed the battery they had gotten from the other military truck. The wind-driven flames were licking up dead foliage not a hundred yards away. The heat washed over Herald, oppressive and threatening, beginning to suck up the oxygen in the air around him. His mask saved him. Luckily, not carrying pure oxygen, the mask didn't catch fire.

He flung the battery like a rectangular bowling ball across the tiled floor of the entryway. It skidded clear across the floor and smacked against the bottom of a display case opposite the door. He grabbed his two tanks again and with two free fingers pulled the glass doors shut behind him. He barreled toward his three teammates.

Bridget stood dumbfounded watching this, all of which happened in four or five seconds that ran in slow motion. She grabbed Herald by an arm as he ran by, stopped him, and held him.

"Please-don't-do-that-again!" she growled through her mask.

He smiled through his.

"OK. I'm OK! Let's go!"

They rushed through the Visitors Center and down the long glass hall toward Pod 1. The glass walls were vibrating from the intense heat. Herald ripped the seals off the door into the pod before the others could even set down their tanks.

"Go!" Bridget called.

Mai Ker unlocked the outer door. They dragged themselves and the equipment in.

"Seal!"

"Sealing," Mai Ker said, still breathless. As quickly as her monitors showed the outer door locked she keyed the air purge sequence.

"You OK?" she called, crying. Her hands nervously pounded the console.

"Yeah," Bridget said, winded. "Did we beat the smoke? What does the screen say?" They felt the air change around them.

"Screen says it's clear," Mai Ker answered.

The warm, moist air of the Solarium was refilling the pod.

"Go," Bridget said to Herald, who ripped the seals from the inner door. He turned, without it being suggested, and began taping them into the cracks of the outer door.

INSIDE Nathaniel and Braden were yanking seals off. Even Sing, against her instincts, had run to help.

"Unlocked," Mai Ker said, gulping her breaths.

They pushed through the door, slammed it, and helped the kids replace the inner seals.

In the scramble, all four of the party had pulled the tape loose around their air masks. Sing was the first to notice.

"Herald!" she cried at her husband. "Your mask!"

He was too winded to do much but gasp.

"I'm OK," he managed between short breaths. "I'm OK." He made a futile attempt to press the sweaty tape back onto his face.

"Well, you don't need it now, dummy!" Sing hollered, sounding very much like her mother.

She grabbed him, pulled the mask off and kissed him. Then she held onto him for dear life as if he might vaporize at any second.

16

Sunday, December 1st, 18 (NC)

The fire had raged around them for nearly an hour yesterday afternoon until the last scraps of burnable fuel on the dead prairie had been lapped up, consumed and reduced to fine, black ash. The flames surrounded the pods so completely that nothing was visible beyond the conflagration around them. It was like being inside a huge furnace as everything around was consumed but they were left untouched.

"Like those three young men," Piper remarked last evening after the flames had departed. "In the Bible."

None of the others knew the story she meant.

At one point, the flames became so brilliant and intense, it looked as if the sun itself had erupted through the atmosphere, crashed to earth and was hammering away at their plastic haven trying to take them, too.

Remarkably, only a small amount of the intense heat passed through the inch-thick Stellar panels. The stuff was so dense and hardened that it not only repelled heat but, as best they could tell from INSIDE, it remained completely unscathed by the destructive fire.

As the wildfire raged, the Solarians had spent the crawling minutes huddled together in the main tent, uncertain if the pods could survive the heat.

The children wondered if these might be their last moments together. They looked at each other with new eyes, as if seeing for the first time. Each face, each feature, each expression, each lock of hair was brought into an intensified focus, driven by the fear that they might never see each other again.

The four explorers bravely tried to distract the others, and themselves, by sharing bits and pieces of what they had seen OUTSIDE. Herald and Piper were careful to omit details they knew would upset the two youngest.

AS THE fire raged, it raised again the question of fixing the crack in the roof of Pod 10. Whatever the usual air pressures were doing INSIDE and OUT, the fire changed the dynamics, at least for its duration. At the peak of the blaze, as flames and heat pushed the smoke up and over the tops of the pods, Pam saw steam, or smoke, or a little of both, seeping in through the crack. She got Bridget and Mai Ker. They watched it through binoculars for several minutes.

"The heat is creating more pressure out there. It's forcing the leak," Mai Ker said.

"Could make the crack worse," Bridget said.

"Could. We've got to do something, Bridget."

"I know. I don't think the air's that bad, anymore but—"

"But we don't know if the fire changed that, either," Mai Ker pointed out.

"I know that, too. But if it did, it was only localized. And temporary. Shouldn't affect the wider atmosphere."

"So?" Pam asked.

"We have to fix it."

"Our air?"

"The leak."

"Tonight?" Pam was horrified.

"Tomorrow. We'll go out first thing. Herald and I are going to have to climb."

"You?" Mai Ker asked.

"You wanna go?" Bridget asked curtly.

"No," Mai Ker said reluctantly. She looked at Pam, then Bridget. "Thought you were terrified of heights."

Bridget looked away, but not up.

"I am."

"You shouldn't try it, Bridget. Maybe I—"

"Nope. Herald and I can do it. He could probably do it on his own. But I'm gonna help."

Once the fire died out and only a few embers smoldered here and there, Bridget and Mai Ker did a quick walking inspection of all the pods. After just a few minutes, it became apparent there was no damage. Whether the project planners had accounted for wildfires—not an uncommon thing in this region—or whether by some other providence, the complex was so solid that the fire had not even left scorch marks on the OUTSIDE of the pods.

Whatever rain had been approaching had been driven away by the intense ground heat of the fire. Bits of blown ash danced up across the pod tops here and there like large blackened insects seeking non-existent prey. The entire landscape around them, having lain dead for years, was now further devastated by the lightning-sparked fire. If ever there had been a vivid image of Hell, they found themselves in the very center of it.

"Everything is dead," Mai Ker commented to Bridget, looking out after the fire had burned itself out. "Smoke and ashes. But here we are."

A grayish striped kitten came prancing by them, thinking one or both were large deposits of food. It chewed playfully at Bridget's pant leg. She captured it and cuddled it. It tried to leap away but after a few failed attempts it succumbed and snuggled itself against her bosom. Who needs food?

Mai Ker was still ruminating.

"No one would believe this, would they? If it was made up," she remarked.

"No. When I was little," Bridget told her, "I had a kitten this color. Used to hold her on my lap when Mom read to me at bedtime." She looked at Mai Ker. "You're right. If mom had told me this story, I'd have said,

'Mommy, that could never happen.'"

They were quiet for a few moments. The kitten meowed. Bridget kissed it and let it run away.

"And here we are," Mai Ker said again.

Bridget just nodded. She had no answers. She had tried at different times to pray about it, to seek answers from God, this God she so little understood. But there was only a wall of silence. Either he couldn't speak, or she couldn't hear.

WITH THE fire past and their nerves calmed, they had managed to make supper last evening. The four who had gone OUTSIDE were exhausted but also starving. The fright and worry of the fire had heightened their hunger.

When they had all finished eating, Pam brought the newspapers they had retrieved from the campground into the living room. She quietly suggested the adults should read them alone and excuse the children to play.

Mai Ker objected. She said whatever they might learn, they should learn together. It was just as important for the children—maybe more so, she said—to understand what happened in those final days. The kids had not experienced what she, Pam and Bridget had lived through. They needed to know.

Sing agreed. She told them her hunger to know things was just as strong as theirs.

Bridget frowned but agreed. All the children were allowed to stay while the moms read from the newspapers.

"Sounds like it was pretty awful," Herald said after one item described mass killings in the suburbs of St. Louis in the final weeks. Thousands had already died from the air, mostly the elderly, the sick, and many small children. But according to the article, large roaming gangs, some young adults, some older adults, went on rampages several nights in a row, killing indiscriminately.

"How could they do that?" Piper wondered, a deeply disturbed look in her eyes.

"Fear," Bridget said. "Not knowing what was facing them. I wouldn't do that. But I can understand it."

"I can't," Mai Ker said. "Nothing could provoke me to do something like that. Go around killing. I would just lay down and die quietly."

"They weren't ready," Pam remarked, after reading one article silently to herself and shaking her head. She spoke as if to herself. "Lot of people never think about death. Their own. Or what's coming next. And if there would be consequences."

"Consequences?" Nathaniel asked, bringing her back into the room. "Like when I hit Braden?" he asked innocuously.

"Yes. Consequences. For how they had lived." Pam shook her head as if considering some impenetrable mystery. "But these people," she said, looking down at the paper, "they *knew*. Death was right there. Staring them in the face." She kept shaking her head slowly as if it was controlled by a small electric motor. "No way out. And still not ready."

"Would be terrible," Sing said.

Pam nodded toward her.

"Maybe all the killing, maybe it was—I don't know— a final rebellion. Against what was inevitable."

"Like that night, all the bombs?" Herald asked.

"Yes."

"I don't know what 'inevedouble' means," Braden said.

"It means a thing is going to happen," Pam explained, "and you're powerless to stop it."

"Aren't we powerless to stop most things?" he asked innocently.

Pam looked at Bridget and Mai Ker. The three shared a look.

"Yes, honey," Bridget said. "We are."

"Was Daddy ready?" Nathaniel asked timidly.

It came out of nowhere. Pam didn't want to answer. Bridget wasn't sure.

With only a slight hesitation, Mai Ker answered.

"Yes, Nate. Daddy was ready." She considered it more deeply and smiled with a newly discovered relief. "If anyone was ever ready, your daddy was."

There were other stories. Accounts of brutality, robbery, assaults of every kind. As things degenerated OUTSIDE, from what the writers said, the question of what was the "human level" of things became very fuzzy. Pointless editorials, hoping to avoid conclusions, held forth on what was humane, or right, or justified, under the circumstances.

But one editor was blunt.

"Man was made a little lower than the angels. I fear he now has sunk into an abyss, a pit lower than any brute animal could call home."

Rational behavior, according to the papers, had become impossible for many. Animal instincts for survival had taken over, stealing food or water, brutalizing anyone who stood in the way.

"They weren't ready," Pam repeated.

Sing picked up a paper. She read aloud a bizarre story of a woman who went around her nearly deserted town with a large shopping cart, piling up not just food but everything she could lay hands on. Someone found her body among floor-to-ceiling piles of stuff in her house, a personal warehouse of stolen goods. "Senseless," the writer commented, "but there it is." The story ended with this: "The neighbor who found her body lugged back home an empty planter she had stolen off his porch. He died two days later."

Nathaniel listened with a furrowing brow.

"Those people were pretty weird," he said. "Why did she want all that stuff?" he genuinely wanted to know.

His mom offered an insight.

"Some people had no purpose in life. All those things made them feel important, somehow" Mai Ker said.

"I knew people like that," Pam said. "Their possessions possessed them."

"Sad," Herald said.

"No," his wife corrected him, tossing the paper aside, "sick."

"Guess people didn't matter anymore," Bridget commented vaguely, her mind somewhere else. "Relationships falling apart," she added. "That was nothing new." She was remembering the older boyfriend who got her pregnant when she was 15, then ditched her and left town in his expensive new car. "Couldn't hang on to each other. But they sure hung on to their junk."

She remembered how she had been forced to give her baby up for adoption. Her heart wrenched, thinking of all the children who had died OUTSIDE at the end, many ignored or rejected by parents consumed with trying to keep themselves alive. Of all the repulsive horrors of those days, that must have been the worst.

Everyone was quiet for a time. Gloom had settled over them like an unwelcome visitor. Pam regretted picking up the newspapers, now. They needed to move on, not keep looking back.

"Well, I can't stand this anymore," she said. "Let's get ready for bed. Herald and his mom have a big job tomorrow."

She met no resistance.

Piper was especially quiet as she got ready for bed. Since Sing and Herald had gotten the tent she and Sing had shared for so long, Piper now bunked in with her mom. Even before he died, Jimmy had given them their privacy here.

Piper buttoned up the long shirt that was her nightgown, a Clayton Block hand-me-down. She reflected on what they heard from the newspapers, especially all the neglected children who had been lost. It sounded so foreign to her, having been raised by parents whose prime concern, always, was the children's safety and health. She couldn't imagine what those kids had gone through.

"Mommy?"

"Yes, sweetie?"

"Do you love me?"

Pam's heart swelled. She gave a contented sigh.

"More than you can know."

BRIDGET ROSE from bed this morning already thinking about the project for the day. She had had a restless night. In addition to the disquieting evening reading, she realized while trying to fall asleep that in their rush to beat the fire INSIDE yesterday they had forgotten their new air, water and soil samples. These were still on the counter in the Visitors Center. The heat of the fire around the building might have altered them. They would have to get new.

The air, scourged by yesterday's fire, was back to its usual color this morning, so she felt safe enough about going back out.

As she had tried to sleep, she woke repeatedly, worried about the climb. It would strain her but she was still pretty fit. Day-to-day life in the Solarium provided sometimes intense exercise. But she would not let Herald climb on his own, even if she would be mainly moral support.

At breakfast this morning she discussed plans with Mai Ker and Pam. They decided, if time and energy permitted, they would bury the bodies of the two guards. They felt an obligation. But they would be buried OUTSIDE. No coffins, just simple markers so the burials would be recognizable to any future generation. If any survived. They knew only their first names from the little plastic nameplates on their S-3 jackets.

"That'll have to do. God knows who they are," Pam

said.

"You need to get out early," Mai Ker said. "It's sunny today. You want to stay ahead of the heat as far as you can. Could get hot up on top."

Bridget took Herald and Nathaniel to gather the climbing equipment and assemble it near Pod 1. The climbing harness Jimmy had used was still lying by itself on a shelf in the shed in #13. She set it aside and got two others from storage. They collected every hundred-foot length of rope they could find. It would all go out on two carts. This was trial and error. They had no idea how they would use the ropes or how much they would need.

Pam, Mai Ker and the other kids made up two new sets of door seals. In the flurry yesterday, they had partly shredded several of them.

The plan was that Bridget and Herald would carry the two bodies up from the basement for Pam and Nathaniel to bury, then make the climb of #10. Piper would help rig ropes for the climb.

"Handling a couple of mummies might do Herald some good," Pam said.

"Maybe settle him down a little," his mom agreed.

"Just don't let him play around. You know how he is," Mai Ker said.

Sing would stay back with Mai Ker and Braden. She was still afraid of going OUTSIDE, not to mention being very squeamish. She didn't want to see any more bodies. With her morning sickness she needed no help to get nauseated.

Mai Ker would again man the control console in the Comm. Center. Sing and Braden would handle the inner door seals.

All was ready a little before 10:00 o'clock.

"Be careful," Sing said, giving Herald a kiss where they stood by the door of #1. "Don't be careless. Like yesterday."

If only she knew, he thought. Thankfully, his mom

had not told the others about his last-minute dash for the spare battery.

He smiled. He enjoyed this fawning over him. He gave her a hug.

"I wanna see our baby, too, you know," he grinned. "Don't you overwork yourself in here, either. Worrying, I mean."

The OUTSIDE team went into #1, the air was transitioned, the seals placed. They moved out, sealed the outer door from the OUTSIDE and went to work.

They all wore air masks again. They were as big a nuisance as before. But Pam and Mai Ker had insisted. They brought out one spare tank each for Pam, Nathaniel and Piper. They took two extras each for Herald and Bridget. Herald remembered how hard he was breathing after his short test climb on #2. He didn't want to run out. If a tank ran low, they could pull another up with a rope.

They reached the front doors of the Visitors Center. The truck they had used yesterday was sitting there. The updraft of the fire racing up the pods had apparently protected it from direct onslaught. The paint was badly scorched and bubbled but it seemed otherwise intact. The low tires proved a blessing. Had they been full, the burgeoning pressure from the heat might have blown them.

Bridget tried the key. Miraculously, it started. She backed it away toward the side of the parking lot out of their way, alongside Clayton's old junker.

She and Herald went back in the building. Mai Ker unlocked the doors into the basement and Control Room. They carried the dead up. Mummified, the bodies seemed nearly as light as the clothing. The trick was trying to avoid bumping into doorjambs or stair railings. The bodies were incredibly fragile. They wanted to bury them as intact as possible.

The team took the bodies to a spot on a low rise just east of the Visitors Center. Yesterday morning it bore the long dead, dried remains of tall prairie grasses, yucca plants and a few small bushes. This morning it was black ash and dust. Appropriate enough, Pam thought, for a graveyard.

They searched around for the grave of whomever it was Paul Bishop's group had buried out here, intending to keep the graves together. But if there had been any marker it, too, had been consumed in the fire.

Bridget, Herald and Piper wheeled the two carts with their tanks and climbing gear along the sidewalks circling the pods until they reached the south side of #10.

The thing didn't look quite as mammoth from out here. Maybe it was because they would be climbing on a solid surface instead of dangling in thin air like high-wire artists. They set the four extra air tanks by the base of the pod and rigged them up in slings so they could be quickly attached to a pull rope if needed. They didn't know if they would need them, or how soon. They wanted them ready.

Pam and Nathaniel meanwhile dug the two graves as deep as they could with a couple of shovels and a small pick ax. Pam realized there was no need to go very deep. Just enough to protect the bodies from wind and weather. The old rule—6 feet down—had been to protect bodies from prowling animals, and prowling grave robbers. They didn't need to worry about either.

She and Nathaniel carefully lowered each body in its grave. They just as carefully covered it over with dirt and small rock. Pam tamped the tops down as best she could when they were done.

"Will they be happier now?" Nathaniel asked as he started placing the rough name markers they had made. He steadied them with some larger rocks.

"Hum," Pam said. "Hope so. Wherever they are."

"I think it was nice. That we buried them."

"Really?" she asked. This seemed so out of character for Nathaniel.

"Yeah. After we buried Daddy, it just seems the right thing. I'd feel bad. Them just sitting down there in the basement forever."

She almost said, "Honey, the basement won't last forever," until she realized the implication about the Solarium itself. Instead, she gave Nate a hug, thanked him for being so thoughtful and hoped it might stick. *Maybe there's the beginning of a heart in the child after all,* she smiled.

She put an arm around Nate and said a quiet prayer over the graves. Then they walked around the pods to where Bridget and Herald were getting ready for the climb.

Bridget was practicing with the suction cups on the bottom of the pod wall. She was focusing her thoughts, trying to shake off the nerves. She didn't look up, even now.

"We'll get as high as we can freehand," Bridget explained, "then we'll each throw a rope as far as we can around each side of the pod. Piper, you and Nate go around each way and tie off the ends of the ropes. With those steel stakes," she pointed. "When you get 'em staked down, we'll tie another rope between them on this side. Kind of," she hesitated to say it, "a catch line. That we can grab. Just in case."

She didn't need to say any more. Everyone got the picture.

"We'll tether to each other. And we'll each trail a line behind us," Herald said, "to pull things up."

They had gone over all this earlier but Bridget wanted to be sure everyone remembered their assignments.

"Yup," said Nathaniel with a burst of energy.

This part looked much more fun than what he had just done. He brushed his frizzy hair back trying to make himself feel stronger. Piper watched, smiling.

Herald and Bridget started up, using the movable suction cups to grip the pod as they ascended. The fine ash left on the plastic by the fire yesterday made it slippery and much more unpredictable than during Herald's test climb on Friday. They edged up inches at a time, making sure the suction cups were tight before pulling against them. They moved slowly, cautiously. There could be no more mistakes, no more mishaps.

It was slow going at first, but once they developed their technique with the suction cups they began to move along more quickly.

"Tell me if you get tired," Herald said.

"I'm tired. Keep going. Tell you when I can't go another inch."

"OK."

The memory of Jimmy's fall haunted Bridget with every step. But the sloping arc of the pod made this climbing much more endurable, and safer. The thing was, not to slip.

Herald had completely blocked thoughts of Jimmy's death out of his mind. He was still grieving but had reached a stage where he just refused to think about it. For the present, at least. There was too much else to do, too much else to think about. There was Sing, and their baby.

Bridget moved like an aged grasshopper up the pod. Herald was not much better. His arms were already tired. At about 60 feet, they rested for several minutes. They were thirsty but didn't bring water bottles up because of the air masks. Breathing the bottled air left a dry, powdery taste in their mouths but there was nothing to be done about it.

Twenty feet further up they decided to try to throw the safety ropes around the pod. Bridget threw hers. It didn't come anywhere close to the top but it didn't need to. Tension from the far side, once it was tied to the catch rope between this one and the one Herald just threw, would hold it secure. Her rope landed, its end just above the ground between Pods 11 and 12.

Herald threw his rope.

"OK," Bridget called down to Pam. "Send 'em around."

Piper and Nathaniel hurried along the walks around opposite sides of the complex. Piper reached Bridget's rope and staked it to the ground.

Herald had thrown his wildly like a hurried shortstop trying to throw out a runner at first base. The rope slid too far sideways.

"Try again," Bridget said, enjoying the extra rest. "Needs to land between number three and number eight."

He pulled the rope back into careful coils and threw it again. This time it landed in the right area and trailed off toward the ground. Nathaniel tried to reach it. He couldn't.

"Shoot!'' Nathaniel cried out.

Herald could just see him through the pod.

"What's wrong?" he called.

"Can't reach it," Nathaniel hollered.

"Crap," Herald said. "What do we do, Mom?"

"How far up is it?"

"I dunno. Maybe 12, 15 feet."

"Can he climb that far?"

"Nate, can you climb up to it?"

"OK," Nate called back.

"What's wrong up there?" Pam was hollering from the ground.

"It's OK, Auntie Pam," Nathaniel called at the top of his lungs over the podwalks. "I can do it. Like climbing a tree."

"Not on your life, young man!" Pam yelled back. But she couldn't leave her post.

"Pam," Bridget called down, "calm down! It's not that far. He can do it!"

Pam was stomping, spitting out choice words just loud enough to be heard. It was not her child, but she knew Mai Ker would never allow it. What if Mai Ker could see him, from INSIDE?

"Piper," Pam finally yelled over the pods, "go help Nate!" She yelled so loud it nearly blew her mask off.

"Good idea," Bridget smiled to Herald up on the pod.

The sun was climbing, too, and the temperature of the plastic was rising. It wasn't unbearable. It was also not fun.

"Be careful," Pam called over the podwalks to Piper and Nathaniel.

Piper, having run around the back of the pods 11, 9 and 8, reached Nathaniel. She boosted him on her shoulders. He now weighed more than she did so it was no easy trick. Nate scrambled freehand 15 feet up the side of the pod. It was steepest here, near the bottom. His foot slipped in the ash and he tumbled back down, landing like a concrete block on his back. It knocked the wind out of him. Herald saw but just looked away, and grimaced. Pam's view was obstructed by a shed in the south part of #10.

"Don't you say a word!" Nathaniel ordered Piper as he regained his breath and she helped him up.

"Toughie," she grinned.

She boosted him again. He scrambled again. His fall had wiped some of the ash down with him. He reached the end of the dangling rope and tossed it to Piper. She quickly staked it down.

"Pretty good team," she said as she stood.

"Pretty, at least," he smiled at her.

"What's happening?" Pam was hollering again.

"Good!" Herald called down. "Done."

The rest break was over. Herald called for Pam to send the middle rope up. It was a hundred feet long and there was only 20 feet between him and his mom but they didn't want to cut any rope. He pulled it up with his trailing line and tossed an end to Bridget. They tied it to the other two ropes, creating a kind of papoose sling around the giant pod.

Mai Ker and Braden had moved into #10 to watch the climb from INSIDE. Against her better judgment, Sing finally joined them. Pam was right. Mai Ker had cringed when Nathaniel started up the pod, not to mention when he fell. But he was on the ground again and she was breathing normally. Sing was not.

It was nerve-wracking for Sing, watching Herald climb. She found herself praying, words that just seemed to come. Someone needed to hold onto them. She couldn't.

The two climbers began to move further up. As the pod arced toward the top, the incline gradually decreased and became more manageable. But everyone knew if either fell, the sling rope stretched below them would be little help. It was so tight against the pod it would be very hard to catch—on the way by.

They only had to reach the crack which was about 15 feet below the peak. They were climbing straight toward it now, and closer to each other, and would reach it in another five minutes. Bridget closed in alongside Herald. She stopped and reached over to check the gauge on his tank.

"Fifty-five percent" she said. "It'll be close. May have to change. Gonna be tricky switching them up here."

"Let's just see," Herald said. He pulled the top of his mom's tank toward him to see her gauge. "Just over fifty percent, Mom."

"Keep going," she said. She was huffing steadily, but wouldn't quit. They were too close.

They reached the crack. Bridget was anxious to make the repair and get down. She got on her hands and knees and laid her face just above the surface. She examined the crack. She could see it was broken clear through.

"What I thought," she said to him. "When we saw the smoke getting in yesterday."

She pulled her mask loose, putting her nose just over the crack. Despite the light breeze blowing, and the still-burnt stench from the fire, she could just detect a filament of INSIDE air seeping out. The smell of its living organisms was pungent compared to the smell of the dead world OUTSIDE.

"Pressure must be a little higher INSIDE. It's pushing out instead of sucking in."

"Which is why our air hasn't changed much."

"Prob'ly. Except during the fire."

Herald looked out toward the east where they had been yesterday.

"Won't have that problem again, Mom. Nothin' left to burn."

"Let's get after it."

They called back and forth to the ground. Using the rope Bridget had trailed from her harnesses on the way up, Pam sent the Stellar patch up. Piper and Nathaniel had rejoined her. They tied a bucket full of glue tubes and torches to Herald's rope. He pulled it up.

He and Bridget were about 20 feet shy of the crest of the pod, so the pod was nearly flat here. He was able to set the bucket on the pod roof without it sliding. Bridget held the patch that was still tied to the end of her rope, the same patch Jimmy had cut for INSIDE. In her backpack, Bridget had brought a bottle of chemical cleaner and two large rags. She laid the patch on the pod and held it with one hand. With the other she helped Herald scrub the pod surface around the break.

The cleaner dried quickly in the breeze. She took the patch piece out of its sling. It was much larger than the 16-inch crack. They smeared glue on it and flipped it over into place. Then, trying not to burn each other, they heated the whole area with the small propane torches. The glue thinned and spread, dripping out here and there at the edges. They killed the torches and watched. The glue solidified quickly.

"Great stuff," Herald said.

"Should be good. The glue'll harden as it cools."

Bridget inspected the edges as Herald stood up.

Until this moment they had been so utterly focused on climbing safely and getting the patch on that they had noticed little except the plastic beneath their feet. As Herald stretched his tired, straining back, he looked out. He looked east again where he could see the tops of some buildings in Las Animas. Then he turned west, the direction the fire had come from.

"Oh my gosh—" he uttered with true astonishment.

"What?" Bridget said with mild panic, quickly looking up at him.

"Look," he said in wonder.

She stood, following his eyes toward the west. There was nothing that astonished her. Then came the realization.

"The mountains," she said. "I forgot. You've never been able to see them, have you?"

"Just pictures."

"Pretty, huh?"

"Yeah. Except they look so small."

"Far away."

"But they're beautiful. Standing against the horizon like that." His eyes ran along the range. "That big one, there. What's that one?"

"That's Pikes Peak," she said. "By where Colorado Springs is—was."

"What's wrong?" Pam yelled up.

"Nothing!" Bridget smiled. "You should see them up close," she told Herald.

"Can we?" he asked excitedly.

"We can't."

He was still wiping sweat from his forehead and arms.

"Why not, Mom?"

"It's just a long way. No reason to go."

He accepted this, though with obvious disappointment. Standing out here, high up, he tried to imagine all the beauty of the former world, as it once was. All the things he had never seen. And never would.

"Too bad," he said.

"Yes," she said.

He looked down at the newly installed patch.

"Should we caulk the edges?" he asked.

"Not a bad idea."

"Not all my ideas are bad."

She smiled.

"Just squeeze a bead of glue around the edges. That'll work," she said.

Her back was more than tired. It was throbbing almost as it had in childbirth. She stood there atop the pod and watched her son. She remembered his birth. She ached. She was feeling old.

"OK. I think we're done," her son said.

She checked his air gauge before he stood. It hovered at 42 percent. Hers was at 34 percent. She really couldn't face the prospect of dragging new tanks up.

"Let's try it," she said. "We won't breathe as hard going down. If we have to change tanks, I'd rather do it closer down, anyway. Not so far to pull."

"After you," he said graciously.

They lowered the gear bucket to the ground team. Then backing, feet first and using the suction cups, they began the slow, careful descent. They didn't breathe as hard, but it was just as tiring. The incline increased the lower they got and this put more strain on their already sore muscles. They were now below the safety rig, which they just left in place.

At about 45 feet, Bridget's left foot slipped out from under her. She fell flat against the steep pod and began to slide. Instinctively, she slapped the loose suction cup in her right hand down hard. Herald at the same instant lunged at her, holding himself with the grip in his left hand. He just reached her but was off balance. It was now he who was in danger of losing his footing, or his grip.

INSIDE, Sing looked up in horror. She spun her face

away. Mai Ker held her, still looking up OUTSIDE.

Pam let out a muffled shriek as Piper and Nathaniel grabbed each other, feeling like this should help Bridget.

But the climbers were secure. Herald managed to cross-brace a leg over his mom's back to steady himself and help keep her from sliding more. He pulled his head close to hers.

"Yeah?" he asked her.

"Yeah," she huffed, trying to control herself.

Slowly she brought herself to her hands and knees. She caught her breath. Herald remained straddled but unmoved.

"OK?"

"OK," she said.

"I think it's OK," Mai Ker told Sing INSIDE. Sing still would not look.

Bridget locked both suction cups tightly onto the pod near her waist. Herald moved his leg away and she began to lower herself down again.

"Should have tied onto the stupid safety line when we got down to it," she said, highly irritated with herself.

"Yeah," he said. "Stupid us."

"Runs in the family, I think," she laughed, trying to regain a little composure.

Their arms and legs began quaking as they neared the bottom and they were breathing hard. Soon they were on the ground, hugged by Pam and Nathaniel and Piper. Mai Ker, Sing and Braden were vicariously hugging them from INSIDE. Sing had been crying the last 10 minutes.

Pam checked their air tanks. Herald's was just over 9 percent. Bridget's was at 3 percent.

"Quick, kids, new tanks," Pam ordered.

They made the quick change, gathered the loose gear and ropes, and headed back around the south end of the complex to the Visitors Center.

"The samples," Pam reminded them.

"Yeah. We need new air samples," Bridget said. "The

heat from the fire might have affected the ones from yesterday."

"You know, Mom, we forgot."

"What?"

"Yesterday. At the reservoir. We went there to get water samples."

They looked at each other. With the scene they had come upon at John Martin, they had completely forgotten water samples.

"Doesn't matter," Bridget said. "We'll get more from the river."

They collected fresh samples and got back INSIDE about 1:30.

Everyone decided on a nap. Bridget and Herald were exhausted, the rest were exhausted from watching.

Sing would not look at Herald or talk to him, and refused to go into their tent. She went, instead, to her mom's tent and laid down on the loveseat. She was wrung out. She slept hard.

Everyone slept well into the afternoon. It was quiet throughout the tents except for Pam's light snore. Mai Ker was the first to awake.

She went into the living room area and sat. She stared at the pile of newspapers still lying on the coffee table. She looked through some again. The solitude and quiet made the reading even more eerie and tragic. As she sat alone, reading of all the devastation, one article caught her eye. She read it slowly.

Bridget heard Mai Ker stirring. Still tired, she got up and joined Mai Ker in the living room.

"What'cha reading?"

"This must have been it."

"What?" Bridget asked.

"This one, from St. Louis. May 25th that year. See?"

She handed her the paper. Bridget read the headline aloud.

"Corporate Heads Ponder Fate Of Researchers." She

read the lead. "Executives of the Lifeline/New World Exploration Corporation have been discussing the fate of five remaining researchers inside the Solarium-3 complex in southeast Colorado."

"Wow. Like they cared."

"You know it wasn't like that, Bridget."

"I still resent it that they kept us in the dark so long."

"I know. Keep reading."

Bridget silently read a brief description of the Solarium. "The facility houses a sealed, self-contained ecosystem designed to test the possibility of survival in such a complex on other planets."

"See?" Mai Ker said. "If the internet was still up, or they saw this story somewhere, it would have been easy for Bishop and his people to figure out our location."

"Yeah," Bridget said. "And they knew we were isolated from the OUTSIDE air."

"That's why they came." Mai Ker looked somber. "You ever have regrets?"

"That we didn't let them in? I sure thought about it yesterday, when we found them by the reservoir," she admitted. "Regrets? No. We did what we had to. I didn't agree with Clayton that day. Remember? But Jimmy and him were right. If we'd opened up and contaminated our air—we wouldn't be here now."

"Or the kids," Mai Ker said.

"See? We can't undo what's done. We might change the future. We can't change the past."

Bridget flopped into a chair.

"I wonder sometimes if we can even change the future."

She let the thought hang. The rest of the family was getting up from their naps. Stomachs were starting to complain. Supper had to be made.

Bridget looked around the table as everyone ate, this tiny band of surviving humanity. She thought about those poor people, the ones they had turned away, dying at that campground. She watched their own precious children.

Had they done the right thing? Forced to end lives, to make new ones possible? A terrible test.

She still wanted to know why.

Her thoughts were interrupted by her elder son.

"I really would love to see the mountains," he said. "Up close," he appealed with his handsome eyes.

"Too far, honey."

"But, Mom, if the air is almost normal again—like you think—what's the harm? We could make it."

Everyone else's ears tuned in.

A new conversation started about all the possible explorations they could make. They knew there was fuel around. If the air were really OK, distance wouldn't be an issue. The kids got more animated as they talked. Bridget said little.

"Think of what we might find!" Nathaniel was saying. "Like explorers coming to the new world. Remember, Mom? Like Jimmy taught us in history?"

"A little different," Mai Ker said. "Then, there was something to discover."

"We have cameras," Herald said. "We could take pictures. Think how different the whole world might look now. After the bombs. And the quakes."

"Lot of wreckage, I'm guessing," Pam said soberly.

"I still wanna see," Herald insisted.

"Yeah, well, before we make any more trips, you're gonna have to work on the alternator in that truck. We're not going anywhere unless we're sure it's fixed."

"I'll do it the next time we go out, Mom," Herald promised.

TALK ABOUT all the places they might go filled much of the evening. As she listened, even Bridget's curiosity began to build. They had been trapped here so long. Why not venture out a little further? Who could tell what they might discover?

On the other hand, the trips might be futile. What, after all, was there likely to be, except more ghost towns, more bodies, more unalterable sadness?

It was one more dilemma Bridget did not really want to deal with, at least not tonight.

"You kids still have chores before bedtime," she told them. "We need fresh milk for the morning. And I don't think the horses were fed all day, were they?"

The kids all looked at each other, hoping someone else would jump to the tasks. The moms had to cajole to get the work done.

"I'm baking some fresh cookies," Pam said casually to Bridget as the kids went out. "Might come in handy. On the road," she teased.

Mai Ker was torn. She could face each day because she had come to rely on the safety of the Solarium. But wasn't life more than just keeping safe? Living in a see-through vault? She began to feel the urge to explore, too. What lay out there? Destruction, yes. But what else?

Herald kept talking about going all the way toward Colorado Springs, to get close to the mountains. Bridget kept remembering the sickening blasts and ghostly mushroom clouds of that horrible night. Radiation could still be a problem, especially closer to the site of the blasts. Yes, the air was apparently regenerating but what were the radiation levels doing?

The bigger question that began to plague her was more long term. Was there any conceivable future OUTSIDE? If so, it would change everything.

All possibilities had to be considered. Bridget, Mai Ker and Pam were researchers at heart and either by genetics or nurture the children all had the same inquisitiveness. Would the world ever be habitable again? What if there were more earthquakes? The questions once again began to pile up.

As she tried to think this all through, the old question reared its head. How in the world were they ever going to repopulate? Until now, the odds were next to nothing. With Jimmy's death, the answer had dropped off the scale of improbability into the blind realm of the impossible.

HERALD NOTICED Sing gone from the group after supper. She had carefully avoided him since he came back INSIDE. He went searching and found her sitting in a deck chair by the swimming pool. She was singing and humming, something she had not done in the days since her father's death.

He sat in another chair that was not too close. He watched her. He listened.

"What'cha thinkin'?" he asked.

"Not really thinking."

"You're singing again."

"Yes," she said gently, almost ashamed. "Maybe I shouldn't."

"Maybe you should."

He moved his chair closer. They were quiet, except for the soft hum from Sing.

"You remember when Daddy taught us to swim?" She asked, looking at the still pool.

"Sure. He was a great swimmer."

"I miss him. Bad." A few tears forced their way out.

Herald noticed she was cradling her stomach.

"Think it's a boy or a girl?" he asked.

"Girl."

"How do you know?"

"Just do."

"Well, let's say you're right, what do you wanna call her?" Herald asked.

"Kai."

"What?"

"Kai."

"That's a name?" he asked.

"Yes. Came to me last week. I like it. And it sounds

like mom's name."

"Kai," he repeated.

"I looked it up," Sing told him. "It meant 'the sea' in Hawaiian. And in Navajo it meant 'graceful like a willow tree.'"

"Huh." Herald thought for several moments. "Yeah, I like it, too."

He pulled her close, his arm around her expanding waist. He patted her stomach tenderly. Her eyes were closed.

"Sorry about today," he said.

"OK."

"I do love you."

"OK."

"You'll be a good mom."

17

Tuesday, June 10th, 19 (NC)

From that moment by the swimming pool last December, the months of waiting flew by for Herald. They didn't for Sing. As she got bigger and bigger, life became even more of a struggle than her young heart imagined possible. The thought of the little human life inside her felt overwhelming. She would stop what she was doing, and sit, and consider it. An amazing thing.

I was once like that, she considered. She felt her abdomen. Even more amazing.

In the last two months, the sheer physical exertion of her days took its toll. Keeping up her daily chores in her very pregnant condition was exhausting, more demanding than she could have foreseen.

"I don't know how you did it twice," she told her mom on an afternoon in April. She was still two months from delivery.

"I remember. You were hard," Mai Ker told her, "my first. Nate was a little easier. But he was bigger, too. I guess it was about even."

The truth was, the hours around the births of both her children were now a mere blur, a washed-out watercolor memory.

As she spoke of this with Sing, Mai Ker could not help but think of Jimmy. His death was brutal. It cut her deeply. Yet, in one way, it had relieved her. She would not have to go through childbirth again. She felt badly that she felt this way because losing him was such a painful and overbearing loss. An unnamed guilt haunted her.

I shouldn't feel that way, she would tell herself. But the feeling was real. Maybe, she rationalized, it was simply because she was starting to grow older and she would rather hold a grandchild than one of her own. It was very confusing.

Her train of thought was broken by Sing's wavering voice.

"I'm afraid," Sing said.

"I know. We're scared of what we don't know yet. You'll be OK. When it's over, you'll be so glad. You'll know something new then, too."

"What?"

"Like when you first realized you loved Herald."

"Yes?"

"Like that."

Sing digested this. The thought of bearing new life into the world, of holding a newborn in her arms, was such a delightful prospect. And yet, for some reason—a reason she couldn't explain even to herself—she felt no one was worthy of such a grand privilege. To create something entirely new. Something that did not before exist. This, too, overwhelmed her.

OVER THE months since December, the Solarians had made more explorations OUTSIDE. They never strayed too far. They explored towns and farms in about a 30-mile radius but that was as far as they had ventured. Bridget was nervous about getting too far from the Solarium. As much as it felt at times like a cage, it was also home. It was safety. It was what little security they had left.

As he had promised, Herald had fixed the alternator in the guard truck they were using. Working from old diagrams in the archives, he was able to get it apart, work it over, and reinstall it in about three hours. Nathaniel had gone out with him to work on the truck, a small adventure, but all were worth taking, especially for the younger Solarians.

Early on in their explorations, they went back to Las Animas and retrieved the siphon pump and storage tank from the broken-down truck at the old gas station. They installed the tank and pump into the back of the one guard truck that was now their primary transportation. As they explored, they came across other gas storage tanks, mostly on old farms. With the siphon pump, they were able to fuel the truck as often as needed. The gas, having sat so many years in storage tanks, made the engine run rough. It made a lot of knocking noise, but it ran.

Herald kept the truck maintained. He knew how to do a basic tune-up, which helped with the deteriorated fuel. They also discovered several spare truck tires, already mounted on wheels, in a storage shed by the Visitors Center. This was good fortune, since two tires on the other guard truck had ruptured in the wildfire. Herald worked over the second truck, too, in case the first one ever gave out. To be prepared, they always carried a spare battery, the one Herald had rescued from the fire.

They were forced to drive slowly because of the roads. Most of the roads were no better than the one they first took to Las Animas. Even with the air poisoned and radiation disbursing, the general weather patterns over southeastern Colorado had continued to be fairly constant through the years. It was as unpredictable as ever. The radical temperature swings played havoc on the roads. In the winter, it was not unusual to have temperatures all the way from 75 degrees to minus 20 degrees. Whether concrete, asphalt or gravel, the roads had broken down. The pavements were so deteriorated that it was often easier to drive along the dirt shoulders or ditches than to negotiate the roadways themselves. There was no longer any grass to plow through so the ditches were pretty clear sailing.

The air OUTSIDE had not changed markedly since

they had first tested it last November. It seemed stable, the oxygen pressure just a few clicks south of what would have been normal before the catastrophic changes in the first year of the Solarium's life.

Each time they went exploring, Bridget—and she alone—would try going with her air mask off for short periods. If she felt OK, she would try it longer. The others wanted to try but she, as leader, always refused.

The only adverse effect was that she sometimes had a headache later that night. Pam tested Bridget's blood each time when they got back INSIDE. The oxygen level in her blood had usually dipped very slightly, but not to a dangerous level. At times she felt lightheaded. Pam laughed, telling her this was "Bridget normal."

The biggest problem was that because travel OUTSIDE had become so apparently safe, almost routine, it was beginning to distract them—especially the children—from work INSIDE. The daily breakfast mantra had become, "Bridget, can we go OUT today?" Her standard answer, "Oh, let me think about it."

What the kids discovered pretty quickly was that if they worked extra hard at their chores, the next day or perhaps the day after that, Bridget was ready for another adventure.

Sing always remained INSIDE. It was her choice but no one argued. Had she ever suggested going along on one of their little "vacations," as Braden called them, Herald would have raised Cain. It was not only that he didn't want to risk the baby. He didn't want to risk Sing. It was selfish of him, he knew, but fortunately she had no desire to go OUTSIDE anytime soon. Herald was able to hide this selfishness behind a mask of love.

EVERYONE WAS working INSIDE today, except Sing. She was moping around in the tents. It was just after 8:00 a.m. She didn't want to even think about chores. She hurt all over. She felt fat and cumbersome, like an overstuffed turkey. Not having slept well for two weeks, she wished the baby could just magically jump from her womb, put on its own diaper, crawl into its crib and feed itself. Sing was not a big woman but at the moment she felt every inch and pound of her body.

At the crucial moment, she was standing at the kitchen sink washing breakfast dishes. She felt a very strange sensation and realized it was happening.

"Mom!" she cried out, as her knees buckled down with pain.

Mai Ker was out of earshot but Pam was close by in the flower garden. She heard the cry and came running.

"Sit down, sweetie," she urged Sing. "I'll get your Mom and Herald."

"Herald? No!"

"But Sing, you want him to be here."

"No!"

"To help."

"Nothing *he* can do!"

"That's not what I mean. I mean it's his baby, too. He'll want to be here. To see her born."

As Sing had sensed last December, an ultrasound in March had shown her baby was a girl.

Sing felt embarrassed and disgusted with herself at the same instant. As much as she loved Herald, she had never thought of letting him watch her give birth. She had witnessed the mess when Braden had been born and found the whole process very strange and unthinkable, both miraculous and ridiculous.

"Oh—" She bit off the word. "Ah—! OK," she gasped, "I need to lay down."

"Not yet, Sing. You've got to sit up till we get things ready."

"It hurts!"

"I know, honey. Just sit still and breathe deep. It won't take me a couple of minutes."

Wisely, Pam, Mai Ker and Bridget, knowing the days

were short, had been keeping their intercom radios close. Pam called the other two. Bridget ran to get Herald from Pod 14. Mai Ker and Pam rushed to get their makeshift birthing bed in the infirmary ready. In three minutes, Herald and Bridget were carrying Sing toward Pod 7 in a chair.

Herald was not squeamish under normal circumstances but he was turning an unusual shade of pale reddish-blue at the moment. The painful, tearful screams coming from his beautiful wife tore at his heart and frightened him. He wished he could make them stop but knew they would go on, probably for hours.

Sweat was pouring from every pore on Sing's body. She was in agony. Herald would not have been surprised to see droplets of blood behind the sweat.

Sing did all the work but the others got exhausted watching. It was nearly nine hours later when Pam got in position to catch the baby. As the ultrasound had promised, it was a tiny baby girl who at this moment was about the same color as her father, who was making just about the same spasmodic, incoherent noises that Kai was making as Herald first beheld her.

Sing's eyes were shut tightly, the result of too much pain and an unwillingness to let even light in for fear it would hurt. With some coaxing from her mother, Sing opened her eyes slowly and saw the eyelids of her own daughter, also pinched shut from pain, eyeballs seeming to quiver beneath the lids, and little catch-breaths beginning to fill her tiny lungs. Kai looked not only hurt but mad, as newborns do.

"Cut the cord, Dad," Bridget said. He did, even though he was sure this would hurt both his wife and his baby as he clipped the surgical scissors shut.

"Breathe, Herald," Pam said.

What no one realized was that Piper, Nathaniel and Braden were hovering like a totem pole with very large eyes near the open door of the infirmary.

Pam saw them first as she moved around the bed. She hurried over.

"Get!"

They did.

"Finally," Sing said with her first deep breath. The tension woven into her face and body began to ease. She cried softly. Mai Ker wiped her nose. Except for all the happy commotion around her, Sing would have instantly drifted into a deep sleep.

Herald took his wrapped-up baby daughter from Pam, cuddled her for a few moments, and then laid her on Sing's chest. Mai Ker propped the head of the bed up a little to make mom and the newest Solarian comfortable.

"Pretty, and perfect," Mai Ker said. "Just like you were, sweetie," she purred, kissing Sing's drying forehead.

"Can't believe it," Herald said quietly several times. He appeared to have drifted away to some distant land where rational thought never happens.

Piper and the two younger boys had run to Comm. Center in Pod 2.

"Maybe we can play some video games," Piper suggested impatiently, pacing, wanting to go back to the infirmary.

"I want to see!" Braden was chirping.

"You will. Later," she said, trying to look nonchalant and in charge. "Guess they don't want us there," she said "Give 'em time to get the baby washed up."

"She's just born," Nathaniel observed. "Why would she need a bath?"

"You wouldn't understand," Piper said as if she did, wanting to sound grown up.

After about 45 minutes, when the baby was clean and wrapped in a small fragment of an old blanket and snuggled in Sing's arms, they let Piper bring the two little brothers back.

"She's so cute," Braden said.

"Lot better than you prob'ly looked," Nathaniel said. "Can I hold her?" he begged.

"Not yet, guys," Herald answered. "We want to let her and Sing keep kinda to themselves for a while. Just a quick look. Now you're outta here. Go play."

The boys protested, with no luck. Herald was shoving them toward the door. Piper slipped over, gave Sing and the baby a joint hug, then followed Nathaniel and Braden to try to keep them out of whatever trouble they were planning next.

"So," Bridget said, "Kai Moua-Block has joined us!"

Sing was just becoming coherent again.

"We thought, Kai Moua-Listner," she said.

All three older women looked surprised.

"Really? Why?" Mai Ker asked.

"Well, not that Herald doesn't love his dad. But he's not a real memory. You know?"

She looked in appeal to Herald.

"See," Herald said, "you two, our Moms, you're the ones here with us. We thought we should honor that."

He and Sing looked anxiously for approval from the three women.

"I guess," Pam said as the only impartial bystander, "you two can name your baby whatever you want."

"Well, we haven't passed any naming laws," Bridget smiled. "Kids, I *am* honored, more than you realize, that you even thought of that. But," she leaned her head slightly sideways in sympathy for their wonderful intention, "the truth is, I'd be even more honored if she could carry on your dad's name, son. Clayton never even got to see you. He was robbed of all the joy I've had with you. Kai could be a link, for me and him, to what he missed." She began to cry softly.

"Don't be sad, Mom," Herald said, going over and holding her.

As she looked up at his handsome face she saw a memory of Clayton looking back.

Herald turned and looked at his wife.

"Sing?"

Sing's lips quivered. She was trying to hold in tears, too.

"I never got to know your dad, either. And yes, if it brings Bridget joy, it is perfect." She looked lovingly at Bridget, who had to bear her son after losing her husband. "Would you like to hold Kai Moua-Block?"

Bridget burst into louder, unembarrassed tears mixed with laughter. She gave her son a long, loving hug, then took baby Kai into her arms.

"Thanks, kids," was all she could say.

Mai Ker was now beaming. Another baby girl, another source of joy. Neither she nor Bridget nor Pam could have imagined this moment that day years ago when they first walked blindly, without a clue of what was to come, through the entry pod into Solarium-3 with their four teammates.

"Life is so unpredictable," Bridget said, "but such a treasure chest."

THE MARVEL of their own survival continued to baffle the original Solarians. In a different way, it troubled them. The old, ever-present question often jumped out of the shadows, if not spoken, at least in the backs of their minds. Why had so many died, yet they survived?

The birth of Kai added marvel on top of marvel. They were still searching for answers but didn't know where to look.

Pam felt that when Jimmy used to read his Bible to them, she at least found food for thought, and sometimes insights that she had never considered before. This felt like that kind of time.

This evening she went to get Jimmy's Bible from his tent. She stood in the doorway, looking into the room. The empty bed. His few clothes and belongings lay where he had left them that morning last November. The women didn't want to disturb his things. It felt wrong. The room had become an unplanned monument to their lost husband so she and Bridget and Mai Ker had agreed to just let things be. Nathaniel had asked for the room so he could split up from Braden. So far they had refused. They had pulled the curtain across the door of his tent, and there it was left, undisturbed.

Pam went into the living room where she sat and read near a tall lamp. She remembered how Jimmy was always telling them, trying to persuade them, about how God always brought new life out of old.

"Even the seasons show that," he used to say.

Maybe, when we had real seasons, Pam thought. What now, when the world was dead?

He simply couldn't believe death could be the final end, Jimmy used to tell her. She held to that hope. She shared his basic faith. But it had been easier to listen to Jimmy say that then, than to believe it now, when death had snatched him away so abruptly, so needlessly.

Still, as she reflected on things they had talked about, and read them over again from his Bible, she couldn't help wondering about Kai. Death continued to lurk around them like an enemy always hidden in the shadows. Every trip OUTSIDE was a grinding and gruesome reminder. Yet with the birth of Kai today, as with the other children before, life kept breaking in, overcoming loss, bringing hope.

Kai's birth renewed in Pam the expectation of some vague something she wanted. She wasn't sure what it was. It, too, lay hidden, just beyond the reach of her mind. Whatever it was, she wanted it desperately, though it still eluded her. She sat quietly, her eyes looking inward, wondering what was missing. This feeling was usually more pronounced when she was around her daughter, who seemed to have something inside that Pam herself lacked.

Bridget came in and sat in a chair next to her. She

didn't speak, just watched Pam read.

"Does it help?" Bridget eventually asked.

"What?"

"Reading his Bible?"

"Well, not really his."

"You know what I mean."

"Yeah. A little. I still don't understand everything. Not nearly. I don't think Jimmy did. But he had such a . . ." She couldn't find the word she wanted. ". . . such a, I don't know, trust. You know? Like nothing fazed him. All the death, the destruction. Willy, Sarajane. Clayton," she added carefully, watching Bridget's eyes. "Somehow, he got beyond it."

"Not always," Bridget said. "Mai Ker told me he struggled at times. Especially toward the end."

Pam was surprised.

"But she told the kids she thought he was ready. To die, I mean."

"As far as any of us can be, I guess I agree with her."

They remained quiet for several moments.

"Anyway," Bridget said, "whatever faith Jimmy had is beyond me. I was pretty stuck on my own ideas, before. But when I try to sort it all out now, Jimmy dying and everything—I come up empty."

"I know."

"What I used to think about God, it was pretty worthless. Just a kind of storybook figure. Jimmy got me thinking. God was just starting to be real. Now—I don't know."

Pam listened, but didn't help.

"I've really been struggling, Pam. How could any God do this? Just rip Jimmy from us like that? How cruel."

She was shaking her head, Pam unconsciously joining in.

"But what's weird, and I hate to admit this," Bridget frowned, "it was facing all the death that began to change me. To realize how much bigger the whole thing is."

"Bigger?" Pam asked.

"Than we are."

Pam thought for several moments. She couldn't think of anything to say. The conversation was becoming Bridget's alone.

"All my bluster," Bridget added vaguely. "I really regret that."

Pam's expression telegraphed that she didn't understand.

"You know, things I said about God. To Jimmy. Even to Clayton. Just an excuse. So I didn't have to go too deep myself," Bridget said.

"Deep?"

"Life, death. I had too much living to do. Why think about death? Before we ended up here, I spent most of my life trying not to think about it. Then the world collapsed around us."

Her mind went back, and further back.

"When I knew my grandma was really sick, that she was gonna die, I just downplayed it. Told myself, 'It's just how it is.' I completely shut it out of my mind. Even when she died."

"I was guilty of that," Pam admitted. "In nursing. Like, just closing the book. 'That life's done. Others to go care for.' But it didn't really help." She shook her head, thinking. "That's why Jimmy's heart was so encouraging."

"Yeah. You know, Piper's like that, too."

"Maybe she got it from him."

"Don't know," Bridget reflected. "Well, you know her better than me."

"Not sure about that," Pam said.

Bridget nodded. Piper was endearing and lovable, yet an enigma to them all.

"It's like there's a kind of secret world going on inside her all the time," Bridget said. "A mystery playing out. But she's the only one who knows the script."

"She's unique," her mom said. "Different. I never doubted that." She shook her head again. "But I haven't figured it out."

"What makes you think you can?" Bridget asked.

"I'm her mom. I should be able to decipher her, huh? But sometimes I can't even tell her mood."

Bridget nodded. Then she told Pam about a conversation with Piper.

"She said one time—this was like three or four months ago—she said how much she missed her Daddy, but she knew she was going to see him."

"She said that?"

"Yes," Bridget said. "Then she said, 'I don't think it'll be very long.'"

Pam stared, then frowned.

"What do you mean?"

"I don't know what she meant."

Pam tried to rationalize it, using what she knew of psychology.

"I think all kids want to think that. When a parent dies."

"No, this was different," Bridget said. "It was like— she just somehow knew. Like she had a direct wire to God himself. And he told her. Like that."

Pam was deep in thought. Bridget almost didn't ask the question, but couldn't hold it back.

"She wouldn't—hurt herself, would she?"

Pam had to consider this only a moment.

"No. I do know her that well. That's exactly the one thing she would never do."

Bridget nodded, relieved. Stiff from her chores, she got up and walked aimlessly around the room.

"She did mention a dream to me," Pam said.

"What about?"

"About Jimmy. I asked her what. But she said she didn't want to say. Just that he's OK."

"Maybe that's her faith coming out. In her dreams."

"But for Piper, it's like they're connected," Pam said.

"Isn't there a lot of dream stuff in the Bible?"

"Yes." Pam looked peculiarly at Bridget. "How is it you seem to have such a better understanding of my daughter than I do?"

"You kidding? Parents are the most blind, when it comes to kids. You know that. I guarantee, you probably know Herald better than I do."

Pam thought about this a moment.

"I guess I do."

"So, will we?" Bridget asked, stretching her arms high, a slow yawn escaping.

"Will we what?"

"Will we see Jimmy again? Or . . . the others?" She wanted to say "Or Clayton?" but couldn't.

"There's hints," Pam said, pointing to the Bible. "But it's not very clear. To me, at least."

"Yeah. Whenever I listened to Jimmy read it, I always thought, If God's so smart, why can't he just make us understand?"

Pam laughed quietly.

"My feelings exactly." She paused. "It's not just this, though," she said, thumbing the edges of the pages in the book. "I just want to believe it. Like Piper. That we'll meet up again. Someday."

"Sounds like an old-time Western roundup," Bridget joked.

"Don't make fun," Pam said.

"Sorry."

"Otherwise, why be here at all? Why know each other in the first place?" Pam said. "That's why it's always bothered me so much."

"What?"

"Dying. Why would God make us, then—un-make us?"

"You're asking me?" Bridget asked, mild sarcasm in

her voice.

Pam set her chin.

"Yes. I am."

Bridget didn't want to tackle this anymore. She was tired of talking. She walked to the door of the tent and looked out at the huge pod. She glanced up. The sky OUTSIDE looked completely black. Her mind felt the same.

"Bothers me, too," she said, still staring out. "I remember that night. When Clayton died. I cried. I raged. Never felt so lost." Fresh tears came. The moment returned. "It was so wrong. I just wanted him back." She turned and looked squarely at Pam, wiping her cheeks. "But maybe that's just us. Just wishing. Something selfish that doesn't want to let go."

Pam looked at her, moved to her core. She couldn't imagine how Bridget had managed that loss, let alone the loss of Jimmy.

She spoke quietly, not realizing she was confirming what Bridget had said.

"Maybe it's something God put in us. So we *wouldn't* let go."

Bridget went and settled in a different chair. Images of Clayton flooded back. Pam could tell what was happening so she just read quietly a few more minutes, her eyebrows working hard trying to connect it all in her mind.

"One thing," she finally said. "Don't know if it helps. Jimmy read something in our family time one night. One of Peter's letters." She had found the spot. "About a new world. Remember?"

"I remember," Bridget said noncommittally.

"Well, look at what's happened," Pam went on. "OUTSIDE. The air. How it could just change back, like it was before?"

"Not exactly like before." Bridget yawned again.

"But still. Think about this," Pam said, one eye

squinting as if she was peering through a telescope. "Are we starting over?"

"Over?"

"A new world. Are we it?"

"Pam, you blind? You've been OUTSIDE! Call that 'new'? It's a mess. Dead bodies. Dead everything." Bridget thought it was an outrageous suggestion.

"No, I know." Pam shook her head like a fly was loose in it. "Maybe it's a beginning, though. My great-grandmother had a saying. 'Out with the old, in with the new.' I was just thinking."

"I'm thinking, too. I think you've been INSIDE too long," Bridget said. "I'm tired. I'm gonna finish chores. Then go to bed."

AN HOUR later, although Pam was just as tired, she went and helped Herald move Sing and Kai back to their own tent. Sing was half-awake as they moved, Kai was sound asleep in her arms.

When they were settled, even though Pam was now more tired, she went to find Bridget. She was still troubled. Her mind would not slow down.

Bridget was at her dressing table, brushing out her hair that had grown much longer than she used to keep it.

"Can I say something else?" Pam said from the doorway.

Bridget had put the last conversation to bed already and didn't really want to awaken it. But she saw the drawn look on Pam's face.

"I suppose."

Pam came in and sat on the edge of the bed behind Bridget. Bridget continued brushing.

"Earlier, maybe you were right."

"Which part?"

"Maybe I have been in here too long. Maybe we all have."

"Maybe," Bridget mumbled. What else could she say?

"But I was thinking. About this new world thing. Jimmy used to talk about 'heaven' like it was a really special place."

"So?"

"Maybe that's it."

"Maybe what's what?"

"Heaven."

"I thought heaven was where people go—when they die."

"That's what I mean. When we die, we go to heaven. That's our new world."

Bridget sat up more straight and tried to picture this. The brush hung in midair. She turned and looked at Pam.

"So, this new world, everybody is dead." Bridget's face puckered like she just bit a lemon. "That what you mean?"

A confused look deepened on Pam's face.

"Oh. I see what you mean." Pam whisked her hands in the air. "Guess I just don't understand."

She hooked her hands together. Then her eyes flickered at a new thought.

"I know, you think this new world is somewhere totally different? Another planet?"

"That's what this place was built for, remember?" Bridget said. "We didn't need God to get us to some other planet. Would have just gone. On our own."

"But we didn't go. Did we." Pam wondered. "Something stopped us."

This managed to send her mystified look over to Bridget.

"Sure as hell did," Bridget said bluntly.

Pam sighed.

"Good night," she said.

She walked to her own room, still wondering.

Piper, who shared her tent, was propped up on her own bed.

"What'cha doing?" her mom asked.

"Thinking. And praying."

"Good. Keep it up," Pam said with a tone of frustration.

"I heard a little of what you and Bridget were just saying."

"You could hear us?"

"Tarps aren't soundproof, Mom."

"Think I'd know that by now?" Pam joked.

"How did that start?"

"What start?"

"Your conversation with Auntie Bridget."

Pam explained what they had talked about earlier, and during the last few minutes.

Piper sat quietly for several minutes as her mom changed for bed.

"I've prayed a lot about this, Mom. Especially since Daddy fell."

Pam noticed that she said "since Daddy fell," not "since Daddy died."

"And?" she asked her daughter.

"I believe it. A new world, like in Daddy's Bible. I believe it's going to happen."

"You sound pretty sure."

"I am."

"Why?"

"God. He gave his word."

"Sweetie, what's in the Bible is what men *think* God said," her mom said.

"No. It's more. Besides, I don't mean just what's written down. God speaks other ways."

Her mom watched her carefully. She hesitated, but asked.

"Does he ever speak to you?"

Piper figured she had to answer. She was reluctant, but didn't want to lie.

"Sometimes. I don't hear a voice. But I hear him." She looked up at her mom, who was hovering near the foot of her bed. "Does that happen to you?"

Piper stared at her mom with genuine curiosity, afraid of the answer, wondering if maybe there was just something wrong with herself.

"I used to think so," Pam remembered. "Long time ago." She sat on the corner of the bed. "In fact, I probably wasn't much older than you. But, I haven't heard anything for a long time."

"So why can kids hear? And grownups can't?"

"I can't tell you."

"Why not?"

"I mean, I don't know." She studied Piper's face. "The stories in the Bible, sweetie, you know, some people said they're just that. Stories. What we used to call myths."

Pam went over and got into her own bed.

"It's not a myth, Mom," Piper said emphatically.

"What?" her mom asked as she settled back. She shut off the small light on her bed table.

"The new world."

"You sound pretty sure again."

"It's not a myth," Piper repeated more softly but just as insistently, wondering how she knew what she knew. She shut off her own light and slid down under her covers. She spoke to her mom, but really to the tent roof. "If God made the world, why would he just let it go?"

18

One of the mares in the barn in Pod 9 was groaning loudly in pain. Her colt was being born. Herald and Bridget were there to pull it, the third of three born to the herd this year. There were 17 new chicks that had hatched and several new bunnies were also inhabiting the Solarium.

"If only we could take all these animals OUTSIDE. Let 'em really breed," Bridget said, thinking aloud.

"Prob'ly could," Herald said. "Except we'd about have to live out there with them. And there's no food."

"I know. Just thinking. The air out there seems about as normal as it's likely to get. But we can't chance it."

"Yeah. You know, there's something I don't understand."

"What?"

"Why isn't anything growing? It can't be the air anymore."

"Could be lots of things. Mai Ker would know better. The soil might be too depleted of nutrients. Could be the radiation levels. Don't know."

They picked up the conversation with Mai Ker later in the morning as they cultivated two cabbage plots in #10.

"I am not really sure," Mai Ker answered. "It might be whatever seed survived—after the plants died—was damaged. Ruined."

"How would bad air damage the seed?" Herald wanted to know.

"Can't be sure. It's one possibility. Or, it might be low

nitrogen levels in the soil. Or radiation. Or a combination. Plants are very sensitive creatures."

"I wondered about the nitrogen. In the soil," Bridget said. "Would the higher levels of nitrogen in the air get absorbed into the soil?"

"Possibly. I am not certain. We don't know all the chemical dynamics that were in play. Air and soil and water interact. Very complex, even before. I cannot be certain what happened—later."

For Mai Ker to admit she didn't have an answer was not comfortable for her. She liked to have answers. But she was being honest. The world had changed. The old rules might not be working. Some of the rules could have changed. With the kind of disaster they had lived through, they could only guess.

"You think it's the radiation? Stopping growth?" Bridget asked.

"That would affect plant development. I do not see why that would completely prevent germination," Mai Ker said, "if there was seed. Unless radiation had corrupted the seed—in its formation." She shook her head. "Why are you asking?"

"Just wondering, now that the air is better, if anything might grow."

"Possible. Something might have survived. Seed. Maybe roots."

Herald stopped his weeding and wiped his face. The pre-noon sun was intense through the pod roof.

"Wouldn't the root completely die?" Herald asked them. "When the top did?"

"It would depend on the kind of plant," Mai Ker said. "A large enough bulb or root might lay fallow. Underground. Maybe come back to life. If the conditions were ever right."

"The problem is," Bridget said, "we don't know when the air started to change back. Might've been several years ago. Could've been more recent, the last year or so."

"Oh, I don't think it was that sudden," Mai Ker said. "Not as recent as last year. The volume of the atmosphere is too huge. It would take time."

"But look how quick it fell apart," Bridget reminded her.

"That is true."

Mai Ker was overheated, too. She took a drink of water.

"I just don't get how it could change back at all," Herald said, tearing once more at a thick, stubborn weed stem. "I mean, when it was so fouled up! How could it just suddenly turn good again?"

Bridget remembered the conversations she and Pam were still having about the world being made over. It was too fantastic to be believed. Her mind drifted there now, though she said nothing aloud. What was happening? The air changes OUTSIDE were certainly an improvement. But a new world? It seemed, in a very real sense, too good to be true.

Besides, she kept thinking, if there was a God over it all—and she still struggled about this—she couldn't believe that a God who was loving or good would destroy so much of his own world. Take all those lives. It didn't make sense.

She missed whatever Herald and Mai Ker said next. Her mind was quite literally in another world, one she dreamed of but was afraid to wish for.

ANOTHER EXPLORATION had been planned for this afternoon. The team would be Bridget, Herald, Piper and Braden. Nathaniel had misbehaved badly on the last trip. First, he took his air mask off when Bridget didn't notice and refused to put it back on, which she was finally forced to do for him. Later, after they stopped at an old farm and took some gas from a storage tank, Nathaniel refused to get back in the truck. He wanted to explore the rickety old three-story house and Bridget wouldn't let him. Who knows what he might have found. Bodies, dead animals, guns, poisons. Anything.

On their return, he was grounded INSIDE for the next month.

During the two most recent expeditions, they had found only slight increases in the soil radiation levels as they moved west, and almost none in the water. They were trying to understand why. Bridget, Herald and Mai Ker had talked this over one afternoon a week ago.

"Surprises just keep coming, don't they?" Mai Ker commented.

They were in the barn, repairing torn leather on two saddles.

"I really thought the radiation levels would be much higher. Especially further west," Bridget said. "Especially in the soil."

"Why is the radiation so much lower in the water than the soil?" Herald asked.

"The soil is essentially stagnant," Mai Ker told him. "Other than wind stripping off the top. The water is mainly rainwater, and runoff from winter snows. It keeps moving."

"Wouldn't the air pollute the rain as it fell?" he wondered. "And snow?"

"Yes. But the air is so much better now. Almost no radiation to pick up," Mai Ker said.

"So it looks like we're mainly dealing with the buildup in the soil," Bridget said.

"Yes," Mai Ker answered. "We certainly could not grow any safe crops OUTSIDE. Even if we used good seed from INSIDE. It just would not be smart."

"Plants absorb natural radiation in the soil, don't they? Even when it was normal?" Bridget asked.

"Yes. Still, with what we're finding in soil radiation, I do not think it would be wise."

"So moving OUTSIDE isn't gonna happen anytime

soon," Herald said.

"No, son," Bridget said. "I know the idea's appealing. But no. We're stuck in here."

"Why keep exploring then?" he asked.

"I agree," Mai Ker said as objectively as she could.

"I know," Bridget said. "There's risks every time we go out. But it gives the kids a chance to see more of the world. And—I hate to say it—it still feels more normal than being locked away in here."

"Even with all the destruction out there?" Mai Ker asked.

"Even with that."

THE FOUR explorers of the day gathered their gear and testing equipment. Wearing their masks and tanks, they went out to the truck. Herald had taken the best of the vehicle batteries INSIDE after their last trip to charge it. He quickly reinstalled it.

Today held a special excitement because his mom had finally agreed to let him learn to drive the truck. Feeling grown-up indeed, he climbed in behind the wheel.

"Now, first—" Bridget began to say, in true mom fashion.

"Mom. I know. I've watched you every time. And it's really not that different from the big tractor. You know?"

He looked and sounded, with his deepening voice, a lot older than she knew he was.

She remembered her first time behind the wheel, too, an old pickup on her grandparents' farm in Canada. Her grandpa decided when she was 11 that she needed to learn to drive if she was to be of any use on the farm that summer. She remembered killing the engine at least six times trying to let out the clutch. After a lot of patient coaching from Grandpa, she finally got the truck to roll forward in first gear, bumping across an open field that Grandpa felt was the safest place for her to learn.

"Yeah," she finally said to Herald, "I know. Just be

glad it's an automatic."

They began today's venture by driving west. As usual, they stopped every few miles to collect soil samples, and water samples if they could find a source. These were often just large puddles left by a recent rain, or a feeble creek meandering toward the river.

They had gone a little distance west on previous trips. Bridget hoped to get further today. She assumed they would find higher levels of radiation in the soil as they moved closer to the Front Range of the mountains. That was where the worst of the nuclear blasts had detonated during that terrible night years ago.

They drove west on the beaten-up highway that ran toward the ruins of La Junta, passing farms and homes where they had stopped before. As they came into the outskirts just north of town, the highway—according to one barely readable intersection sign—became "Old Trail Road."

"What trail?" Braden asked.

"The old Santa Fe Trail, I think," Bridget said.

"It was," Piper said. "I looked it up, after the last trip. The Santa Fe trail carried lots of settlers west into this part of the country. Headed to California."

"You're a regular encyclopedia," Herald said as he swerved carefully to miss a piece of missing asphalt.

"Careful!" Bridget yipped.

"Mom . . ."

"There was even a railroad named after the trail. It mostly followed the trail. Faster than covered wagons," Piper explained.

"Faster than Herald's driving," Braden complained.

"You want to take over?" the older boy said, glaring.

"Sure!"

"Forget it."

North of La Junta they turned north onto an even more broken-down highway that led toward a tiny community that had been called Cheraw. The map showed there had been a small lake there. On the way, they drove past the old airport. It had been a bomber base during the Second World War, later converted to a community airport. The remaining runways that had been in use when the great catastrophe hit stood out like the tops of aircraft carriers on a perfectly calm, black sea of ash. A few months ago there might have been at least some dead plant stubble helping to hide them among the overgrowth. Now, since the wildfire had blazed through the area in December, they sat exposed like two giant strips of gray tape stuck across the blackened land.

Unfortunately, when they got to Cheraw, they discovered the lake had drained out. The remnants of what had been an earthen dam remained but there was a large swath cut through near the middle. Whatever water the lake once held had spilled into a smaller pond beyond the dam, then run down an irrigation canal to the east.

The only signs of moisture they could see were a few damp spots where recent rainfall had already drained into the sandy soil. They could have scraped the dampness at the surface but it would have been impossible to differentiate any water contamination from the soil contamination.

"Let's not give up," Bridget encouraged them. "There were two more lakes on the map. Here," she pointed, "to the west."

They got back in the truck, Herald still chauffeuring them, and worked their way west along another skinny highway and some gravel roads. Not surprisingly, the gravel ones were in better shape than the paved ones.

The next lake west was called Holbrook Reservoir. It, too, had been created by a manmade dam which, when they finally found the spot, was still intact. There wasn't much water in the lake but enough to sample. They walked along the irregular, muddy bank until they found some water more than a few inches deep.

"Mom, what's this yucky green stuff?" Braden asked

as he bent to draw water into one of the test canisters.

Bridget bent down and stared, almost speechless. Her eyes grew wide.

"I don't believe it," she said in complete amazement.

"What?" Herald asked, bending behind her to see.

"Can't be . . . it looks like algae," she said.

"What's that?" Braden asked. He pulled off his shoes and socks and waded into the water for closer look.

"You've seen it. When water collects in a low spot and sits. And the saltwater kind—you know—on the rocks by the beach?" She was so engrossed, it didn't dawn on her what Braden had done. "Get out of the water! You'll contaminate the test!"

He promptly did.

"It's ugly," Braden said.

"It's alive," Bridget said.

She was dumbfounded. In all their treks so far they had found not one single living thing. The water samples had not yielded any microorganisms. And suddenly, here was living algae. In front of her nose.

"Impossible. This is major," she said. "Herald, get another canister. Piper, get a piece of paper from your notebook. Scratch some of this stuff on it to dry. Mai Ker's gotta see this!" She found herself laughing like a giddy teenager. "She won't believe this!"

Piper had been standing and watching, sketching on a pad of paper. After staring several moments at the silliness that had overtaken Bridget, she did what Bridget asked. With her pencil eraser, she captured a little bit of floating green scum. It was such a faint green it was almost invisible. She pasted the stuff carefully onto a piece of folded paper and carried it ceremoniously back to the truck as if it was to be an offering for some great king.

Braden had beaten her back to the truck, looking for something to use to wipe the sand out from between his toes. As he pulled a rag from the floorboard and walked toward the tailgate to sit, he saw—for just an instant—a faint sparkle floating above the bed of the truck.

He stopped as if he had banged into a wall.

"What was it?" he asked Piper, who just reached him.

"What was what?"

"That—little flash thing."

She frowned.

"Where?"

"Right there," he pointed emphatically, "above the truck." He stabbed the air several times with his finger.

Piper looked up, trying to see what he meant.

"No," he said, "not far off. Right here. Just above the truck bed."

Piper refocused. She looked.

"Don't see anything."

"It was there!"

"What did you see?"

"Like a little—I dunno—a little blink of light. Quick. Then gone."

His vocabulary was not very large yet.

"I don't see a thing," Piper said. "It's your eyes. You're not used to this much sun. Used to it getting filtered through the pods."

"I saw *something*," Braden insisted.

"OK. If you say so."

She didn't really doubt him, she just didn't see anything. She attached no importance to it.

Braden's toes were brushed dry and most of the sand was gone. He pulled his shoes back on and ran toward his mother, who was walking back to the truck with Herald.

"Mom, there was a funny bright thing."

"What?" she asked, her mind elsewhere.

"By the truck. There." He pointed to where he thought he had seen the faintly glittering light.

"What was it" she asked.

"I dunno. Like a flash. In the middle of nothing." He was gesturing and making less sense now than he had with Piper.

Herald laughed.

"Didn't know you believed in fairies," he teased.

Braden scowled.

Bridget's mind was far away. Braden's imagination didn't interest her nearly as much at the moment as the algae.

"Come on. Let's go. I wanna make one more stop."

They all got in, Braden shaking his head, his feelings hurt.

They drove west again a few more miles to the last lake of any size shown on the map. It was called Dye Reservoir. It was, however, another disappointment. The outline of what had been a small reservoir was still visible, reamed by water into the landscape. All that was left was the shallow creek bed that had run through the bottom of what had been the reservoir.

The creek bed was mostly dry. They could see a few small pools of stagnant water here and there. But this, at this moment, excited Bridget more than if a mighty river had been pouring into the empty lake. Stagnant water was perfect. She led the children down to the creek bed.

"Walk both edges. See if you can spot any more algae," she directed.

Two walked each side, slowly, looking down, checking the puddles of stagnated water for any sign of green.

After 30 minutes, they came up empty.

"I don't get it," Bridget was saying, as much to herself as to the kids. "Why at Holbrook, but not here?"

"Just luck, I guess," Herald said as they walked up to the truck.

"You believe in luck, Herald?" Piper asked.

"Sure."

"Maybe it wasn't."

Piper stopped and turned. She looked across the desolate landscape. Everything dead, forsaken. Except the tiny sign of life at Holbrook. She wondered.

Herald and Bridget got into the truck. Piper reached the truck but waited on Braden who was holding the door, balanced on one foot, shaking bits of gravel out of the other sandal. She looked at him curiously, then hugged him gently.

"Maybe you did see something," she whispered to him.

The other two didn't hear as Herald started and revved up the popping engine. Piper and Braden climbed in and they started home.

THEIR ARRIVAL back at the Solarium was like a circus. Bridget had called to Mai Ker as soon as they were back in radio range. Like a barnstorming stuntwoman, Bridget bailed out of the truck and ran toward Pod 1 as fast as she could, her air mask dangling by her waist and a canister of water from Holbrook carried like a football. The kids worked to keep up.

Mai Ker was ready in the Comm. Center to pass them through the airlock. Pam and Nathaniel had come running, too.

From Pod 9, Sing heard the yelling and thought something horrible must have happened. She dropped the horse brush she was using to clean the new colt, left poor Kai hanging from a fence post in her canvas carrier, and ran panicked toward Pod 2.

"What's wrong?" she almost shrieked as she flew through the door of the Comm. Center. All the others were hovering around something on the counter by Mai Ker's control panel. Sing caught her breath and exhaled hard when she saw Herald standing there, perfectly all right.

"You scared me to death," she almost shouted at them all.

"Where's Kai?" Herald asked innocently.

"She's— I don't know. She's—by the barn!"

Mai Ker came over to Sing.

"It's OK, sweetheart. Something really exciting! Come here. Look."

She pulled Sing to the counter. Sing looked down at the open water canister and a piece of folded notebook paper with a faint green smudge on it.

"This some kind of joke?" she asked them. She was sure they were playing with her.

"No, Sing, look," Herald said. "We found it in the water at an old lake."

"What is it?" Sing asked, still unsure what she was looking at.

"It's algae," Bridget said. "And it's alive!"

Finally, Sing recognized what was so important.

"You mean—?" she began. "Something has started growing? OUTSIDE?"

"Yes," Bridget said, wanting to dance. "The first thing we've found alive. In all the trips."

"Wow," Sing said. "Fantastic!"

"You couldn't pick a better word," Bridget beamed.

"So we were right about the air?" Pam asked. "Something can live out there?"

"This was," Bridget said, pointing to the water canister. "If simple organisms can survive, maybe more complex ones can."

"Like us," Mai Ker said.

"Now *that* would be fantastic!" Herald said.

Bridget's smile faded a little as reality set it.

"Yeah, but let's not be hasty," she said. "Radiation is still high in places. Moving out there—for the long term—that's still a long way off."

"I am perfectly fine here at home," Sing said. She put a special emphasis on "home." "And so is Kai."

Herald laughed.

"We're not gonna rush out of here, if that's what you're worrying about."

"Not what you sounded like a second ago," she said.

"Just thinking ahead, Sing. Gotta think ahead. It's exciting! The future might be longer than we guessed!"

THIS EVENING Bridget called a family gathering. Their entire discussion focused in on the possibilities that lay before them. The world OUTSIDE appeared to be slowly healing, thus growing bigger in their minds. The air was probably safe to breathe for longer periods of time, although Bridget had continued to make them wear the air masks when they went exploring.

"And," Mai Ker cautioned, "we don't know that it won't go foul again. We don't know what happened. Before. What if it happens again? And we're living out there?"

"She's right," Pam said. "Still kind of scary."

Mai Ker's bigger concern was the residual radiation. It seemed to have washed from the air. But it was much higher that healthy limits in some of the soil samples they had taken, and several of the water samples. To live outside would mean longer-term exposure. And she questioned whether they would be able to safely drink OUTSIDE water, or eat foods grown out there, anytime in the near future.

Still, just the thought of having an entire world to live in, instead of this shell, was fascinating to everyone, especially the children.

"Living OUTSIDE would be fun," Nathaniel said enthusiastically. "All that room!"

"You're not listening well, son," Mai Ker said. "As usual."

Bridget was more sympathetic.

"I understand the worry, Mai. And, I grant you, everything is still pretty much dead out there," Bridget said. "But finding that algae—it makes me believe life can be regenerated. Out of the ruins."

"Maybe we should be praying. Asking for guidance." Piper said it with innocence but also assurance that guidance would in some way be given.

Her comment brought the conversation to a screeching halt. Although some of them found themselves praying—privately—they had never prayed together since Jimmy died. It was impossibly hard. The three older Solarians, especially, feared that they would pray, then what they asked for wouldn't happen.

"We could," Pam said, trying to sympathize with her daughter. "Once we know what to pray for."

"Mom," Piper said, "that's not what I meant."

Pam looked at her and didn't know what else to say. While Pam still felt shy about her faith, her daughter was the opposite. Always speaking as if God was in the room, or at least in the next, Piper acted as if he was watching every move and turn they made. Pam loved her deeply but she found Piper's confident faith unsettling. *Maybe the problem is with me,* Pam often wondered. *Maybe I have grown up, and lost something.*

"Honey, we can all pray. In our own ways," she told Piper, but really everyone.

"Not what I meant."

Piper scrunched her lips into a knot. Everyone waited. Piper said no more.

Bridget jumped in to steer the conversation back to the possibilities opening up before them.

"If we're gonna pray, I suggest we pray for more children. If we need anything, we need that."

"Doing the best we can," Herald said with an embarrassed smile.

"I know," Bridget said with a motherly nod. She looked with an awkward disappointment at the children, remembering how closely the rest were related. "Just not sure how it's all going to work out."

"Yes," Mai Ker said. "So few. Even if someday we moved OUTSIDE, how could we repopulate a whole world?"

Piper was sitting on the arm of one of the couches

near the door of the tent. She was getting more irritated with how stuck they all sounded but she said nothing more.

"Maybe we can talk about it some other time," Bridget said, trying to shift to a less awkward topic.

She talked more of their discovery today and stressed to the children that the algae were living organisms. If algae could survive, life OUTSIDE was not beyond possibility.

"What I would like to know," Mai Ker said, "is where did it come from? How did it survive?"

"And how could it survive the fire?" Herald asked. "The whole area over there was burned, too."

The explorers had already described what they had seen today. Just as on previous excursions, the destruction of the huge December wildfire was everywhere, everywhere they had gone so far. The smell snuck into their nostrils even with the air masks on.

"Not sure," Bridget said.

"Those tree stumps?" Braden asked.

"Maybe." She looked at him, then back at Mai Ker. "There was a thick cluster of dead stumps. Along the west shore. Must have been a grove of trees on that side once. Maybe the stumps created a fire break. Enough to protect that edge of the lake. That's where we found the algae."

"And the heat didn't hurt it?" Sing asked.

"Well, living in the water like that, maybe some got scorched. But just under the surface, maybe it was enough protection," Bridget said.

"Could the algae have grown inside the stumps?" Herald asked. "The stumps went right down into the water."

"Possible," Mai Ker said. "Still, how did it survive at all? Before? With the atmosphere? I can't understand that."

"Maybe it's new," Braden suggested with the

simplicity of a young mind.

"New, how?" Mai Ker asked. "New, from where? It had to come from something."

Her studies in chemistry, biology and genetics had convinced her that there had to be some direct, biological cause for any organism.

Piper, sitting near the door, slipped out quietly during this exchange without being noticed. She wasn't bored. She was frustrated. There was something they were missing. Every time they had discussions like this, about really big questions, she felt the same frustration. They were looking at toothpicks, not trees.

She decided to go for a swim in the pool in Pod 5, which they now again used regularly. She slipped into her and her mom's tent to change. Her mind was in a whirl. She needed some quiet.

No one had yet noticed she had left the Meeting Tent. She went off by herself, swam for half an hour, then sat on one of the deck chairs, thinking.

But nothing became clear. Memories of her dad took over. She could hear his voice in her head, teaching them about God, reading from his Bible. He spoke of a promise, a new hope, and a new world. The words flooded her mind. Her faith was deep. But her vision was still slight. And she missed the reassurance of her dad.

She thought over their trip OUTSIDE today. Still destruction everywhere, except for one little flicker of life. Some miniscule, faintly greenish organisms in the midst of chaos. She felt exactly like one of those little creatures. Faint, pale, not quite real, no apparent purpose, suspended in the middle of near-nothingness, trying to hang on to something she knew but could not seem to pin down.

New life? Were they it? A few shards of humanity safe INSIDE? Or little clumps of green algae OUTSIDE, whose existence could be snuffed out tomorrow?

Too many questions. Piper felt more confused than

ever. Her mind became a jumble. She wished she could shut it off for a while. But this was always hard for her. Her mind always dug deeper, even when she slept.

She was fairly well dried off. She got up, pulled a dry shirt on over her swimming shirt, and started walking back through the podwalk that connected the Rec. Pod with #10. Her eyes fixed vacantly on the sidewalk, trying to let her thoughts wind down. She looked up as she neared the door into #10. Far across the complex something caught her eyes, the flicker of what looked like the end of a small flashlight pointed directly at her. But the light appeared to hover, disconnected from anything, high over the water in Pod 12. It faded, then popped out more brightly again.

She had never seen anything like it. It wasn't really a light but seemed to dance between light and shadow.

Her heart raced and her breathing quickened. She made a dash across the fields and walks of Pod 10 and raced into the podwalk that led to the ocean. Almost to the door into #12 she stopped, hesitating. Did she want to go in? What might she see?

She slowed down but walked purposefully through the door. Just as slowly, she approached the water's edge. There it was again. What had seemed just a faint twittering of light when it first caught her eyes was now more distinct, yet still undefinable. She thought maybe it was a reflection. Perhaps one of the pod lights high up was dying, flickering and reflecting off the roof. She looked up. The lights were all fine, and perfectly still.

She stared. The strange thing she was seeing appeared to be little more than a mirage but it had some kind of substance. The more she looked the more she was certain. What seemed like an area of light—though she was still not sure it was light—took on a definite form for just a moment, then changed again. It was not a form that could be measured or contained but was nonetheless a body of some kind. It started to move. Then it darted sideways, without appearing to turn.

This movement so startled her that she was shaking. She felt a person nearby, although "nearby" did not accurately describe it. It was not nearby in a physical sense but near to her own spirit in a way that frightened her, yet consoled her. Whatever it was, it was somehow connected to the light—but not in the light.

Her heart was now racing faster than her mind.

She heard words that were not normal words. They weren't audible as far as she could tell.

"You will lead them, Piper."

She didn't understand but her name was unmistakable. She had been praying almost nightly for some kind of guidance. Here it was, and she was frightened, and she didn't understand what it meant.

"I don't understand." She spoke as to herself, which frightened her more.

"Listen, and prepare. Watch," the non-voice said.

Then it was gone. The light too, if it was light, disappeared and the sense she had felt of someone or something near passed as abruptly as it had come.

Piper realized she was still quaking. A flood of tingling rushed down the full length of her body as lightning passes into the ground after it has exploded its full energy. But this tingling was a pleasant sensation that actually calmed her. It seemed to last a full minute. The quaking subsided. She realized she had not breathed since her last words. She gasped.

"What was *that?*" she whispered to no one.

19

Kai let out a miniature scream as Sing put her down into her crib.

"I'm sorry!" Sing said, tears seeping into her eyes. "Sweetie, what did I do?"

She picked Kai back up. The baby let out another yelp.

"What in the world is wrong?" Sing asked the squirming baby who could not answer.

Herald heard it, jumped up from his lunch in the dining tent, and came running.

"What's wrong?" He was panting.

Sing had found the problem.

"It's these stupid diaper pins you concocted. Why didn't you use steel wire? This brass stuff keeps bending. It stuck her again! See?"

Sing was irritated at Herald about a number of things and this was the perfect excuse to blow up at him.

"Sorry," he pleaded. "I'll make some better ones. Just be careful."

"Yes, always telling *me* to be careful! Look at you! Always dashing off OUTSIDE like some big hero. You don't have to impress *me,* you know."

Having straightened the offending pin and dabbed up a tiny spot of blood with a piece of cloth, she tucked their baby girl in again for her afternoon nap.

"Not trying to impress anybody," Herald griped. "I just like exploring."

"Thought maybe you'd rather spend time with me. We have such little time by ourselves anymore."

"Well, that's partly Kai's fault."

"Oh, really? She's the primary decision maker in the family now?"

Herald was effectively rebuked.

"You know I didn't mean that."

"You go right on making your own decisions, Herald. But I'd think you'd want to spend a little time with me and Kai." She turned her back on him and went about folding some homemade baby clothes. "It's like you don't even care! You wanna go run around the countryside, go on." She was wiping back tears. "Just don't be mad when I get upset. 'Cause I'm stuck in here doing all the baby chores!"

"I try to help." He walked to her and cuddled her shoulders from behind.

"Sure. Men helping with baby chores is like rats sweeping the floor," she said.

"Well, which is it? You want me to help or not?"

"I don't know," she said, being honest.

"Well, I'll stay back more if you want."

"That would be nice," Sing said, calming down. "I know you love our baby. I just want you and me and her to be together more."

"Not like I can nurse her or anything," he said.

She shot an affectionate scowl at him, then laughed.

"Plenty else you can do. Just hold her more. Cuddle her. She wants to get to know her Daddy, you know?" The thought stung, because she still missed her own so much. "You know, instead of just making pins, maybe you could actually pin one on once in a while?"

Herald avoided diaper duty as far as humanly possible.

"You're better at it," he said.

"You're a coward."

"I know. Let's go finish lunch."

The young mom and dad gave a loving look at little Kai who, despite the commotion over her head, was sound asleep. Neither of them could know that Kai would be the last baby born in Solarium-3.

"I THINK after lunch I'm going to re-test those last water and soil samples," Mai Ker was saying to Bridget as the two came into the dining tent.

"Can I come watch?" Piper asked.

"Sure."

"Yeah," Bridget said. "Maybe we've missed something. I still can't understand why the soil radiation isn't higher."

"I don't think we have missed anything," Mai Ker said defensively. "But it does not hurt to double check."

After eating, Piper went with Mai Ker to Pod 3 and helped key up the test programs on the computer while Mai Ker very carefully prepared precise samples.

Mai Ker saw the unusual expression on Piper's face.

"Something wrong, honey?"

"No," Piper said.

But she was preoccupied. As hard as she tried to drive it from her mind, she kept thinking about what she saw last night above the ocean. The strange words kept repeating themselves in her head.

Listen for what? Prepare? What am I supposed to watch for?

She thought for a moment about telling it all to Mai Ker. She was afraid Mai Ker would think she had gone crazy.

She had the test programs ready. Her mind wandered again. *Was that not real last night?* she worried. *Did I imagine the light—or whatever it was? Am I crazy and don't know it?*

She forced her mind back to the present.

"What happens if the radiation isn't that high?"

"How do you mean?" Mai Ker asked.

"Well, could we really live OUTSIDE?"

"It's so ugly out there. Don't think I want to."

"But *could* we?" Piper pressed her.

"Possibly. Yes. But it would depend on a lot of things."

"The test programs are set. Like what things?"

"Start test 31. Well, like, can we rebuild some farms, get the soil tillable again? And we'd have to rehabilitate some housing."

"We live in tents. Couldn't we out there?"

"Yes. But remember, in here we're protected from the violent weather. OUTSIDE, the tents wouldn't be much protection. Especially when it turns cold."

"No. Didn't think of that. Never gets cold in here." She considered the lightweight shirt and shorts she had on. "Wonder what that would feel like? I don't think I'd like it."

"I never did," Mai Ker said.

"But we could make it happen. Couldn't we? If we did those things you said?"

"It's more complicated, honey. OK, key test twenty-six. See, the question is, would we grow out there? I mean, our numbers."

"You mean, more people."

"More children."

"I understand."

Piper thought about this for several moments. She had thought about it many times before. But she was afraid to ask the moms. It felt very embarrassing.

She could not imagine getting married to one of her brothers. *Yuck.* She wondered if Herald could have two wives. She wasn't sure she liked that much, either.

"Well, I don't really understand it all," she told Mai Ker. "I know how babies are born. I mean, how they get made. I s'pose, when I'm older, I could have babies, too? But what about my brothers?"

Mai Ker wanted to change the subject rather than

explain all this to Piper.

"It's difficult."

"Why? I mean, other than the getting born part?"

"Genetics, Piper. You know. We've studied this in school. Except for Herald, you and Sing and the boys share the same father. It would be difficult to have children, and not problems."

"Problems?"

"Complications. The babies could have problems."

"Defects," Piper said.

"Yes."

"I see."

Piper sat quietly. She unconsciously twirled a length of hair hanging behind her ear. "Maybe the boys wouldn't like me, anyway. I'm not very pretty."

"You are too."

"Not like Sing."

"You don't need to be like Sing. You're pretty in your own way. Your mom is nice looking. And your dad," she couldn't help but smile, "he was a very handsome man."

"I guess."

"Maybe we should just finish these tests," Mai Ker said. "And worry about it later."

"OK," Piper said, her mind drifting again.

Long speculations about life and the future would have to wait.

The tests yielded exactly the same results as the first time. Mai Ker was pleased. Bridget seemed less pleased when she heard. They found her next door, sitting on a bench by the empty aviary in #6.

"Why are you looking so funny?" Mai Ker asked as Bridget scanned the results.

The noise of boys filtered in from Pod 5 even though the podwalk doors were closed. Nathaniel and Braden were having another wild afternoon swim.

"Well, because it complicates things," Bridget said. "Doesn't it? Promising results. That means, at some point, maybe we really have to decide. If OUTSIDE is viable again."

"Yes," Mai Ker agreed.

"Till now," Bridget said, "it was never an issue. Never even thought about it."

"Isn't it funny?"

"What?" Bridget asked.

"Well, not funny. Strange. I mean, what made us go out?"

"The crack."

"No," Mai Ker said. "Jimmy's death. Because we did not want to risk a climb again. From in here."

"He never would've let us go out, would he?" Piper asked.

"No," Mai Ker said. "Your dad dying forced us to try. And look what we've found."

"Huh," Bridget said. Her mind bent into mental acrobatics trying to comprehend this.

"Daddy's death made us risk everything," Piper said, her own mind swirling. Listen. Prepare. Watch.

"Risk everything. And maybe find a new life," Mai Ker said.

"Maybe not so strange," Piper said so softly that Bridget and Mai Ker missed it.

"We can't be sure about the radiation yet," Bridget said. "Unless we make some longer trips, closer to the Front Range. Where the main blasts were."

"The radiation should be pretty static," Mai Ker said. "After this many years. At least, we've gotten pretty consistent readings around here."

"Why don't we go?" Piper asked.

Bridget heard this one.

"Where?"

"The mountains."

"Well, we . . ."

"You just said that's where we'll really find out. Why don't we go?" Piper asked with a certain insistence.

So far, Bridget had not seriously considered venturing that far from the Solarium. The element of the unknown was much higher. She shook her head unconsciously.

"It's a really long way, Piper."

"Doesn't look too far on the map."

"You checked?"

"Yes. Herald and I talked about it the other day." She said it as if acknowledging that they had discussed some terrible, forbidden subject.

"Maps are deceiving. You don't get the true sense of distance. It's just a picture."

"Could we make it that far?" Piper asked, excitement growing in her voice.

"Oh, probably," Bridget said. "We'd have to have extra tanks, supplies."

"Some food," Mai Ker said.

Bridget pondered such a trip. She let out a frustrated sigh.

"See. That's our problem. Isn't it? The Solarium is like a big cage. But it's safe. I get nervous the farther we go."

"Maybe I could go this time," Mai Ker said.

Bridget looked at her dumbfounded. In all the months of exploring, this was the first moment Mai Ker had shown even remote interest in ever being OUTSIDE again.

"Thought you didn't want to be out there?" Bridget said.

Mai Ker nodded several times.

"I didn't."

"Why now?"

"While we were redoing those tests, Piper kept asking. About if we could live out there. I started wondering. And I realized, I've been chicken. You guys have gone. How many times? And I hide in here."

She nodded her head once more. "I do not want to be a coward."

Bridget shook her head but smiled.

"Besides," Mai Ker added, "I always loved the mountains."

"It feels really strange, Mai," Bridget said.

"I am sure it will. I look out through the pods. My eyes tell me everything is different. My mind still wants to remember what was." She sat on the bench by Bridget and stared into the empty aviary. "For a long time, I tried not to think of this. Now, I will think of nothing else."

"Because Jimmy's not here," Bridget said quietly.

"Yes. That, too."

It was a somber moment, but Piper couldn't help breaking in.

"So, we can go?" There was a thrill in her voice.

"Move outside?" Bridget asked.

"Go to the mountains."

Bridget shrugged her shoulders, also unconsciously. As the leader, she knew she would have the final say. Life had been drudgery. This sounded exciting. Something in her felt like a bomb about to explode.

"Let's try it," she said with a burst of enthusiasm she had not felt for a long time.

Then she realized there was about to be raging competition for seats in the truck. This trip could be an amazing adventure for the children. The problem was, who would get to go?

A piercing cry rang through the podwalk door from #5. It was one of the boys. They couldn't tell which. It was the sound of gasping pain interspersed with unsuccessful attempts at crying.

They ran through the podwalk. Nathaniel was kneeling over Braden who was crumpled on the ground about 10 feet beyond the pool, under a 30-foot elm tree.

"Don't touch it!" Braden squealed, batting away

Nathaniel's attempts to help. The younger boy was trying to cradle his right leg but even his own attempts to hold it shot pain through the rest of his body.

"What happened?" Bridget demanded, barreling to a stop.

"He fell!" Nathaniel said.

"No kidding!"

Bridget and Mai Ker were now kneeling over Braden trying to calm him and get him still.

"I didn't make him!" Nathaniel protested, assuming everybody would think he had.

"It's all right, Nate," Mai Ker said. "Nobody said you did."

"He was bored swimming. So he went climbing."

"With wet hands and feet," Bridget said, looking up at the elm and shaking her head. To herself she thought, *That was stupid.* But her son was in so much pain she wasn't about to say it out loud. "It'll be all right, sweetheart," she told him.

"I think it's the tibia," Mai Ker said as she very gently ran her hands over the lower part of his right leg. "Can't tell if it's clean through. But I'm sure it's broken."

"Piper—" Bridget started to say, but Piper was already scurrying toward the podwalk.

"I'm getting Pam," she said as she ran off.

Nathaniel had begun crying violently, feeling he must have done something wrong, but mostly suffering the same shock waves that had torn through him when he saw his father fall to his death.

"I'm sorry!" he howled, taking several steps back, almost falling into the pool.

Mai Ker now had to tend him. She got up and took him into a careful hug.

"Nate, it's OK. You didn't do anything. He was careless. Not your fault, darling."

"I saw Daddy again—" He was shaking uncontrollably.

"I know, honey. I know."

Mai Ker was trying hard not to imagine the same horror herself. She hadn't seen the fall but she had seen the aftermath.

"Braden will be OK, honey. He broke his leg. But he'll be OK." She hugged him tighter. "Just sit down. Till we take care of him. OK?"

He couldn't form words yet, but he nodded an *OK*. He plopped down, whimpering. Gradually, his sobbing abated. He tried to remember how to breathe normally.

Pam arrived with Piper and sent Bridget to the infirmary for an air splint. She wiped Braden's sweat and tears with the dishrag that was still in her hand.

"Braden, we're going to have to move you—"

"No!" he shouted. He hurt so much he couldn't imagine being moved an inch.

"We have to move you," she said again patiently, "to the infirmary. We'll have to set the bone."

"No!" he pleaded again.

"I'll give you something that will make it not hurt so bad."

This, finally, sounded like a great idea to Braden. He was very much in favor of less pain.

"OK," he said with resignation. "But don't hurt me."

"I would never do that," Pam said.

In fact, when they got him to the infirmary the stick of the syringe did hurt, but only for a second. Compared to the pain and muscle spasms in his leg, this was nothing—and well worth it once the painkiller kicked in. Pam also gave him a sedative that would relax the muscles around the break.

Herald and Sing ran to the infirmary when they realized what had happened. They hovered in the background but Herald encouraged his little brother, assuring him, "Everything will be OK, buddy."

Pam pulled the portable X-ray machine over Braden's leg and shot a quick picture to be sure what she was dealing with. The X-ray showed his shinbone was broken clear through. The jagged, displaced bone ends were chomping into the muscles.

The sedative worked. Braden had fallen into a mild sleep. Pam shooed all the children out and gave instructions to Bridget and Mai Ker how to hold him while she set the bone. They didn't have materials for a rigid plaster cast. For some reason, of the tons of supplies the Solarium planners poured into the place, this was one of the obvious things they missed.

Pam jerked hard on the leg, fighting the muscle spasms and pulling the broken bone ends back into alignment. She felt along the area of the break to make sure it felt right. It did. She replaced the air cast over his leg, then placed a rigid strap-on cast over the air cast to keep it completely immobile. It barely fit but the straps were just long enough.

"I'll check on the other kids," Mai Ker offered. She was tense, the muscles in her own legs fighting her, and mainly wanted a chance to sit down.

"We'll stay with him till he wakes up," Bridget said. "Hey," she said, catching Mai Ker.

"Yes?"

"Try to convince Nathaniel he's not in trouble, would you?"

"I'll try," Mai Ker said, knowing full well it was hard to convince her son of anything.

DINNER WAS somber. Braden was awake but only slightly coherent. The sedative kept working and he was still feeling its aftereffects. They sat him sideways to the table with his cast leg propped up on a second chair. He ate little, barely awake enough to chew.

After supper, Bridget told them she wanted to talk. They all moved to the living room in the main tent.

"You know, we've been kind of struggling lately." By "lately" she meant every day and month since Jimmy's death, and they all knew it. "Piper and Mai Ker and I were talking this afternoon. About whether we could ever move. OUTSIDE. I've thought a lot about it. But we need to realize, it's an attractive idea but there's a lot to it."

"But the other thing. We're still going, right?" Piper asked.

"OUTSIDE?"

"No. The mountains?"

"Yes. We're still going to the mountains."

"Oh, that would be so great!" Herald said.

He didn't notice Sing's sideways glance.

Renewed excitement burbled among all the children, except Braden, who still hurt too much to care about anything, and Sing, who was quietly glaring at her husband.

"Piper made a really good point today," Mai Ker told them. "The only way we'll find out how bad the radiation was—maybe still is—is to get close to the Front Range. And test there."

"That's where the blasts were," Bridget told the children.

They all knew this from their school hours. Jimmy and Bridget had lectured them more than once about the insanity of it all—not only building all the nuclear weapons in the first place but the sheer insanity of setting so many off when the human race was all but dead, anyway.

"So, we're going to make a trip farther west, right up to the mountains," Bridget said. "We'll need to wear protective gear. We've got those lightweight radiation suits in supply. That should help."

"You mean those funny looking coveralls?" Herald asked.

"Yes."

"Going to be awful big on Piper," Pam pointed out.

"We'll pull them up with belts and things," Bridget said.

"So. Where we headed?" Herald asked.

"Oh, I thought we'd go northwest, toward Colorado Springs. That's where NORAD was."

"What was?" Nathaniel asked. He apparently slept through that lesson.

"North American Aerospace Defense Command," Herald explained.

"That place in the mountain," Sing told Nathaniel. She must have stayed awake.

"Yes," Bridget said. "There used to be a bunch of other military facilities around there, too. The reason so many nuclear weapons were targeted there."

"I want to go," Herald said with energized enthusiasm.

Sing looked at him again.

"You have a very short memory," she whispered.

"What?" he stammered, as if he didn't know.

"Why can't I go and you stay?" she said.

"You *want* to go?"

She glared at him again.

"No."

"I'll stay if you want," he said.

Sing pursed her lips.

"No."

She knew it was pointless. This would be the biggest adventure ever. And she knew he would be impossibly restless if he missed the trip. He would be no use in helping with Kai and she would hear about it for a long time.

"Just go if you have to."

Herald looked at his mom with brighter eyes.

"Can I?"

"Well, there'll only be four of us. We can't get more in the cab comfortably."

"Could you take the other guard truck, too?" Pam asked.

"Rather not. We know the one we've been using is reliable. Going that far, I'd rather not chance it."

"Except, what if it breaks down?" Pam asked. "You'd be too far to reach us."

Bridget hadn't considered this.

"Might be right. If one truck quit, we'd have the other as backup."

"The other one runs OK, Mom. We can look it over again, to be sure," Herald said.

"So. Who will go?" Pam asked.

"Well, I'll go, of course," Bridget answered. "Herald wants to go. Anyone else?"

"Can I—?" Nathaniel barely got out.

"You're still grounded. Sorry," Mai Ker said. She looked around. "I'll go this time."

Everyone was surprised except Bridget and Piper who had talked with her earlier.

"Really. Thought you didn't want to be out there," Pam said.

"First time for everything." Mai Ker felt tension in her chest as she said it.

"I'd like to go. If I can," Piper said. She was hesitating but knew she had to go. She was supposed to go. She wasn't sure of much, right now, but she felt sure of this.

"OK," Bridget said. "Anyone else?"

"There is no one else," Pam pointed out. "If Mai Ker's going, I need to stay back to operate the doors. And I'll only have Sing and Nate to help with the inner seals."

She nodded toward Braden, who was dozing off. Everyone realized he wouldn't be going, and wouldn't be able to help with the seals either.

"Well, we won't be crowded. Two to a truck," Bridget smiled. "Herald and I will drive."

Herald smiled even bigger.

Sing was not smiling. But under her frustration, she felt happy for him. She knew he loved adventure. And she had the baby to worry over.

"We'll take extra gear and supplies. All the air tanks we can manage," Bridget said. "And food."

"Why don't we try without masks?" Herald asked.

He didn't see her but Sing almost lost it. She was too upset to say a word. Bridget saw her, though.

"No, son. Not going that close to the mountains. We want all the protection we can muster. Heavier clothing. And the masks stay on. No fooling around."

"I guess," Herald said, disappointed.

He loved exploring but he hated the air masks. They were, to him, nothing but an irritation.

Bridget was planning out loud.

"We'll gas up both trucks at that second farm, just west of here. And top off the storage tank in the truck bed. That should get us there and back."

"We need to take the Geiger counters," Mai Ker said. "We are going to be that close to the center of things, we have got to be really careful."

"Yeah," Bridget agreed.

"If it gets too hot—"

"Hot?" Nathaniel asked.

"The radiation, son," Mai Ker said. "If it gets too hot—as we get closer—we are coming right back and do a decon."

"De—what?" Nathaniel was having trouble following.

"Decontamination," his mom said. "Don't worry, honey."

She didn't realize this was telling him to turn back from the path she had just sent him down.

Bridget nodded that they would need to be careful. She didn't want to press what little luck they had.

"And plenty of sampling containers. We can collect

samples along the way," Mai Ker added.

The excitement was growing.

"I can print maps out from the archives," Herald offered.

"Yes, you should," his mom said, leaning back and stretching out her sore neck. "Not sure the best route. We could try taking Highway 50 into I-25. That was the main route. If there's anything left."

"Yes. I-25 ran right along the Front Range. There might be a lot of damage that way," Mai Ker said.

"Maybe there's a back way," Herald said.

"It was pretty open country," his mom said. "Not sure what the roads would be like."

"I'll check the maps," Herald said.

"We need a little prep time," Bridget said. "Let's work stuff up tomorrow. And make the trip Thursday."

HERALD AND his mom studied over the maps archived in the Comm. Center computers after supper and chores. The maps showed several possible routes along backroad routes going north and west from where Rocky Ford had been. The most promising route was old Highway 71 north past a little burg called Ordway where the map showed a good-sized reservoir. They could take water samples there. About 40 miles further north, in what looked like the middle of nowhere, was an intersection with old Highway 94. It ran straight west into Colorado Springs.

The trip would be about 130 miles each way, about 20 miles longer than going up Highway 50 to I-25. But it would keep them away from where they guessed the worst road damage might be.

Bridget lay in her bed long after nightfall with a note pad making a list of all the gear they would take. She believed in being prepared. Nothing, however, would prepare them for what they would find when they reached the end of their trip on Thursday.

20

Thursday, July 24th, 19 (NC), Morning

The excitement and anticipation about the planned journey had not diminished since Tuesday night and had only grown yesterday. The short excursions they had made so far had been close by. Today they were undertaking a major expedition.

The trip, if all went well, would consume the whole day if they left very early. With a few stops, they guessed, it would take three to four hours to reach Colorado Springs, maybe longer, depending on the roads. Stops would have to be brief. Bridget was adamant that they had to be back before nightfall.

The condition of the roads would determine whether they reached Colorado Springs at all. Most of the roads they had traveled so far were broken up in spots but still passable. At best, they usually made about 35 miles per hour. In open country, if the road could stand it, they might do better.

YESTERDAY MORNING had been beautiful, a bright day with a few broken clouds to the west and no storm clouds in sight. Bridget knew that could change overnight, and often did. They hoped for good weather for the trip.

Piper prayed silently throughout the day for fair weather for their trip. After listening to Bridget lecture them about sticking tightly to a schedule, Piper did not want to be turned back by unexpected storms. Hour after hour on Wednesday, she had felt a stronger and stronger impulse to see the mountains. Why she felt so strongly, she couldn't decide. Her experience by the ocean Monday night still haunted her. She still wasn't sure what she had seen. A strange, flickering, moving thread of light. A voice she didn't think was audible. She was more than ever worried something might be wrong with her but she was not about to talk about it, even to her mother.

Bridget and Herald went OUTSIDE early Wednesday, taking freshly charged batteries to put into the two guard trucks. They had tested the engine of the second truck—without driving it—twice before. It ran poorly. Herald brought a large toolbox, several quarts of reasonably clean, recycled oil for each truck, and a new set of spark plugs for the second one. Jimmy had taught Herald mechanic skills from the time he was about 8. And Herald enjoyed making things work better. In an hour he had the second truck running more smoothly. Not perfect, but better. Bridget aired up all the tires and the two spares.

The large fuel storage tank and siphon pump they had robbed from the old gas station in Las Animas was now bolted into the bed of the one truck. It held about 100 gallons and was three-quarters full. Every gas tank they came across on their trips got siphoned.

For this next trip they would top off the storage tank and both truck tanks at the little farm down the road. There was a thousand-gallon aboveground tank there that was nearly full when they discovered it. They had also found, by accident, an even larger tank underground. It, too, was almost full. From the depth of the tank, they guessed there might be as much as 6,000 gallons in it. They weren't likely to run out soon.

When they discovered this farm several months ago, they also discovered the farmer and his wife, whose badly decayed remains were in the farmhouse. It looked like they had stayed home through their final days. Both doors into the house and one into the cellar had been boarded up from the inside. It took some work to get in.

Food and other supplies in the house were pretty much gone. The remnants of what was probably their final lunch together were dried to plates on the metal-topped kitchen table. Two shriveled corncobs with a few hardened kernels left. There were scraps of what must have been some kind of meat, along with salad fixings that had first turned to slime and then dried. A small plate held a hard lump of what Bridget thought might have been homemade butter. But it was impossible to tell.

The farmer and his wife had fallen asleep in their easy chairs in the living room. Unlike those who died in the riots or the nuclear blasts, these two appeared to have gone as peacefully as possible, under the circumstances. Their chairs were drawn close together. A Bible lay open on the lap of the wife.

These images were running through Bridget's mind as she and Herald finished up work on the guard trucks yesterday.

"I think it'll run fine, Mom," Herald said, jerking her back to the present.

"You're amazing, son. Smart. And a great mechanic. Glad Sing didn't think you're too bad looking."

As if on cue, Herald pushed a shock of sandy brown hair up off his forehead, leaving a nice streak of grease across his brow.

"Yeah, well she's not too happy with me lately."

"I can tell. But I don't butt in."

"She thinks I care more about exploring than being with her and Kai." He tightened the last new spark plug into place.

"Do you?"

"No," he said, wiping more grease across his head. "I love exploring. That part's true. But I love them, too. It's just, how can I do everything at once?"

"You can't," his mom said. Her mind drifted backward again. "It was easier for me and your dad."

"Why?"

"We didn't have a choice of going anywhere. Except another pod," she laughed. Her face became somber. "Wish I'd had more time with him, too." She got quiet. She looked at Herald who looked so much like his dad. "Life is what it is. You get the time you get. You try to enjoy it."

"Yeah."

"The trick is, try not to worry about what you don't get."

"Sound pretty philosophical today, Mom."

She carried the air tank behind the truck, set it on the ground and checked the spare tire under the back.

"Not really. Just, at times, I still miss him. Never really got much past the honeymoon."

"I don't think Sing thinks we're on the honeymoon anymore." He frowned under the hood where his mom could not see.

"Don't worry. She loves you. It's just all the crazy changes we're living through. You two having a baby, that *really* changes everything. *That* is weird to me." She crawled back to her feet. "You have to expect she'll be upset at times. Just keep showing you love her."

Bridget looked out across the sterile, blackened prairie. Her face darkened. "Maybe Sing's right. What's the point of running around out here? We know what we're gonna find. Nothing."

"Still interesting."

"Because you never experienced it before."

"And we did find that algae."

"Yeah. That's crazy, too. Nothing should be alive out here. I still can't figure how that pond scum is there. Did it survive? Or somehow come back to life?"

"The way the air went, it couldn't have survived. Could it?"

"Probably not. So, it came back to life." Just as with Mai Ker, this was a dead-end thought. Bridget could not explain it.

Herald was done under the hood. They radioed Mai Ker to get ready to bring them back in. Pam was in the Comm. Center with Mai Ker going over the door procedures for Pod 1. Pam was writing some notes. She wanted to be sure she could get them out and—more importantly—get them safely back in.

While Herald put his tools away, Bridget walked to where the two guards were buried. The graves were undisturbed except that a little dirt had blown off the tops. She bent down and tamped the dirt down more with her hands, then piled a few more small rocks on both graves. Herald watched her, waiting in the door of the Visitors Center. She patted the graves a last time.

"Sleep tight," she said as she got up.

AS THE sun rose this morning, everyone except Braden and baby Kai were hurrying around, finishing necessary chores in the pods. It was an unbendable Bridget rule. Regular daily chores had to be done before the explorers went out.

Nathaniel's nose was severely out of joint because he couldn't go, especially since there would be ample room in the two trucks. Sing tried to pacify him.

"I need your help, Nate. I can't do those door seals by myself. You can have the step bench and do the top ones. OK?"

It wasn't much, but at least getting to do the seals high up felt like some kind of privilege to Nathaniel. He agreed, and nodded his head.

"Braden sure isn't gonna be any help. Dummy. Why'd he have to go break his leg right now?"

"Nate, it's your own fault you're grounded. Running off like that. Even if Braden could help me, you wouldn't be going."

"I know," he moaned.

They were carrying several new seals and tape to Pod

1. The four explorers had assembled their gear there last evening. They were now bringing food and water to add to the pile. Pam had baked a pan of special "Explorer Cookies" with miniature Solarium-3 flags in the icing.

"But we don't have a flag," Braden said from his chair as he had watched Pam working.

"We do now," she said. "Maybe they can put one somewhere in Colorado Springs. You know, a marker. 'The Solarians were here.'"

Braden thought it was a completely dumb idea, but he didn't say so.

When everyone was assembled by Pod 1 and Pam was at the control panel in #2, Bridget ran down her final checklist.

"Got everything?" she asked for the tenth time.

"Mom, we've got everything," Herald said impatiently.

"Sure?"

"Mom." Herald gave her an embarrassed look. "Can we just go? Man, I'm gonna cook in these coveralls."

"They're bulky but they won't feel so funny if we run into some high radiation. If not, maybe we can take them off later," Mai Ker said.

"Ready?" their leader asked.

Nods all around.

"OK," she said, "let's go."

It was just before 7:00. The migration through Pod 1 went smoothly except for one small bump. Pam unlocked the outer door but forgot to relock the inner door. As they started out, the air pressure change pulled the inner door open just a crack. Bridget hollered.

"Pam!"

"Sorry." She fidgeted for a moment over the keyboard trying to figure out what she had done wrong.

Nathaniel, quick to react, had grabbed the handle of the inner door and yanked it back shut. Pam managed to relock it.

"Sorry," she said over the radios.

"Sure you can get us back in?" Bridget asked. She glared toward Pod 2 but Pam, inside the Comm. Center, couldn't see her.

"I'm sure," Pam said innocently. "Relax. We're good."

Braden was propped up behind Pam watching. *Boy, I sure hope so,* he fretted.

Once in the trucks, they headed west on Highway 194. Mai Ker rode with Herald. At first, she wanted to drive but said nothing. She didn't want to disappoint Herald. Then she remembered the day she came to Solarium-3, when she had gone into the ditch along this same stretch of road.

Better that he drives, she told herself.

They fueled the trucks and the storage tank at the farm a couple of miles west of the Solarium and headed on. No house calls today.

They couldn't get to Rocky Ford along Highway 50. They had discovered on an earlier trip that the bridge was out across the Arkansas River at the north edge of La Junta. One whole end of the bridge was now in the riverbed, so this first leg of the trip would be tricky. Herald had printed several sections of maps showing the county roads along the north side of the river. They went near Holbrook and Dye Reservoirs again and then reached the intersection with 71.

A dilapidated sign pointed south, toward where Rocky Ford had been.

"They used to be famous for watermelons," Mai Ker said.

Herald looked at her oddly, then glanced down the road that direction.

"Prob'ly not in season," he said as he turned north.

Somehow, he had inherited his father's humor.

Back at the Solarium, Pam heard only broken, scratchy bits of speech. The team was going out of radio range.

They were following close behind Bridget and Piper in the lead truck. Bridget was driving slower than he thought she should. He was anxious to get wherever they were going. He blinked his headlights a couple of times, then honked at her once. She stopped abruptly, and came hurrying back to their truck.

"What's wrong?" she said with a worried look.

"Nothing," he said.

"Why'd you honk and flash the lights?"

"Want you to go faster."

She looked at him.

"Herald. Are we going faster right now?"

He gave her a look.

"Do not flash lights or blow the horn unless you need to stop," she said again, reminding him of her instructions. "Remember?"

"Uh-hum," he said, looking at the floorboard.

"Thought we had all this down last night. Bathroom stops, truck problem, emergencies. Otherwise, lay off."

She had left her mom hat at the Solarium and was in her invisible Leader hat.

"Sorry. Just anxious."

"What's wrong?" Piper asked when Bridget got back in the truck.

"Nothing."

"Why did he—?"

"Let it go," she said, exasperated. She felt like a junior high teacher on a field trip.

Just south of Ordway they saw Lake Meredith, a large lake compared to most in the area. It still held a lot of water, helped by this spring's rains. They collected soil and water samples. They would wait to take air samples until they were closer to the mountains.

From there north, the landscape was completely nondescript. Beyond boring, it was mind numbing. Nearly flat rolling hills panned out in every direction.

Dead vegetation spread as far as they could see. The fire last November had not come this far.

The highway was as straight as the side of a carpenter's square as it ran across the desolate land. Minutes crawled along with the trucks.

Herald, one hand on the wheel, was fidgety and wanted something to break the boredom. He picked up the map with the other hand and was trying to read it when he had to swerve suddenly to miss a large chunk of broken asphalt sticking up in center of the pavement.

"Careful, Herald!" Mai Ker snapped. "I don't want my first trip out here to be my last!"

"Sorry."

"You're worse of a driver than me," she said, trying to recompose herself.

"Really?" he asked quite seriously.

"How could anything have lived out here?" Piper asked Mai Ker over the radio.

"After?"

"Before," Piper said, wonder in her voice.

"Got me," was Mai Ker's answer.

After a quick rest stop about 20 miles later, they forged on like two lost ships trying to find land in a fog. The air was clear in its light purple kind of way. Not a cloud was in sight. It got hotter as they drove.

"Almost 95 degrees," Bridget radioed Mai Ker, "according to the dash."

"I don't think we need to worry about storms," Mai Ker replied. "Too hot and too dry."

An hour and a half later they saw—unexpectedly—a crossroad. It jumped up out of nowhere. Everything was so flat, the other road just blended in.

They had reached the intersection with Highway 94. There was nothing to mark the intersection except the stubby, broken remnant of a wooden post that had once held a stop sign, and the rubble of buildings on three corners. The wind had long ago carried the stop sign and its companion opposite to some distant land to the east. The weathered pavement was so faded that it was virtually indistinguishable from the soil.

Bridget saw the intersection at the last second and hit the brakes. Herald, who was following a little too closely, almost rear-ended the first truck.

"Herald!" Mai Ker yelped again.

"My gosh, quit picking! You're just like Sing!" he barked.

"Well, I wonder why?"

Bridget got out and came back to their truck. Piper followed.

"OK, I didn't honk!" he said.

He was breathing hard, a little shot of adrenaline pumping through him. He had stopped just inches from the other truck.

"No. Just tried to ram us, that's all," she laughed.

"Next time, holler before you jam the stupid brakes!"

"Check your copy of the map. You think this is it?"

He looked at his map of the area. He looked out around the countryside.

"*Guess* so," he said.

"We're guessing?"

"Mileage looks about right," Mai Ker said. She had clocked their progress by the mileage on the odometer.

"No markings," Bridget said, concerned. "What if this isn't 94? Don't want to get us lost."

"I think we've been lost a long time," Mai Ker said.

Bridget nodded at the irony.

"Let's try it, Mom," Herald said. "The buildings don't show on the map, but this must have been a main intersection."

"Only one I've seen in miles," Piper said.

Some buildings had stood at three corners where the highways met. They were mere rubble now, ground into the landscape. Either by fire, weather or perhaps the blast edges of a misguided warhead, they had been all but obliterated. Short, jagged pieces of rusty sheet metal poked out of the ground in several places, suggesting there had been several trailer houses on one corner.

"Map says this was Punkin Center," Bridget said.

"What a funny name," Piper said.

"Center of what?" Herald wanted to know.

"Nowhere?" Bridget wondered, looking at the empty terrain surrounding them.

She looked out across the barren plains that surrounded them. She shivered in the heat.

They collected more soil samples. As Herald and Piper walked through what had been the yard of one of the trailer homes, he saw some bones peeking through the topsoil, once covered, but now uncovered, by the wind.

"Stay there," he told Piper, pointing behind himself. He walked over and knelt down. At first he feared it had been an infant. A closer look made plain that it was a small dog, probably a pup.

"It's OK," he said.

"What is it?" Piper asked tentatively, stepping closer cautiously. Her nose and cheeks crinkled. A wave of nausea hit her. She clasped a hand over her mouth.

"Must have been a pet," Herald told her.

"Poor thing."

"Yeah."

He got up. He scraped some dirt over the bones with his boot and packed it down. He looked at the low pile of building rubble in front of them and wondered what might lie beneath it.

"Come on. I don't wanna get any closer," he said.

Piper did not need persuading. They went back to the trucks. She looked up at him several times as they walked.

"Must have been horrid," she said in a hushed whisper.

He said nothing, but nodded.

The team talked a little more and decided to take the left turn, hoping this was the right road. If it wasn't, out here they could be lost for hours. Or days.

Thankfully, about five miles further west the road jogged south diagonally for a mile then straightened out. This corresponded to the map. They had made the right decision. They were on Highway 94.

As they traveled west, they began to see clearer evidence of the nuclear blasts. Although there had never been many trees in this area, those few that had stood as lonely sentries along the road had been blown to shreds and charred. What remained were weathered-down stumps, most only a few inches above the dirt.

The explorers passed the wreckage of several old rotary irrigators that used to paint giant, green circles on the land during the short Colorado growing seasons. What was left were strips of large tires blown off the wheeled support sections and bits of twisted pipe thrown about, as if an army of enormous locusts had ravaged the fields, eating the irrigators and spitting out the bones.

The day had worn into the late morning. What would have been a trip of just less than two hours before was turning into half-a-day's drive. The clock in the dash of Bridget's truck was nearing 11:00 and the city was nowhere in sight.

The mountains, however, were. Looming ahead of them, like great titans who had laid down to sleep and never awoken, the lesser peaks began to show their ragged backs and scraggly hair. Most impressive, sitting watchful as the chief warrior who never slept, was the face of Pikes Peak. Still many miles off, it grew with each mile not only in sight but in imagination.

To Herald and Piper, it was a truly spectacular view. The many pictures and satellite images they had seen of mountains in the archives were a joke by comparison. Nothing could have prepared them for the stunning size of these mammoth wonders. As each mile passed, the marvel of the Rockies began to imprint its image into their minds.

A quiet "Wow" was all Herald could manage as they came over a low rise and saw the great peak in its full stature for the first time. Mai Ker smiled at his childlike astonishment.

In the truck ahead of them, Bridget gazed at the still-indistinct mountain peaks. She was overcome by a different impression, by the thought of how everything at a distance looks so unclear, so indistinct, so unreal. Yet they were as real and distinct as they would soon appear up close. As she tried to focus on the still-distant peaks, most of them seeming to be only a blue-gray haze, she realized how life was like this. At a distance, every future moment and event seems fuzzy, indistinct. Yet as each moment rolls into the present, it can be seen that it was always *this* moment, this exact, particular moment. And every coming event, though at a distance, is equally real and can be no other.

"Look at that," Piper said to Bridget, breaking her thoughts. "Never realized they were so huge."

"Enormous," Bridget smiled.

After the many years since she last saw them, they were still impressive. There they lay, immovable.

"I'd almost forgotten."

She glanced at Piper.

"That big one in the middle, that's Pikes Peak."

"So beautiful."

Piper was enjoying the wonder. She leaned forward on her seat as if getting a few inches closer would speed them on their journey.

"Can we go up there?" She looked at Bridget with pleading eyes.

"Don't think we have time, honey."

"What if we don't come back here?"

"We might. Sometime."

"But what if we don't?"

There was an urgency in Piper's voice that Bridget didn't understand. She looked over at her.

Piper was leaning, both hands pressed against the dashboard, urging the truck forward. She glanced back and forth between Bridget and the stunning peak as if one or the other might suddenly disappear.

Bridget couldn't account for why but she, too, felt a growing desire to see the top of the peak, a place she had once visited as a child. She slowed the truck, stopped in the road, and walked back to Herald and Mai Ker.

"Piper wants to go up the mountain." Why she put the impetus on Piper she was not certain.

"The big one?" Herald asked excitedly.

"Yeah. Pikes Peak."

"There is no reason to do that," Mai Ker said. She frowned toward Bridget. "We don't have enough time."

"Man, I'd love to see everything from way up there," Herald said, already enlarging the dream that had captured his mind. "We'd be able to see the Solarium!"

Just as inexplicably as the desire had come over her, Bridget was losing her nerve.

"Well, Mai Ker's right. It would take time," Bridget said. "I know there used to be a road up the back side. But who knows what it's like now."

"Can't we go see?" Herald asked.

Bridget and Mai Ker's eyes held a brief conference. They knew it was risky to stay out longer than need be. Their reason for coming was simply to get samples from the Colorado Springs area. So far, the Geiger counter readings were very low. But still, they were above normal. It could take several hours to go up and back down the peak. Mai Ker was silently shaking her head.

"Let's wait and see," Bridget finally said. "Once we're in the city."

"Let's go!" Herald said, putting the truck in gear with Bridget's arm still on his windowsill.

"We need to change air tanks first."

Herald shifted back into Park. They switched out all four tanks, collected some soil and air samples, and drove on.

Bridget looked at her watch. It was 11:45. It would be foolhardy, she told herself, to try the mountain today. But, as Piper hinted, how could they know if they would ever come back this way?

Bridget remembered the fantastic view. She had been on top of the peak once on a family vacation. Though the memory had faded, she remembered the awe, the sense of reverence that crept over her with chills as she had gotten out of their car at the summit. The thin air, dizzying her brain, added to the otherworldly sensations she had experienced as she tried to take in the immensity of the world that stretched out below her.

Yes, it was risky. But her heart tugged at her. She wanted her son to share that experience with her, if only once.

She called Mai Ker on the radio.

"Hey, check your maps. I'm sure there was a highway up the back side. But I was just a kid. I might have it wrong."

Mai Ker could tell from the sound of her voice that Bridget was changing her mind despite Mai Ker's advice. She shook her head again, and scanned over the map.

"There is a road. Looks like we would go west into a place called Manitou Springs. Then up old Highway 24."

"Let's look it over when we get into the city," Bridget said.

Piper began smiling broadly.

"Thanks."

"Well, don't hold your breath. Not a sure deal yet. All depends on time."

Bridget glanced at the dash clock and her watch. She pressed the accelerator a little deeper. They were doing more than 40 miles per hour, which was dangerous considering the rotten pavement. Her hands began sweating. She put her eyes and brain on alert, watching for chuckholes and blown-out asphalt.

She pressed the accelerator down a little farther.

21

Thursday, July 24th, Afternoon

They had come more than 50 miles since Punkin Center when they reached the outskirts of what had been Colorado Springs. The scattered remnants of small commercial buildings and trailers that had lined the highway lay like confetti along the roadsides.

Standing—somehow—at a corner where a country road intersected the highway was a lone road sign, listing sideways on its bent metal post. The once-green sign was now a deep brown, but readable.

"Enoch Road," Bridget read aloud.

"Enoch. Hey, he was in Daddy's Bible," Piper said with surprise.

"Oh," Bridget said, remembering. "That one who got carried off to heaven."

"No, that was Elijah. Enoch just 'walked with God.' I think that's right."

"Maybe he *walked* into heaven?" Bridget said smiling, half-teasing her.

"Don't know." Piper pondered this. "Can't picture that."

Not long after, they came to an intersection where Highway 94 merged into Highway 24. As they approached the intersection about to turn left, Bridget slowed and stopped. She caught her breath. An unspeakable panorama opened before them. Talking stopped abruptly in both trucks.

Ahead of them lay the ruins of an entire subdivision. The buildings that once stood there had been shredded into small, charred remains, debris piles of wildly scattered brick, concrete and lumber. Glass had disintegrated. Destruction on this scale had been hard to picture until they saw it. An entire village of homes, stores, people, pets—wiped away like burnt crumbs of toast from a counter top.

Both trucks crept forward as the four Solarians tried to take in the devastation. Any souls who had survived the deteriorating air could never have survived these blasts.

For the next several miles, the Solarians were mute, watching. Slowly, they worked their way into town. To the south was a large open area that had been the local airport and an Air Force base. Little was left.

The highway became a wide city street. It, too, was badly damaged but passable. At one overpass, the bridge had collapsed. They drove down a side ramp and back up the other side. Fallen trees, the larger ones that had not been consumed in the heat flash, had rotted with age and could easily be driven over. It was like driving through sand.

Finally, they reached the core of the city, stopping at a wide, divided street. All four got out of the trucks. They had still not spoken. The unnatural silence around them was oppressive in the heart of what had been a beautiful city. Around them were devastated buildings on all four sides. A wonderland of ruin.

Buildings once called skyscrapers were now reduced to carcasses, some lying atop each other in piles, others looking like tall cardboard boxes whose sides some giant had kicked in, buckling the tops over at an angle.

Glass, metal, paper, rubber, bits and pieces of every conceivable substance and building material were strewn in every direction.

"Nevada Avenue," Bridget said somberly, looking up from the map. "It was the main street down here."

Herald remembered the street name.

"Mom, remember? In the archives last night? There

was a picture of a big statue. By the high school. The guy who founded the city, I think."

"Palmer?" Bridget asked.

"Yeah. Could we find it? The school, I mean. I've never seen a big school."

The truth was, he and Piper had never seen a school of any size, except the area in the Meeting Tent that was their own school, and pictures in the archives.

"Palmer High School," Bridget read from the map. "Couple of blocks that way."

They looked north. No statue. No school.

"Let's look," Herald said.

They decided to walk the short blocks. They had been stuck in the trucks most of the day. Bridget's watch read 11:45.

"Can't we eat first?" Mai Ker asked. "I'm starved."

It felt strange to think about eating here, in the midst of such complete destruction. Then it dawned on them. They ate that way every day.

Their stomachs were beginning the noon growl. They usually didn't go this long without food. They downed some pork sandwiches and leftover fried potatoes brought along in a cooler, washing lunch down with cups of safe water from the Solarium.

Feeling better with something in their stomachs, they walked north, estimating the blocks as best they could, considering the condition of the streets. They arrived at what should have been Platte Avenue. The incinerated heap of concrete and steel on the northeast corner, they decided, must have been the high school.

"Too bad," Piper said.

"Hope they were all home," Herald said soberly.

They found the spot where the statue of General Palmer had stood in the middle of the intersection. "Spot" was an accurate description. What was left was a hardened lump of what appeared to be melted bronze or iron, most of which had poured off the concrete footer and dribbled into the intersection.

Herald's disappointment was manifest.

"Shoot. He was on a horse. It was really sharp."

"Slow horse," was Bridget's sardonic comment.

She stared at the demolished school. Her mind ran off with Herald's thought. She remembered the missiles had fallen in the middle of the night. Hopefully all those kids were home with their families when the hour had come.

Mai Ker had been monitoring her Geiger counter closely. Readings were still a little high, but not dangerous. She was amazed.

"Maybe we should start back," she said, looking at her own watch. We'll have plenty of daylight. If we start now."

"Bridget?" Piper's eyes were pleading again. It was a mixed look of hope and yearning that probably no living person could refuse.

"I know, honey. But I said it wasn't a sure deal. Remember?"

"Yeah."

"It is getting late. Mai Ker's right. We should start back."

"Are you afraid?" Piper asked.

"Afraid of what?" Herald wanted to know.

"Heights?" Piper smiled at Bridget.

"'Course not," Bridget lied.

They all knew she was. They all knew what a miracle it was that she had climbed #10 that day with Herald.

They started walking back to the trucks. Bridget was glancing down at her watch again when the ground began rolling violently.

Piper lunged sideways and fell. Herald reached for her but landed on top of her. Mai Ker purposely dropped to her knees to try to steady herself. Bridget alone managed to remain standing. The wreckage of buildings around them shook violently. What saved them was that everything near them that could possibly fall had fallen long ago.

The quake was violent but short-lived, about a minute and a half. A few seconds after the quake subsided, two of the partially collapsed skyscrapers about six blocks away came the rest of the way to the ground. They made their own quake.

Dust rolled toward the Solarians.

"Headgear!" Mai Ker shouted.

They pulled the head covers of the radiation suits they were wearing over their heads and faces. They had not needed them, until now. Radiation trapped in the soil around the buildings would quickly be stirred up.

Piper was crying, and praying. She was praying very loudly.

"Jesus! Help us!" she shouted.

It was short, to the point.

As if in a completely antagonistic reply, the sky had begun to darken rapidly. A violent storm was blowing in from the west over the mountains. As the Solarians were trying to regain their bearings, dark clouds roiled over the peaks and began to race down the slopes along the west side of the city. It looked like a flood from the sky, untamed, intent on swallowing Colorado Springs once and for all.

They had nowhere to go but the trucks. They were up and running. The wind felt like an approaching hurricane. They were in the trucks, the windows up, before the rain hit. It came with vicious force, blowing sideways like a monsoon. Both trucks rocked like a kiddie ride at an amusement park. There were four terrified kids inside them.

The thunderstorm crashing over the peaks brought slings full of lightning with it. Flashes catapulted across the sky. Thunder joined with several aftershocks of the quake that shook even the footings of the mountains.

It seemed endless, but lasted only a few minutes. The powerful winds raked up soil and dust, mixing them into a radioactive soup with the pounding rain, and blew the storm east as quickly as it had descended. As sheets of water fell from the trucks, the Solarians crawled out. All were shaking. Pickup trucks were not a Solarium. They had been sheltered from storms there. Now they had faced one head-on, with almost no protection.

"OK," Bridget said, breathing hard. "Everyone OK?"

Mai Ker's Geiger counter was mad, and snapping more loudly.

"Bridget!"

"I hear."

"Let's go!"

"Where? We can't go east, behind the storm," Bridget said. "If the wind's stirring up the soil, we'll drive right into more radiation!"

Mai Ker shook her head.

"I know. But there's radioactive dust all around us! We must not just stand here!"

The kids were frightened, eyes wide, listening.

"Well?" Bridget almost demanded.

"We try to get above it," Mai Ker said.

"How?" Piper cried.

"Just get higher. All the moisture in the air will help settle the dust particles. To the lowest areas. We've got to get up higher."

"I'm not goin' up in one of those buildings!" Herald said emphatically.

"No. Up there." Mai Ker pointed to the hills at the west side of the city. "We go up, to a higher elevation."

Herald was yanking map pages of the city from his front seat. He pointed a route for Bridget.

"Here. We might be able to cross the river here."

"After that rain?" Piper asked.

"Have to chance it."

"He's right," Bridget said. "Let's just not stand here."

They piled back into their trucks.

Bridget drove west, picking their way through debris-strewn streets out of downtown. This took the better part of 30 minutes. They came to where a viaduct had crossed the wide valley of Monument Creek but the viaduct had been destroyed in the blasts.

Despite the downpour, the runoff had not yet piled up in the creek. Slowly, they were able to drive down, cross the 1-foot-deep water, and get back up the other side, toward the old I-25 freeway. Mai Ker looked behind them. The creek was quickly rising where they had just crossed.

The freeway presented a worse hurdle.

"Gonna be tough cutting across the interstate," Bridget radioed as they came out of the creek bed. "That overpass is collapsed, too."

"We'll never squeeze under that," Mai Ker agreed.

Herald quickly surveyed the obstacles.

"Maybe we can follow that onramp over there to the right. Up to the main lanes. Then cut across somehow," he said.

"Let's try," Bridget said. "You lead, Herald."

Even in his panicky state, Herald grinned. He headed for the ramp.

Mai Ker's Geiger counter was still carrying on its own erratic conversation.

They drove up the ramp, then drove sideways across the north and southbound lanes of the broken up freeway. They bounced down the embankment on the far side. Fortunately, the trucks sat high off the ground so they were able to clear several large rocks.

They made it to a frontage road that sat along the highway. This wound past several streets until they got back to what they hoped was Highway 24.

"Well done, son," Bridget called on the air. She called to Mai Ker. "How high?"

"I will tell you when we get there," Mai Ker said, her eyes and ears glued to the meter.

"West," Bridget ordered.

Herald kept the lead. They moved slowly up the old bypass highway that ran around the ruins of Manitou Springs.

"Bridget. Look." Piper's voice was intense, suddenly full of awe.

Bridget looked.

"Herald! Stop!" she radioed.

She parked in the middle of the road and got out. Piper was out her door, too, looking up.

A huge, brilliantly white, circular cloud had settled over Pikes Peak.

"Spectacular!" Bridget said. "I've never seen one before."

"What is it?" Piper asked.

"A lenticular cloud. See. It's the winds, circulating around up there. And downdrafts. The cloud swirls in place. Like it's stuck."

Mai Ker and Herald had walked back to them, also glancing up at the peak.

"We need to keep going," Mai Ker insisted. "Higher!"

"Yeah. But look at that," Bridget said with wonderment. She had seen dozens of pictures of these clouds, but never a real one.

"I know," Mai Ker said. "Very perfect. Come on. Let's go."

"Wait. Look. How it's—it's kind of sinking," Piper said, pointing.

As the four watched, the circular, slowly rotating cloud was settling gently down over the top of the peak like a halo. It kept sinking. In half-a-minute, the crest of the mountain reappeared, shrouded by the great yoke of white cloud.

Even Mai Ker became entranced. She looked steadily at the peak, then beyond.

"Not even the whisper of clouds behind to the west. Very odd."

Then she noticed the oddest thing of all. The bowl-like cloud had a strange luminosity about it.

"See it?" she asked the others.

"There's no more lightning. What is that?" Herald asked.

"It looks so bright," Piper said.

It wasn't the sun, which was still high and to the south.

"Is it—?" Herald almost didn't want to say it. He sounded almost childish. "Like, glowing?"

Almost a full minute passed. No one said anything, or moved. Just watched.

Finally, Mai Ker came to her senses.

"Come on," she said firmly, "we have to get higher." Her Geiger counter had slowed as they rose in elevation. "It's better. But still pretty talkative."

She and Herald hurried back to their truck. Bridget got back behind the wheel of hers.

"The winds and fire do his bidding."

Piper heard the words clearly as she climbed back in.

"What?" she asked Bridget.

"What?" Bridget said, looking at her blankly.

"What did you say?"

Bridget frowned.

"Didn't say anything." She watched Piper, whose face went slightly white. "You OK, honey?"

Piper didn't answer right away.

"Uh-huh," she finally said, but wasn't really sure.

She had heard the words as clearly as if over a loud speaker. Obviously, Bridget hadn't. Piper felt, more than ever, that she must be losing her mind.

The truck started forward, following Herald's. Piper stared through the top of the windshield at the strange cloud that hung atop the mountain.

"We've got to get up there," she told Bridget.

"We're getting higher. We'll be OK."

"No. Up there!" Piper said, pointing upward at the big peak.

"It's too far, honey."

"Bridget!" the girl said passionately. It was her tone of voice that meant this was not something to argue about. "Please listen. Don't you see? We're halfway there! *Why* are we halfway there?"

Bridget couldn't answer. But she understood. Events, completely unplanned, were driving them upward. They were only a few miles, she was sure, from where the Pikes Peak Highway used to turn off.

"Herald, stop," she called on the radio.

He and Mai Ker hurried back to them again.

"Piper's really set on going up there." She gestured toward the peak.

Mai Ker frowned deeply. She checked the Geiger counter. It was slowing, but still chattering. She realized they could not go back down yet. She looked through the windshield at the plea on Piper's face.

"How long?" Mai Ker asked.

"Depends on the access highway. If it's even still there," Bridget said. "Couple of hours, maybe. To reach the top."

"So—one-thirty-five, now. Two-thirty-five, three-thirty-five. Back down by, maybe six-thirty?" Mai Ker was calculating aloud and not smiling. She looked at Bridget. "And if we hit trouble?"

"I know." Bridget raised her eyebrows. She looked over at Piper, then back at Mai Ker. "No way to know. The headlights do work."

"It will be pushing our luck," Mai Ker said. She caught again the expectant look in Piper's eyes. Herald's looked like their reflection.

"We've got to go," Piper insisted. She hesitated, afraid she would sound completely insane. She was afraid of her own words. "I think the lights are calling us."

Herald stared at her through the windshield. *What's with her, now?* he was thinking. He thought she meant the glow in the cloud. This confused him. But too often in the past, Piper seemed to have some hidden insight into things that confused him.

Bridget heard her remark but was preoccupied, feeling anxious watching Mai Ker looking anxious. She turned and looked up. She remembered again her family vacation and the beauty of the world from atop this peak. The brilliant, almost pulsating cloud hung in seeming stillness. She knew they had to go.

"Is it steep?" Mai Ker was asking her.

"The mountain?"

"The road."

"Pretty much."

Mai Ker looked at their two trucks.

"These old clunkers going to make it?" she asked Herald.

"We can find out," he grinned.

His father's son.

Bridget looked at her map.

"Look. We just keep following this bypass around Manitou. A few miles past this junction there's this little burg," Bridget pointed, "see? Cascade. That's where the road up the mountain takes off."

Mai Ker nodded. They were close. She was outnumbered. And Bridget was their leader. Right now, they were simply wasting time.

"All right. If we're going, we need to go," Mai Ker said. "Daylight can disappear early in these canyons."

Herald crinkled his mouth. With an embarrassed look, he handed his truck keys toward Mai Ker.

"You wanna drive?" It was a polite but sincere question.

Mai Ker almost glared at him.

"You nuts?"

Herald almost sprinted to their truck. Mai Ker didn't.

They nudged forward and picked up speed. The bypass climbed steeply and passed Manitou Springs.

The cloud was still tucked neatly around the top of the peak like a vaporous shroud.

"Pretty," was Piper's comment as she watched it.

"Yes," Bridget said.

At the ruins of Cascade, they were baffled. The buildings, roads and intersections were so badly damaged that it was impossible to be sure which road led to the Pikes Peak Highway. They went past the town, turned around, and circled back east. Bridget, taking the lead, pulled to the side—out of habit—got out, and looked around.

"Maybe we just should go back," Mai Ker suggested, walking up to her.

"You think it's safe down there yet?"

"I do not know."

Bridget looked at Piper. She was still in the truck and seemed oblivious to the conversation.

"Mom," Herald called out his window. "See how that one goes up real quick? Over there. To the right?"

He was pointing with an arm across the windshield of his truck but Bridget still wasn't sure which road he meant.

"You wanna lead?" she asked.

"Sure."

Mai Ker got back in with Herald, who pulled around to be the lead truck again. They turned down a road through the wreckage of the town. This connected with another street that was wider than the others and soon curved left. Just beyond what seemed to be the edge of town they passed a large parking area. He was sure this was the way.

The road climbed, made a dogleg turn to the left, and climbed steeply again. Everyone's breathing had picked up. They were beginning to feel the altitude.

"That's so strange," Mai Ker said to Herald as they reached a spot where the road leveled out briefly.

"What?"

She gestured up the mountain.

"That cloud. The way it just sits there. Did you notice when we stopped? There is a pretty good breeze from the west." She stared. "Why does the cloud just sit there?"

"Maybe it likes mountains," he said.

"And no other cloud in sight."

The circular cloud was rotating ever-so-slowly but seemed tethered to the peak. It looked thick with moisture but there was no rain. The glow had changed to a brighter hue, snow white against the light-purplish sky.

"Whad'a'ya think, Mai?" Bridget called on the radio.

"I think it ought to rain any minute," Mai Ker said, her eyes on the cloud.

"Shoot!" Herald exclaimed. He pulled to a stop.

Bridget slowed behind them.

"What?" she called back.

"Trouble," he said to Mai Ker. "Look."

Not far ahead was a large dam and lake. Herald looked down at his map on the seat.

"Must be Crystal Creek Reservoir," he said.

Bridget walked up to his window.

"So?"

"I don't like how the dam looks, Mom." He pointed. "See those cracks? Down the water side? Probably some on the outer side too."

The four of them walked the short distance toward the dam. A number of large cracks were visible above the water line but it was still holding back the large reservoir. Bridget looked at the map in her hand.

"What about this way? This loop road? Goes down below the dam—down there—then links back with the main road."

They walked a little farther to where the loop road cut downhill.

"Don't think so," Herald said.

"Never mind," Bridget said.

Not more than 500 feet off the main road an entire

section of the loop road was gone. A landslide below the dam, triggered by the nuclear blasts, had torn the road from its mother.

"Can't believe the dam survived," Mai Ker said.

"Should we chance it?" Herald asked everyone.

They looked up at the dam. They looked at each other. Piper said nothing.

"Maybe go back," Mai Ker said. She was winning chicken of the day.

"We've come this far," Bridget said, looking up at the north side of the peak. "Piper?"

"We can make it," Piper shrugged.

"To the top?"

"Across the dam."

They were walking back up to the road.

"Not sure," Bridget said. "Looks pretty dicey."

"We can make it," Piper repeated.

Her confidence was infectious. Bridget nodded very slightly.

They got back in the trucks. The dam was solid concrete. Despite lots of cracks, it was holding back millions of tons of water and apparently had for years. The nuclear blasts didn't take it. Surely it would hold their little trucks.

This, at least, they all hoped.

As Herald was about to drive forward, something strange happened. The halo-like cloud shifted position, and shape. They all saw it.

Herald was sure for about two seconds that it took the appearance of a face, but it was no face he had ever seen, or imagined. It was not human. It was more than human. But this made no sense to him.

Where's Piper when I need her?

He realized he was holding his breath. Like a diver surfacing, he gulped some air, and called Piper over the radio.

"What's it doing?

Piper watched, transfixed. A thousand thoughts and emotions flooded her. She felt as if it her whole body was being twisted into a tight knot. But she couldn't say a word.

"Piper?" Bridget said. She had never seen this consumed look on Piper's face before.

Piper could only shake her head a little from side to side. Though it was perfectly warm in the truck, she felt she might freeze.

"Piper!" Bridget said forcefully. "Sweetie, what is it?"

Piper's eyes unfroze.

"They are. They're calling."

"What?"

"The lights," Piper said.

A new expression broke over her face, replacing what had looked like confusion with mild fear. But then, for no apparent reason, she instantly relaxed.

"It's OK, Bridget. I'm all right."

She looked at Bridget. The fear was gone and serenity was now in her eyes.

In the other truck, Mai Ker was getting impatient.

"Are we going?" she called to Bridget.

"Go."

Both trucks inched toward the dam.

Bridget hated moments like this, when Piper was so sure of things no one else could even sense. But like Herald and the rest, she had learned to trust Piper's instincts. They couldn't understand where these intuitions came from but Piper was rarely wrong. It was like that day when she and Sing were young and Sing had been so sick. Piper had been certain Sing would get well. She knew.

"Take it slow, Herald," Bridget ordered.

Mai Ker closed her eyes as they eased out onto the road atop the dam.

"Don't look down," he told Mai Ker.

"Watch the road, Herald," she said intensely, her eyes

locked shut.

Herald eased along until they were about halfway, then got nervous and gunned it on across. It was the smoothest section of road they had been on all day.

Bridget followed suit. They were on the far side, and safe.

"That was nervy," Bridget gulped.

"We *did* make it," Piper grinned. She was more excited than ever. "Can I switch with Mai Ker? Be in the front truck?"

"No," Bridget said. "You stay with me."

She tried to make it not sound harsh. The road had a very steep drop off in places and she felt better with Piper next to her. She promised Pam to look after her, but she was fairly certain that in some reverse way Piper was also looking after *her*.

Herald drove on. The road wound and climbed for the next 30 minutes. The truck engines were straining. Herald began to wonder if this was such a great idea.

They began to see small pockets of packed snow deep in the valleys and crevices, shaded from the sun by the huge mountain.

"It's like winter and summer at the same time," Herald said to Mai Ker.

Mai Ker didn't answer. She had caught her breath, which was becoming harder as they gained altitude. But her heart had not slowed down much since crossing the dam. All she could think about was that before long they would have to cross the stupid thing again on the way down.

She felt restless but was trying to calm herself. Looking up across the treeless landscape they were approaching gave her a perfect view of the beautiful cloud, still hovering—weightlessly, it appeared—just below the top of the peak.

"You remember the cloud in the wilderness?" Piper was asking Bridget in the other truck.

"What?"

"In the Bible," Piper said.

"Oh. Yeah. After the Red Sea. A pillar of cloud by day, a pillar of fire at night. That part?"

"No. When they got to that mountain, and a cloud settled on top of it. Remember? How it sat there for days and days?"

Bridget looked up. The sun had moved to the west and, from their angle, was now partly behind the peak. A bluish glow shown through the cloud, mixing with a faint shade of amber.

"You think it was like that?" she gestured with her head.

"I dunno. Maybe not."

Piper got quiet. The truck bumped along for another 15 minutes. Her heart, too, was now racing, for different reasons. Disconnected events and memories, some far back in her childhood, began to fall together in the back of her mind. *Is this it? Is this what that was about?* she wondered.

"Keep going, Herald," Bridget said over the radio. "I wanna be on top by 3 o'clock, if we can."

"Gonna be slow once we drive into that cloud."

"Take a good look when we get up there," Mai Ker radioed back. "We can't stay long. We'll lose the sunlight. I am not going back over that dam in the dark."

"Good thing the cloud's below the summit," Herald told her, "or we wouldn't see a thing."

His truck's right front wheel bounced hard into a gaping chuckhole. He steadied the wheel. He radioed Bridget to dodge the hole but his mirror confirmed she already had.

They were nearly to the base of the cloud. Above the long-dead timberline now, the winds were stronger. The cloud continued to circle but not move. It looked as if someone had taken a huge spatula and carved off the bottom of it so that it sat perfectly level across the angle of the peak, like a white, watery crown. From down below they had seen some packed snow up at the top of the mountain. But from here they could no longer see the summit because of the size of the cloud.

Then a very unusual thing happened. As Herald looked into the flattened base of the cloud, it seemed he was looking at a crystal ceiling. What was stranger was that as he stared at this glass-like barrier, he couldn't shake the feeling that instead of looking up he was looking down through a transparent floor into a great depth. His stomach did a summersault. He felt a sensation of falling into a deep abyss where light and dark danced in unison in the midst of nothingness. He blinked. By reflex, his foot reached for the brake pedal and he slowed, still watching.

The other three Solarians saw this strange sight, too, but each saw something entirely different.

The first thing Mai Ker noticed was that her Geiger counter, which had slowed drastically as they climbed, went totally silent. She stared at the cloud. It looked to her like a transparent, dark-skinned animal as big as the mountaintop. The animal was alive, circling, menacing, ready to pounce.

Bridget saw only the clear ceiling-like barrier that separated them from the interior of the cloud. But it reminded her of a beautiful crystal serving plate her great-grandmother had used to put out cake and treats for her visitors. The plate was handmade, simple yet ornate.

What Piper saw was crystalline light radiating down into the air around them like a summer sun, melting the four of them together, like grains of sand on a vast beach, into a golden, living tapestry.

Herald edged his truck forward but suddenly jumped in his seat with fright and jammed the brakes hard. His heart pounded, his fingers trying to tear through the steering wheel. Bridget, staring and not reacting quickly, jammed her brakes, too, but not in time. She smacked into the back of the lead truck, knocking Mai Ker sideways against the dash.

Bridget unconsciously locked the truck into Park. She continued to stare. Alongside her, Piper was entranced.

Something was moving in the cloud.

Herald got out of his truck and cautiously walked a few paces forward, toward the base of the cloud. Mai Ker didn't move.

Before he realized it, his mother and Piper were alongside him. They watched intently.

Slowly, their minds grasped what they were seeing. It was not something moving in the cloud. It was some *things*. Several distinct shapes were visible just inside the near perimeter of the cloud. The shapes were moving toward them. Flying? Drifting? Walking? What?

"Mom, what are those?" Herald stood rigid, his eyes unblinking.

"Altitude, maybe," Bridget tried to convince herself. She did not want to see what she was seeing. Out here. Alone. Not knowing. She stared harder. "Maybe not . . ."

"My God," Piper said in a breathless whisper.

The body-like figures in the cloud were alive. Several had an indistinct yet human appearance. But nothing was clear.

The three Solarians stood like trees, unable to move. Without realizing it, they had taken each other's hands. In the truck, Mai Ker was trying to shrink into the seat and was sinking deeper into panic.

"It can't . . . they can't be—people," she was muttering.

She trembled, her eyes squinting in disbelief. She brushed an uncontrolled tear, not of sadness but of fear, from her face.

Then the unimaginable happened. As they watched, a figure appeared from the cloud, walking toward them. Unspeakable dread struck Bridget. Even her clothes shook.

It was the figure of a man, and he kept coming toward them. He walked confidently but cautiously, as if he knew he had frightened them. More frightening was the fact that the glow from the cloud accompanied him, or followed him, or filled the air around him.

As the three Solarians tried to take this in, two more men appeared behind the first one. The first man was real, solid. These two looked faint, not yet real. But as they walked, they took clearer form, like mist turning into water and then into living flesh.

Stunned, Mai Ker forced herself to keep watching through the windshield. Panic had given way to curiosity and wonder. *An illusion,* she told herself. *I'm hallucinating.*

The three men came closer. The three Solarians stood dazed. They felt disconnected from reality with no way to digest what was plain before their eyes. They knew everything was dead. Knew it with certainty. Nothing— and *no one*—could have survived those years OUTSIDE.

Bridget bolted backward, dragging Herald and Piper with her. They scrambled between the trucks where they braced themselves into a protective knot. Piper, dizzy and trying hard for more air, had a vice grip on Bridget's arm.

Mai Ker, out of nothing but desperation and fear she might die cut off from the others, climbed out of the truck and enfolded herself into the human knot. Only with their help was she standing. Despite the cool air, sweat was dripping from her forehead.

They huddled together tightly, grabbing hands and arms, to protect themselves from—they didn't know what. Herald and Piper had heard of ghosts. Bridget and Mai Ker didn't believe in them.

But these were no ghosts. The three men stopped about 20 feet away. Herald began to feel sick again. His half-digested lunch started coming up. He swallowed hard and forced it back. He was not about to chicken out.

The first man came a few steps nearer and stopped.

The other two waited further back.

Except for the strange glow around him, he was ordinary looking, with a dark complexion as if he had been in the sun a lot. His clothing was common looking and outdated, plain woolen pants and a dark green, poorly tailored shirt. His face was pleasant but uncommon, with a forceful jaw and cheekbones.

He examined the four Solarians closely, as though he was curious yet at the same time quite certain about them.

"Hello."

He spoke the simple greeting but didn't move or offer a hand. He knew he should not come closer.

"Who are—? I mean, where are—?" Bridget's lips felt as if they were three days' frost-bitten. "Where are you from?" she finally managed.

While Bridget mumbled, Piper was beginning to loosen the hold on her arm.

"Oh, no . . ." Piper said with a worrisome tone.

Her mind was spiraling up and down at the same time. Like Herald, she began to feel her whole universe was turning upside down—or right-side up. Her eyes remained fixed on the man.

"Really?" she asked him with obvious relief, though the man had said nothing more.

An unexpected smile broadened across Piper's face. The stranger's eyes began to sparkle.

"Yes, Piper," he finally said. "Sorry it's sudden. But I did warn everyone, didn't I? 'When you least expect it'?"

Piper was laughing almost hysterically with joy. She let go of Bridget's arm and flung herself against the man's chest.

Bridget, Mai Ker and Herald listened dumbfounded to Piper and the man, but they still didn't grasp what was happening. Several more shadowy figures were emerging from the cloud, seeming, as before, faint at first then becoming more solid.

"I have to say, you've all been very patient," the man said as he comforted the child in his arms.

"What?" Mai Ker asked, her mind more boggled by the appearance of even more people walking up behind the first three. She wanted to sit down but couldn't. Her legs felt like boards and her lungs kept trying to overfill.

The man didn't react to her obvious distress, but answered her in a calm voice.

"I only mean, you've been waiting for me a very long time, haven't you?"

"Mom?" Herald muttered. He looked from Bridget to the man and back to his mom, as if she should be able to explain. "I don't—understand," he said, stepping backward. "Tell me I'm not awake."

The words were just out of his mouth as dizziness overtook him. He fainted and fell to the ground.

Look for **ReGeneration**
Book Three of the Solarium-3 Trilogy
wherever books are sold

Life In The Midst Of Death

In *Haeven* (Book Two), the Solarians and their children have struggled to survive INSIDE Solarium-3 against insurmountable odds.

Mankind's desire for a better world is now nothing but a bad dream. Life has become the perfect exercise in futility. Daily they wonder, *Why go on?*

Forced OUTSIDE to repair an air leak in the main pod, they faced new risks and old horrors. Searching for answers, they have begun to explore what seems an utterly godforsaken planet.

Now, a day's journey has brought four of the Solarians to the ruins of Colorado Springs where unforeseen events drive them to the summit of Pikes Peak. Then comes a mystifying, staggering confrontation.

Life is about to take an unexpected turn, new realities are about to erupt around them—and the last thing they ever imagined will be the greatest surprise of all.

ReGeneration

Venture Into Life

www.solarium-3.com

About The Author

John R. Spencer grew up in Kansas and Colorado, and holds a degree in English Literature from the University of Northern Colorado, where he was, for two years, editor-in-chief of the campus literary magazine *NOVA*.

In addition to writing, he has enjoyed a diverse career as a police detective, emergency medical technician, coroner's investigator, social worker, and community corrections supervisor. He has also worked as a dramatic director for several community and children's theaters in Colorado, Wisconsin and Illinois.

The father of three grown children, he lives with his wife, Candice, in eastern Iowa.

9 780986 372728